THE FITFUL SLEEP OF IMMIGRANTS

Orlando Ortega-Medina

AMBLE
PRESS

2023

Dear Reader,

Sitting in my law office in leafy South Kensington in London, overlooking the campus of Imperial College, it's incredible to believe that twenty-three years ago, my partner and I were wrapping up our lives and professions in San Francisco and kissing our families goodbye, about to embark on a journey into the unknown. Our inability as a same-sex couple to marry, coupled with our refusal to settle for second best and live a life of indefinite insecurity, forced us to seek another country that would offer us the liberty and respect denied us in the United States. That country was Canada, where we were welcomed with open arms in August 1999. I swear, I kissed the tarmac when we stepped off the plane at Pearson International Airport in Toronto.

I'd never felt freer in my entire life as we went about setting ourselves up in our new country. I was delighted to find the fact we were a gay couple was a non-issue for anyone we met. As I embraced that reality, I felt as if a heavy weight had been lifted off my back. Nevertheless, there was a sting in the sweetness of those early days. There was no denying, we were starting from scratch: no home, no jobs, no recognized credentials, no friends, and no family. My partner coped a bit better with this, focusing on the positive as he helped set up our new home. I, however, experienced a crisis of identity. I'd gone overnight from running my own thriving law practice to working temp jobs in Toronto law offices, resentful I'd been relegated to making photocopies and serving coffee.

To cope with the strain of my new reality, I started work on a memoir, where I recorded what my partner and I had experienced as a couple and how it had affected my professional life. I continued work on my memoir throughout a long, dark Toronto winter, growing ever more bitter at having been ejected from my country of birth. It became clear to me, however, that a memoir forged in anger made for an unpleasant read. I was too close to the material and lacked sufficient objectivity to produce anything better than 200,000 words worth of sour grapes. And so, I shoved the manuscript into a drawer and focused, instead, on re-inventing myself as a foreign legal consultant, specializing in, of all things, United States immigration.

Two decades after shelving my aborted memoir, I happened across the material, dusted it off, and began the process of reimagining it as fiction—as an alternate universe version of the real events—a format I felt better suited the subject. The result of this work is my third novel *The Fitful Sleep of Immigrants*. In this alternate universe version of the facts, I explore what would have happened had my partner and I chose to remain in the United States and fight his case. As such, it represents a kind of self-therapy, something that confirmed for me, once and for all, that our decision to leave was the right one.

These days I'm often asked whether we'd ever consider moving back to the United States now that marriage equality is the law of the land. Our answer to this question is a resounding __no__. Although I count myself as a proud American Expat and enjoy our annual visits to California to reunite with our families, once my partner and I tasted life outside the United States, including the liberal social policies we sought, there was no going back for us.

There's still a long way to go before we who are LGBTQ+ are on equal footing with everyone else, given that close to 50% of the US population still considers us to be counterculture. Along our journey, we've encountered several other couples with similar stories, and it is to them, that I have dedicated *The Fitful Sleep of Immigrants*. I'm hopeful that my book, as a cross-over novel, may engender some empathy for our cause and help swing the pendulum of public opinion a bit more to our side.

Enjoy!

Praise for
The Fitful Sleep of Immigrants

"Orlando Ortega-Medina has written a compelling novel set within fraught familial, religious, legal and romantic realities of gay love."

—Rabbi Steven Greenberg, author of *Wrestling with God & Men: Homosexuality in the Jewish Tradition*

"There's plenty of drama inside and outside the courtroom . . . plus stalking and 90s homophobia—in this deeply moving novel with depth and heart that explores how difficult it is to find a place called home in a world filled with hate."

—Lev Raphael, author of *Winter Eyes*

"The thrills in this legal thriller come not only from its plot but also from its rich portrait of the varieties of American estrangement."

—Michael Lowenthal, author of *Sex with Strangers*

"Orlando Ortega-Medina's *The Fitful Sleep of Immigrants* is equal parts love story, legal thriller, and social commentary that powerfully weaves together disparate narratives to produce a provocative, big-hearted page-turner of a novel. What a triumph!"

—Daniel A. Olivas, author of *How to Date a Flying Mexican: New and Collected Stories*

"Ortega-Medina"s novel is a quiet thriller, simmering with tension, a story of exile in which the most haunted fugitive turns out to be the man on the run from himself"

—Hilary Zaid, author of *Paper is White* and *Forget I Told You This*

Amble Press

Copyright © 2023 Orlando Ortega-Medina

Print ISBN: 978-1-61294-263-6

Unplugged Book Box Special Edition
published by arrangement with Amble Press

Amble Press First Edition: April 2023

Cover designer:
TreeHouse Studio

Amble Press
PO Box 3671
Ann Arbor MI 48106-3671

www.amblepressbooks.com

*To the countless multinational same-sex couples
forced to emigrate due to marriage inequality and to those
progressive countries that welcomed them with open hearts.*

Chapter 1

The sun begins its slow, aching descent over the Negev Highlands. It sets alight the azure expanse above Kfar Kerem with mad swirls of yellow, orange, deep red. As I hurry to wrap up a day's work picking grapes in the community vineyard, I pause for a moment in the waning light to take in the beauty of my surroundings: the lush fields, the vine-covered hills. A warm desert breeze, deliciously laced with the scent of orange blossoms, dries the perspiration from my face. I draw it in, hold it, and release it, once, twice, three times. Then I trudge across the field to pack away my tools. On my way back to my bunkhouse, I catch sight of beautiful Simon. He waves at me from the other side of the field, beckoning me over to the baseball dugout, our rendezvous point, and, for a moment, I forget to breathe . . .

A knock at my office door jarred me out of my meditation.

"Mr. Mendes, this came in over the fax machine," my legal assistant Vlad said as he pushed open the door and tossed a three-page document onto my desk. "It's from the Xanadu lawyer."

I skimmed the letter for half a minute and tossed it aside with a groan. It was nine thirty on a Tuesday morning, my first day back at work after a long weekend. It hadn't gotten off to a good start: by nine, all the parking lots in downtown San Francisco were full, and the nearest available meter I could find was at the summit of Telegraph Hill, a twenty-minute hike from our Jackson Square offices.

Now that I was at my desk, poring over the latest evidence collected in our sexual harassment claim against Xanadu Hotels, I was having trouble concentrating. The air conditioning was on too high, and a few members of the office staff were gathered outside my door, catching up on everything they'd done over the weekend.

"Sorry, folks," I called out in as diplomatic a tone as I could muster. "Do you mind taking the noise somewhere else, please?"

An awkward silence hung in the air as the five clerks scattered, each to his or her own workstation. Frustrated, I rested my head on folded arms. The weekend hadn't been long enough.

I raised my eyes and focused on the framed photograph of Isaac Perez, my lover of six years, and felt my heart rate slow. He had a warm, open smile that reminded me of better days, in contrast to my usually serious expression. Marc Mendes, the serious lawyer—it's what my colleagues called me. Thirty-something, bearded, prematurely gray, and haggard. As much as I loved the law, my daily routine was grinding me down. My relationship with my senior partner, Ed Haddad, had become strained due to our diverging visions for the firm, and I was having serious issues with the cases he was tossing my way. To cope with my growing dissatisfaction, I found myself retreating more and more into daydreams of happier times. Better that, I figured, than giving in again to the bottle or worse. There was no question about it: I needed a new lease on life.

Reluctantly, I returned to the Xanadu file. I was just getting into reading the latest caustic fax from the company's defense lawyer when Ed's ever-calm voice lilted out of the intercom.

"Marc, can you take a call on line three?"

I looked up from the file and cast about the room. In the three years Ed and I had worked together, he'd never personally asked me to take a call.

"What's up, Ed?"

"It's Silva. Seems he's got a problem and wants to speak to

2

you about it."

I glanced at the Xanadu file and noted the plaintiff's name. "Alejandro Silva?"

"The same," Ed said. "Line three. Come see me when you've finished."

Alejandro Silva had appeared at our offices about a month earlier with a typical sexual harassment claim. The kind that was difficult to prove. Silva had been employed by Xanadu Hotel on Market as a junior mechanic. According to Silva, Jimbo Harrison, Xanadu's plant manager and Silva's immediate supervisor, had called Silva to his office on a pretext and offered him oral sex. When Silva refused, Harrison told him to think about it and suggested Silva would get a promotion if he capitulated.

One week later, Harrison called Silva to his office again and engaged him in idle chitchat for a few minutes. Then he pounced on Silva. Harrison held him down and tried to kiss him on the mouth; he pleaded with Silva to sleep with him at least once. But Silva was adamant he wasn't interested in Harrison, calling him an old queer. Humiliated, Harrison released Silva, who ran out the door and returned to his duties. An hour later, Silva was called to the personnel department and handed his walking papers with a check for two weeks' severance pay. The hotel had terminated his employment at Harrison's request.

Xanadu's position was that the case was impossible to substantiate since the alleged harassment had taken place behind closed doors. In other words, the case was nothing more than a he said/he said affair.

Nevertheless, we did have a few facts that lent credibility to our side. First, Silva made for a sympathetic witness if his case ever went before a jury. He was young and handsome, in contrast to Harrison, who was well past middle age and not particularly attractive. Second, there had been chronic gossip and speculation about Harrison's sexual orientation among the hotel staff ever since he'd arrived three months before. But most damning to the

3

hotel's defense was the information that had recently come to light: Harrison had been transferred to Xanadu's San Francisco property from Xanadu Seattle because of a similar complaint.

At our first meeting, Silva had struck me as one of the most charming persons I'd ever encountered in all my years of practice. He was in his mid-twenties, of medium stature, with an eye-wateringly handsome, open face. Longish brown hair, beautiful hazel eyes, a honey-colored complexion, and a distinctive oval birthmark that I found sexy, despite myself. He spoke quietly, politely, rarely raising his smooth voice above a whisper, always keeping his striking eyes firmly locked on mine.

He explained that he'd been born in San Diego to a single mother to the great disappointment of his grandfather, the owner of a chain of body shops in Southern California. As punishment, his grandfather had sent him and his mother to live with extended family in Jalisco, Mexico, where Silva was raised to the age of fourteen. Then his grandfather had summoned him back to San Diego and enrolled him in a local Catholic school for boys. Even though his grandfather had taken charge of his education and upbringing, he was, according to Silva, harsh to the point of abusive, frequently beating him for even the slightest misstep. He promised to leave Silva his chain of body shops if he proved worthy, forcing him to work ten-hour days on the weekends so that he could learn the trade.

By age seventeen, Silva had had enough and ran away without a dime to his name, first to Los Angeles where he worked in restaurants and garages and roomed with coworkers, and then to San Francisco, where he eventually landed a job at Xanadu. Ever calculating, Ed was sure we could make good use of these facts if Silva's case ever went to trial. In his words, Silva was clearly a serial victim. Personally, I just felt sorry for the guy.

I picked up the telephone.

"Mr. Mendes," said the voice at the other end of the line, "I don't have much time. I need to see you *right away*." He sounded agitated, almost panicked.

"What's going on, Mr. Silva?"

"I'm in jail!"

It took me a moment to register the word. "Jail?"

"Yes. The West County Detention Center in Richmond. Come see me, please!"

"Wait, what happened?"

A male voice in the background growled, "Finish it up, you! We've got a line forming here."

"Please hurry, Mr. Mendes!" Silva said.

There was a click, and the line went dead. I immediately looked up Contra Costa County's booking information number and placed a call. I was shocked to hear Silva was being held pending a parole violation hearing. If Silva was on parole, that could only mean he'd previously done time in state prison for a felony of some sort, something he'd failed to mention.

I kicked myself for not asking the handsome Mr. Silva a very standard question at our first meeting: "Have you ever been arrested or convicted?" Apparently he had. Big time.

I took a deep breath and stepped into Ed's office. Tall, dark, and dignified, at forty-five my Lebanese-American business partner could have easily passed for thirty. He looked up from his computer and regarded me with a fixed smile.

"What happened?" he asked.

"Silva's in jail."

"That much I gathered; *why* is he in jail?"

"He didn't have time to tell me much. According to booking information, they've got him on a parole violation. That's pretty much all they know. I'm going to have to go see him."

Ed shook his head and looked up at the ceiling. "How did we not know about this?"

"Somehow it slipped my mind to ask, sorry. It won't happen again."

Ed leaned forward and cut his eyes at me. "You do realize

5

this could fuck up the whole case for us, don't you? He's our *only* witness. If the other side finds out he's a felon, his credibility is as good as dead, as is our case."

"Easy there, Ed. It may not be as bad as all that. Leave it with me."

Ed fixed me with a cold stare. "You've had your head up your ass lately, Marc. I suggest you pull it out and get back with the program."

We regarded each other for a beat as I chewed on his words.

"I'll see you when you get back." He turned his attention to a file on his desk.

I grabbed my briefcase and a notepad and ran downstairs.

"Susan, I'm stepping out until after lunch," I said to our receptionist as I sped past her desk.

"Mr. Mendes, wait!" She waved a telephone memo at me. "Your mother called from Los Angeles and said to remind you about the, um"—she glanced at the message—"about your family's Passover Seder on the twenty-first."

"Thanks." I groaned inside as I snatched the memo out of her hand and ran out the door, mentally pushing aside another impending disaster, and focused instead on my immediate task.

I sprinted out of our two-story brick office building, up Montgomery Street, crossed Broadway, and hiked the rest of the way up Telegraph Hill. I was wheezing and soaked with sweat as I approached my Range Rover a few minutes later. My chest tightened at the sight of a parking ticket fluttering in the breeze, pinned to the windshield. It was my tenth one this month. I yanked it off and tossed it into the back seat along with the other nine.

I drove across the Bay Bridge and headed north on the 80 freeway. The stress of the morning had called up an urge for something strong, a drink, anything. I gritted my teeth and pushed back against the craving as I'd been doing now for a couple of years. I'd stopped attending NA meetings some time ago, as they'd eaten into my schedule, and I'd been white-knuckling it ever since. As long as I could ride out the cravings with deep breathing and a couple of mindfulness exercises, I'd be okay. *I'll be okay.*

As I took the 580 turnoff to Richmond, my thoughts turned to Silva and the predicament we were in. I couldn't believe this was happening. How could I possibly have missed asking him about his police record? Was I that charmed by his good looks, or was my head really that far up my ass, as Ed had said? And what could he have done to get on parole? Whatever it was, I was going to have to find a way to fix this. There was no way I was going to give Xanadu the pleasure of unfairly firing Silva with impunity.

At the gates of the jail, I flashed my driver's license and my bar card. The guard examined them for a moment and waved me through. I parked and marched into the visitor's center, where I was given a guest badge and directions to Silva's blockhouse. The sally port slid open with a grinding steel-on-steel sound, and I passed through unescorted.

I walked along a sidewalk that meandered through a grassy area and followed it to the blockhouse where Silva was being held. It was a large, octagonal two-story structure with a wide center area open to the top of the building and a perimeter ringed with cells. There were inmates scattered everywhere. Some were playing cards, others were watching TV, and others moved in and out of a set of double doors at the back of the building leading to a playing field. In the middle of the room sat a paper-thin, pimple-faced guard at a desk, talking on the telephone.

"Excuse me," I said after a few seconds of being ignored, "I'm here to see Alejandro Silva. I'm his lawyer."

The guard set down the telephone and motioned me into a small interview room equipped with a wooden table and two plastic chairs. A couple of minutes later, Silva stepped into the room and sat in the chair opposite me. His face was ashen, and his hands were trembling.

"Mr. Mendes, thank you so much for coming," he said in a low voice. He folded his hands to hold them steady. "I can't tell you how much I appreciate it."

He drew a breath and flashed a pained smile that lit up his eyes and showed off his perfect teeth. I'd been impressed with his good looks at our first meeting. But here was something new. A sexy vulnerability I hadn't noticed before. It touched something inside me that hadn't been touched in a long time. Not since Simon.

"What happened, Mr. Silva?" I asked gently, refocusing on the reason I was there.

Silva tossed a glance over his shoulder. "My parole officer had me arrested. He says I stole my roommate's car. But it's not true! He told me I could use it anytime I needed it, I swear. He was just sore at me because I'd fallen behind in my rent. So he sicced my parole officer on me."

"Just a second, Mr. Silva. Let's start with why you were on parole in the first place."

Silva closed his eyes and shook his head. After a moment, he opened them and met my gaze. "You're not going to like this."

"You're probably right. But if you want me to help you, I need the full story. I'm your lawyer; you can trust me."

He drew a deep breath and nodded. Then he leaned across the table and, in the confines of that tiny room, uttered the words that sent my already messy life into a tailspin: "I killed a man," he whispered. "Five years ago, in San Francisco."

My head snapped up. "You did what?"

"I can explain."

"Yeah, I think you'd better."

Silva grasped my wrist with a cold hand, tears now coursing down his face. He proceeded to tell me the chilling story of how he'd been sexually assaulted by the owner of a hair salon who'd been letting him live rent-free in his house.

"He thought I was gay," he said. "He kept trying to sleep with me. And then that night he got me really drunk, and I passed out. When I woke up, I was naked, and he was trying to stick his . . ." Silva closed his eyes and shook his head slowly. "I shoved him, hard, and he fell and split his head open."

Silva paused and searched my shocked face. "It was an accident, Mr. Mendes, I swear. I kind of went nuts. But I didn't mean to kill him. I just wanted him to stop."

"What were you convicted of?"

"Manslaughter. I got a six-year sentence and was paroled in three."

I pulled back my hand and sat up, processing what he'd just told me, trying to recover from the shock of the revelation. Silva wiped his face with the back of his sleeve and crossed his arms. He stared at me from across the table, waiting.

"Why didn't you mention any of this to me before, Mr. Silva?"

"Call me Alejandro. I hate that Mr. Silva stuff. Makes me feel old."

"Fine. Alejandro. Why didn't you mention any of this to me before?"

"Because you never asked me. Plus, I didn't see how my getting fired from Xanadu had anything to do with my doing time. Anyway, they didn't know about it at the hotel."

"Are you sure about that?"

"I'm pretty sure, yes. But my problem *now* is the parole violation. My hearing's coming up in a couple of weeks. Can you help me with that?"

"I'm not a criminal defense lawyer, Alejandro. But I'm sure the parole board will assign you a perfectly competent panel attorney—"

Silva shook his head. "I don't want a panel attorney. They're just hired guns who don't care. I want *you* to help me."

I stood and waved to the guard, suddenly needing to regroup.

"You've laid a lot on me, Alejandro." I squeezed his shoulder reassuringly. "I'll see what I can do."

"But what about my parole violation hearing?" he asked, craning his neck around as I pushed open the door.

"I'll get back to you on that."

Chapter 2

A quarter of an hour later, I was driving back to the city across the Bay Bridge, my mind swirling.

I kind of went nuts . . .

All lawyers know that clients rarely tell the complete truth. But Silva's not mentioning he went to prison for manslaughter was a damned serious omission that could have a devastating impact on his suit against Xanadu. For as much as I wanted to help him, Silva's omission was reason enough for us to drop his case. I was sure that Ed would see it that way. But before I would allow such drastic action, I needed to know how much of what Silva had told me was the truth.

I kind of went nuts . . .

I exited the bridge at Fremont Street and drove past the Greyhound Bus Terminal. But instead of going back to my office, I made a beeline to the Criminal Courts on Bryant Street.

The building that housed the criminal courts, the police department, the coroner's office, and the San Francisco County Jail was hands down the ugliest structure in the city. It was, for all intents, a massive, window-deficient concrete rectangle that took up an entire block. Its heavily guarded front doors opened onto Bryant Street in the industrial SoMa district, and an elevated portion of the 101 freeway skirted its backside. I'd never been inside.

I parked in a lot across the street that, amazingly, had one available space. Grabbing my notepad, I jaywalked past a contingent of San Francisco's finest on their lunch break and ran up the concrete slab steps leading into the building.

I followed the signs to the clerk's office on the third floor and requested Silva's case file. One of the ten deputy clerks told me to wait while he tracked it down. The room, which was decorated in dark marble, was soft-lit and quiet. The only sounds were the rustle of papers, the light tapping of fingers on keyboards, and the occasional clearing of a throat.

The chirping of my cell phone broke the funereal silence, and ten pairs of eyes suddenly focused on me. I recognized the incoming number as that of Landis, Murray, Smith, and Damji, the SoMa law firm where my lover, Isaac, worked as a paralegal. I took the call in the hallway.

"Where *are* you, Marc?" Isaac said, sounding ready to take my head off. "We're supposed to meet for lunch."

I looked at my watch and winced. We'd made a date for twelve-thirty, and it was already approaching one. "Isaac, I'm sorry. I'm at the Criminal Courts."

"What are you doing there?"

"I'll explain later. It's related to a case we're working on at the office."

The line went silent for a moment. Then Isaac spoke again; his voice sounded further away. "This is the third time this month you've stood me up."

"You're keeping count now?" I said a bit too sharply, then took a moment and pushed down my anger. "Come on, Isaac, you work in a law office. You know how it is with lawyers, one crisis after another."

"You could have at least called me, couldn't you? I've been waiting for twenty minutes. Should I keep waiting, or what?"

"No, you go ahead and eat without me."

No response.

I thought I'd lost the signal. "Hello?"

"Call me later." Isaac's voice was pregnant with disappointment. Then the line went dead. I tried calling him back, but it went straight to voicemail.

I felt sad that our once vibrant relationship had lately turned into one long, boring bicker-fest filled with suspicion and petty jealousies. The truth was we'd always had an intense love-hate thing going on from the start, with nothing much in between. I remember Jacob, my twin brother, had once quipped that my relationship with Isaac was bipolar, ever swinging between the heights of manic happiness and the depths of the dark blue sea. We had laughed at Jacob's little joke, Isaac and I, back when we still knew how to laugh. Now it was all tension between us. Despite that, I loved Isaac deeply. He was the best thing that had ever happened to me. My relationship with him had stabilized me back when I was nothing more than a rudderless ship on a churning ocean. And any success I'd achieved so far in my life I owed in large part to our relationship. But I was fucking things up lately, with him, with everyone. I looked again at the cell phone I was gripping with damp fingers, steeling myself to try his number when the door to the clerk's office swung open.

"*There* you are," said the deputy clerk who was helping me. "Your file's ready."

As much as it pained me, Isaac would have to wait.

I had a moment of déjà vu as I opened Silva's case file. In my second year of law school, I'd clerked for the Los Angeles County Public Defender's office. One of my duties was writing one-paragraph case summaries for use by the deputy public defenders based on my review of the case files assigned to me. I still found it amazing a single defense lawyer could walk into court armed only with my notes and represent fifty defendants at a time, never having met most of them.

Silva's file was thin as far as felony cases go. It consisted of a sealed police report, a felony complaint, a forty-page transcript from the evidentiary hearing, a plea form, the sentencing transcript, and the clerk's handwritten notes. I read the complaint: one count of first-degree murder. I stared at the words for a moment, hardly believing what I was seeing, almost afraid to read on. First-degree murder required premeditation and carried a penalty of twenty-five to life. But Silva was out . . .

I moved on to reading the plea form executed two months after his arrest. I was relieved to see that he had pled no contest to voluntary manslaughter, as he'd told me, and was given the mid-term sentence of six years in state prison. With *good time/work time*, he would have been out in three. Something had obviously happened between the time he was arrested and charged with first-degree murder and the time a judge was willing to accept a no-contest plea for manslaughter. I settled into reading the transcript.

Three witnesses had testified, all for the prosecution. The evidence developed by the prosecutor was straightforward: the victim, Charlie Stewart, a well-liked and colorful figure in the San Francisco gay community, had befriended Silva, a drifter whom he found one afternoon sitting on the curb in front of his Castro Street barbershop. Newly arrived in town, Silva had no money, no job, and nowhere to sleep. Against the better advice of the owners of neighboring businesses, Charlie offered him all three. He gave Silva a job sweeping floors at the barbershop and let him sleep on a sofa bed in his Mission District flat. After work, the two of them were frequently spotted drinking martinis at Harvey's, a popular hangout on the corner of Eighteenth and Castro.

Things had gone well for a few weeks. Then, one Tuesday morning, Charlie had failed to show up at his shop. For the past ten years, he'd been absolutely religious about opening his doors at nine thirty sharp each morning. By noon his Castro

Street neighbors began to worry. This was a district where business owners watched out for each other. Ever since he had taken up with Silva, his neighbors had been predicting disaster, suspicious that Silva was a grifter who preyed on older men. At seven o'clock that evening, two police officers had arrived at Charlie's flat and found the front door half open. They knocked twice, waited a few seconds, and moved in. Two minutes later, they found Charlie Stewart's body stuffed under his canopy bed. The back of his head appeared to have been bashed in, and there were deep, thick puncture wounds on the left side of his face.

An all-points bulletin was put out for Silva. One hour later, a patrolman spotted him huddled under a railroad bridge in Hunter's Point. In a matter of moments, an army of police officers had surrounded him, their rifles and revolvers trained on him. They took him into custody without incident, and by midnight, he had confessed to killing Stewart the night before. The story he told the police was the same one he had told me. Verbatim. They obviously didn't buy it.

A forensic investigation of the scene confirmed that Charlie's head had made forceful contact with the wall to the left of his fireplace, after which he appeared to have fallen onto an iron grate, explaining the wounds to his face. Blood streaks on the hardwood floor leading from the living room confirmed the body had been dragged to his bedroom and shoved under his bed. This was all supported by the medical examiner's report, which concluded that what had killed Charlie was the blow to his head. The puncture wounds on his face came afterward.

The prosecutor's theory of premeditation boiled down to three key facts: A victim with a bashed-in head, his body deliberately hidden under his bed, and a perpetrator who fled the scene. Simple.

In her summation, Silva's defense attorney argued that his spontaneous statement—"I kind of went nuts the last time he tried to touch me"—along with the almost superhuman

15

force with which he had shoved Charlie did not indicate the premeditation or malice aforethought necessary for a charge of first-degree murder. She asked the judge to dismiss the charge or, in the alternative, hold Silva to answer for one count of voluntary manslaughter or, at worst, second-degree murder. The judge declined and bound Silva over to stand trial in the Superior Court as charged.

From a strictly legal point of view, I agreed with the defense attorney. The prosecutor had not presented any evidence suggesting Silva's attack on Stewart was planned, or cool and calculated. On the contrary, the prosecution's own evidence indicated, at worst, a sudden, frenzied attack. It was a perfect case for a manslaughter defense. If this case had ever gone to trial, there was a good chance a jury would have acquitted him.

This must have been the line of thinking in the prosecutor's office. They wouldn't have wanted to lose the case completely. So they offered him a deal, and ten days after the preliminary hearing, at his Superior Court arraignment, Silva entered his no-contest plea to manslaughter, and the judge sentenced him to six years. All things considered, it seemed perfectly reasonable to me.

I looked through the rest of the file to make sure I hadn't missed anything of significance. I hadn't. The sentencing transcript showed Silva's attorney had advocated for therapy instead of custody, drawing the court's attention to his troubled childhood. Focusing on his victimization as a teenager by an abusive grandfather, she argued that Silva should be pitied rather than punished. On the other side, a large delegation of the Castro Street business community had expressed outrage at the court's leniency. The judge ignored both sides and stuck to his sentencing script.

So that was it. Silva had told me the truth, which was somewhat of a relief. Still, a manslaughter conviction wasn't something Ed and I were going to be able to make disappear.

Not to mention that damned parole violation. I was going to have to come up with something pretty fast if I was going to convince Ed to keep Silva as a client.

Slamming shut the file, I returned it to the clerk and walked out.

Desperately needing to decompress before heading back to the office, I grabbed a takeout lunch at the café in the San Francisco Museum of Modern Art. Then I crossed the road for an impromptu picnic amid the rolling lawns, flowering trees, and waterfalls of Yerba Buena Gardens. On a stage set up in the middle of the park, a string quartet performed an homage to Aaron Copland. I ate my lunch slowly in the warm sun, taking in the peaceful scene in an attempt to exorcise the negativity of the morning.

A schoolteacher was leading a group of children behind the waterfalls where the city had created a grotto monument to the ideals of Martin Luther King. There, in the cool dampness of the grotto, one could read the words from some of King's most famous speeches inscribed on a marble wall:

I have a dream that my four little children will one day live in a nation where they will not be judged by the color of their skin, but by the content of their character.

My thoughts turned to my grandfather, Rabbi Gabriel Mendes, who fled his native Syria with my grandmother in the late 1930s in search of just such a nation. Violent anti-Jewish hostilities had broken out in Aleppo, the city where our ancestors had lived for centuries, and they barely escaped with their lives. They ended up in Cuba, where my father was born. Tragically, my grandfather died five years later, bereft, the same year my grandmother was run down by an army jeep as she crossed the boulevard. The jeep never stopped, and those responsible were never identified.

Twenty-three years after my grandparents fled Syria, my father and mother had left Cuba, escaping from the Castro government, which wasn't tolerant of religion in general, least of all the Jewish faith. They settled in Los Angeles, where my father took up the post of associate rabbi of an established Sephardic community. Jacob and I were born a year later.

We were a family of emigrants, on the move from generation to generation. Forced to flee our homes because of intolerable situations imposed on us by those in power. The United States was meant to be the last stop on that journey. A just society with equal opportunity and equal protection for all, regardless of creed, race, gender, or sexual orientation.

I have a dream . . .

I took a bite of my sandwich. It's still a dream, I mused.

"What did you find out?" Ed asked once I'd arrived back at the office.

I closed the door to the boardroom and leveled my eyes at him. "He did three years in prison for manslaughter."

Ed jerked upright. "What?"

"He slammed his roommate against the wall for sexually assaulting him. That's the story he told the police and the story he told me. The evidence bears it out."

Ed took this in for a moment, then closed his eyes and pressed his temples the way he did whenever he felt a migraine coming on.

"His roommate was another man, I suppose?"

"Yes."

"A gay man?"

"Yes."

"He killed one gay man for making a pass at him and is suing another for the same thing."

"To be fair, it was more than a pass, Ed," I emphasized.

Ed waved off my comment. "A jury might think he's a little oversensitive."

I nodded. "Or just plain homophobic."

"Not to mention his entire credibility can be impeached with his felony conviction."

We sat in silence, each of us adrift in our thoughts. The quiet was broken by Vlad's voice pulsing out of the intercom.

"Mr. Haddad, you have a call on line two. It's Jerry Ulrich from the *Chronicle*."

Ed didn't react.

"Vlad, tell Ulrich that Mr. Haddad is tied up in a meeting. And hold all calls until we're done in here."

"Sure thing, sir."

Ed stood and stretched. "Silva withheld vital information from us. We could bail on the case."

"Hang on, Ed. The other side doesn't know about the conviction."

"What do you mean?"

"Silva says they don't know anything, and I haven't had any indication from them that they do. So let's just continue with the case and see if we can get a settlement offer. They made him one before."

"Yes, and he turned it down."

"That was then. We can always withdraw from his case if they find out. If they *never* find out and they settle, then all the better for us."

"What about the parole violation?"

"That's just a misunderstanding between Silva and his roommate. Something about Silva using his car without his permission. The hearing's next week. I'm going to go speak with the roommate and Silva's PO. If I can clear it up, then hopefully Silva won't be in jail when Xanadu is ready to depose him. In the meantime, I can let them know we're ready to settle. Maybe they'll bite."

Ed took in my words, stone-faced. After a moment, he nodded.

"Thanks, Ed." I stood, readying myself to go. "Oh, one more thing."

He narrowed his eyes at me.

"Do you mind covering the WEBINC pretrial tomorrow morning for me? All of this has thrown off my schedule, and I missed a lunch date with Isaac. I'd like the extra time to try and make things up with him."

"Sure. Talk to the roommate, then go home and relax," Ed said, nodding at the door. "I'll handle the pretrial."

According to Silva's file, his last known address was an apartment in Oakland's Lake Merritt district. I tried calling the telephone number we had for him, but there was no answer, so I decided to drive out there to investigate.

As I rounded the vast inner-city lagoon that was Lake Merritt, I was impressed by how beautiful it was, surrounded by verdant parkland, expensive houses, and glitzy apartment blocks. There was even a boating center and small amusement park along its grassy shores. It was a universe away from the gritty, urban image of Oakland that had stained its reputation.

I pulled up in front of Silva's building. It was a well-maintained five-story structure that looked straight out of the 1930s—pink stucco, clay-tile roof, exposed wooden beams, Moorish arches, and an incongruous tower that echoed the Giralda in Seville. I buzzed his apartment and waited. A moment later a soft male voice answered from the intercom.

"Good afternoon," I said. "I'm sorry to disturb you. I'm here about Alejandro Silva."

There was a long period of silence followed by a muffled response: "Who is this, please?"

"I'm Mr. Silva's employment lawyer. I'd like to have a word with his roommate if possible."

After a moment, the entry buzzer sounded. I pushed open the heavy, carved wood front door and stepped into the cool of a vaulted foyer, which was tastefully tiled in decorative terracotta. An antique cage elevator carried me to the penthouse level, where I was met by a rail-thin man in his late sixties or early seventies with watery green eyes and a receding blond hairline. He was dressed in an elegant blue velour housecoat with matching slippers and a pair of red linen trousers. The gentleman, who identified himself as Professor Emeritus Peter Miller, graciously accepted my business card and invited me inside his well-appointed, antique-filled apartment. I noted a fully stocked wet bar at the back of the living room.

"Please," Miller said, gesturing at a plush love seat.

I sank into the love seat. He sat opposite me in a high-backed wooden chair and studied my business card, then looked up and flashed an icy smile. "Now then, Marc Mendes, Attorney at Law, how may I help you?"

"I understand my client Alejandro Silva lives here."

"You mean he lived here," Miller corrected. "Past tense." He continued to smile, baring a perfect set of bleached teeth.

"Got it. Anyway, as I said earlier, I'm interested in speaking with Mr. Silva's roommate. Is he in?"

Miller stared at me for a beat. "There's no roommate, Mr. Mendes. Only me. This is my home, and Alejandro was occupying my guest room." He gestured toward the back of the apartment.

I was taken aback at that, having imagined Silva's roommate to be closer to him in both age and station. Or perhaps I'd begun to suspect otherwise and was hoping against hope that I was wrong.

"I understand from Mr. Silva that you reported him to his parole officer, claiming he stole your car. Is that correct?"

Miller sighed and passed his fingers through his thinning hair. "Yes, Mr. Mendes, that's correct. He took my Jaguar without asking and disappeared for three days. What else was I to think?"

I sidestepped the problematic three-day absence and pressed on. "Mr. Silva seems to think it had something to do with not paying his rent on time."

Miller smothered a titter and wiped his eyes with the back of his hand. "Oh, please. That boy never paid me a dime of rent in the four months he lived here."

"I don't understand. Was he meant to pay rent, or were you letting him live here rent-free?"

"What I mean, Mr. Mendes, is that your lovely client Alejandro charmed his way into my life, leading me to believe he was interested in me." Miller's face became serious. "Can you imagine that?" He stood and drifted to a large window that overlooked the lagoon. He stared outside for a moment and looked back at me. "He needed a place to live. I offered my guest room, and he promised to pay five hundred dollars a month once he was on his feet financially. Silly me, I agreed."

The room fell silent for a moment while I processed the information and worked out my next set of questions.

"I'm sorry," Miller said abruptly. "I've forgotten my manners." He stepped over to the wet bar and picked up a tumbler. "May I offer you something to drink, Mr. Mendes? Some lemonade? Perhaps something stronger?"

"No, thank you. I'm all right."

He poured himself a whiskey and dropped two cubes of ice into it. Then he took a sip and closed his eyes, a blissful smile breaking out on his face. It took all I had to tear my eyes away from that glass and refocus.

"How did you and Alejandro meet?" I asked.

Miller crossed the room and sat in front of me again. "He was waiting tables at a French cafe that I frequent in Piedmont. I invited him for drinks after work, and he accepted. He told me he'd recently been laid off by the Xanadu hotel chain and was between apartments." Miller swirled the amber liquid in his glass and stared at it pensively. "What can I say? I felt sorry for the young man. He was young, attractive, and very well mannered. I liked him; I thought he might like me, too. My mistake was to play the Good Samaritan and offer him a room in my home."

"Were the two of you lovers?"

He took a sip of his whiskey, then set aside the tumbler and frowned.

"You don't have to tell me if you don't want to," I said. "Don't feel any pressure. But it might be helpful to Alejandro's case."

"And what makes you think I want to help him?" he asked, meeting my gaze.

"You may not. That's your prerogative, of course. I'm just trying to understand the facts. Nothing more."

Miller nodded. "What did he tell you? About us being lovers."

"He didn't tell me anything. But with all due respect, sir, I can't see how you would have let him live here rent-free on a promise unless you were getting something from him in return."

Miller picked up the tumbler and drained it, then set it down noisily on the coffee table. "We *weren't* lovers. I had hoped for more, of course. But he soon made it clear he wasn't gay. That said, the boy didn't mind my taking certain liberties from time to time while he feigned sleep. And he seemed happy enough to be seen on my arm whenever we went out together. As long as I paid."

"I see." I loosened my tie, feeling suddenly discomfited by what I was hearing.

"Over time, I grew very attached to him and our arrangement.

Then he pulled that disappearing act with my Jaguar. I was sick to death with worry. Not paying rent was one thing, but vanishing with my car without a word was unforgivable. I dug around in his things for some clue as to where he'd gone. That's when I found his parole officer's business card. I couldn't believe it. I had no idea the boy was on parole."

Miller reached into the pocket of his housecoat, produced the card, and handed it to me. I noted the name and number of Silva's parole officer and handed it back.

"Keep it," he said, rising from the chair and refilling his glass. "Anyway, I hope that young man learns his lesson."

"You don't really believe he intended to steal your car, do you?"

Miller shrugged. "Does it matter at this point?"

"Actually, yes. There's a big difference between a joyride and intending to permanently deprive an owner of his car."

Miller barked a sarcastic laugh. "Three days is an awful long joyride in my book, Mr. Mendes."

"Fair enough. But did he clear out his room?" I pointed in the direction of the guest room.

"No, it's all still there. I've boxed most of it up."

"Well, then?"

"Fine, let's say he didn't actually intend to steal my car. Nevertheless, what he did wasn't right. Was it?"

"No, it wasn't," I said. "But if it was only an irresponsible, extended joyride, it might make a difference to his parole officer and to the parole board."

Miller shook his head. "I'm *not* going to change my story if that's what you're suggesting, Mr. Mendes."

"Nothing like that at all, sir. I was just stating a fact." I stood and readied myself to leave before I got myself into trouble. I didn't want anyone flinging a charge of witness tampering at me. "I've taken enough of your afternoon. Thank you very much for the time. I appreciate your candor."

Miller shrugged and raised his glass soberly. "Blame it on the spirits."

As I exited the building, I punched the number of Silva's parole officer into my cell phone. He answered on the first ring. I explained that I was Silva's lawyer and filled him in on my conversation with Miller, offering the theory of a misunderstanding between roommates instead of straight-up auto theft. The phone went silent for a moment; then the officer spoke, his voice hard as granite.

"I brought in your client on a report of auto theft from Professor Miller. We found him passed out in the vehicle on the side of the road and took him into custody. But that's not the basis of the violation, counselor."

"It's not?"

"No, it's not. Your client tested dirty for cannabis and psilocybin. *That's* the violation. The hearing's just a formality. Your guy's going down for six months."

I ended the call, reeling from a mix of disappointment, anger, and confusion. My head felt like it was about to explode; I couldn't take any more of Silva or his case today. Stumbling to my car, I fired up the engine and headed back to the city across the bridge.

Chapter 3

By the time I got home, it was seven-thirty in the evening. It had taken me nearly an hour and a half of battling rush-hour traffic to drive the thirteen miles to the Marina district apartment I shared with Isaac. We lived on the eighteenth floor of a high-rise with a panoramic view of the San Francisco Bay. It cost us a small fortune each month, but nothing could beat the serenity of that view after a long, stressful day at the office or in court.

I sank into an overstuffed armchair, put my feet on the coffee table, and watched the sun begin its final descent behind the Golden Gate and into the Pacific. The moment it made contact with the water, its rays exploded from the glowing ball of fire, flooding the surrounding hills, the sky, and the water's surface with wide and twisting shafts of blinding gold, blood red, and darkening purple. After a few minutes, it dropped below the surface of the water, leaving in its wake a twilight that painted the sky with a palate of electric blue, a tinge of pink and violet, before finally giving way to the black of night.

"Get your feet off the table, please," came a voice from the front door. It was Isaac, arriving with his mother, Miriam, who was sporting braids and a rust-colored poncho. A sharp-witted woman in her seventies, Miriam had been part of our household ever since Isaac and I had moved in together. That was part of the deal.

Lugging a veggie-stuffed paper bag in her thin arms, Miriam lifted her head at me. I jumped to help bring in the groceries from the hallway.

"It's all right, Mamá. We've got them," Isaac said, easing the bag out of her arms and pushing it at me. He gave me a quick hug and turned his attention to the rest of the groceries. Miriam brushed my cheek with the back of her hand and hobbled to her room to watch the latest installment of her favorite telenovela.

Isaac and I had met in Los Angeles the month after I graduated from law school, following five years of rabid dissipation, including a ninety-day enforced lockdown in rehab. I was volunteering at a legal clinic specializing in Central American asylum cases. He was the clinic's Spanish-language interpreter.

One afternoon, an elderly couple whose son had been tortured by an opposition group in Guatemala came into the clinic and asked for help filling out the forms to request asylum. Although I knew Spanish reasonably well, I was having trouble understanding the couple. They spoke with a peculiar accent, sprinkling their sentences with indigenous words I'd never heard before. After a few attempts, I rang the secretary and asked for the clinic's interpreter. Several minutes later, a tall young man with a warm smile popped his head through the doorway. His short black hair, dark eyes, and prominent cheekbones paired nicely with a crisp white dress shirt, close-fitting blue jeans, and black oxfords.

"You called for an interpreter," he said, in a voice as cool and smooth as a chocolate milkshake. It was more a statement than a question.

I stood and held out my hand. "I'm Marc Mendes, the volunteer law clerk."

He grasped my hand and held it firmly, never taking his

eyes from mine.

"I know. I'm Isaac Perez. How can I help?"

He let go of my hand.

Isaac didn't understand the couple any better than I did. But between the two of us, after two and a half hours, we were able to piece together their story well enough to fill out the forms. At the end of the ordeal, we were all exhausted, the elderly couple included. They thanked us profusely and, after showering us with an abundance of tears and hugs, left us alone in the office.

A few moments of silence passed in which we organized our notes and traded interested glances. Then, Paul Landry, the clinic's neo-hippie director, strode into the office, running his fingers through his shoulder-length mane of hair.

"Are you guys *still* here? Jesus Christ! I thought those people would never leave."

"We had to get their story, and that's how long it took," Isaac said, gathering up his notebook.

I was impressed by how he responded to Landry, confident and unintimidated by the director's position. Landry didn't appear to have noticed.

"Yeah, well, good job! Both of you," he said. "I think you guys deserve some dinner. El Pollo Loco for the two of you. My treat." He held out a ten-dollar bill.

Isaac halted in the doorway.

"Thanks, Paul." I snatched the bill out of his hand and pocketed it. "Your generosity floors me. Want to join?"

"Nah, you guys go on alone. I have some work to finish up."

And with that, Isaac and I were out the door.

We strolled to the restaurant, ordered our food, and sat at a red Formica table to wait for our number to be called. Lively mariachi music blared out of a cracked loudspeaker, and a little boy of around five years old was doing what looked like a Mexican hat dance on a nearby table. His embarrassed mother grabbed at him, trying to pull him down, but he was doing a great job of evading her.

Isaac watched the scene with delight, laughing with infectious enthusiasm. After a few moments, the little boy's mother was able to yank him off the table. Just as quickly, he wriggled out of her arms and took off around the restaurant, hopping and dancing like a little bronco. Finally, the manager snapped off the music, and the little boy returned sheepishly to his table.

I was still processing the scene when Isaac turned to me and asked, "Are you married?"

The question sideswiped me. The last thing I'd expected was something so sudden and direct.

"You look surprised." He flashed a beautiful smile.

"No," I said. "I mean, *yes*, I'm surprised."

Isaac whirled around to see if our order was ready. It was. He jumped up and brought our food to the table.

"I like the chicken here," he said, with an air of nonchalance.

I tentatively nodded my approval of the food.

"And, by the way," he added, "I'm not married, and I don't have kids."

I stared at him as he casually sliced into his chicken and stuffed the pieces into a corn tortilla.

"What makes you think I'd want to know that?" I asked.

"Because you do. I can tell. You've been curious all afternoon. I've been curious, too. About you."

I glanced around the restaurant, which was filling up with diners. It suddenly felt stuffy and hot. After a beat, I looked back and found Isaac staring at me, waiting, holding the dripping tortilla over his plate. Cautious of what I was getting myself into, I let out a long breath and put on my best poker face.

"What's wrong?" Isaac asked.

"Look," I said, lowering my voice, "I'm flattered by your interest. But I'm not ready for this."

He put down his tortilla and leaned forward. "Ready for what?"

"For this." I moved my hand back and forth between us.

"Why?" he asked. "Are you in a relationship?"

"No, I'm single."

"You *are* attracted to me, right? Or was I misreading the signals?"

"You weren't misreading anything. If it's sex you're looking for, I'm down for that. We can go to my place once we're done if you like. I've got all night."

Isaac's face clouded over. He lowered his eyes and poked at his food with a fork. After a moment, he lifted his head. "I was hoping we might see each other outside the clinic in a more formal way. You know, dinner, the movies, some clubbing, the beach, maybe a museum." He flashed a sad smile. "Sex, too, of course. But not that, mainly. That's easy enough to find."

I held his gaze. It had been a long time since I'd dated a nice person. My eyes teared thinking of how alone I'd felt since I'd gotten clean. I swiped at them with the back of my sleeve, angry I'd allowed myself to lose control of my emotions so easily.

Isaac leaned toward me. "What's the matter?"

"I have to warn you, I have a past." I was surprised by how hard my voice sounded.

He blinked at me. "I assume so."

"What I mean," I said, softening my tone, "is that I have issues I'm working through that would make a relationship more challenging than normal. For me and for whomever I'm dating."

"What kind of issues?"

Noticing the restaurant was now packed, I fell quiet, feeling exposed in the presence of so many people.

Isaac placed his hand on my arm. "Why don't we go for a drive? My car's over there." He pointed at a dark blue Toyota Tercel parked across the street.

We rode in silence to Venice Beach through the tail end of rush hour. When we got to the boardwalk, Isaac kicked off his shoes, rolled up his jeans, and walked out onto the sand. The sun was dropping below the horizon, and a cool breeze was kicking up. After a moment of hesitation, I removed my dress shoes, picked my way across the cold sand, and dropped down next to him. He flashed a crooked smile and leaned against me.

"This is nice," he said as the sky darkened with the deepening twilight.

I nodded. Much of the tension I'd been feeling was easing away. It had been so long since I'd relaxed, naturally, without the need for medication, prescribed or otherwise, that I'd forgotten what it felt like. I stared out at the ocean and focused on my breathing.

Isaac pivoted away from me and sat Indian-style. "So you were saying . . ."

I studied him for a beat, considering the wisdom of laying myself bare to a virtual stranger, as sincere as he appeared. That said, wisdom was never my strong suit. So I drew a breath, closed my eyes, and felt my way forward.

"I'm a recovering addict," I started. I kept my eyes closed and waited for a response, but all I heard was his breathing inches away. So I continued. "I've been clean for over a year now. It had gotten so bad I spent an entire summer in rehab." I opened my eyes and found Isaac staring out at the open sea, unblinking. "On top of that, I've never been particularly good at relationships, which was another problem, or maybe part of the same problem. I don't know." I shrugged. "I didn't pick well, I guess. A lot of reckless sex, countless partners. I'm lucky to be alive."

Isaac pried his eyes away from the ocean and looked at me. "Wow."

"Yeah, so that's me."

His face had turned pale. "Have you been tested?" he rasped, "You know, like, for HIV."

"Yes, sure. I get tested regularly. I'm negative. Thank God."

Isaac looked away and raked his fingers through his hair. After a few moments of silence, he looked back at me.

"Not much of a catch, are you?" he said, his mouth pulling back into a half-smile. His eyes looked sad.

"That's what I've been trying to tell you."

Isaac nodded. "But you're clean now. And you're healthy."

"Yes, thank God."

"Well, then—"

"There's one more thing you should know," I interrupted.

"There's more?"

"I'm afraid so. My father's a rabbi. A rabbinical judge, actually. He had a tough time with my addiction stuff, as you can imagine."

"Okay."

"We haven't spoken in a couple of years."

Isaac frowned. "Why? Did he disown you?"

"No, nothing like that. I just haven't wanted to answer to him or my mother about my personal life. So I've kept away."

"Does he at least know you're gay?"

I shook my head. "No. Which is why I wouldn't be sharing any of this with my family if it became serious, except for maybe my twin brother Jacob."

"You have a twin brother? Don't tell me he's gay, too," Isaac said half-serious.

"No, he's straight. But he knows about me and has been running interference for me with my parents for a while."

"Jesus Christ." Isaac rolled his eyes. "Anything else?"

"No. That's it."

"Are you sure you haven't murdered anyone?" he asked with a wry smile.

"Ha-ha. Not yet."

"Just asking."

"I wouldn't think I'm capable of that."

"I was joking, of course. Anyway, I think that's enough for now." Isaac stood, slapped the sand off his jeans, and picked up his shoes. "I need to go home and process all of this if that's all right."

"Yeah, of course."

He held out his hand and pulled me to my feet.

We trudged across the sand in silence back to the boardwalk. When we reached his car, I paused before climbing inside.

"What is it?" Isaac asked.

"I'd appreciate it if you kept everything I've told you confidential."

He'd narrowed his eyes at me for a moment and nodded. "That goes without saying."

After that evening, Isaac and I had become nearly inseparable. After a month of seeing each other every day as friends and confidantes, we transitioned to spending the nights with each other and found ourselves sexually compatible to a fault. Isaac became my new addiction, and I became his. Six months into our tempestuous courtship, he trusted me enough to tell me his own story, how he and his mother had fled the brutality of El Salvador's civil war; how they ended up in the United States, undocumented, on a grant of temporary asylum, and subject to deportation in some distant hypothetical future. But by then we were well on our way to merging our lives. And at that point in our relationship, such details didn't seem to matter a great deal. Little did we know how much our future would hinge on our respective pasts.

Isaac dropped into the sofa across from me and crossed his arms and legs. "What was so pressing that you had to stand me up for lunch today?"

"I'm sorry about that. One of our cases turned crazy. Threw off my whole day."

"What do you mean 'crazy'?" Isaac leaned forward on the sofa, his eyebrows meeting in the middle.

"I can't go into the details, sorry. Confidentiality and all that…"

"You can give me an idea, can't you?"

"All right, fine," I said. "We have this sexual harassment case that, up until this morning, we thought was clear-cut. Then the shit hit. Now it's a crazy case with the plaintiff in jail on a parole violation."

"Parole violation? Why were they on parole? And is it a he or a she?"

"It's a *he*. And I can't tell you more than that. Sorry."

Isaac waved his hand dismissively. "So *that's* why you were at the Criminal Courts today?"

"The Criminal Courts to review the case file and, before that, the county jail to interview the plaintiff who, frankly, has turned out to be a piece of work. Then this afternoon, I had to drive to Oakland to interview the complaining witness in his parole violation. Believe me, I've had quite the day."

As if on cue, Miriam came out of her bedroom and asked us what we wanted to eat. The interruption helped dispel some of the tension in the room. We opted for her veggie-stuffed cabbage with rice, and she disappeared into the kitchen.

Isaac uncrossed his body. "I'm sorry to hear that."

Satisfied we had put the issue to rest, I rotated my neck, which had stiffened in the last few minutes.

Isaac reached over and gave my shoulder a squeeze; I swung

around and offered him my back. After six years together, he knew by instinct when my muscles were tightening up and where to apply firm and steady pressure to work out the knots.

"What does Ed have to say about all this?" he asked after a few moments.

My muscles tensed up again, and I disengaged from Isaac's hands. "We're both hoping the defendants will settle before they find out about the problem. But after what I've discovered this afternoon, I'm not sure we should stay on the case." I moved to the window and looked out at the darkened bay. My chest felt tight, and I had a horrible feeling in the pit of my stomach.

"On top of all of that, there was this." I pulled out the crumpled memo with the message from my mother.

"What's that?" Isaac snatched it out of my hand and read it.

"She keeps leaving me reminders about Passover as if I'm going to forget," I said. "As if I *could* forget."

Isaac handed the memo back to me. "It's coming up soon."

"God!" I stuffed it back into my pocket. "I'm dreading it."

"Not about them meeting me, I hope." Isaac glanced at me reproachfully.

"No, of course not. More about my seeing them again after so long, about having to talk about the whole gay thing. Especially with my father."

"The 'gay thing'?"

"You know what I mean."

At that moment, Miriam hobbled out of the kitchen, balancing two hot serving dishes, one in each hand. "Time to eat," she announced.

Isaac ran to help her. "We'll take care of it, Mamá. You go watch your program."

Miriam gave him a quick peck on the cheek, grabbed her plate of food, and hurried back to her bedroom, calling over her shoulder, "Leave the dishes in the sink! I'll wash them later."

Isaac and I shared a tired smile across the empty room; then he called me over and pulled me into his arms. I relaxed into his embrace and rested my head against his shoulder.

"I'm sorry I pushed," he said. "I didn't realize—"

I kissed him on the forehead. "It's all right, no worries. I'll figure it out." I moved to the sideboard to retrieve a pair of candlesticks for the dinner table. "In the meantime, let's eat. I'm famished."

Isaac watched me light the candles and place them on the table, as was our nightly custom. Then he disappeared into the kitchen and brought out the plates, cutlery, and a nice bottle of nonalcoholic Shiraz. I pulled the cork and poured a glass for each of us, including a small glass reserved for Miriam. This nightly ritual lent a comfortable predictability to the end of my day. It reminded me of the same comfort I'd felt throughout my childhood in my family's weekly observance of *Shabbat*, the Sabbath. Isaac and his mother had become part of the ritual of my adult life. The fact we always made sure to include at least one dish on the dinner table from our respective home cultures added an extra dimension to our shared experience.

As we polished off Miriam's homemade Syrian-style walnut baklava, which she'd baked for my benefit, Isaac flashed a wide smile.

"What?" I asked.

"Tonight's supposed to be the best night for viewing the comet."

"What comet?" I put the last piece of baklava in my mouth and slid the fork onto the empty dessert plate.

"Hale-Bopp—*the* comet."

"Right . . ." I said, racking my tired brain to remember when we'd discussed it.

Isaac gave a sigh of exasperation. "We promised each other last year when I was taking that astronomy course that we'd go out to see it when it arrived."

Vaguely recalling the subject, I nodded, drained my coffee

cup, and reached for the serving pot for some more.

Isaac intercepted the pot and moved it out of my reach. "Tonight's the night. It's the perihelion."

"We're not going to be able to see it very well because of all the city lights."

He gathered up the dirty dishes and matter-of-factly stated, "Well, we're not going to miss it. We promised each other. And besides, we're not going to be here the next time it comes around in two thousand years." He lifted his head and nodded at our bedroom. "Go change into something more comfortable and get yourself ready."

"Ready for what?"

"We're going to Napa."

"Napa? That's over an hour away," I said, looking at my watch.

"It doesn't matter. Get ready," he insisted. "We're not going to miss it."

We drove in silence across the Golden Gate Bridge, up Highway 101, and took the Highway 37 turnoff to Sonoma. The sky was clear, and we could see Hale-Bopp rising in the night sky. As we rounded the vine-planted hills of Sonoma in search of an isolated field, all the problems of the past day fell away. We carried on past shadowy wine country chateaus and villas and crossed into Napa County.

"A few hundred yards beyond the Napa River, we accessed a narrow dirt road that looked promising. After a few minutes of blind driving, it branched onto a country lane that led us to a cozy little clearing bounded on two sides by flowering vineyards and at the far end by a narrow estuary of the Napa River. It was perfect."

I switched off the engine and cut the headlights, and for an instant Isaac and I were plunged into darkness. After a moment, our eyes adjusted to the absence of artificial light, and our surroundings came into a clearer, mellower focus, illuminated by the soft glow emanating from the sky. Isaac squeezed my hand and stepped out of the car in an attitude of reverence. I followed.

Light from countless millions of stars shone down on us from a cloudless and moonless sky. The air was sultry and sweet with the scent of orange blossoms from a nearby grove. We cleared a few stones and extended a sleeping bag on the ground. I stretched out on it and rested my head in Isaac's lap.

Hale-Bopp was clearly visible above us at around eighty degrees from the zenith. Its tail extended an impressive distance from the head of the comet itself. As we gazed at the sky in stunned silence, Isaac raked my hair with his fingers, their tips making soft contact with my scalp.

"It's beautiful," I said after several minutes.

Isaac pointed at the sky. "The last time that comet visited the Earth was in 2214 BC." He looked down at me. "Incredible, isn't it?"

"I can't even fathom that. And that's just one comet. What about all the rest of the things out there? All those stars and galaxies, and the things we can't even see or begin to imagine. Black holes and quasars."

Isaac chuckled. "Aren't you glad I dragged you out here?"

I sat up and gave him a big hug. "To be honest, I'd completely forgotten about the comet. So, yes, thanks."

"You've had a lot on your mind."

"I *have* had a lot on my mind. More than just that case."

"You don't have to talk about it if you don't want to."

"No, it's okay." I gazed up at the comet and drew a deep, calming breath. "We've been taking on more and more cases—too many cases for two lawyers to handle. Ed and I need to recruit another associate, but we haven't gotten around to interviewing anyone yet."

"Maybe it's time for a change," Isaac ventured after a long silence.

"Like what? I can't exactly give up my job."

"Why not? You've made a lot of money already. Why don't you slow it down a bit? We could—"

"What?"

"Well, we've always liked it up here. Wouldn't it be great to *live* here? We could buy a small house, and you could open up your own office in town."

"Don't you think it's too quiet?"

"It is quiet. But consider the quality of life. Beautiful open spaces, clean air, vineyards everywhere." He kissed me and looked back up at the stars. "Besides, it's only an hour from the city."

"I don't know," I said. "I'd have to dissolve the partnership. God knows how long that would take." I sighed at the thought of separating from Ed. The logistics would be a nightmare. "I'll think about it."

Isaac kicked back on the sleeping bag and shut his eyes, smiling. "Okay. You think about it."

Giving in to my exhaustion, I closed my eyes and relished the serenity of the moment, wishing I could stay there forever, frozen in time with my beloved Isaac. He slid closer and stroked my face with the back of his hand. Opening my eyes, I found him staring into my face. His eyes were shining in the starlight. I smiled, and he kissed me, first on the cheek, then on the mouth. I drew him closer, and we kissed tenderly, deeply, enjoying the warm press of our bodies against each other. Then we sat up and helped ourselves out of our clothes and made love for the first time in months in full view of the comet.

Chapter 4

I rose early the next morning and saw Isaac off to work. Then I got back into bed and slept for another two hours. The rest was wonderful, and by the time I was rinsing off under the warm water of the shower, I felt ready to take on the day.

Since I wasn't expecting to drive to a deposition, to court, or anywhere else, I pulled on a black tracksuit and power walked to work along the Embarcadero. When I reached our office building twenty minutes later, my legs were ready to give out. It was ten fifteen.

Through the ground floor window, I could see a small group of women milling about in the waiting area. Vlad intercepted me as I stepped inside.

"Mr. Mendes, your nine thirty appointments are here. They've been waiting."

"What nine thirty appointments?"

Vlad tilted his head toward the waiting area. "Those women in there. They retained the firm yesterday afternoon. Ed set up the appointment for you since he had to go to the WEBINC pretrial this morning in your place. I was supposed to call you to let you know, but it slipped my mind. Sorry."

I glanced in the direction of the waiting area. "What kind of case is it?"

"Ed left a memo on your desk about it. The tall one is Ms.

Hudson, their spokeswoman." He tapped my shoulder and lowered his voice. "Good luck with her."

I popped into the waiting area and was confronted by the sight of three expensively dressed middle-aged women. One of them was sitting on the couch, stroking a tiny silver shih tzu. Another was perusing our collection of paintings and vintage photographs. A tall woman in heels, Ms. Hudson apparently, was pacing the room, a fur pillbox hat nicely balanced on her blonde pixie cut.

"Good morning, I'm Marc Mendes," I said, reaching out a hand to the pacing woman. "Ms. Hudson, is it?"

All heads in the room turned in my direction, and the pacing woman arched an eyebrow at my extended hand.

"Yes, that's right. When is the lawyer arriving? We've been waiting forty-five minutes."

I pulled back my hand. "I'm the lawyer."

"*You're* the lawyer?" She turned and glanced doubtfully at the others, then looked back at me.

"Yes, I'm the lawyer."

She frowned at my tracksuit. "Why are you dressed like that?"

I drew a deep breath and forced a smile. "I'm dressed like this because I was exercising, and I didn't want to perspire in my suit. In any event, I'm sorry to have kept you all waiting. Please accept my apologies." I waved Vlad over. "I believe you've all met my assistant. He'll escort you into the boardroom now. I'll join you in a moment. I won't be five minutes."

I dashed down to the lower level, where Ed and I'd had the foresight to install a full bathroom, and jumped in the shower for a sixty-second rinse. It took me another three minutes or so to change into a fresh suit and tie. Then I ran back upstairs to my desk and pushed aside Ed's memo. Gritting my teeth, I punched in the number to the law firm defending against Alejandro Silva's claim. Seconds later, I had the lead attorney on the line.

"I'd like to reopen settlement discussions," I said once we'd exchanged the customary pleasantries.

"I thought your client wasn't interested in settling," she stated dryly.

"I wouldn't be calling you now if that were still the case," I said, matching her tone.

"What makes you think *my* client is willing to extend another offer?"

"Because they're not going to want to go before a jury with this one."

She paused and rustled some papers in the background, then she spoke again. "May I ask why your Mr. Silva is suddenly so eager to settle?"

A knock on my door jarred my concentration. Vlad stuck in his head and pointed downstairs with an exasperated look on his face. I held up my hand and shooed him away.

"To be frank," I said, refocusing, "the process is wearing Mr. Silva down, and he's keen for some closure. But only at the right price."

"Fine," she said. "I'll talk to my client and get back to you."

"Just make sure you come back to me with a hundred and fifty thousand, or it's no deal."

"That's fifty thousand more than we originally offered," she fired back.

"That's our counteroffer. They can take it or leave it," I said.

"I'm not sure that's going to be possible. But we'll see."

"I strongly suggest you remind your client that the facts look bad for them given the perpetrator's history, and we'll be dredging for even more dirt," I said, bluffing my way forward. "We're preparing to lay it all out to a jury in full-blown Technicolor. So you can tell them it's either pay or play. They've got until the end of April."

I ended the call, took a breath, and grabbed the memo Ed had left for me. It took me thirty seconds to speed-read it:

Marc.

We were retained yesterday afternoon by three female hair stylists: Gertie Ford, Millicent Hudson, and Barbie Shoenfeld. They seem to have a solid gender discrimination claim against the Saint-Cloud Salon and Spa on Nob Hill. I've scheduled them for an appointment with you tomorrow morning at 9:30 a.m. Get their stories, send out a representation letter to the defendants ASAP, and see if you can get CNN *or the* SF Chronicle *interested in doing a story. I'll see you when I get back from the pretrial.*

Ed.

When I stepped into the boardroom, Ms. Hudson was peering at her watch. She looked up at me, and her expression changed from one of hostility to one of surprise as I sat at the head of the table and pulled out a notepad.

"My, don't you clean up well," she said.

The other women nodded in agreement.

"Thank you. Now then, I'd like each of you to introduce yourselves, which will help me once we get into the details of your claim against Saint-Cloud." I turned to Ms. Hudson. "Let's start with you if that's all right."

"I'm Millicent Hudson," she said, drawing herself up. "I'll be doing most of the talking for the group since we all have the same or similar stories. There's no point in repeating ourselves, is there?"

"We'll see," I said. "And the rest of you?"

"That's Gertie Ford." Millicent pointed to the woman with

43

the shih tzu. Gertie flashed a quick smile and lowered her eyes at her dog. "And on your left is Barbie." Barbie nodded at me and exchanged a a quick glance with Gertie.

"We've written everything down so we don't have to waste any time." Ms. Hudson handed me a few sheaves of paper, which I skimmed. Someone had taken the time to set out the facts with a calligraphy pen in small printed letters.

"Who wrote this?"

"I did." Ms. Hudson shifted forward.

"I'll take a few minutes to read this if you don't mind." I rose from the table. "I'll let you know if I have any questions."

"You shouldn't have any questions," Ms. Hudson said. "We've been very thorough."

I smiled politely, then excused myself and went upstairs to review their statement.

Dear Law Firm of Haddad and Mendes,

We the plaintiffs (Millicent, Barbie, and Gertie) wish to thank you from the bottom of our hearts for taking our case against our former employer, Saint-Cloud Salon and Spa on Nob Hill, San Francisco, California, USA. We feel we have been unfairly treated and discriminated against by Saint-Cloud because we are women and not gay.

The whole thing began one year ago, I think it was in February, when Saint-Cloud hired a new manager who was both a male and a gay (homosexual) person. His name is Brent Hart. We knew he was gay from the beginning because of his gay mannerisms and because his gay friends were always visiting him. We (the plaintiffs) would always comment to each other about how inappropriate it was for him to be bringing his personal life into the store. Not that we have anything against gay people or anything! But since we could not relate to the new manager's way of doing things or to his off-color sense of humor, we kept to ourselves and maintained our high level of service to the salon's long-standing clients.

Then one day at the end of February, right after our Valentine's Day promotional event, Brent started finding fault with everything I (Millicent Hudson) did. He constantly picked on me. He told me I didn't know how to treat the salon's clients well, and that I was favoring some over others. Can you imagine that? After three years with an impeccable service record, this new person tells me I don't know how to treat our clients. I patiently bore his abuse for a full two or three days; then, I couldn't take it anymore. I had to say something. I told him that I knew how to do my job and didn't need him to teach me how to treat people. After all, he wasn't Mr. Amiable himself. Well, he fired me right there on the spot for "insubordination." That was on February 25, 1996.

By the next day, he had hired someone to replace me. It was one of his gay friends I had seen in the store before. His name is Alex Borrego. (Alex is very flamboyant and unquestionably gay. His boyfriend comes by every evening to pick him up.) At first, I thought it was just a coincidence that Brent had replaced me with a gay man. Then, in mid-April, Brent started to pick fault with the other plaintiffs. (I was still in touch with them since we had been co-workers and friends for so long.)

One by one, over the next few months, Brent found some excuse to fire each one of them. And each time he did he replaced them with a gay man. Now the only women left at Saint-Cloud are Brent, his friends, and a couple of so-called females who enjoy socializing with them and who go to bars with them after work.

These are the facts, plain and simple. I am sure you will agree that Saint-Cloud, through our manager Brent Hart, discriminated against us (the plaintiffs), harassed us, and then fired us simply because we are heterosexual women. The proof of all of this is the fact that we were all replaced by gay men.

We swear that these are the true facts,

Millicent Hudson
Barbie Shoenfeld
Gertie Ford

I set aside the letter and rubbed my eyes as I digested what I had read. I had a sick feeling in the pit of my stomach. Up until then our firm had distinguished itself as the San Francisco law firm *par excellence* in defending the rights of gays and lesbians in the workplace. I couldn't fathom the thought of representing a group of plaintiffs against gays and lesbians as a class, and I couldn't believe Ed was fully informed about the facts of the case.

"Ladies," I started as I walked back into the boardroom, which was humming with enthusiastic chatter. The conversation died down, and the three women moved forward on their seats and stared at me. "I have a few general questions about this case."

Ms. Hudson glanced at the others and shook her head. "Wasn't my synopsis clear enough?"

"Yes, very clear, insofar as your perceptions of the facts are concerned."

There was a moment of pregnant silence. Ms. Hudson cleared her throat, took a sip of water, and dropped her glass on the table. "What do you mean by my 'perceptions'?"

I felt a tugging at my left sock and looked down. The shih tzu was using my leg as a scratching post. I picked it up, handed it to Gertie, and continued. "I mean, I have to be prepared to respond to *their* side of the story."

Millicent glared at me, and the other women looked back and forth between the two of us.

"In other words," I said, "what reason is Saint-Cloud going to give for your termination?"

"I have no idea," Millicent snapped. "It's not *my* job to think of those things."

"Another issue is you were terminated more than one year ago. The statute of limitations in a wrongful termination case is one year. That means you had to have filed a claim against Saint-Cloud no later than one year after the date of your termination, or February 25, 1997, to be exact. Otherwise, you forever lose your right to sue. And, since today is April 2, 1997 . . ."

Millicent's mouth fell open. "But I didn't know that! There must be some exception for that sort of thing."

"Unfortunately, there isn't, unless the defense fails to raise it, which isn't likely."

"What about us?" Barbie asked. "We weren't terminated until after the second of April."

I winced inwardly. "Yes, well, then the rest of you would be fine as far as he statute of limitations is concerned. But that still leaves the issue of—"

There was a light knock on the door, and Ed stepped into the boardroom.

"Mr. Haddad!" Ms. Hudson said, throwing me a sidelong glance. "It's so good to see you."

He raised an eyebrow and took a seat at the table next to her. "How are things going here?"

"Not very well," Ms. Hudson said. "Your colleague, Mr. Mendes, doesn't think I have a case."

"There's a statute of limitations issue with Ms. Hudson's claim," I said.

"How so?" Ed asked.

"She was terminated on February 25, 1996. That's over a year ago."

Ed looked down and nodded. Everyone in the room watched him. He and I had been partners for over three years, and I knew how his mind worked. Even before he opened his mouth, I sensed the angle from which he was analyzing the statute of limitations problem. I could also tell by his lack of questions that he was, in fact, apprised of the basic facts of the case, which annoyed me to no end. After a moment, he raised his eyes to me.

"Well," he began, "just because Ms. Hudson was replaced by a gay man doesn't establish a recognizable pattern of discrimination. It could have been a mere coincidence. The pattern didn't become obvious until Saint-Cloud had replaced each of these women with a gay man. Therefore, we could argue the statute of limitations didn't begin to run for Ms. Hudson until she became *aware* she'd been a victim of a demonstrable pattern of discrimination, which wouldn't have been until, *at the earliest*, May or June 1996."

"I beg your pardon?" Millicent said. "You lost me there."

"That was a lawyer's way of saying: 'Don't worry about anything, ladies, everything is going to be just fine!'" Ed said with a broad, uncharacteristic smile. And with that, he shook their hands, patted me on the back, and slipped out the door.

The women were all hugs and tears and laughter. I thanked them for coming and promised we'd be in contact in the next few days. After a few minutes, I ushered them out the door with great relief and marched upstairs to have it out with Ed.

The door to Ed's office was closed when I arrived. Just as I raised my arm to knock on the door, his fifty-something secretary Marjory Hammer intercepted me. She was dressed in a severe dark gray suit and black oxfords. "Mr. Haddad would like you to review these, Mr. Mendes." She pushed a one-inch-thick folder into my hands. "It's more discovery from the WEBINC case, something turned over to him this morning at the pretrial. The one he covered for you."

I frowned at the folder and looked up at the closed door.

"He's on an important call. I suggest you speak with him later." She spun around and marched across the room to her desk, and I pushed open the door to Ed's office.

Ed was indeed on the telephone when I stepped inside. He looked up and pointed at the chair in front of his desk, then swiveled around and gave me his back. I tried not to eavesdrop on the personal conversation he was having with his fiancée. After a few moments, I felt so uncomfortable that I got up and started back toward the door, but he swung around and held up his hand. At that moment, there was a loud knocking at the door; Ed took advantage of the interruption to cut short his conversation and hung up.

"What is it?" he called out.

The door opened with a violent shove, and Marjory advanced into the room. "Is everything all right, Mr. Haddad?"

"Everything's fine, Marjory."

"I tried to stop him, but he barged right in."

"Everything's fine," Ed repeated. "Really."

Marjory hesitated, glowering at me with poison-tipped daggers in her eyes, then whirled around and all but goose-stepped out of the room, slamming the door behind her.

"Why is she so rude to me?" I asked.

"She's not rude. It's just a foible. We all have them," Ed flashed a sly smile. "In any event, she keeps us all in line."

"She keeps *you* in line. The rest of us, she just harasses."

"Speaking of harassment," he said, the smile vanishing from his face, "what do you think about the Saint-Cloud case? Sounds like a winner for us, what with all the publicity it could generate for the firm."

"You've got to be kidding, Ed. That case is a killer! We're supposed to be defending gays and lesbians against discrimination and harassment in the workplace, not suing them."

"I disagree. This firm is dedicated to fighting discrimination and harassment in the workplace, period, regardless of who commits it. It's clear to me those women were fired solely because they weren't gay. And that's wrong."

"Maybe so, but we don't have to be the firm that litigates their case."

"Why not? Just think of the publicity—"

"It's bad publicity for us as far as the gay community is concerned. Rightly or wrongly, we'll get a name as an anti-gay firm, and nobody from the community will seek us out anymore."

Ed shook his head.

"Besides," I continued, "there are plenty of other firms in the city that would salivate at the chance to embarrass the gay community with a case like this. Let *them* litigate it."

The room grew quiet. Ed leaned back in his chair, closed his eyes, and pinched the bridge of his nose. The antique clock I'd given him for his last birthday chimed the half hour on the back wall. I was drained to the dregs, and it was still only eleven-thirty in the morning.

I turned away from him and stared out the office window to the street below. It was alive with activity. Cars were cruising up and down the street in search of that elusive parking space; three meter maids were converging on our block to ticket any vehicle that had overstayed its one-hour welcome; couriers dashed in and out of offices with packages bound for other offices. Pedestrians on their way to lunch and tourists juggling cameras and tour books jockeyed for space on the crowded sidewalks. A stirring in the room brought me back to myself. I turned and found Ed staring at me.

"Marc," he said, dropping the volume of his voice. "Do you remember when you joined this firm three years ago?"

I nodded.

"You were very impressive. Smart, ambitious, and above all a fast learner. I'm glad I hired you. You've been a great asset to this firm, and that's why I made you a junior partner after only one year. But lately, I'm afraid, you've been allowing your . . ." He closed his eyes and shook his head. After a moment, he opened them and leaned in toward me, speaking with a renewed intensity. "You've allowed your ideals to interfere with your duty to zealously defend the interests of the firm's clients."

"I'm sorry, Ed, but I can't take on a case I know will conflict with what I believe is right. That's why I'm recommending we allow a different firm to handle the Saint-Cloud case."

Ed regarded me with a rigid expression, then grabbed a folder off his desk. "That may well be. But I'm the senior partner of this firm, and I still have the final say in these matters." He held the folder out to me. "My decision is that we are going to represent those women in their suit against Saint-Cloud, and I'm assigning *you* as lead attorney. This isn't negotiable."

A hot flash raced through my body. For a moment, I feared I was going to black out from the shock of what Ed was throwing at me. I snatched the folder out of his hand and considered it, weighing my options.

"Now then," he said, "let's talk about the Xanadu case."

My head snapped up at that.

"How did things go with the roommate?" he asked.

51

"It went fine. But he's not going to be of much help."

"That's unfortunate." Ed tapped his pen impatiently against his desk.

"I also spoke with the PO. He said Silva tested dirty."

"Shit."

"Yeah."

"So that's it then."

"Not necessarily," I said. "I called Xanadu's lawyer this morning and told her we were ready to reconsider their offer. She said she'd speak with her client."

Ed leaned forward. "If they don't go for it, cut Silva loose, Marc. He's trouble."

"We can't just throw him under the bus and let Xanadu get away with the unfair dismissal, Ed! Don't forget, Silva's a victim. If anything, we might be able to string Xanadu along until he gets out."

"No, Marc. Either they settle, or Silva goes." He stood and held his hand out at the door. "Trust me, Marc, it's for the best. Learn from this experience. It'll make you a better lawyer in the long run."

I'm standing with Simon at the edge of a massive crater, the makhtesh, just outside the tiny clay-mining town of Mitzpe Ramon, in the middle of Israel's Negev Desert. The quality of light here, at the edge of this amazing geological formation, makes everything seem surreal as the afternoon sun splashes the scene with an eerie vermilion luminescence. I imagine I'm looking at the earth the way it looked fifty million years ago—orange and black patterns, flat, twisting, massive shapes.

I close my eyes. The hot desert wind blows through my shoulder-length hair and caresses my bare chest. I am still sweating from our hike to the makhtesh, and the moisture causes my white linen

drawstring pants to cling damply to my legs. To avoid dehydration,
I take a long swig of water from my army issue canteen and pour the
rest over my head.

"What are you doing?" Simon asks. The memory of his sweet voice
makes me cry, and my tears merge with the water from the canteen.

"Marc!" A hand shook me by the shoulder.

I opened my eyes and blinked at my surroundings. I was back in San Francisco, sitting on a bench in a little park of redwood trees in the shadow of the Transamerica Pyramid. Isaac was on the bench next to me, balancing a large takeout bag from a Pasqua cafe in his lap and staring at me. The park was filling with office workers on their lunch break.

"What's wrong?" he asked.

"Sorry." I flashed an embarrassed smile and wiped my face with the back of my hand. "I was just on one of my trips."

He considered me for a moment, then handed me the bag.

"Israel again?"

I nodded and fished around inside, looking for my sandwich. "Which one's mine?"

He pulled out a plastic foam container and handed it to me. "Grilled tofu with vegan pesto, as usual."

We ate in silence for a few minutes. A quartet had set up in a corner of the park and was performing a set of jazz standards. After a few mouthfuls, I set aside my half-eaten sandwich, stuffing it back into the bag.

"Not hungry?"

"Not much."

Isaac shook his head. "Are you going to tell me what's wrong?"

"Nothing's wrong." I looked away from him and stared across the park. "I'm just swamped at work."

I could feel Isaac staring hard at me. "You're shit at lying."

I swung around and looked him in the eye. "Imagine that—a lawyer who's shit at lying."

The corners of his mouth turned down. He edged forward

53

on the bench, ready to bolt in typical Isaac fashion.

"No, wait!" I took hold of his arm. He shook off my hand and beamed an icy stare at me.

"I'm sorry," I said.

"Sorry about what?"

"About lying to you, about snapping at you." I raised my shoulders. "I don't know."

"You can start by telling me what's going on."

"All right, I'll tell you." I stood and stretched my legs. "But let's take a walk, please. I'm feeling claustrophobic."

Isaac looked around the park then back at me. "What do you mean? We're outside, in a park."

"I don't know—" I waved my hand at our surroundings, "—it's this place, these buildings, everything. I can't breathe. I just need to get the hell out of here."

Isaac washed down what was left of his sandwich and followed me out of the park. We marched down Washington toward the open space of the Embarcadero and walked out onto Pier 3, where I stopped to draw in the cool ocean air, grasping the iron rail, staring out over the water. Isaac stood by, rubbing my back, waiting. After a few minutes of quiet, I turned around and leaned heavily against the rail.

"Better?" he asked.

"Better."

"Good," he said, holding my gaze. "So you were saying?"

I spent the rest of the lunch hour telling him about the Saint-Cloud case, careful not to reveal the identities of the parties. I explained the ethical dilemma I was facing and recounted what had happened between Ed and me. He listened to all of this, making only the most minimal of comments. When I finished, he kissed my cheek.

"Thank you," he said. "You'll figure it out."

I cocked my head to one side. "That's it? That's all you have to say?"

"Marc, if there's anyone who knows what to do in a situation like this, it's you. You're a rabbi's son, for God's sake. You were raised in a home where you discussed ethics from sunup to sundown. You know as well as I do that you already know what you have to do."

"Then what was that all about?"

"It's not good to keep things bottled up inside. It only makes things feel worse than they are. So, you're welcome."

He checked his watch, and his eyes went wide. "Oh, damn! I'm late." He drew me into a quick hug, then spun around and sped away. "I'll see you at home," he called over his shoulder as he rushed off in the direction of his office.

Chapter 5

The following morning, I finished up a deposition in Benicia three hours earlier than expected. So with a "what the hell" attitude, I took the Highway 35 arch-in-the-sky turnoff from Interstate 80 and gunned it toward Napa Valley.

Ed's insistence that I lead the Saint-Cloud case, and his harsh words from the day before, kept replaying in my mind. And as I made the thirty-minute drive to Napa, my frustration with the situation morphed into an unambiguous resolve. I was ready to cash in my chips. In that moment, I determined to make Isaac's and my dream a reality. We *would* buy a place in Napa and live a peaceful life, free from complications. If I felt like practicing law again, it would be on terms I could live with comfortably, in a way that didn't conflict with my personal ethics. No more playing the law-whore.

I drove straight into the heart of downtown Napa and searched for a real estate agent. In a matter of minutes, I was sitting in the too-cold office of Mavis DeAngelis, a chain-smoking woman in her mid-sixties with a dyed blonde bouffant. I spent a few minutes describing the kind of place I was looking for, and we narrowed down her available inventory to the three most suitable properties. Then she hustled me into her tobacco-trap Cadillac Coupe de Ville for a grand tour.

Mercifully, the first property we viewed was only a twenty-five-minute drive from her office, in the hills overlooking the town of St. Helena. I emerged from her car in a cloud of smoke, my hair and my clothes reeking like an ashtray. When my eyes cleared of the fumes, I saw we were standing in the sloping driveway of a charming, well-cared-for two-story Victorian. I drew in a deep cleansing lungful of mountain air and started the walk-through.

From the moment I set eyes on that one-hundred-and-ten-year-old architectural wonder, I knew it was the one. Its roof, plumbing, and wiring had been replaced a year earlier. Its kitchen and two full bathrooms were updated and modernized, and its hardwood floors were pristine. There was a decent-sized bedroom on the ground floor and two larger ones on the second floor. One of them overlooked a lovely manicured English garden behind the house. But my favorite was the main bedroom, with its unobstructed vista across the lush valley. If that weren't enough, the property also boasted four acres of terraced vineyards, which were part of the deal.

"This is perfect," I said to the agent, who was hovering in the doorway.

She crinkled her brow at me. "Really? Don't you think you should at least see the other two?"

To be frank, I can't recall the other properties Mavis dragged me to that afternoon. She could have taken me to the Taj Mahal and back for all I remember. All I could think of was that Victorian in the hills. I could picture Isaac and me living there for the rest of our lives. The bedroom with the vineyard views would be ours, and the one overlooking the garden would be our home office. Miriam would be delighted to have the bedroom on the ground floor with access to the kitchen. Isaac would work in the garden as he loved to do. And he would finally be able to have the Labrador retriever he always wanted. And I—I would have to practice a hell of a lot of law to afford the mortgage payment.

When we got back to Mavis's office, I booked an appointment to see the house the next afternoon with Isaac. We would drive to the property in our own car. Mavis gave me all sorts of facts and figures and a few photos of the property to take with me, and I was out the door.

Of course, I couldn't resist the temptation to drive back to the house and take my time walking around the garden and the vineyard. This was definitely the right place. I knew Isaac would fall in love with it, too.

Taking the cell phone out of my pocket, I punched in his office number. It rang five times; then his voicemail picked up.

"Isaac, this is Marc," I said. "I have a surprise. Meet me after work at the Cypress Club, and I'll tell you all about it then."

I hadn't been this excited since I'd received word that I'd passed the bar exam five years before. I jumped into the car and drove straight to my office. I found a couple of messages from Silva asking for another visit, which I set aside. I wasn't ready to deal with that yet. Instead, I spent the rest of the afternoon taking stock of the various other cases I was handling, planning how best to wrap them up and how long it would take.

At around five o'clock, I finished up and strolled around the corner to the restaurant. The host gave me a nice booth with a street view, and I ordered a cranberry juice. Half an hour later, I'd started on my second glass, and Isaac still hadn't shown up.

Outside, the weather was taking an odd turn. Low clouds had gathered over the financial district, and it was beginning to drizzle, turning the streets and sidewalks dark and damp.

I called Isaac's office and got his message machine again. Then I called him at home. Miriam told me she hadn't seen him, but she would ask him to call me if he showed up. By six o'clock, I was worried. Then I saw him walking, head down, toward the restaurant. Relieved, I rose to meet him at the door.

Isaac followed me to the booth and sat facing me. His eyes were red and moist. He rarely discussed work, but I knew his job was stressful. Landis, Murray, Smith, and Damji was one of the foremost public interest firms in the Bay Area, and Isaac's boss, Sylvia Pratt, handled some of its most high-profile cases.

"Hard day?" I asked.

Isaac shook his head. "I have something to tell you," he said in a low voice.

"No, wait. I have something to tell you first." I was sure he'd feel better once he heard about the house and about my decision to leave the firm.

"But I—"

"Hold on a second," I said. "The deposition ended early today, so I took a drive to Napa. I saw a house I think would be perfect for us. It's a beautiful Victorian in mint condition, four acres of land with a wonderful garden. I'm sure you'll love it as much as I do. We have an appointment to see it tomorrow afternoon."

Isaac lowered his head and rubbed his forehead. I noticed with alarm he was crying.

"What is it?" I asked.

He reached into the breast pocket of his coat, pulled out a white, legal-size envelope, and slid it across the table at me. I looked at it and noted the return address: U.S. Department of Justice, Immigration and Naturalization Service.

I reached inside the envelope, pulled out an official notice addressed to Isaac, and read it carefully. It was a summons. Isaac was to present himself before the United States Immigration Court next week for a Removal Hearing.

A cold wave of fear washed over my body. This was the letter we both knew would come one day, the one we tried never to think about. And yet, here it was. I knew everything was about to change forever. I reached across the table for Isaac's hand, but he pulled it away.

"That's it," he said, his voice trembling. "Everything's over. They're going to send me back."

"We'll hire a lawyer," I said, putting on a brave face and trying my best to maintain my composure. "Someone who specializes in these kinds of cases."

A bitter laugh escaped his lips. "What good would that do? Didn't you read the letter? They're going to deport me."

"That's not what it says." I held the letter out to him. "What it actually says is you're going to have a removal *hearing*. That means the court is going to *hear* arguments for and against your deportation. In other words, it's not a foregone conclusion."

Isaac flashed angry eyes and jumped to his feet. "Don't try to convince me everything is going to be fine. I know about these things. People get deported all the time. Everything's over!" he shouted.

I was dazed by his reaction and watched helplessly as he bolted from the restaurant. The other patrons stared at me, murmuring surreptitious comments as I fumbled a few bills out of my wallet and paid the check.

Chapter 6

I stumbled out of the restaurant, still clutching the letter. A bank of dense, low clouds had gathered over the city, and what began as a drizzle had turned into a pounding rain shower. By the time I reached my car, my suit was sopping wet, and I was sloshing about in my oxfords. As I went for the door, a sizzle of lightning momentarily blinded me. Thunder exploded all around, and I ducked into a nearby doorway for cover, afraid of a lightning strike.

Pulling out my cell phone, I punched in my home number. Miriam answered: Isaac wasn't home, and she had neither seen him nor heard from him. I quickly ended the call before she could ask me anything.

At that moment, utter panic seized me. I'd never seen Isaac so distraught before. The thought of him wandering around in a raging storm filled me with fear. Fear of what might happen to him and fear of what he might do to himself.

When I finally made it into my car, I drove up California in the direction of Van Ness. Rainwater streamed down Nob Hill, and cars slid and spun haphazardly in front of me as their tires made slippery contact with the cable car rails running down the middle of the street. I engaged my four-wheel drive for additional traction and slowed down in time to avoid plowing into a startled group of tourists who had launched themselves off a cable car to dash into the nearest hotel. One of them beat my windshield with her umbrella before being yanked along by her companion.

Spotting a parking space, I pulled into it to wait for the rain to let up and closed my burning eyes. A moment later, my cell phone rang. Hoping it was Isaac, I answered.

"Mr. Mendes?"

It wasn't Isaac.

"Yes, who is this please?" The rain was letting up a bit, and I was keen to continue my search.

"This is your client, Alejandro Silva," said the last person on the planet I needed to hear from right then.

"Alejandro, I'm busy at the moment."

"I've been waiting for you to get back to me about my case," he said. "I called your office a few times today. Your assistant finally gave me your cell number."

"Which assistant was that?" I asked, feeling extremely annoyed.

"Vlad, your secretary guy. I want to know whether you're going to help me with my hearing. It's scheduled for the day after tomorrow at eleven in the morning."

"Alejandro, I spoke with *both* Peter Miller *and* your parole officer. Why didn't you tell me you tested dirty?"

"What?"

"Your parole officer told me you failed your drug test."

The line went quiet for a moment.

"Alejandro?"

"Come see me, please."

"I'm sorry, Alejandro. I don't have time right now, and I don't know what my day will be like tomorrow. I'll see what I can do."

I snapped off the phone and pulled away from the sidewalk, yielding carefully to the passing traffic. As I drove through the rain, which was coming down hard again, I tried to think of where Isaac could have possibly gone. SoMa, the Castro, Union

Square, Golden Gate Park, the Embarcadero. My God, the list was endless.

I drove for another thirty minutes or so, my nerves fraying more and more with every passing moment before I gave up and headed home. Just as I pulled into our garage, my cell phone rang again. It was Isaac.

"Where are you?" I shouted.

"Don't scream at me."

"I'm sorry! I've been going crazy looking for you."

There was an uneasy silence at the end of the line. In the background, I could hear canned music. Then, the phone clicked and sounded as if the connection was breaking up.

"Isaac? Hello?"

"I'm here," he said, his voice shaking with emotion. "I just wanted to thank you for everything you've done for me. And I wanted to let you know I'll be returning to El Salvador as soon as I can book a flight for my mother and me."

My heart leaped into my throat. "Wait! What?"

"I'm sorry, I can't take any more pressure," he said, sounding on the verge of tears. "You have no idea, Marc. I haven't wanted to say anything, but I've been killing myself at work, which is a total nightmare. On top of that, things haven't been very good between you and me for a while. And now this fucking thing. I just don't have the energy to fight."

"Babe, I get it. But you can't just leave like that. I love you. We've made a life together." I felt like a blubbering idiot, tearfully confessing my love for Isaac in my idling car. But I couldn't help myself. Isaac's wasn't the only tragedy unfolding. After six years, our lives were inextricably and inexorably joined. I wasn't about to let us be wrenched apart by the legal system. Not without a fight. "Isaac," I said, "please just tell me where you are."

"All right," he whispered. "I'm at the Stonestown Galleria, in the food court. They're about to close up for the night," he said, and the telephone went dead.

I sped west on Lombard, made an illegal left onto Divisadero, and cut across Pacific Heights toward the Castro. Ten minutes later, I was racing south toward Daly City. I could barely see a hundred yards ahead of me in the storm. Stonestown Galleria was coming up on my right, so I pulled into the parking lot and drove to the entrance nearest the food court. Isaac was standing outside under an awning, clutching a takeout coffee from Peet's in his hand.

Pulling to the curb, I parked, turned on my flashers, and hopped out of the car. Isaac was cold and shivering. I took off my jacket and draped it over his shoulders, but he shrugged it off.

"Isaac, get in the car, please."

"Why?"

"Because you're freezing. Come on." I took him by the arm, and he reluctantly followed me.

When we were finally inside, I turned up the heater and pulled back onto the highway, heading away from San Francisco. The fog was less dense south of the city, and the rain had let up. We drove in silence with Isaac turned away from me, staring out the window into the darkness. When we reached Highway 92, I decided to head toward Half Moon Bay to travel the coastal route to Santa Cruz. We'd always done our best talking on long drives.

"Where are we going?" Isaac asked once we were cruising along the edge of the Pacific.

"Anywhere you want to go."

He looked at me skeptically, "What do you mean?"

"You want to go back to El Salvador? Let's go. Or if you decide to stay here and fight it out, I'm with you."

Isaac reached into the glove box and pulled out a pack of gum. He unwrapped a piece, placed it in his mouth, and chewed it thoughtfully. "Would you really go with me to El Salvador?" he asked after a moment.

"Of course I would if that was our only option. But I don't

think it is, that's all. I think we should fight to keep you here. If we lose, we lose. If we win, then all the better. But win or lose, I plan on following you to wherever. Even if that means going to El Salvador."

"What about your career? Your family?"

"What about them?"

"You're not going to leave everything for me, are you?"

I pulled into the parking lot of a beachside restaurant and turned off the engine. Then, taking Isaac's hand in mine, I looked him in the eye and said, "Isaac, you're my family. If we were a straight couple, we would've been married by now, and we wouldn't have this problem in the first place."

"Yeah, I know. I've been thinking about that, too." He rested his head against the window.

"And as for your job, you can quit and look for another one. There's no reason for you to suffer in silence. Not for a damned paycheck."

We sat quietly for a few minutes. Isaac relaxed a bit, absently running his finger across the back of my hand, his eyes half closed. He hummed a little melody in a barely audible voice. It was one of his mother's favorites. I would often find her singing it to herself in the kitchen while she cooked. When he came to the end of the tune, he opened his eyes and looked at me. His eyes were wet. "You know, I love you," he said.

"Of course I do. That's why I don't understand why you ran away like that."

"I don't know." He wrapped his arms around himself. "I guess I was trying to push you away so it would hurt less."

"So what would hurt less?"

"Losing you." The corners of his mouth curled down, and he blinked back tears. "*Everyone* I've ever loved has been taken from me, except Mother. My father, my brothers. Everyone! And now you."

"No one's going to take me away from you."

Isaac held my gaze "Is that true, Marc? You'll stay with me no matter what happens?"

"Yes, no matter what. I promise."

Isaac nodded and allowed himself a slight smile.

"Now *you're* going to have to make me a promise," I said.

"Okay, yes, I promise."

"You don't even know what I'm going to say."

"That's all right." He rested his head on my shoulder and closed his eyes. "I'll promise you anything now."

His body relaxed, the grip of tension giving way to exhaustion. He reached up and kissed me on the cheek, then returned his damp head to my shoulder. I ran my fingers through his hair, lightly massaging his scalp.

"Promise me you'll never run away like that again," I said. "You need to trust me."

He squeezed my arm tightly, then lifted his head and looked at me, searching my face. After a moment, he smiled broadly and drew me into a hug. "I promise I'll never run away from you again. *Ever*."

"And we're going to fight to keep you here. Agreed?"

Isaac yawned and reclined against me. "Tomorrow, we'll fight. Right now, let's just go home."

Chapter 7

"Mr. Mendes, are you in there?" Vlad's voice blared out of the intercom. I spun down the volume.

"Yes, what is it?"

"Someone named Lyle Chesney's calling on line three. Says he's an immigration lawyer. Returning your call, he says."

"Thanks. Put him through."

"Mendes, how the hell are you?" boomed Lyle Chesney's *basso profundo* voice. I held the receiver away from my ear. "The last time I saw you was five years ago in the bathroom at the Pasadena Convention Center."

"Excuse me?"

"Hell, yes, don't you remember? Second day of the bar exam. You were losing your lunch into the sink. Nerves, I think."

I cringed. "Oh, right. Thanks for the reminder."

I'd met Chesney in law school, where he'd earned a reputation as a brilliant, hypercompetitive prick. He'd graduated near the top of our class and, after passing the bar exam, had hung up his shingle, opening a cutting-edge immigration practice.

"Anyway," I said, steeling myself, "thanks for calling me back, Lyle. I hear things have been going well for you."

"Never better! Plenty of foreigners wanting to crash our party. That's my bread and butter, you might say. I hear you've been getting rich suing all the deep pockets in town."

There was no question about it: Chesney was still the same type-A jackass I'd known as a student. But I needed to start somewhere, so I resisted the temptation to end the conversation and pressed on. "Listen, Lyle. I've got a situation. Something personal. Can I come see you?"

"Oh, hell, Mendes, I thought you were going to refer me some work."

"It's not a referral. It's an actual case. My case, or rather, my partner's case. I was hoping we could come in for a consultation. This afternoon if possible."

"Why, yes, surely. How's four o'clock?"

"Can we make it five?"

"Five o'clock it is, Mendes. Can you give me a heads-up or your partner's name at least?"

"His name's Isaac Perez, but I can't really go into it right now, sorry."

A loud rumble emanated from the receiver as Chesney cleared his throat. After a moment, he rasped, "See you at five-o, buddy. You and your partner."

Something told me I was going to regret calling Chesney, but I put that down to nerves. After a moment's hesitation, I called Isaac and made arrangements to meet him at the lobby of Chesney's building at five o'clock.

The smell of brewing coffee brought me out of my office. Vlad intercepted me as I filled a large mug to the brim with Italian roast.

"Don't you know caffeine is bad for you?" he said.

Susan, the receptionist, strolled up to us. "He's right, Mr. Mendes. That stuff will stunt your growth for sure." She flashed a wicked smile at Vlad.

"No, seriously," Vlad said, turning to Susan. "It makes him irritable and nervous. Some days, if he's had more than a couple of those humongous mugs, he actually yells at me."

"He's never yelled at me." Susan winked at me.

I downed a sip of coffee and held out my mug at the staircase. "Who's answering the telephone?"

Susan rolled her eyes. "It's routed to voicemail while I get a cup of herbal tea." She filled a cup with hot water and beat a hasty retreat downstairs to her desk. Once she was out of earshot, I turned to Vlad.

"Did you by any chance give out my cell phone number to Alejandro Silva yesterday?"

"You're not going to yell at me, are you?" he shot back, eyeing my coffee cup with renewed suspicion.

"That's a private number. It's *not* to be given out to clients."

"He was calling so much, I figured I'd put him in touch with you directly."

"Call Cell World right away and change the number. And, don't let it happen again, please." I moved back toward my office.

"Coincidentally," Vlad called out, "he's holding on line four. Mr. Silva, that is."

I turned around and stared at him. "How long has he been holding?"

"I don't know, ten minutes or so. I was going to patch him through to voicemail, but he insisted on waiting."

"That's just great," I said. "Anything from Xanadu's lawyers yet?"

"Nope, nothing."

I returned to my office, pushed the door closed, and took the call.

"Sorry to keep you waiting, Alejandro. I was on an important call."

"Are you going to come see me? I have to talk to you."

"Something has come up. A family emergency. I'm not going to be able to make it out there. I'm sorry."

"Will you at least be at my hearing?"

"I don't think I can, Alejandro. But it won't make a difference to your case anyway. According to your parole officer, they're

69

going to give you six months for the dirty test."

"I know. The panel lawyer told me that, too. I was just hoping you'd come to support me."

"If I can, I will. But I can't promise anything. On a positive note, I've reopened discussions with Xanadu about settling your case. I'm hoping they'll offer the one hundred thousand they offered before or something close to that. If they do, I'll bring you the settlement agreement for your signature."

"I thought we were taking them to court."

"That was before I found out about your felony conviction, Alejandro. They could shoot down your case on that alone. So we'll be settling it if we can. Okay?"

"Whatever you say, Mr. Mendes. I trust you."

I ended the call and attended to a couple of other client emergencies. Then I put in a follow-up call to Xanadu's defense lawyer, who was tied up in a meeting.

At around four thirty, I grabbed my coat and ran to meet Isaac. Chesney's offices were in the Embarcadero Center, a good ten-minute walk south on Fremont Street. When I arrived at the lobby, Isaac was waiting for me by the security station, dressed in a dark blue suit, white shirt, and brick red tie. I took him by the hand, and we rode the elevator to the twenty-fifth floor. On the way up, Isaac held my hand tightly.

"Are you all right?" I asked.

Isaac nodded.

The elevator doors opened onto a vast reception area dedicated to Chesney's operation. It was decorated in a nautical theme. Dark wood paneling, model ships, a large anchor mounted on a dais, and a spyglass set up by the window pointed in the direction of Alcatraz. The receptionist, an attractive, well-proportioned redhead in her late thirties, peered at us over her rhinestone-encrusted glasses as we approached.

"Yes?" She glanced at the wall clock with a frown.

"We have an appointment with Mr. Chesney at five

o'clock," I said.

"I doubt that," she said lightly, turning off her desk lamp. "We close at five."

"I made the appointment with him myself."

She had already gotten up and was slipping into a powder blue angora sweater.

"Do you mind checking?" I nodded at her desk. "The name's Marc Mendes."

"I'll look in the calendar. But as I said, I doubt it." She flipped through a book on her desk. "Well, I'll be damned. He did it again!" She threw up her hands in exasperation. "I hate it when he does that."

"Is Mr. Chesney here, Miss?" Isaac interjected.

She grabbed the telephone, punched in a few numbers, and announced, "Lyle! Your five o'clock's here." Then, slamming down the receiver, she snatched up her purse and swished to the elevator, unsteady in her stiletto heels. "Next time, make an appointment during business hours," she snapped as the elevator doors slid shut.

"Not very professional, is she?" Isaac said.

"No, but she doubles as a legal secretary and types ninety-five words a minute," a voice croaked from behind us.

I turned, expecting to see Lyle Chesney. Instead, I was confronted by a funhouse mirror version of the hirsute Adonis I'd gone to law school with. In the five years since I'd last seen him, Chesney had managed to pack on a good fifty extra pounds and had lost most of his hair.

"Mendes! You haven't changed one goddamned bit." He vigorously pumped my hand.

"Thanks for seeing us so late in the day, Lyle. This is Isaac Perez, my partner."

"Partner? Why, that's great!" Chesney turned to Isaac and flashed a wide smile. "Perez, it's a pleasure to meet you." He flung his arm around Isaac's shoulder and shepherded him toward an open door. "Come on back to the war room."

Chesney led us to an antique-filled boardroom with a sweeping view of Twin Peaks. When we had settled around the table, Chesney stretched out his arms, indicating the spread. "Not bad, eh?"

"No question about it, Lyle," I said. "You've done well for yourself. Congratulations."

"I can't get over the irony of it. Here we are, two guys who went to a second-rate law school, earning six-figure incomes just like the guys from Stanford and Harvard." Chesney cleared his throat and reached across the table for a notepad. He was apparently ready to get down to business. "Now then, Mendes, what can I do for you?" He cast his eyes back and forth between Isaac and me. "Does this have anything to do with your firm?"

Isaac looked at me. "Your firm?"

"What are you talking about, Lyle?" I asked

Chesney put down the notebook. "You said Mr. Perez here was your partner."

"Yes, that's right." I shifted in my seat. "But he's not my business partner. When I said Isaac was my partner, I meant that he's my life partner."

"Come again?"

"My lover."

"Your lover?" Chesney glanced at Isaac, who was shaking his head, and looked back at me. "You're gay?"

"Yes, Lyle. I'm gay, and Isaac is my lover, and we have a personal immigration matter to discuss with you. But if this is going to be too much for you, we can go elsewhere."

"No, no, no. I'm sorry, Marc." His face had turned red as a turnip. "It's just that I didn't realize you were gay. I mean, I heard you were a player and all that. But I always assumed you were— well, you know. I mean, you had that spectacularly beautiful girlfriend. What was her name?"

"Lisa Perelis. She was my friend, not my girlfriend."

"I see." Chesney studied me for a moment, then reached for his notepad again. "All right, fine. So you're gay. We're in San Francisco, the gay capital of North America, after all. Nothing to be surprised about."

"Sorry to interrupt this epiphany, Mr. Chesney," Isaac said. "But I'd like to discuss my situation now. Is that all right?"

Chesney blinked at Isaac and nodded his head like an obedient schoolboy. "Please, go ahead, Mr. Perez."

We spent the next hour going over Isaac's family history, his journey to America, his claim of temporary asylum, and his relationship with me. To his credit, Chesney listened attentively, occasionally pausing to take notes, sometimes copiously. I found the exercise of laying out the entire situation to be cathartic. At any rate, it was a relief to be sharing our problem with someone who might be able to offer some valuable guidance. When Isaac wrapped up his story, Chesney sat staring at his notes. Then, placing his pen diagonally across his notepad, he looked first at Isaac, then at me.

"I'm not an expert in asylum cases. Not by a mile," he began. "But it seems to me Mr. Perez has a compelling claim. It has all the right elements, and the facts are very sympathetic."

"Great!" I said. "But is there enough time to prepare the case? The hearing's a week away."

"That's the Master Calendar hearing," Chesney said. "All they'll do there is take Mr. Perez's plea and schedule the full asylum hearing for later in the year."

Isaac and I exchanged a relieved glance.

"That said," Chesney continued, "I'm not the right lawyer for the case. You gentlemen need an expert in asylum law, someone who regularly appears before the court, someone the judges know. What I *can* do, Mr. Perez, is appear in court with you next week and ask the judge for a lengthy continuance to allow you time to find that expert."

"Can't you recommend someone?" I asked.

Chesney shook his head. "I don't give recommendations. If something goes wrong with the case, it always comes back to bite me on the ass."

Isaac leaned forward in his chair. "But what if the judge doesn't want to grant a continuance?" The reality of the upcoming hearing was hitting him, and I could see the tension etching itself on his face.

"Don't worry about a thing, Mr. Perez." Chesney rose from the table and patted him on the back. "Continuances are routinely granted, especially at a first hearing."

I helped Isaac to his feet and shook Chesney's hand. "Thanks for everything, Lyle. I appreciate your help."

"Not a problem," Chesney said. "But do yourselves a favor."

"What's that?" I asked.

"Trust me," he said. "Leave this first hearing in my hands and relax. Both of you."

"All right. Thanks again, Lyle," I said.

"Yes, thanks," Isaac echoed in a whisper.

"Oh, one more thing," Chesney said as we stepped into the elevator. "Make sure you're there at nine thirty sharp. The court doesn't take kindly to stragglers."

Chapter 8

Isaac and I arrived at Immigration Court at nine on Wednesday morning. As the elevator doors opened onto the eighth floor, we were confronted by a throng of angry and nervous people of every race, culture, and language. The din of so many people talking-whispering-shouting-swearing-sobbing in multiple tongues was, frankly, intimidating. Taking a deep breath, I grabbed Isaac's clammy hand and pushed our way into the crush of humanity.

We tried our best to excuse-me-sir, pardon-me-madam, and sorry-was-that-your-hat-I-knocked-to-the-ground our way through the crowd, trying to get to the court calendar, which was posted on the far wall. When that didn't work, we pushed, plowed, and elbowed our way across the room to the bulletin board. I was surprised to see Isaac's name wasn't listed and exchanged a glance with him. His naturally tanned face was taking on the color of curdled milk; marbles of sweat jiggled on his furrowed forehead before detaching and running down his nose.

"Wait here," I said, squeezing his arm. "I'll go check with the clerk's office."

"I've got to find the restroom," he responded in a shaky voice. "I'll meet you back here."

I watched him hurry away, about to lose his breakfast. Then scanning the walls above people's heads and turbans, I spotted what looked like the clerk's office angled in an awkward corner of the floor. I could barely make out the information window and tiny counter through the milling crowd.

After squeezing through the press of potential deportees and their lawyers, I managed to maneuver my way to the information window and catch the attention of a young woman in her early twenties with a cherry blonde bob, shuffling papers behind two-inch thick security glass. Her eyes lit up, and she waved me forward to the counter.

"Excuse me, Miss," I said, lowering my head to the document slot.

She flashed a bright smile and disappeared from view. A moment later, I heard a faint whistle and turned around. The young woman was standing at a door, waving me over. I followed her into the inner sanctum of the court clerk's office. When we reached her desk, she thrust out a petite hand at me framed by the sleeve of a lacy sweater.

"I'm Tina Kelly."

I shook her hand hesitantly, not sure why she'd called me into her office.

"You're Mr. Mendes, right?"

"Yes. But how—"

"My boyfriend Vlad Williams works for you. He introduced me to you last year at the office Christmas party. Remember?"

I peered at her for a moment, reaching back into the fog of my long-term memory. "Yes, of course. I remember now. Your hair was longer then."

She clapped her hands. "That's right! Plus, I'd gotten a perm."

"I didn't know you worked here. Vlad never mentioned it."

"Oh, God, I've been here forever. But what are *you* doing here?"

"I'm here with a friend who's scheduled for a Master Calendar hearing this morning. We can't seem to find his name on the board."

"Oh, that's easy." She sat at her computer and flashed her teeth. "What's your friend's name?"

I hesitated a moment. Vlad had probably mentioned Isaac to her. After all, everyone at the office knew about our relationship. Her eyes grew wider as she waited. *What the hell*, I thought.

"Isaac Perez," I said.

If she recognized the name, she didn't show it. She simply typed it into her docketing program, and we waited while the system performed its search.

"Isaac Edgar Perez? she asked.

"That's him."

"Okay, the case is set for nine thirty in room 835." She scooted back from the computer. "That's Judge Tanaka's courtroom. He's nice. I like him."

"Why wasn't it on the calendar outside?"

She glanced at her screen again and scrolled down a couple of pages. "It looks like the case was reassigned to Judge Tanaka yesterday afternoon."

"Oh." I didn't like the sound of that. "What does that mean?"

Tina looked again at the screen and read through the notes. "It doesn't mean anything, really. They always shift cases around so all the judges have roughly the same number of cases on their docket." She flashed a timid smile. "You'd better get over to the courtroom. It's probably already started."

I thanked her and rushed out the door into an empty hallway. I rounded the corner toward room 835 and found Isaac sitting on a bench, looking like he was on the verge of hyperventilating. He barely acknowledged me as I walked up and laid a hand on his trembling shoulder.

"How are you doing?" I asked.

Isaac reached up and touched my hand. "Where were you?"

"I went to find out whether you were on the calendar."

"Am I?"

"Yes, we're in room 835." I pointed to the door at the end of the corridor.

Isaac nodded and searched the empty hallway. "Where's the lawyer?"

"I don't know. Let's wait for him in the courtroom." I took him by the hand. He rose weakly from the bench and allowed me to lead him to Judge Tanaka's courtroom.

Pushing open the door, we were greeted by a wave of warm, fetid air. The smallish room was crammed with people. All the benches were packed tight, and everyone else was either standing in the aisles, pressed against the walls, or sitting on other people's laps. I scanned the crowd for Chesney, but it was difficult to see whether or not he was there. Isaac looked like he was about to swoon.

"Ladies and gentlemen," said the judge's clerk, a personable Ivy League type with short black hair and piercing blue eyes. "Our air conditioning unit is out this morning. Please bear with us. The judge will be coming out in a moment. He will hear attorney-represented matters first, in the order indicated by the sign-in sheet. Then he will hear the matters of those of you who are not represented by a lawyer."

As the clerk repeated what he'd said in Spanish, I made my way up to the front, flashed my bar card, and located the sign-in sheet on his desk. Chesney's name wasn't there.

"Excuse me," I said to the clerk.

He smiled at me. "How can I help you, Counsel?"

"Have you heard from Lyle Chesney? He's representing my partner Isaac Perez this morning."

The clerk flipped through his message pad and shook his head. "Nothing yet."

I thanked him and went back to Isaac.

"It's hot," he whispered.

I pulled him out into the corridor. "Wait here. I'll come get you when they call your case. Hopefully, Chesney will get here soon."

"I don't want to be alone."

"It's too hot in there. I'm on the other side of the door if you need me."

Isaac nodded with a tight, unhappy smile.

Chesney arrived at eleven thirty with poor nervous Isaac in tow. The sight of them at that hour made my blood pressure spike. Late was one thing, but two fucking hours? The judge was in the middle of battling over a complex legal issue with an ancient and rather long-winded lawyer, so I took the opportunity to push Chesney back into the corridor.

"Where have you been?" I shouted.

Chesney looked startled. "What do you mean?"

"It's eleven thirty! Court started at nine thirty and 'doesn't take kindly to stragglers'! Where the hell were you?"

"I called ahead and spoke with the clerk. He knew I was going to be late."

"The hell you did!"

Chesney held up a hand. "I understand you're angry, Mendes, but it's not my fault. I was elsewhere in the building, tied up in a conference. You're a lawyer; you know how these things work. Your *boyfriend*'s isn't the only case I have."

"My boyfriend?"

Chesney snorted and tried to move past me. "I'm sorry, Mendes, but I don't have time for this right now—"

"Forget it, Lyle. You're fired!" I marched back into the courtroom to join Isaac.

Chesney followed me inside, protesting. The previous hearing had ended, and there was a brief lull in the proceedings. Judge Tanaka peered over his bifocals at us—a rugged-looking man with a salt and pepper crew cut; I was sure he was ex-military.

"Mr. Chesney, it's good of you to join us," he said.

Chesney bowed awkwardly and blurted out, "I apologize for my tardiness, Your Honor. I had another matter to attend to on the ninth floor. I called earlier and informed your clerk."

"Mr. Zane?" Judge Tanaka said, turning to his clerk.

"I have nothing, Your Honor," his clerk said, flipping through his message pad.

"Mr. Chesney," Judge Tanaka said, cutting his eyes at Chesney, "would you care to explain?"

Chesney loosened his tie. "I meant that I left a message on your clerk's voicemail, Your Honor. My apologies for any confusion."

I moved forward. "Excuse me, Your Honor, if I may."

Judge Tanaka looked at me, as did his clerk and Chesney.

"Who is this?" Tanaka asked.

"This is Marc Mendes, my client's partner," Chesney said. "He's also a lawyer."

Tanaka raised one eyebrow and cleared his throat. "What is it, Mr. Mendes?"

"Your Honor, I have just fired Mr. Chesney. So, if it pleases the court, I will represent Mr. Perez this morning."

Tanaka shifted in his high-backed chair and adjusted his robe. Then he peered at me over the top of his glasses. "Are you an immigration lawyer?"

"No," I said.

"Mr. Mendes, the decision of whether or not to fire Mr. Chesney belongs to the respondent, Mr. Perez, not to you." He focused on Isaac. "Mr. Perez, are you following this discussion?"

"Yes, Your Honor, perfectly well."

"Well, then, which of these two lawyers would you like to designate as your representative today? The one that practices immigration law and arrived two hours late, or the one who practices some other variety of law and is probably unfamiliar with our procedures here?"

"Your Honor—" Chesney said, raising his hand.

"Silence, Mr. Chesney," the judge shot back. "You've said enough."

"But I haven't said anything yet," Chesney said.

"Well, Mr. Perez, the court is expectantly awaiting your momentous decision. Will it be the talkative Mr. Chesney or the arrogant Mr. Mendes?"

"I'll take the arrogant Mr. Mendes, Your Honor," Isaac answered.

"Thank you, Mr. Perez." Tanaka pointed at Chesney. "Mr. Chesney, either take a seat or step out the door. Mr. Mendes, please come up here and fill out a form EOIR-28 for the court and a G-28 for Ms. Blair, counsel for the Immigration and Naturalization Service. In the meantime, the court is in recess."

Judge Tanaka stood and unbuttoned his black robe. Underneath, he was dressed as if ready to play a round of golf as soon as he finished up for the day. "Mr. Zane, let me know when the forms have been filled out," he said, addressing his clerk, and strode out of the room to his chambers.

I felt lightheaded. What was an EOIR-28? I turned around for Chesney and saw he was no longer in the room. Taking a breath, I stepped up to the clerk's desk. He smiled and winked one of his steely blue eyes at me.

"So what's an EOIR?" I asked.

He slid an orange form and a blue form across his desk. "These are substitution of attorney forms. Fill them both out, have Mr. Perez sign them, then bring the orange one back to me and give the blue one to Ms. Blair."

He pointed his pencil at counsel for the immigration service, who was coming into the room. Early forties and lanky, mid-length blonde hair, royal blue suit, black pumps.

I thanked the clerk and spent the next few minutes completing the forms. When I'd distributed them according to his instructions, he buzzed the judge. Moments later, Tanaka emerged into the courtroom, buttoning his robe. He cast an eye at the wall clock, sat at the bench, and said, "Call the case, Mr. Zane."

"Matter of Isaac Perez, case number A98-589-437."

Following the example of the twenty or so lawyers before me, I shepherded Isaac to the respondent's side of the table and sat next to him.

"Marc Mendes for the respondent, Your Honor," I said.

"Not yet, Mr. Mendes," Tanaka said. "We're not on the record." He exchanged a look with Isaac, and Isaac punched my leg under the table.

Tanaka adjusted his microphone, then activated a tape recorder that sat to his left. When he spoke again, his voice had taken on an officious tone.

"We are now on the record. This is Judge James Tanaka of the United States Immigration Court. It is April 18, 1997. We are in the Removal Hearing of Respondent Isaac Edgar Perez, case number A98-589-437. This is the first Master Calendar hearing in the matter. The respondent is present, as are his counsel and counsel for the Immigration and Naturalization Service. Please state your appearances for the record."

"Marc Mendes for the respondent."

"Mindy Blair for the Service." Ms. Blair discreetly suppressed a yawn.

"Mr. Mendes, how do you wish to proceed this morning?" Tanaka asked.

"Your Honor, I'd like to request a short continuance of two weeks for my client to find a lawyer."

Judge Tanaka peered over his half-glasses at me the way he had at Chesney. That was a sure sign of trouble. I braced myself.

"Mr. Mendes, you *are* a lawyer. Request denied. Please proceed."

"But Your Honor, it's my understanding that the granting of a short continuance is routine, especially at a first Master

Calendar hearing. My client should have the opportunity to be represented by competent counsel."

"As I said, Mr. Mendes, your request for a continuance is denied. Do you have a copy of the NTA? If not, my clerk will give you a copy."

I had no idea what an NTA was. I looked over at the ever-helpful clerk. He was one step ahead of me, holding up a sheet of paper with a few lines of text. I took it from him and skimmed it on my way back to my seat. The heading said, NOTICE TO APPEAR. The rest of it was a brief recitation of the allegations.

Respondent: PEREZ, Isaac Edgar

The Service Alleges that:
1. You are not a citizen or national of the United States.
2. You are a native of El Salvador and a citizen of El Salvador.
3. You entered the United States without inspection at San Ysidro, California, on or about February 14, 1986.

Based on the foregoing, it is charged that you are subject to removal from the United States . . .

"I have a copy of the NTA, Your Honor," I said.

"Have you had a chance to review it?" Tanaka asked.

"Yes, Your Honor."

"Are you ready to enter a plea on behalf of your client?"

After having watched two full hours of lawyers entering pleas on behalf of their clients, I felt reasonably sure of what I was supposed to do at this point.

"Yes, I am," I said, feeling my way forward, "we admit paragraphs one, two, and three and concede deportability."

Isaac turned to me, wide eyed. "What are you doing?" he whispered.

"Don't worry," I whispered back. "This is the way they get to the asylum claim."

He shook his head, closed his eyes, and sat back, rubbing his temples to ward off a migraine. "Whatever," he muttered under his breath.

"All right, based on that plea, the court finds the respondent removable," Tanaka said. "Will you be designating a country of removal at this time, counselor?"

"No, Your Honor. We'll reserve that for the time being."

"What type of relief, if any, will your client be seeking?"

I nudged Isaac under the table. He opened his eyes and sat forward. "Respondent will be seeking asylum, and in the alternative, voluntary departure."

Tanaka nodded. "All right, counselor. I don't suppose you have an estimate of how long the asylum hearing will take, do you?"

"I have no idea."

"Fine." He turned to his clerk. "When do I have a four-hour block available, Mr. Zane?"

The clerk swung to his computer and typed a few commands. "Looks like your next four-hour slot is Tuesday, April 23, 1998, at eight thirty in the morning."

"Counselor, will that date work for you?" Tanaka asked.

I flipped forward in my calendar and examined the empty page, processing the date. Then I glanced up at Tanaka. "That's over a year from now."

"Yes, Mr. Mendes, shall we set the asylum hearing for that date?"

"That date will be fine, Your Honor. Thank you." A wave of relief washed over me at the lengthy reprieve. I turned to Isaac. He was nodding in agreement, his mood noticeably lightening.

"Ms. Blair, I assume your office will have someone here on that date?" Tanaka said.

Ms. Blair raised her hand in agreement and noted the date in her calendar.

Tanaka turned his attention back to his tape recorder.

"Respondent has requested an asylum hearing. All parties have agreed to April 23, 1998, at eight thirty. The asylum application should be filed within the next ninety days, and all supporting documents should be served on all parties no later than one month before the hearing. Agreed?"

I agreed.

"This then concludes the Master Calendar hearing." Tanaka switched off the tape recorder and rushed out of the courtroom, hurriedly unbuttoning his robe.

Isaac and I sat at the counsel table, both of us in a daze. Ms. Blair gathered up her things and strolled out of the room, half-waving good-bye to the clerk, Mr. Zane. He came around from behind his desk and approached me.

"Call this woman." He placed a scrap of paper on the table with a name and number scribbled on it.

I studied the name. "Phoebe Thistlewig?"

A smile hovered on the clerk's lips. "She's the best damned asylum lawyer in the city, hands down." He glanced in the direction of Tanaka's chamber. "Best of all," he said, lowering his voice, "Judge Tanaka likes her."

Chapter 9

I stared out the window of the plane on our short-hop flight to Los Angeles, bound for my first family Passover in eight years. To combat my mounting anxiety, I focused on the thunderheads that threatened a bumpy ride and tried to empty my mind.

Isaac squeezed my clammy hand. "Earth to Marc."

I tore my gaze away from the window. "Sorry, I'm just so damned nervous."

A trolley loaded with alcohol rolled past us, and I felt a sudden and disturbing urge for a stiff drink.

"It must be a combination of everything," I said, drawing a deep breath and refocusing. "The stress of seeing my parents again after so long and everything going on at work—"

"And my immigration hearing." Isaac's eyes drifted away.

"More than anything, it's about seeing my father," I clarified. "I'm dreading the whole thing. I don't know why I ever accepted the invitation."

"Maybe he's dreading seeing you, too."

"Why would he dread seeing me?"

Isaac lifted his shoulders. "You're the one who blew *him* off." He closed the seat-back tray table and crossed his arms. "Or maybe it's something else."

"Like what?"

"Like maybe you're ashamed of me."

"Why would you even think such a thing?" I asked, frowning.

"I don't know. Maybe because I'm going to be the pink Catholic elephant in the dining room?"

I rolled my eyes. "It has *nothing* to do with you, Isaac."

"It has *everything* to do with me!"

"I'm sorry, but you're completely wrong about that. I'd feel the same if it was just me. The fact you'll be there is the icing on the cake, not the cake itself. *I'm* the one who's going to be facing interrogation—the gay ex-druggie rabbi's son. I'm the one who's going to have to give an account of myself. And all of that in the middle of a major religious festival celebrating freedom from slavery. I can't even imagine what it's going to feel like sitting around the dinner table, everyone staring at me, judging me: Abba, Ima, Jacob, his wife. Your being with me is the *only* thing that's going to make it bearable."

Isaac's face relaxed at that. "That's sweet."

"The fact I'm in a healthy, long-term relationship with a nice person will go a long way, believe me."

Isaac rubbed my arm. "So maybe it won't be so bad."

"Maybe."

"At least you'll have Jacob on your side."

I nodded. Jacob had been supportive of my relationship with Isaac from the start, with reservations, of course. And when he felt the time was right, he had gently broken the news to my parents.

"I have a feeling he had a lot to do with this reunion," Isaac said.

"I wouldn't be so sure about that."

"What do you mean?"

"Listen, Isaac, Jacob loves both of us, I'm sure, but he has mixed feelings about officially bringing you into the family."

Isaac frowned. "You never told me that."

"Well, I'm telling you now. So be prepared."

A chime sounded in the cabin. "*Ladies and gentlemen,*" came the voice of the captain. *"We are beginning our descent into the Los Angeles metropolitan area—"*

My heart climbed into my throat.

Passover—*Pesach* in Hebrew—was the most significant holiday at my parents' home. We celebrated it with a ceremonial meal, the Seder. It was the time we remembered the exodus of our people from Egypt and their subsequent wanderings. It was also the time we, as a family, reflected on our own wanderings.

Our ancestors had been expelled from Palestine by the Romans in 70 CE, chased out of Spain by the Inquisition in 1492, booted from Syria in the thirties, and forced to leave Cuba in 1965—all of this dislocation because of intolerance, bigotry, and hate.

But Pesach was also a spring festival, a celebration of rebirth and revival, bursting with new possibilities. I was banking on *that* chance of a fresh start as I directed our driver to pull over at a flower shop on La Cienega Boulevard. Isaac and I picked out a gorgeous bouquet of blue hydrangeas, crème roses, white mums, and alstroemeria, the "Lily of the Incas," imported from Peru. I knew my mother would love it, as it was the perfect addition to the Seder table.

The limousine dropped us off in front of my parents' sprawling, white stucco Mediterranean-style house with the fastidiously manicured dichondra lawn. Even though I'd spent over half my life there, the house looked strangely unfamiliar. It was an unpleasant, disorienting feeling. I double-checked the address to make sure we'd arrived at the right place.

Just then, the front door opened, and my mother came bounding down the flagstone path to where we stood. She looked thinner than I remembered but still stylish in a subdued floral dress, light gray cardigan, and a delicate white headscarf.

I handed Isaac the bouquet and ran to meet her halfway up the path.

"Marc, my son! Thank God you're here." She enveloped me in her slender arms and planted wet kisses all over my face.

"Hello, Ima!" I lifted her off the ground, close to tears myself. "It's good to be home."

Jacob raised his hand at me from the doorway, wearing an unconvincing smile. Shoulder-length black hair, full beard, blue embroidered silk shirt, and dark blue jeans, he looked the opposite of the conservative math professor that he was. I extricated one of my arms from my mother's hug and waved back.

"Let me look at you." My mother stepped back, her eyes shining. She held both her hands against her mouth, suppressing an overflow of emotion.

"Ima," I said, "this is Isaac."

Isaac stepped forward and thrust out his hand. "It's a pleasure to meet you, Mrs. Mendes."

My mother wiped the tears from her eyes and looked at him curiously. After a moment, she said, "*Baruch haba*, Isaac."

Isaac tossed a glance at me.

"It means *welcome* in Hebrew," I explained.

He looked back at my mother and held out the bouquet, flashing a friendly smile. "These are for you, Mrs. Mendes, for the table."

"They're lovely, thank you." She linked arms with me and shepherded me up the path toward the house, leaving Isaac behind with our suitcases, still holding the flowers. "Have you explained everything to him?" she asked in a low voice.

"Yes, Ima."

"About your father?"

"He knows everything, Ima. You go on ahead." I disengaged from her arm, grabbed our bags, and lugged them up the walkway.

Isaac caught me by the elbow and shot me a questioning look.

"Later," I whispered, feeling like a condemned man moving toward the gallows.

My mother was waiting on the porch as we climbed the steps to the house. She pressed a skullcap into my hand. "Wear this *kipa*, please. For your father. It's the one from your Bar Mitzvah."

I ran my fingers over the kipa, royal blue with a Star of David in the center, that my grandmother had knit specially for my thirteenth birthday. I nodded at my mother and kissed her cheek, then made for the front door without putting it on.

She shook her head. "Always such a stubborn boy."

I brushed the tips of my fingers against the stone mezuzah on the doorpost and brought them to my trembling lips.

As I stepped across the threshold, Jacob drew me into a rough bear hug, and we held each other for a bit. The house was filled with the aroma of the banquet my mother was preparing for our celebratory Aleppo-inspired meal, which brought back memories of my childhood. The dining table, visible in the next room, was laid out with my mother's best tablecloth, her Passover china, the family's antique silver, and an arrangement of flowers. Everything was exactly as I remembered it, my childhood preserved in amber. When we finally let go of each other, Jacob reached out his hand to Isaac, who was following close behind with my mother. "Welcome to the jungle, man," he said, subtly glancing at my mother.

"Jacob!" my mother shot back. "What a way to greet a guest. And on Pesach."

"It's a joke, Ima. I'm sure he doesn't mind. Right, Isaac?"

"Ignore him," I said, squeezing Isaac's arm and guiding him into the living room. Someone had placed a white satin kipa on his head while I wasn't looking. I put my hand to my head and was surprised to find I was already wearing mine.

"Jacob, help your brother with the suitcases, please," my mother said. "Marc, you'll stay in your old bedroom; I've fixed up the guest room for Isaac. Isaac, come this way."

Isaac shot a glance at me over his shoulder as she led him into the kitchen. He was in enemy territory now, out of my control and protection.

"The guest room?" I said to Jacob.

"Baby steps, buddy." Jacob pulled his hair into a ponytail, securing it with a bungee hook. "You're lucky to be here at all."

I glanced nervously in the direction of my father's study off the foyer. The door was open, the light off, and the desk empty. Everything was happening too quickly. Time had sped up and was sweeping Isaac, my family, my father, and me toward an unknown unfolding of events.

"Where is he?" I asked Jacob.

He frowned and pointed in the direction of the family room in the back of the house. "You've got guts bringing your friend here, you know," he said.

I locked eyes with him. "We were invited."

"Yeah, yeah, I know all that. But you *do* realize it's going to be awkward, right? Don't expect a happy reunion."

"Awkward I can handle. I just don't want a lecture from Abba."

Jacob lowered his voice. "Of course, you're going to get a lecture. He's a jurist, for fuck's sake."

I nodded, and we fell silent. We were startled a moment later by the kitchen door swinging open. Jacob's wife, Margalit, bounded across the reception room and blew me a kiss. "Greetings, brother!"

She always managed to get a laugh out of me even when I was at my lowest.

"Greetings, wife of my brother. Look at you!" I stepped back and admired her outfit, a close-fitting blue embroidered midi dress and matching headscarf.

She pirouetted to show off her ensemble. Then she slunk up to Jacob and rested her head on his shoulder. "We *are* gorgeous, are we not? Color-coordinated and all that!" Narrowing her eyes, she reached out and touched her finger to the Star of David pendant around my neck. "My, my, this is nice! White gold?"

"It's platinum. A present from Isaac when I turned thirty."

She drew in an exaggerated breath. "And all along I thought *you* were the sugar daddy."

Jacob rolled his eyes. "Come on, you loons. Quit being silly. This is Pesach, remember?"

"Oh, I remember all right." Margalit bent down and rubbed her knees. "They're still raw from spending half the night on them searching for *hametz* with your mother, not to mention all the cleaning and scrubbing." She turned back to me and playfully adjusted my shirt collar. "Speaking of Isaac, it looks like your mother recruited him as her *sous-chef* in there." She cocked her head at the kitchen. "Maybe you should go rescue him."

I strode across the room, heart racing, and pushed into the kitchen. I was greeted by the sight of Isaac and my mother, both in dark blue chef aprons. Isaac was forming *charoset* balls with an ice cream scoop out of the wine-soaked, chopped-apple, dried-fruit-and-nuts concoction meant to symbolize bricks and mortar. My mother was hovering over him. "Carefully, carefully, Isaac. Don't make them too big. Ay! Too much there."

Isaac froze mid-motion, balancing a half-formed ball in the palm of his hand. My mother passed the back of her arm across her damp forehead and forced a smile. "Never mind, dear, just keep rolling."

I cleared my throat in the doorway, and my mother looked up. "Where have you been? Poor Isaac here has been bored out of his mind, putting up with me."

Isaac laughed and shook his head. "Not at all, Mrs. Mendes. This is fun."

"Such a sweet boy," she said to no one in particular, removing her apron and stowing it in the cupboard. "Now then, *motek*—" she leveled her eyes at me, "—it's time to say hello to your father.

I know he's anxious to see you."

I glanced at Isaac, who was focused on finishing up his assignment, trying his best to ignore our conversation. Reading my thoughts, my mother brushed Isaac's arm, and he looked up. "Isaac, you can join them later."

The family room was a short walk from the kitchen, through an adjacent den, and then through a pair of French doors. I approached the doors, which were ajar, and peered through them. In the far corner of the sparsely furnished room, in the most comfortable chair in the house, sat the man in whose presence I had dreaded to find myself for the last eight years—my father the judge, studying Talmud by the warm light of an antique Berber lantern. He was dressed in a pair of loose-fitting trousers and a housecoat and wearing his dress kipa. He held the largish tome in his left hand and unconsciously stroked his chest-length beard with the other.

Watching him from across the room, I was transported to my childhood, when I used to sneak into his office and hide under a table to watch him while he studied. I would spend hours that way, imagining what he might be reading, what he might be thinking. And now, after so many years, here was the same man, that same serene expression, the same quiet and compassionate intensity so many in our community had sought out over the years. Here was a man whose heart was tender but whose mind was as sharp as an incisor.

My father's door had always been open to me. He'd always been there when I needed him. And yet, although I'd never lacked a father, I'd always felt deprived of a dad. My father was simply too high above me, like God. For as much as God loves and cares for his people, he lacks true immanence, in my experience, regardless of what our sages taught. There was no warmth, no hugs, no kisses, no playing rough and tumble in the yard, no baseball, no outings, no camping trips, no bike rides. I'd felt lonely as a child.

Jacob never needed any of that. He was self-sufficient. Strong and tall, a natural athlete. Like my father, but without the superior intellect. Jacob was a regular guy, admired by his peers. And that was all he needed.

I needed more. *More!* My mother knew it. I'm sure my father knew it as well. But all he could offer me were his hopes that I would one day become a rabbi like him and my grandfather before him. In the presence of our congregation, he frequently announced I was a rabbi in the making, often adding that I was an intellectual with a strong sense of the spiritual. What he didn't know was that I was a spiritual intellectual with a secret: I liked other boys.

I pushed back the deluge of memories, steeling myself for the encounter. And then he looked up. Our eyes met. He set aside the book and nodded slowly at me. It was one of his signals; he was granting me permission to enter the room. I moved toward him, short of breath, feeling a tightness in the middle of my chest. At sixty, his once black hair was now salted through with white. But as he rose from his armchair, he stood as tall as ever, and the fire in his large, black eyes told me his mind was as sharp as it had ever been.

I reached out, and he tenderly took my hand and pulled me toward him. He encircled me with his muscular arms and held me against his chest. I could feel his heart beating as strongly as mine, and I wrapped my arms around him and held tight. After a few moments, he removed my kipa and stroked my hair.

"My son," he whispered. It was the first time I'd heard his voice in nearly a decade. I braced myself for the lecture, the questions, the recriminations. But they didn't come. Not yet. Instead, my father released me from his embrace and placed the kipa back on my head. Then he held my face in his large hands and kissed me on the cheek.

The sound of clinking glass made me turn around. My mother swept into the room, carrying a silver tray on which sat three hand-painted demitasses of cardamom-spiced Syrian coffee.

"We'll be starting the Seder in a few minutes," she announced. "But first, take a bit of coffee."

My father nodded in the direction of Isaac, who had poked his head through the doorway. "Is this our guest?"

"Yes, I'm sorry, Abba." I waved Isaac over. "This is my partner, Isaac Perez. Isaac, this is my father, Rabbi Gabriel Mendes."

Isaac pumped my father's hand earnestly. "Rabbi Mendes, it's so great to meet you. Thank you for inviting me to spend Passover with you and your family."

My father nodded and allowed himself a brief smile. "Let's have coffee while my wife finishes the preparations, shall we?"

My mother withdrew, closing the French doors as she left. Isaac and I sat next to each other on one of the couches, and my father positioned himself across from us in the love seat. He motioned for us to take our cups.

I sipped some of the sweet, strong coffee. It was still searingly hot. I swished it around in my mouth before swallowing. My father did the same. Isaac took a tentative sip and closed his eyes thoughtfully. "Very nice." He set down the little cup and flashed his teeth. "Strong, but good."

My father smiled politely. "Isaac." He drew out the word slowly. Isaac looked up. My father's black eyes met his and held them. "Isaac is a Hebrew name; did you know that? It means *to laugh*."

"Yes, sir, I knew that. My mother named me after the Isaac in the Bible."

My father raised his eyebrows. "Your mother is a religious woman?"

"Very much so. She's a devout Roman Catholic."

"I see." My father nodded and took a long sip of his coffee.

"She was quite old when I was born, like Isaac's mother Sarah in the Bible. I was a complete surprise. That's why she named me Isaac."

My father arched an eyebrow. "The birth of Isaac was not a surprise," he said, his voice edged with emotion. "It was foretold."

Isaac took a moment to think. "Well, I wasn't foretold. I just happened unexpectedly."

My father sipped some more coffee, deep in thought. After a moment, he set down his cup and looked again at Isaac. "My son Marc was raised to be observant. Did you know that?"

"Yes, sir, he told me."

"He told you," my father echoed. He looked sideways at me. "Yes, I have no doubt he told you."

"He told me he kept kosher, too," Isaac said, a bit too eagerly.

"He told you he kept kosher?" My father's gaze settled on me. "Yes, my son kept kosher."

"Abba—"

My father raised his hand at me and turned to Isaac. "Did my son *also* tell you he meticulously observed the Sabbath and celebrated all the Holy Festivals? Did he tell you he donned *tefillin* every morning and prayed three times a day, and upon waking, before each meal, and before going to bed at night? Did he tell you he attended *yeshiva* from kindergarten through high school? And that he was a brilliant and engaged student of the Talmud?"

Isaac shifted uncomfortably and looked at me for some help.

"I am sure he also told you about the year he spent in Israel, allegedly to contemplate his future after graduating high school."

"Abba, please—" I said.

"Gabriel," my mother called, poking her head through the French doors. "The table's ready."

My father held up his hand in response.

"Please, Abba, not tonight," I pleaded.

"Not tonight? Why not tonight?"

"Because it's Pesach." I put my arm around Isaac. "And, because we have a guest."

"I want to know what happened to you, Mordechai," my father said, calling me by my Hebrew name for the first time. "I've never asked you this, my son, and God is my witness that I'm not angry with you, but I must know now—before we begin the Seder. What made you change?"

"Abba, please, now isn't the time. We can talk about all that later. The fact I'm here should be enough for now."

My father peered at me, pulling on his beard.

"Gabriel, did you hear me?" my mother called from the doorway.

"Hannah, please join us for a moment," my father said. My mother entered the room and sat next to him on the love seat. She'd changed into a lovely pastel pink dress.

"Marc, Isaac," my father said. "I wanted to take a moment to explain something to you. To both of you." He placed his empty demitasse on the table and dabbed his beard with a napkin. "A generation ago, perhaps not even so long as that, a situation such as yours would have been met, shall we say, with great negativity. I'm referring now to your special friendship." His gaze drifted up to my arm draped over Isaac's shoulder. "Men such as yourselves often found themselves banned from their homes. Some parents went so far as to hold funerals for these estranged sons. I can attest from having witnessed such things that nothing good ever resulted from these extreme actions. In fact, it is my opinion that such reactions were evil and did not carry the blessing of *Hakadosh Baruch Hu*, blessed be His name." He stared at me for a beat. "Do you understand me?"

I nodded.

"Do you really?"

"Yes, Abba, I understand."

He glanced at my mother and looked back at me. "So then," he continued, "eight years ago, without any explanation whatsoever, you withdrew from us."

I opened my mouth to respond but was silenced by my

father's raised hand.

"Eight years of estrangement," he said. "Eight years! Do you have any idea how long eight years is for a father? For a mother? You don't. Six long agonizing years passed before I had *any* idea why you'd withdrawn from us. At first, I assumed it had something to do with your addictions. Thank God you won that terrible battle. But it was your brother who finally told us the truth. And it has taken me two years to forgive you." He paused. "It took me two years to forgive you for abandoning us without any reason, not for being a homosexual."

"I couldn't face you," I whispered, my throat constricting with emotion.

"What do you mean, my son? When did I ever discourage you from coming to me? When did I ever reject you?"

I shook my head, tears welling in my eyes. "Never, Abba. You were always there for me, I know. But I needed space, Abba. I needed to know myself, to love myself as I am, without feeling guilty. You were always so righteous and pure—"

"Pure?" My father's eyes widened. Then he startled all of us by breaking out into the biggest laugh I'd ever heard from him in my life. When he finally regained his composure, he wiped his eyes with the back of his hand and said, "*Hijo*, you don't know anything. I'm far from pure, believe me. In any event, I've forgiven you. And although I can't accept your lifestyle as ideal, I'll never stop loving you as my son."

I nodded. "Nobody's perfect, Abba."

I'd meant to make a joke to lighten the mood. But the lengthening silence in the room felt oppressive as my father regarded me, his large chest rising and falling.

"Tell me this," he said, drawing himself up, "now that you've had your space, have you learned to love yourself?"

The question hung in the air for a moment. Isaac placed his hand on my knee, and I glanced down at it. "Once I was a slave, Abba," I said, reciting a refrain from the Passover Seder. I took

Isaac's hand in mine. "Now I'm free."

My father's lips curled back into a joyless smile. "Well said, *hijo*." He rose and kissed my forehead. Then he moved to Isaac and placed his hand on his head. "Isaac," he said, "welcome to our home. Please join us at the table. The Seder is about to begin."

My father took his place at the head of the table, Jacob and Margalit to his right, my mother to his left. I stood opposite my father, and my mother directed Isaac to stand to her left as she lit the festival candles and recited the appropriate blessing. We responded with a unanimous *amen* and took our seats.

My father held up his *Haggadah*, a new edition I'd never seen before. "In honor of our guest, tonight we will be using a special Haggadah, one with an English-language translation."

Isaac picked up his copy and beamed. "Thank you, sir."

My father nodded, raised his glass, and initiated the Seder with the blessings over the first cup of wine and the festival.

The three-hour-long ritual progressed slowly: the recitation of the story of the Exodus, accompanied by the asking and answering of traditional questions; the eating of symbolic morsels; the breaking and partaking of matzah; the four cups of wine—grape juice for me. My father's voice faded into the background, and I was conscious I was reading and responding by rote. I looked around the table at my parents, my brother, his wife; at Isaac, and I saw smiles. But behind each of these smiles, I sensed pain.

During the holiday meal itself, I caught my mother alternating her gaze between my father, Jacob, and me, with moist eyes. She'd lost weight, much more than I'd noticed earlier. By the light of the candles, she looked gaunt. My father also was grayer, haggard, and careworn. His voice was still strong as he chanted the prayers, but there was a weariness behind it that betrayed his years of suffering—all on account of me.

I wish I could report that the separation from my family made no difference that night, that the years melted away and everything was as it had been before. But I can't. Smooth as the evening went, I no longer felt the joy I'd felt as a child, and later as a young man, sharing the Passover with my family. Instead, we had all gone through the movements in an atmosphere of nostalgia and some sadness. It was then I came to realize I'd committed a grave, irreparable error by shunning my family for all those years.

After the Seder, we retired to the living room to drink cardamom tea. It was past eleven, and the conversation was lagging, as we were all exhausted from the long evening. My mother had just brought out the Syrian nut cake she'd been saving for dessert when Isaac's cell phone fired off. He whipped it out of his coat and answered it. My father shook his head. He wasn't accustomed to having holidays interrupted by technology. I was about to ask Isaac to take it in the hall when I noticed the blood had drained from his face.

"Who is it?" I whispered.

Isaac put his hand on my shoulder to support himself. "Yes, yes, I understand," he mumbled into the phone. "I'll call there immediately . . . No, you did the right thing. Thank you, Laura." He snapped shut the telephone.

"Who's Laura?" my mother asked.

"She's our cleaning lady, Ima. Isaac, what happened?" I asked.

Isaac rose to his feet, still using my shoulder to steady himself. "It's my mother," he said, his voice trembling. "She fell. Laura found her unconscious in the tub. She called the ambulance, and they took her to the hospital."

"Dear God." My mother moved to my father's side.

Jacob and Margalit watched helplessly as tears streamed down Isaac's cheeks. "Please, Marc," he said, handing me the phone. "Call the emergency room at UCSF. Please. I can't—"

He dashed out of the room, and a moment later, we heard the front door open and close.

"Where did he go?" Margalit asked.

"Ima, would you please go after him?" I asked.

My mother picked up a plate of cake and sped off in pursuit of Isaac. I dialed the hospital and, a few moments later, was talking to one of the duty physicians. Miriam had broken her collarbone and had also managed to knock her head hard against the edge of the bathtub. She was unconscious, but her general condition had stabilized. The doctor believed it was safe to perform an emergency procedure to set the bone, but he needed Isaac's consent to do so. I found Isaac sitting on the front porch next to my mother, his head resting on his knees. I explained the situation to him.

"He said it was safe?" he asked. "Are you sure?"

"He needs to talk to you." I pressed the phone into his hands. "He'll explain."

Isaac listened silently. After a few moments, he lifted his eyes to me and said into the phone: "Are you sure . . .? No, of course. But doctor—all right, yes. Please, doctor, take care of her. She's all the family I have. Please . . . Yes, thank you. Tomorrow, yes."

Isaac handed me the phone and turned to my mother. "They're going to operate." His voice was trembling.

"Don't worry," my mother said, squeezing his hand. "If the doctor said it's safe, then it's safe. They're the experts. Thank God it wasn't more serious."

Isaac nodded and drew a deep breath. "I need to catch the first flight out."

Jacob and Margalit stepped outside. "Where's Abba?" I asked them.

"Inside," Margalit said, nodding at the doorway, "praying."

I knelt next to Isaac and whispered in his ear, "I'll be right back."

I found my father in his study, his body bobbing gently back and forth, talking to God. He didn't seem to notice as I pushed open the door and approached him from behind. After a few moments, he spoke, his back still turned to me. "Your friend's mother?"

"They're going to operate on her tonight. She's still unconscious, but the doctor thinks she'll be all right. She's a strong woman."

"Thank God. And your friend, how is he?" he asked, turning to face me.

"He's afraid, Abba. She's everything to him."

My father raised his head questioningly.

"The rest of his family is dead. Killed in El Salvador during their civil war."

My father's expression changed to incredulity and sorrow, and his eyes misted over. "All of them?"

"Yes, Abba. Both his brothers, one of them in his presence, and his father as well. All dead. Now all he has is his mother."

"And you." He touched my chest with his broad palm.

I pressed my hand against his and felt my throat tighten. "Thank you, Abba, for everything. I'm sorry it took so long."

He rubbed my chest softly. "Go comfort your friend. Tell him my prayers are with him and with his mother." He kissed me on the forehead. "We'll talk again once this is all over."

Chapter 10

Isaac insisted we return home right away. So, after saying our hasty good-byes, we hopped a cab to the airport, bought two tickets on the first flight back to San Francisco, and sat in the concourse to wait for our gate to be announced. Apart from the janitorial staff washing the observation windows and polishing the floors, we were the only people in the terminal.

Isaac rang the hospital every half hour or so to check on his mother while I bit my tongue and nursed endless streams of lukewarm coffee from a vending machine. At three in the morning, the surgeon called to report that Miriam's operation had been successful; he'd transferred her to the ICU for recovery and further observation. This news calmed Isaac enough to allow him to close his eyes and rest for a couple of hours. I, on the other hand, was buzzing from the caffeine. I deliriously paced the halls of the terminal until, thank God, at a quarter to six, a mellifluous female voice announced our flight over the loudspeaker.

The ride from SFO to the hospital was more harrowing than the flight from Los Angeles, with Isaac urging the ancient taxi driver to press the pedal to the metal, and the driver only too willing to oblige. Minutes later, he brought his vehicle to a screeching landing in the hospital's handicap zone, and Isaac flew out the door, leaving me to deal with the fare.

When I got inside, I found him coming out of the gift shop, carrying a crystal vase full of spring flowers. He hurried past me to the elevators.

"Hey, remember me?" I said.

Isaac jammed his finger into the elevator call button. "They told me the ICU's on the eleventh floor," he said in an unfamiliar strangulated tone of voice.

The elevator doors slid open, and we pressed our way into the packed car. Isaac fought a path to one of the corners and turned his back to the crowd to protect the vase. By the time we arrived at the eleventh floor, the flowers were mangled.

The elevator doors opened onto the ICU station. A parchment-thin nurse behind the desk peered over his half-glasses as we stepped onto the floor.

"I'm here to see Miriam Perez," Isaac said, stepping up to the station.

The nurse frowned at the wilted flowers and looked up at Isaac. "What's your relationship to the patient?"

"I'm her son," Isaac explained. "This is my partner."

"I see." The nurse ran his finger down a clipboard and paused for a moment. "Oh, yes, Perez." He drew a breath and nodded at the waiting area. "Please wait right over there. I'll call Doctor Sybert."

"Is everything all right?" I asked.

"As I said, I'll call Doctor Sybert. You'll discuss the matter with him. Please, wait over there." He poked his pencil at the waiting room and turned his attention to his computer screen.

Isaac threw me a worried glance, and I led him to the waiting area. A feeble old woman, whose body was racked with shaking, was sitting in a corner, mumbling to herself. She glanced back and forth between Isaac and me, grimacing and nodding conspiratorially. We tried our best to ignore her, but her behavior unnerved me, so we moved closer to the main hallway.

After a few tense moments watching nurses and orderlies race back and forth about the halls, a grim gentleman in green scrubs approached us. I quickly scanned his nametag: John Sybert, M.D., F.A.C.S.

"Mr. Perez?" He looked first at me, then at Isaac.

"That's me." Isaac stepped forward, the vase of flowers in one hand. "I'm here to see my mother, Miriam Perez. I was told she was moved here to the ICU ward early this morning. She had emergency surgery—"

"Yes," the doctor answered, "I was the attending physician."

Over his shoulder, I saw a nurse hovering in the distance, and my hands went numb.

"I'm sorry," he began in a low voice, "I'm afraid your mother went into cardiac arrest an hour and a half ago. We did our best to revive her, but—"

Isaac's head cocked to one side. His brow spasmed into deep furrows as the doctor's words hit home. "What are you saying?"

"I'm very sorry, Mr. Perez. Your mother never regained consciousness. She went peacefully."

The old woman in the waiting area screamed at an explosion of glass, water, and flowers as the vase dropped to the Formica floor from Isaac's hand, followed by his limp body.

Chapter 11

Springtime in San Francisco gave way to a cold and windy summer. A wildfire in the Oakland hills snowed ash over the city for days, and a moderate earthquake, a precursor to *The Big One*, jangled the nerves of natives, transplants, and tourists alike. While my fellow San Franciscans twisted themselves into knots over the impending apocalypse, I tended to Isaac, who'd refused to leave the apartment ever since his mother's funeral two months earlier. The stress of it all reawakened long-suppressed appetites in me, and I found myself tempted to reach for the telephone more than once to scream for help. My old contacts from NA were only a phone call away. But it had been so long since I'd talked to them or been to a meeting, I'd forgotten how to ask for help and was ashamed to ask now. So I never made the call.

In the days immediately following Miriam's passing, Ed had blasted publicity about the Saint-Cloud case all over the media. There were articles, interviews, news stories, and the telephone was ringing off the hook in the office throughout the day. As I expected, the publicity drew a bad response from certain reactive elements in the gay community, which led to anonymous death threats against the firm and some minor incidents of vandalism directed at our building. Despite it all, Ed held firm, determined not to be intimidated into withdrawing from the case. Worst of all, he continually put me forward as the face of the firm, which was all the more difficult for me, considering the tragedy of Miriam's recent passing and Isaac's emotional crisis.

Then came the call from Xanadu's lawyers. They'd agreed to settle the case for the original one hundred thousand and not one penny more, and I jumped on it. Within the hour, they couriered over the settlement agreement for Silva's signature. It was a rare moment of celebration in the office, especially for Ed. He was so pleased I'd pulled it off that he promised, after a few glasses of champagne, to increase my share of ownership in the firm in the new year. Personally, it was enough for me to be putting the case to bed, considering how badly it could have gone.

Silva had been transferred to San Quentin to serve the sentence for his parole violation. So I'd put in a call to the prison administration, advising I'd be coming to see him later that morning. When they finally escorted him into the glass-enclosed booth in the attorney visiting area, I was shocked to see the state of him. His jumpsuit was rumpled and dirty, three ugly scratches angled across the right side of his face, and his hands looked as if they had soaked in a bucket of grease. He looked utterly pitiful.

"Thanks for coming, Mr. Mendes," he said, making a brave attempt to look happy.

"What happened, Alejandro?"

He glanced at his reflection in the glass and shook his head. "I look like crap, right?" He waved his hand. "It's nothing. They have me rebuilding car engines. I was working on one when you got here."

"How'd you get those scratches?"

He brought his hand to his face and winced. "I got into a

scuffle with some guy the other day. It's not a big deal." He flipped back a lock of hair that had fallen in his face and shrugged.

I brought him up to speed about the settlement and handed him the agreement. He skimmed it briefly, then signed it and slid it back at me.

"Thank you, Mr. Mendes. You can go ahead and deposit the money into my bank account."

I slipped the signed agreement into my briefcase and looked up at him. "Not that it matters much now, Alejandro, but why didn't you tell me about the dirty test? I'm just curious."

"I didn't know about it when you came to see me."

"You had to know they'd tested you."

"Yes, but my probation officer never told me the result. He made it seem like I was just being done for GTA. It wasn't until you told me over the telephone and my panel attorney confirmed it later that I had any idea. If I'd known, I would've told you, I swear."

I nodded, thinking through his explanation. "You tested positive for cannabis and psychedelics. What was that about?"

"I went to San Diego to see some friends. They invited me to a party where everyone was smoking. I had maybe like one hit. The rest was just secondhand, I guess. Then someone must have slipped something into my drink because I blacked out. The next thing I knew, I was being arrested. I know it sounds crazy, but it's the God's honest truth."

"It does sound a bit crazy. But if you say so . . ."

He shrugged and smoothed back his hair with both hands, then produced a rubber band from the pocket of his jumpsuit and pulled his hair into a ponytail.

"What do you think?" he asked, flashing a sly smile.

"I thought they would have given you a buzz cut."

"They don't do that anymore." He checked out his reflection in the window and grinned, apparently happy with what he saw.

At that moment, my eye was drawn to the oval birthmark

gracing his left cheek. It was more or less the size of my thumbnail and added an element of intrigue to Silva's handsome face, like Jupiter's mysterious red spot.

Noticing my distraction, a faint blush colored his cheeks, and he sat up. "You like this, don't you?" He touched his index finger to his birthmark.

"I beg your pardon?" I said, recovering myself, trying my best to look nonchalant.

"My birthmark," he said. "You were staring at it."

"No, I—"

"It's okay. People stare at it all the time." He let out a chuckle. "You couldn't take your eyes off it the first time we met at your office."

"I'm sure that's not true, Alejandro."

"Nope, it's true." He raised his eyebrows. "When I was little, my mother used to tell me it was proof I'd been kissed by the Aztec god *Xōchipilli*."

"That's nice." I picked up my briefcase and stood. "Anyway, I'll make sure the funds are deposited to your account once they're available."

"Hang on a second, Mr. Mendes. Don't leave yet!"

I hesitated a moment and sat down again.

Silva glanced around the room; then he beckoned me forward with a wave of his hand.

"What is it?" I asked.

He looked down and said, almost shyly, "You remember the first time I came to see you, right? About my case?"

"Yes, of course."

"Well, I sort of felt like—I don't know how to say it, really, but I felt something from you. Aside from the birthmark thing." He lifted his face and looked at me. "Do you know what I'm saying?"

The temperature in the booth suddenly felt as if it had increased ten degrees. I shifted in my seat and tried hard not to avert my eyes from Silva.

"I know I'm probably not explaining myself very well," he continued. "What I mean is there was something in your eyes when you looked at me as I was explaining my problem. Like you were really listening. Not just because of the money, but because . . ." he inhaled deeply, ". . . because you understood me; you cared about me."

My breath caught in my throat.

"And then when you came to see me at the jail, it was the same thing. I felt you understood me." He leaned forward and peered into my eyes. "I've never felt that from anyone before."

"I care about all my clients, Alejandro."

"It wasn't like that, and you know it, Mr. Mendes. I mean, I know you have to say that because I'm a client. But you know it's not true. We click, you and me."

"We click?"

"We click." Silva laid his hand on my wrist and smiled. "So, what I wanted to ask you was, now that the case is going to be over, do you think we could keep seeing each other?"

"What do you mean?" I gradually moved my arm away from his hand. He gently pulled it back.

"I don't want our acquaintance to end with this case," he said softly but firmly. "I'd like to be able to see you every once in a while, but not just as a former client and his lawyer, more like friends. I have important things I need to talk to someone about. I think you'd understand them."

I checked my watch. It was nearly two in the afternoon, and I hadn't eaten yet. I had to bring this thing to an end.

"Let's wait until you're out of prison, Alejandro. We can talk then."

Silva shook his head. "That could be months from now!"

"All right, then maybe sooner. But you should know, I'm a busy person, and I'm not usually available for impromptu prison visits."

"Don't worry, Mr. Mendes, I know you're busy. I understand . . . But when do you think you'd be free?"

"I'll let you know, Alejandro. Right now, though, I've got to get going. It's late, and I have other things to attend to."

Silva frowned for a moment, then he nodded. "Thank you for everything, Marc. I can call you Marc now, right?"

"Not at the office, please."

Silva forced a smile.

In the two months that passed after that meeting, I put in one call to Silva to let him know his check had been deposited. He never called my office again.

"Isaac." I pushed open the bedroom door with my foot. "Have some soup." I'd driven home from work at lunchtime to make sure he ate something.

Isaac lay on his side in bed, still in his underwear, contemplating a picture of his mother on the nightstand. I stood with the tray in my hand and stared at his back.

"Do you want me to feed you?" I asked and immediately regretted how rude the question sounded.

"Put it on the desk."

"Your throat sounds dry. Have you had any water today?"

He rolled over and looked past me, his eyes a glassy red and outlined in puffy purplish circles. "No, I haven't. Not yet. Bring me some, please."

When I came back with the water, Isaac was sitting up in bed, running his fingers through his overgrown blue-black hair. He accepted the glass and drained it in one long gulp. "Thanks." He pushed the empty glass back at me.

I sat on the bed next to him. Miriam's pet Abyssinian, Nilo, jumped into my lap, ran his rough tongue across my hand, and curled into a ball and dozed off.

Isaac stared at him with teary eyes. He lifted the beaded macramé collar Miriam had made for Nilo and rubbed the sweet spot on his neck. Nilo mewed and slinked into Isaac's lap. Isaac ran his hand along the length of Nilo's ruddy coat and allowed a slight smile to play on his lips.

After a few moments, Isaac let out a long, steady breath and rested his head on my shoulder, closing his eyes.

"What time is it?" he asked.

At the sound of Isaac's voice, Nilo raised his head and jumped out of his lap. Isaac watched him slink under the writing desk.

"It's one o'clock," I answered. "Why?"

"I don't know. Just wondering."

"Do you want to take a walk?"

Isaac shook his head. "Not really." He sat up in bed.

I stood and cleared my throat. "Isaac, you know, I realize you're going through a hard time. We both are. And—"

Isaac squeezed his eyes shut and held up his hand. "Stop, Marc, please. I can't. I don't know why, but I just can't. I'm sorry."

"Then maybe we should see someone. A doctor or something. I don't think this is normal."

Isaac's eyes blazed. "A doctor isn't going to bring back my mother, is he?" He wrapped his arms around himself and held tight. "A doctor probably killed her."

"I don't know about that," I said, battling to keep my temper in check. "But locking yourself away in this apartment isn't going to bring her back either."

Tears spilled out of Isaac's eyes and down his cheeks. "I've lost everyone and everything, Marc. Don't you understand that?"

"Not everything." I rubbed his leg reassuringly, but after two months the gesture felt wooden. "You still have me. More importantly, you still have yourself."

Isaac jerked away. "I'm not ready yet, all right? I'm not goddamned ready!"

He bolted out of bed and ran to the bathroom, slamming the door behind him.

I pounded on the locked door, and the sound reverberated through the room. "Isaac, open up."

"Leave me alone; I'm busy in here," came his muffled response.

"Isaac, come on. Let me in."

"Go away!"

I drew back, on the verge of kicking the door, when I was startled by the loud ringing of the telephone.

I hurried into the living room and snatched up the receiver.

"Mr. Mendes, it's Vlad."

I felt an instant of disorientation.

"—from the office."

"Oh, Vlad." I drew a deep breath and regrouped. "Why are you calling me here?"

"Because you weren't answering your cell phone, obviously."

I felt the inside pocket of my coat and noted with annoyance that my cell phone was missing.

"I must have left it in the car. What is it, Vlad?"

"Some lawyer's been trying to reach you all afternoon. She says it's urgent."

I frowned. "Why didn't you pass the call to Ed?"

"She said it was an urgent personal matter, for your ears only. She's got a strange name: Phoebe Thistlewig. She said she'll be at her office all afternoon."

"Yes, fine, thank you."

"I looked her up. She's an immigration lawyer in Cow Hollow. It may be about your partner's thing."

My heart sped up as he uttered the words.

"How do you know about that?"

"My girlfriend Tina let it slip. I meant to tell you before, sorry."

I suppressed a hot flash of anger as best as I could, taking a deep breath before I spoke again. "I'd appreciate it if you would keep this to yourself, Vlad. And please pass that along to your girlfriend."

"Don't worry, boss. Wild horses and all that. Do you want her number?"

"Whose?"

"The lawyer's."

"I've got it, thanks."

Still stinging from the conversation, I staggered back to the bathroom. "Isaac, open up, please."

"Who was it?"

I sat down on the floor with my back against the door. "It was Vlad. The immigration lawyer finally returned our call. She left a couple of messages."

"Which immigration lawyer?"

"That Thistlewig woman Judge Tanaka's clerk recommended, remember?"

My announcement was met with silence.

"Did you hear—?"

"Yes, I heard you," he snapped. "What about it?"

"I think we should start dealing with our immigration problem."

"You mean *my* immigration problem," he corrected.

"No, I mean *our* immigration problem. Time's getting short, and the hearing will be here before we know it."

Nilo crept out from under the desk. He glanced at me before padding out of the room. I checked my watch and saw it was already two in the afternoon.

"I think we should go see her."

"You go see her." Isaac's voice had withdrawn deeper into the bathroom. "I'm not going anywhere."

My eye twitched. "All right, Isaac, have it your way." Rising to my feet, I steadied myself against a sudden head rush. "You stay right there in the bathroom. I'll see you tonight." The pressure in my eye was morphing into a throbbing migraine.

Traffic was light as I drove to Phoebe Thistlewig's office. Opening the glove compartment, I whipped out my spare bottle of aspirin, dry swallowed a couple of tablets, and reflected on my brief conversation with her moments before. Her phone had rung seven or eight times before she answered with a curt, "Thistlewig here. Is this Mr. Mendes?"

I lowered the sunshade against the dizzying afternoon glare. "Actually, yes. Don't you have any other clients?" I asked half-serious.

"Call me psychic. Are you able to come to my office this afternoon?"

"I can come right now if that works."

She gave me directions to a three-story lavender Victorian house on Gough Street. I passed it a few times, looking for someplace to park. After several minutes, I gave up on the idea of finding something close and ended up fighting off a Federal Express driver for a parking space at Steiner and Broadway. I loaded the meter with quarters and hoofed it downhill, making it to Thistlewig's in less than fifteen minutes, sweat streaming down the sides of my pounding head.

I knocked on the locked door and waited. A few moments later, I knocked again, this time more loudly. Stepping back to the sidewalk, I craned my neck to look at the house's pentagonal tower and debated whether or not to throw a pebble at one of the windows. Thinking the better of it, I stepped up to the door again and cursed myself for not noticing a buzzer panel hidden behind a fern. Locating Thistlewig's name, I pressed the button next to it. Instantly, a loud chime echoed on the porch. Pushing open the door, I stepped inside the house.

The deserted foyer opened onto a musty library furnished

with a scattering of secondhand furniture. At the opposite end of the room hung an antique portrait of the Romanoffs. I tried flipping the light switch, but nothing happened.

I returned to the foyer and searched for some indication of Ms. Thistlewig's office. Finding nothing, I climbed the creaky stairs to the second-story landing, where I located an arrow-shaped sign with the word *Thistlewig*, urging me up the next flight of stairs. When I arrived at the next floor, I found myself confronted by a long, bare hallway. At this point, the only thing keeping me from abandoning my search was Tanaka's clerk's glowing recommendation.

"Hello?" I called into the empty hallway. The muted sounds of traffic penetrated the walls and made the house feel all the lonelier. "Ms. Thistlewig?"

I ventured deeper into the hallway and found a door with a sign on it, which read:

Phoebe Thistlewig, Esq.
Attorney at Law (CA)
Barrister and Solicitor (Eng.)

And to one side, a small wooden plaque was inscribed with the words:

Please Knock
Gently

Feeling like Alice in Wonderland, I raised my fist to the door and knocked gently. The door flew open, and I was greeted by a tall, slender woman in her mid-fifties draped in a dark blue floral caftan and sporting a red bob. An assortment of chains and necklaces hung around her neck, and a pair of tiny prisms dangled from her earlobes.

"Mr. Mendes, I presume?" She regarded me with her jade

green eyes and an unnerving expression that was both intense and welcoming. There was something cat-like about her features, all angles and sharp edges.

I nodded and peered around her into the room. It looked empty, apart from some wooden chairs and a writing table.

"Please, come in." She retreated into the room. "I was about to put on some *yerba mate* tea, direct from Argentina. Would you like some?"

I followed her inside and cast about the room. My gaze settled on a threadbare couch. "Water would be great, thanks."

"Of course. Please step into my office. I'll be with you presently."

"I thought this was your office."

"This? Oh, for heaven's sake, no. This is the waiting room. My office is through there." She pointed a blue lacquered fingernail at a side door and disappeared into another room I assumed was the kitchen.

I moved into her brightly lit, cluttered office. It was dominated by an enormous desk strewn with files. Also on the desk was a glass bowl stuffed with Hershey's chocolate kisses, a basket of fresh-cut daisies, and a plaque that read: *Kindly keep your neuroses to yourself.*

"Have a seat anywhere," she called out.

Looking around, I found a red velveteen settee pushed into a corner. I dragged it in front of the desk and sat down to wait. Every inch of wall in the little office was covered by some kind of picture, plaque, diploma, or certificate. I was relieved to see Ms. Thistlewig's law school diploma and her admission certificate on the wall behind her desk. Next to these was a yellowing photograph of her standing proudly on the Great Wall of China in military khakis. I continued looking around the room and noticed a plaque hanging on the wall behind me that said: *Probably guilty.*

"That's a good one, isn't it?" Thistlewig said, nudging open the door with her foot and carrying in an ornate brass tray loaded with a cast iron teapot, yellow ceramic sugar bowl, two wooden cups, and a pair of matching brass teaspoons. "Would you mind terribly clearing a place for this on my desk?"

I grabbed a pile of folders and put them on top of another pile of folders on the floor.

"Thank you." Thistlewig placed the tray on her desk, poured herself a generous cup, and loaded it with three teaspoons of sugar. "Your water's there." She nodded at the other cup. "There's plenty of tea in case you change your mind."

"Thanks." I drained the cup of water and slid it back onto the tray.

Picking up her steaming cup, Thistlewig passed it under her nose and breathed in the aroma. "Mmmm, yerba mate. It's the perfect recipe for soothing those bothersome migraine headaches."

"You have a migraine?" I asked, a little incredulous.

"No. You do." She took a large sip of her tea and smiled.

"Oh, right, I'd forgotten. You're psychic."

"It was your eye that gave it away."

"My eye?"

"The left one." She gestured towards my flushed face. "It's exhibiting the same telltale redness my late husband Theodore's eye used to get whenever he was stricken with a migraine headache."

"Theodore Thistlewig?"

She frowned and lowered her voice, "Heavens, no. Thistlewig is *my* family name. Theodore's last name was Popov. The late Doctor Theodore Popov of the University of San Francisco. We met in Durham in the sixties while he was there on a Rhodes scholarship. We fell in love and promptly married. Do you know Durham?"

"No, I—"

"You really should visit there one day. The cathedral

is magnificent, and the university, well, that's where I met Theodore."

"It's your hometown?"

"Not at all. I studied applied physics there and was eventually made a lecturer. I'm originally from Wells, another English cathedral town."

"Physics, eh?" I'm not sure why I allowed Thistlewig to engage me in pointless small talk. Perhaps I needed to disconnect my brain for a while from more pressing subjects. In any case, I found her mildly amusing. "I think I'll have that cup of tea after all," I said.

"Excellent! I was certain you had a migraine."

I pointed at the sign above my head. "Guilty."

"They usually are." She poured me a cup. As she handed it to me, we were interrupted by the ringing of her telephone.

I thanked her and took a sip. "Aren't you going to answer?" I pointed at the phone.

"I never allow myself to be disturbed when I'm with a client." She leaned over and yanked the telephone cord out of the wall. "Now then, how's your tea?"

"Very nice, thank you. Ms. Thistlewig, may I ask you a question? I apologize if this sounds rude. But are you currently an active member of the California State Bar? I mean, do you actually practice law and represent people before the courts of this state?"

Thistlewig's expression grew dark. "Why, yes. Of course, absolutely, yes. Why do you ask?"

"Well, all of this—" I waved my arm around the room, "—the clutter, the files on the floor, the fact you don't have a receptionist, a secretary, or even an answering machine. I mean, you're a nice woman and all that, and you did come highly recommended, but—"

"Mr. Mendes." Thistlewig set her cup firmly on the serving tray. "I'm quite aware of my eccentricities, thank you. But rest assured that I *do* practice law, professionally and ethically and in accordance with my own style and instincts."

"Well, I'm sure—"

"Please don't interrupt. I have *never* had a complaint regarding my work. Not from my clients and not from the judges before whose august benches I appear. And I don't ever expect to. Now then, if we are proceeding to business matters, how may I help you?"

"Ms. Thistlewig, I'm sorry. I didn't mean—"

"I repeat, Mr. Mendes, how may I help you?"

"Well, for starters, it's an asylum matter."

"I would expect so." Thistlewig pushed the tray to one side and snatched up a steno pad and pencil. "I do, after all, practice asylum law. What exactly is your situation?"

"It's not my situation, per se."

"It isn't?"

"No, not exactly. It's more my partner Isaac's situation. Actually, it's both of our situation. My partner's and mine, that is."

She tapped the pencil against the steno pad and waited.

"When I say 'partner,' I mean my 'life partner' or my 'lover'—"

"Yes, yes, Mr. Mendes, I understand all that. This is the nineties, after all, and we're all thoroughly modern grownups here. Where is he, by the way?"

"Who? Oh, you mean Isaac. He's at home."

At that, Thistlewig raised an eyebrow. "And may I ask why?"

"His mother died a couple of months back, and he's still depressed about the whole thing. She was all the family he had. The rest were killed in El Salvador. I haven't been able to get him out of the house in over two months." My eyes stung as I fought back a sudden surge of emotion. "I'm sorry, but it's been a difficult time for both of us, what with his mother's passing and this immigration problem."

Thistlewig shook her head slowly. "I'm quite sorry to hear

that. Where do you live?"

"Pardon me?" I pulled out a handkerchief and wiped my eyes.

"What's your address? The place where you and your partner reside?"

"We live in the Marina, Fontana West, eighteenth floor."

"Very nice. And what's your suite number?"

I told her.

Thistlewig carefully printed the address in her steno pad and looked up at me with a tight smile. "I'll be there at eight o'clock tomorrow night."

"Thank you, but it's really not necessary. I'm familiar with the facts of the case, if I may—"

"You, Mr. Mendes, are not the client." She pushed back from her desk and stood up. "And if the client is unable to come to me, then I shall have to go to the client."

"But I don't know whether he'll be up for it. I have to speak with him first."

Thistlewig rounded her desk and pulled me up by one hand. "Eight o'clock sharp, Mr. Mendes. Now please, I have work to do. Yours isn't the only case on my docket, you know."

And with that, she ushered me out of her office, her neck chains all ajangle, and slammed the door at my back.

Chapter 12

By the time I got back to the office, I had three hours left in my day and a mountain of work awaiting me. On top of that, Ed had signed up three new clients in the last week that I had to get up to speed on. I asked Susan to hold my calls, then collected the various files and took up residence in our comfortable boardroom. I spread everything out on the mahogany conference table and dove in with a plan to tackle each matter one by one. Two hours later, my eyes were crossing, and my headache had intensified.

Setting aside the file I was reviewing, I locked the door and shifted into one of the reclining armchairs Ed had installed in the room. A slight trembling in my chest alerted me that the shakes were threatening to come on. Determined to get them under control, I closed my eyes, put one hand on my chest and one on my stomach, and breathed. I concentrated on my expanding and contracting chest, feeling the rising and flattening of my stomach. It was a yoga technique that often worked for me. After a few cycles of deliberate and measured breathing, I was aware only of the coolness of the air, the quiet of the room, and the rhythm of my inhaling, my exhaling—in . . . out; in . . . out.

I called up the image of Israel's Negev desert at dusk. The dry breeze rustling my white cotton tunic; the multi-hued palate of the makhtesh, deepening with the painfully slow dip of the sun toward the vast horizon. The peace and solitude of it washed over me, with Simon at my side, his sweat-dampened skin glistening in the nacreous light.

"Mr. Mendes, are you in there?" came Susan's muffled voice from the other side of the door.

Just ignore her, I thought.

There was a moment of silence followed by a tapping on the door.

"Are you okay, Mr. Mendes?"

Surrendering to the inevitable, I opened the door to Susan's headphone-framed head, tilted in curiosity.

"I was resting, Susan."

"I'm really sorry, sir," she said. "But there's someone here to see you."

"Who?"

She nodded toward the waiting area. "It's Mr. Silva!"

"Silva?" I did a quick calculation. Silva had four months yet to serve.

I peered into the waiting area and did a double take. Milling about the room, examining the pictures and news articles on the wall, was someone who looked strikingly like Simon in profile. That same focused gaze, the aquiline nose, the gymnast's body, the confident way he carried himself. Only, it wasn't Simon. How could it be? Simon had been gone for over twenty years. I shook my head and refocused. No, it was *Silva*, barely recognizable from the Silva I'd last seen two months ago in San Quentin. New fashionable haircut, crisp white dress shirt, well-fitted linen trousers, and a pair of Wayfarer sunglasses pushed up on his head.

Seeing me, he waved and picked up what looked like an expensive gift hamper perched on the coffee table. Then he ambled over on his powerful legs, flashing a warm smile that showed off his perfect teeth.

"Marc!" He tossed a quick glance at Susan. "I'm sorry I didn't make an appointment."

I pulled him into the boardroom. Once the door was closed, he set the hamper on the table and embraced me. He held me against his muscular chest for a few seconds, and I allowed myself the briefest fantasy of being in Simon's arms once again, his warm breath on my neck, the faint smell of tobacco. The resulting surge of emotion that rose inside threatened to reduce me to tears. Then he stepped back and beamed. I'd always been impressed with Silva's good looks, but his resemblance to Simon that afternoon floored me. His white shirt perfectly set off the same lovely hazel eyes, long black eyelashes, and thick eyebrows.

"It's good to see you, Alejandro," I said, stepping back and wiping my eyes. "How is it you're out of prison so soon?"

"They released a bunch of us a couple of weeks back," he said with a relieved smile, oblivious to my emotional state. "All over the state. Everyone who was in for less than six months. Budget cuts, they said."

"You've been out for a couple of weeks?"

"More or less. My grandfather died while I was inside. So I had to rush to San Diego to take care of some family stuff. But I'll tell you all about that later. I literally just got back to the city, and I wanted to bring you guys a thank you gift." He patted the hamper.

"Thank you, Alejandro. That's very thoughtful of you."

"This is for Mr. Haddad and the rest of the firm. I have something else especially for you since you were the one that fought so hard for me."

"That's really not necessary, Alejandro."

"No, Marc. I insist. I was hoping to give it to you over dinner. I've booked a table for two just over the road at Bix for seven o'clock—that is, if you're available."

A short rap on the door startled us. A split second later, it swung open, and Ed poked his head into the room. His eyes opened wide as he saw Silva.

"Mr. Silva," he said, "what a surprise . . ."

The slightest hint of a frown rippled across Silva's face at the interruption. Then, just as quickly, he composed himself and shook Ed's hand. "Hello, Mr. Haddad. I'm back."

Ed scanned Silva top-to-toe. "I can see that." He took in the gift hamper and raised an eyebrow. "Am I interrupting something?" he asked, shooting me a questioning look.

"I brought you a gift," Silva said, laying his hand on the hamper. "It's for you and the firm in appreciation for all you guys did for me."

Ed regarded the hamper for a moment. "Thank you, Mr. Silva."

"Alejandro was just filling me in about his early release." I rolled out a chair at the table. "You're welcome to join us."

"I'm busy dealing with an incident, Marc. Come see me once you're free."

"I'll be right out."

Ed nodded, and his gaze returned to Silva. Silva picked up the hamper and held it out to him. "Don't forget this, Mr. Haddad."

"You can leave it there, Mr. Silva. We'll open it later. How long have you been out?"

"Pardon me?" Silva frowned and glanced in my direction.

"I asked when you got out of prison." He glanced between the two of us.

"Oh, that was a couple of weeks ago now," Silva explained.

"Did you know about this?" Ed asked me.

"I only just found out."

"I see." Ed paused in the doorway. "Well, thank you for the gift, Mr. Silva."

"Yes, sir." Silva nodded.

"Make the best of your newfound freedom." Ed stepped out of the room and shut the door with more force than was typical for him.

"He seemed mad," Silva said. "I didn't do anything wrong, did I?"

"Don't mind him. He's just stressed." I gave his arm a reassuring squeeze. "I've got to go help him."

"What about tonight? Can we get together?"

"That might be difficult."

"Please, Marc, I know it's short notice, but if there's any way you could make it, I'd really appreciate it. I have things I'd like to talk to you about. Plus, it's been a long time since I had a nice dinner with a friend. This will be my treat."

I was caught between the need to rush back home to pick up from where I'd left off with Isaac and my curiosity about Silva, particularly this new incarnation of Silva. In the end, I accepted his invitation. Silva was so happy that he hugged and thanked me to the point of embarrassment. I managed to escort him out of the building after repeatedly promising I would really show up at the appointed time and place. When he was finally gone, Ed was waiting for me at reception.

"Why were you so rude to Silva?" I asked.

"Never mind that," he said. "Someone spray-painted a swastika on the back of the building at the patio level."

"What?"

"Vlad saw it when he went out for a cigarette break this afternoon. I've reported it to the police. They promised to send someone over tomorrow."

"How many incidents is that now, Ed?"

"You can't blame this one on the Saint-Cloud case. It's a blasted swastika. For all we know, it could be directed at you."

"Why at me?"

"You're the only Jew at this firm as far as I know."

"Fuck you, Ed."

"I'm just stating a fact, Marc."

"Again, fuck you. Anything else?"

"Yes. Once you're finished in there," he said, nodding at the conference room, "come see me in my office."

A few minutes later, I stepped into his office and closed the door. Ed was waiting for me, standing against his desk with his arms crossed.

"What's up?"

"Marc, you're not sleeping with Silva, are you?"

A wave of anger washed over me.

"What the fuck is wrong with you today, Ed? Of course I'm not sleeping with Silva. I'm in a relationship, remember?"

Ed waved his hand dismissively. "Now that his case is over, I don't want him hanging around the firm. The guy's trouble. And if you're smart, you'll keep your distance from him."

"Thanks for the sage advice, Ed. But I'm not stupid."

"Nobody's suggesting you're stupid. I just want you to be careful."

"Thank you. Anything else?"

Ed stared at me for a beat, then shook his head.

An hour later, I emerged from my office. Everyone had gone home, and an eerie silence hung in the air. Grabbing my coat, I made my way downstairs and locked up. Billows of a dense summer fog were roiling past our building. Cars cruised past at reduced speeds, their rumbling engines audible long before they emerged from out of the chowder, only to be re-enveloped a moment later, their amber lights bending crazily in San Francisco's strangest climatological feature.

I carefully stepped off the curb and crept across the street in the general direction of Gold Alley, where the Bix Supper Club was located. The sound of my footsteps reflected back from the century-old cobblestones and fog-damp bricks.

Guided by the blue glow of the restaurant's neon sign, I made my way across the alley and stepped inside. I was greeted by the sight of a soaring candlelit dining room, Corinthian columns, dark wood paneling, a lovely mural spanning the breadth of the bar, and a collection of fine art displayed on the walls. White-jacketed waiters crisscrossed the floor and ascended and descended the stairs to the balcony, and a jazz trio was playing softly in a corner. I had lunched there often with Ed throughout my time at the firm. But I'd never been there for dinner.

The black-jacketed *maître d'* led me up the stairs to a quiet booth overlooking the main dining room, where Silva was waiting. A half-empty wine bottle was sitting on the table next to a pair of twinkling tea candles, and he was nursing what was left of a glass of red.

"I see you started without me," I said.

"You made it!" Silva stood on wobbly legs and pulled me into a tight hug. He smelled of Santos de Cartier. I squeezed him back and counted to ten before disengaging from his embrace and sitting across from him.

"Seven o'clock, right on the nose." I pointed at my watch. "What time did you get here?"

"Six-thirty. I didn't want to be late." He held up his hand at a passing waiter. "One bottle of Dom Perignon, please." The waiter smiled and sped away.

"I'll have a cranberry juice, thanks."

"Why not some champagne?"

"I don't drink."

Silva squinted at me for a moment, then nodded. "We'll order your juice when he gets back." Reaching into his blazer, he produced a small rectangular gift box and handed it to me with a wry smile.

"What's this?" I shook the box.

"It's a present for you. Open it."

I handed the box back to him. "I'm sorry, Alejandro, I can't accept this."

The corners of his mouth turned down. "Why not?"

"It's not really necessary. The gift basket was enough."

Silva frowned at the box. "You mean you're not allowed to? You've never accepted a gift from a former client? Not even for Christmas?"

"I wouldn't say that. Of course, for Christmas."

Silva handed the gift box back to me. "Then, consider this a Christmas present, seven months late or five months early. Whatever works."

I turned the box over in my hands and considered the situation. We had, of course, received mementos from appreciative clients before, but I was reluctant to accept a personal gift from Silva for fear of committing an ethical violation or, at least, of being seen to. On the other hand, I was flattered by the gesture and curious as to what he'd gotten me.

I unwrapped the package and was shocked to find myself holding a limited edition Mont Blanc ballpoint pen—a pen so expensive I would never have considered buying it for anyone, least of all myself. Dumbstruck, I stared at it for a few awkward seconds, then raised my eyes to meet Silva's.

"What's wrong?" he asked. "You don't like it?"

"No, it's not that. It's beautiful."

"I picked it out special, just for you. Read the inscription."

I rolled the pen over and found the inscription. It was in Spanish:

Para MM, Con Cariño de AS.

"What do you think?" Silva asked, his hazel eyes fixed on mine.

"Like I said, it's beautiful. But why? Alejandro, this pen is much too expensive."

"Don't worry. I can afford it now. I have the settlement money from Xanadu, plus I inherited some more from my grandfather. Can you believe it?" He barked a sarcastic laugh. "I guess the old man didn't hate me as much as I thought he did." He held out his arm and showed off a diamond Rolex shimmering on his wrist. "He even left me this."

"Wow," I said, looking closely at the watch. "That's quite a gift."

"So you don't have to feel bad about accepting the pen."

I examined the pen again, then put it back into the box and folded my hands over it. Something still didn't feel right.

Silva's face reddened. "You don't think I stole it, do you?"

"Not at all, Alejandro. That never even crossed my mind."

At that moment, the waiter glided up to the table with a bottle of champagne and two glasses. Before we could say anything, he'd popped the cork and filled the two glasses.

"We'll have a glass of cranberry juice as well," Silva said quietly.

The waiter nodded as he nestled the champagne bottle in a nearby bucket of ice.

Once he'd gone, Silva dug into the pocket of his trousers, pulled out a piece of paper, and pushed it over at me.

I picked it up. "What's this?"

"Read it. I'll be back." He got up from the table and descended the stairs.

I unfolded the piece of paper. It was a receipt for a Mont Blanc Meisterstuck Solitaire Ballpoint Pen from the Dada Pen Boutique on Jackson. Total price: $1,383.10, tax included. Name of purchaser: Alejandro Silva. Method of payment: Cash. I stared at the receipt, barely noticing when the waiter returned with a tumbler of cranberry juice and placed it at the edge of the table.

As I sat waiting for Silva to return, my eye settled on the champagne glass in front of me, riveted by the gleam of the liquid in the dim light, by the rising bubbles shimmering around the edges. After the day I'd just had, it hit me: *that glass of champagne was exactly what I needed.* That disquieting realization sparked a deep hunger. A sense of terror overcame me as I watched my hand creep toward the glass. Gritting my teeth, I closed my eyes and willed it back. I grasped both sides of my chair and held tight, impotently drawing deep breaths, fighting against a slow, inevitable slide over the precipice. *One sip*, I heard in my head. One sip was all I needed. *Go for it! After that, you can regroup.* I let go of the chair and exhaled in a final attempt at control. *Fuck it*, I thought and reached for the glass. Glancing around to make sure no one was looking, I took a quick swallow and then another longer one and pushed it away. Easy as that. My first drink in seven years. I waited a few seconds for the ground to yawn open and swallow me. When it didn't, I wiped my mouth and took a deep breath. An instant later, Silva was back at the table.

"Where did you go?" I asked.

"Restroom." He gestured at the receipt. "You see, I didn't steal it."

I handed it back to him. "Exactly how much money did your grandfather leave you, Alejandro?"

He returned the receipt to his pocket. "Seven hundred and fifty thousand, after taxes. I have a copy of the check back at my room if you don't believe me."

"I believe you, Alejandro, and I *do* appreciate the gesture. I just don't think you should have spent all that money on me."

Silva leaned across the table and beamed a smile. Up close, his handsome face was open, innocent, and vulnerable. There was no hint of the volatility he'd been accused of in his criminal case. I was having trouble accepting that this soft-spoken man could have ever committed a violent act against another human being.

"Don't worry," he said, "I didn't spend it all on you. See, I bought new clothes and got this haircut." He stood up and turned around. "Do you like it?"

"You look great, Alejandro. Much better than the last time I saw you. Almost like a different person."

"My God, I know!" he said as he sat down. "I looked horrible. But now all that's changed. I even got myself a nice room at the

Headlands Hotel on Lombard Street. And I'm looking for a job too. I'm hoping to land something at a luxury car dealership this time, if they'll have me. No more hotels."

"I'm glad to hear it, Alejandro. I'm proud of you. And thank you for the pen. It's really lovely."

We ordered dinner, and Silva spent the rest of the evening recounting his adventures since he'd been released from prison a couple weeks back. After getting permission from his parole officer, he'd gone to San Diego to settle up his inheritance. He'd deposited the inheritance check and hung out with friends there, waiting for the funds to become available. He confessed he hadn't wanted to contact me until he was fully back on his feet.

As we finished our last course, his voice took on a more intimate tone as he spoke about the great respect and affection he felt for me, how he believed there was a special bond between us. He'd sensed this at our first meeting; he'd felt it again when I visited him in jail; he was sure of it now.

The waiter broke in on our conversation and offered us the dessert menu. I declined anything, seeing it was nearly nine-thirty.

"Have some coffee at least," Silva said. "You don't need to rush off, do you?"

"I've had a really nice time, Alejandro. The best in a long time to be honest. But it's getting late. My partner will be worried."

Silva set down his wine glass. "You have a partner?"

"Yes, I do. We've been together for six years."

Silva frowned at me. "Is your partner a woman or a man?"

"My partner's a man, Alejandro."

"Does he know you're at dinner with me?"

"No."

"Why not?"

Silva's rapid-fire questions unnerved me. I poured myself a glass of water as my mouth had suddenly gone dry. Searching my mind for some reasonable excuse, I opted for the truth.

"We had a disagreement earlier today. I wasn't keen to get back home too soon. But now, it's pretty late, and I have to be at work early tomorrow. So . . ."

Silva nodded. He called over the waiter and wordlessly settled the bill. Then I followed him downstairs, and we made our way past the other diners toward the entrance. As we reached the door, I asked him to wait for me while I made a quick pit stop at the restroom.

Speeding to the back of the restaurant, I dipped into the men's room and stationed myself in front of a urinal. A moment later, the door opened, and Silva took up a position at the adjacent one. He unbuttoned his trousers and shamelessly pulled up his shirt to give me a clear view of what he was packing. As he relieved himself, he looked sideways at me, and our eyes met. Then he looked down and pointedly checked me out before winking at me and buttoning up.

"I'll catch you out front," he said, flashing a wicked grin.

I found him outside, waiting for me across from the restaurant, reclining against a brick wall in the fog, smoking. He flicked the cigarette aside as I approached, and it sputtered across the alley. Then he drew me into an embrace.

"Thanks for meeting me, Marc," he said once he released me. "I'll call you again soon if that's all right. Maybe we could meet up for lunch."

"Next time's on me, Alejandro."

"Okay, fine."

"Alejandro?"

"What?"

"That was a bit weird in there." I jerked my thumb at the restaurant. "In the restroom."

Silva chuckled. "It was just a bit of harmless fun. You weren't offended, were you?"

"I was surprised, that's all."

"Okay, sorry. Let's pretend it never happened. Deal?"

"Sure," I said, doubtful I'd ever be able to unsee what he'd shown me. "Anyway, my car's that way." I pointed toward the Sansome Street end of the alley. "Can I give you a lift to your hotel?"

"Thanks, but no. I'm meeting someone later tonight at the Transformer Club in SoMa."

"The sex club?" I asked incredulously. The Transformer Club was the sort of place I'd frequented before I got sober and had avoided like plutonium ever since.

"You know it?"

"Not personally. But if you live in San Francisco long enough, you hear about these places. I think the one you're talking about attracts a fetish crowd, right?"

He nodded. "That's the one. I met one of the managers at the gym. He has a contact at the Mercedes-Benz repair center on Folsom and promised to help score me an interview. I'm going to go talk to him about it. Don't worry; I can catch a cab."

"All right," I said, pulling out my car keys. "But be careful, Alejandro. Remember, you're still on parole."

"Yes, Daddy, I *promise* to behave." He gave me a double thumbs-up and headed away from me toward Montgomery, disappearing into the fog.

Chapter 13

Isaac was snoring softly when I entered the bedroom. I undressed in the dark and slid under the blankets next to him. His back felt warm against my chest, and I placed my arm around his smooth torso. I lay listening to the regular rhythm of his breathing and was drifting off when he stirred and woke me. I waited for his breathing to steady again. Instead, his body jerked a few times. He was having one of his bad dreams where he was back in El Salvador. I stroked his side firmly to alter his dream cycle, but the jerking escalated, and he began to moan.

"Isaac, wake up," I said, nudging him gently.

His moaning grew louder, and he began to shout the same words he always shouted, words in Spanish: "*Hermanos, no hagan esto! No hagan esto!*" Brothers, don't do this! Don't do this!

"Isaac, wake up!" I shook him by the shoulders, and he opened his eyes wide as hockey pucks. "Wake up, Isaac, it's all right." I turned on the nightlight and ran my fingers through his sweat-soaked hair. "It's all right. You're awake now."

He shook his head and blinked at the nightlight. "Oh, man," he said, looking at me after a moment. "That was a bad one."

I held him tight and kissed his neck. He hugged me back, then pulled away and sat up in bed.

"What time is it?" He rubbed the circulation back into his face.

"It's ten thirty. Are you all right?"

Isaac licked his dry lips and scanned the room, still getting his bearings. "Yeah, I think so." He wrinkled his brow and looked at me as if for the first time. "Where were you?"

"I had to work late, sorry. I meant to call you, but—"

"I called your office. A couple hours ago." He narrowed his eyes. "No one answered."

"I finished work at seven, then drove around the city for a while." As I spoke, I saw my reflection in the mirrored closet doors. It was the face of a liar. I averted my eyes.

"You drove around? Where did you go?"

"No place in particular. I just drove around, mostly down Mission, then I cut over to the coast and drove along Sunset Beach. I parked there for a while."

"What were you doing?"

"Just thinking. I had a lot on my mind, and I wasn't ready to come home. I guess I was still upset with you for this afternoon. You know, the bathroom, the immigration lawyer. I needed to cool off."

Isaac grabbed a couple of pillows and reclined against them, never taking his eyes off me.

"I'm sorry, really. It won't happen again."

Isaac lowered his eyes and nodded. After a moment, his face relaxed. "By the way, before I forget," he said, "your mother called today."

"Did she? Anything special?"

"Not really. She wanted to find out how I was doing." Isaac smiled. "She's starting to act like a real mother-in-law."

"Who would have thought?"

"They're coming up for a visit," he continued.

"They who?"

"Both of them. Your mother and your father."

I hadn't seen my parents since Miriam's funeral. It was a shock to both of us when they showed up at the Mass and stayed on for a week. In those difficult days following Miriam's passing, both my parents had shown themselves to be warmly supportive of Isaac. A bond, if not of friendship, at least of respect and genuine affection, had grown between them, especially between Isaac and my mother. She now called him at least once every couple of weeks.

"When are they coming?" I asked.

"At the end of August."

I was actually excited at the prospect of a visit from my parents. "You know, it would be really nice to take them to Napa, wouldn't it?"

He put his arms around me and held me tight. "I'm sure I'll be fine by then. I'm starting to feel better already. You'll see. Just give me a few more days."

"All right, let's hope so."

"But promise you're not going to disappear again like you did tonight without calling me first." He let go of me. "I'm liable to think you've got someone else lined up to replace me."

"I promise I'll call you first. Oh, before I forget, Phoebe Thistlewig's coming by tomorrow night to talk to you.

"Who?"

"The asylum lawyer, Phoebe Thistlewig."

Isaac stood up. "She's coming here?"

"That's right. She wants to talk to you in person and offered to make a house call."

He shook his head. "Why would you agree to that? You know I'm not ready to see anyone."

"Don't give me a hard time about this, okay? We've got a hearing coming up, and this is happening whether you're ready or not."

The following evening, at precisely eight o'clock, our dinner was interrupted by a *rat-a-tat-tat* at the front door. Isaac lowered his forkful of rice and beans and frowned.

I pushed my chair away from the table and got up. "She's here."

Isaac grabbed his plate and scurried to the bedroom.

When I opened the front door, Thistlewig strode past me into the apartment, hefting a large black leather satchel. "Good evening, Mr. Mendes. Where's our patient?"

I pointed to the bedroom door. "He's in there. I'll go call him."

"No need for that." She moved toward the bedroom. "Is he dressed?"

"Yes, but Ms. Thistlewig, really—"

She disappeared into the bedroom, firmly closing the door behind her. I prepared for an incensed Isaac to come bursting out of the room at any moment, but the minutes passed, and then an hour, and then I lost track of the time.

I was in the middle of unloading the dishwasher when I heard the bedroom door creak open. I glanced at the kitchen clock. Two and a half hours had passed since Thistlewig had cycloned her way uninvited into our bedroom.

Isaac poked his head through the doorway and motioned me into the living room. Thistlewig was seated on the couch, reading through some notes she'd scribbled during her meeting with Isaac. I cleared my throat, and she looked up.

"Ah, Mr. Mendes, please have a seat."

Isaac sat next to her on the sofa, and I dropped onto the ottoman opposite them.

"I've reviewed the photocopies of the original asylum application Isaac filed back in 1986," she said. "We've also discussed his claim at length."

"Phoebe thinks I've got a tough case," Isaac said.

"Phoebe?" I asked, perplexed.

"Phoebe to Isaac, Mr. Mendes. Thistlewig to you." She

peered at me over her reading glasses before continuing. "Now then, first of all, it's my opinion we should amend the asylum application to add certain details missing from Isaac's story. The original was completed by some sort of paralegal service in San Diego, so it's not surprising the materials are below par. Second, we must add a claim based on Isaac's homosexuality. I have some excellent reports published by various human rights watchdog groups, such as Amnesty International, that detail the persecution faced by homosexuals in Latin America, including in El Salvador. Are you with me?"

"You haven't lost me yet." I smiled weakly.

"I didn't expect I would, but one never knows." She arched an eyebrow at me. "In any event, although Isaac's is a compelling case, it will be a difficult one given the changed conditions in El Salvador now that the civil war is over. Sadly, we've lost more than a few such cases as of late. But one may always appeal to the Board of Immigration Appeals, the Federal District Court, and on up to the Supreme Court."

"Do you think that would be necessary?" Isaac asked.

"Possibly, if things don't go well for us at the hearing. On the other hand, even if you were to lose at the hearing, the case could be tied up in the appellate system for years."

"How many years?" I chimed in.

"As many as ten."

"And then?" Isaac asked. "If I lost all the appeals, I'd have to leave, right?"

"That's correct, Isaac," Thistlewig answered. "You'd have to leave the United States, not necessarily destined for El Salvador, mind you, but you wouldn't be able to remain here any longer unless something were to change in the law."

A silence fell over the room. Thistlewig closed her steno pad and removed her glasses, carefully folding them and slipping them into her satchel.

"We're going to fight this all the way," I said. "I'm sure

we could make some calls to our local congressperson or our senators. Surely that could make a difference."

Isaac and Thistlewig stared blankly at me.

"I have a friend who works for the *LA Times*," I continued. "She might be able to help generate some good publicity for the case. There's got to be some way to get the system to work for us."

"Interesting suggestion, Mr. Mendes," Thistlewig said dryly. "I'll give it some thought." She drew a long breath and turned to Isaac. "I don't see any point in waiting a year for this hearing. We might as well know where we stand as soon as possible."

"Do you think you can push up the date?" he asked.

"It's worth a try," she said. "What I'd like to do, with your consent, of course, is to prepare the amended application and then hand-walk it to Immigration Court tomorrow. I might be able to convince someone over there to give it some priority."

"What do you think, Marc?" Isaac turned to me.

"I'm not sure," I said, processing the sudden change of course. I searched Thistlewig's eyes. "I mean, as long as you have time to prepare a solid case, we might as well know where we stand as soon as possible. Just as long as there's no danger of immediate deportation."

"Not a chance," Thistlewig said. "You'll have plenty of time to plan your contingencies. So then, Isaac, do I have your consent to begin?"

"Yes," he said. "Go ahead."

"Good boy." Thistlewig rose to her feet and shouldered her satchel. She gave Isaac a motherly hug. "Now, don't forget what I said." She winked at him, and he responded with a warm, open smile, something I hadn't seen in months. I suddenly found myself feeling grateful to this strange, wonderful woman.

"I won't forget," he said. "Thank you for everything, Phoebe."

Thistlewig turned her head in my direction. "Mr. Mendes, please escort me out."

I followed her to the front door. She stopped in front of it and indicated the doorknob with an open hand. Taking the hint, I opened it for her and stepped back. As she walked past, she took hold of my arm and pulled me into the hallway.

"I suggest," she said in a low voice, "that you begin investigating other options, Mr. Mendes. For Isaac's sake as well as your own."

"What do you mean other options? We're going to fight this to the end, aren't we?"

"Do you really want to tie up your lives for the next ten years? Always uncertain of the outcome? How will you *ever* be able to make plans for the future? How will that dear boy in there ever be able to call any place home? Can you imagine the two of you, ten years from now, both of you ten years older, forced to uproot and start all over again from zero in a God-forsaken place like El Salvador?"

"Ms. Thistlewig, I'm sorry, I don't understand. What are you suggesting?"

"Mr. Mendes, why in heaven's name are you so determined to remain in the United States, a country that won't give a decent, hardworking man like Isaac a chance to remain here, despite the fact he's educated himself and worked hard, stayed out of trouble, and paid his taxes for over ten years—a country that shamelessly denies you the right to remain here with your partner of six years. You do realize that if you and Isaac were a heterosexual couple, you wouldn't have this problem, don't you?"

"Yes, I realize that."

"Well then, be smart and look elsewhere."

"Elsewhere?" I repeated slowly.

"There are other countries in the world besides the United States. Or hadn't you noticed?"

"Of course."

"Then do some investigating. Find out where the two of you can go. Someplace where you'll both be welcomed with open arms, living the life you want to live. Someplace to put down *permanent* roots. Someplace you and Isaac can truly call home. He deserves some stability, don't you think?"

I stared at her. The suggestion that we leave the United States was the last thing I expected to hear from anyone, least of all Isaac's immigration lawyer. Up until then, even entertaining such a thought was tantamount to total capitulation, to giving up the ghost, a prospect I wasn't ready for. In a strange way, though, in some alternate universe, it did make sense. It reminded me of those occasions when you know something is right, but you're not sure why—until you've chewed on it for a while. Then, what was once hazy becomes clear. But at *that* moment, standing there in the freezing hallway in my stocking feet, I hadn't yet come to such a moment of clarity.

Thistlewig wished me a good night and moved toward the elevator.

"Phoebe," I said.

She halted with her back to me.

"You know, if Isaac can call you Phoebe, then I should be able to as well."

She turned and looked at me with an enigmatic smile.

"I'm sorry I doubted you," I said. "Can you find it in your heart to forgive me?"

"Yes, Mr. Mendes, yes, you're absolved. Now have a good night. The both of you." And with a brisk nod, she disappeared into the elevator.

I found Isaac in the bedroom, wrapped in a towel and blow-drying his hair in front of the closet mirror.

"She's great, isn't she?" he shouted over the roar of the dryer.

"What are you doing?" I yelled back.

"Huh?"

I pulled the cord out of the wall, and the blow dryer fell silent. "I asked what you're doing?"

"Oh, I felt like taking a shower." He moved to the dresser and pulled out a clean pair of striped underpants.

"You had a sudden urge to take a shower?"

Isaac dropped the towel and grinned. "I feel like going out." He pulled on his underpants and slid open the closet doors.

"Really? Isaac, really? That's great!"

I peeled off my shirt, came up behind him, and wrapped him in my arms. He turned around in my embrace, and we kissed deeply. Then he buried his head in my neck, and we held each other. The sensation of his bare chest against mine awakened an appetite that had lain dormant for weeks, and my body started to react.

"We'd better get going if we're going to go at all," he said, lifting his head.

I ran my hands down his back and pulled him tight. "We could always stay home."

"You're kidding, right?" he said. "After all this time of you begging me to go out, when I finally want to, you suddenly want to stay home?" He reached into my trousers and treated me to a nice squeeze. "We can take care of this boy later. Right now, though, we're going out."

Chapter 14

The only thing happening in San Francisco on a Thursday night in those days was a trendy Latino dance party held in the ever-cool basement of a Japanese-Peruvian restaurant on Valencia. Very gay and very San Francisco. Things didn't get going until well after midnight. But the doors opened at ten o'clock, and it was best to get there early if you wanted a good view of the dazzling go-go boys. By the time we arrived, at around eleven, there was a line of people winding halfway around the block.

We fell in at the tail end and inched forward every few minutes. We'd both dressed up for the occasion. Isaac sported a new pair of 501s and a white polo shirt, and I broke out a nice pair of tan linen trousers and a new black silk T-shirt. Isaac was excited and talkative for the first quarter of an hour or so. But as time dragged on, he fell progressively quieter and ended up staring at the street, the pedestrians, the passing cars.

"What's wrong?" I asked.

Isaac turned to me and smiled. "I don't know." His eyes were wet. "I mean, I *do* know, but I don't know why."

"You want to go home?"

He shook his head and looked away. "No, I want to stay out all night and get crazy. But—"

A group of people we knew marginally well sauntered by and waved at us. One of them, a plus-size queen in pink leather named Maxie, disengaged from the group, swished toward us, and threw his arms around Isaac's neck.

"Isaac, my love, where have you been? I've missed you." He planted a lingering kiss on Isaac's cheek.

"Thanks, Maxie." Isaac wiped his face with his sleeve and winked at him.

"He'll catch up with you inside, Maxie," I said.

Maxie shrugged and sashayed away to rejoin his friends at the back of the line.

Isaac shook his head and chuckled. "He's crazy."

"Yeah, a real hoot."

The line moved forward a few more feet, and Isaac stepped ahead of me.

"So," I said, "what's bugging you?"

He swung around. "I guess I'm feeling guilty."

"You mean, because of your mother? Still?"

Isaac nodded.

"Isaac, I'm sure that's normal. After all, this is the first time you've gone out of the apartment since the whole thing happened. It would seem strange to anyone. It's a big enough accomplishment we're here at all."

"I'll be all right." He moved up a few more feet. "I just want to get in there and have a couple of drinks. I can taste them already." He searched my face. "You don't mind, do you?"

I lifted my shoulders. I needed the drink as much as he did. In some ways, more. But I felt terrible about my slip the night before with Silva and was determined not to be stupid again. "I guess not," I said, suppressing my apprehension.

When we finally reached the front of the line, Isaac handed a twenty-dollar bill to a young Asian guy working the ticket window. The rhythms of the salsa music filtered up to the doorway from the basement, and I was ready to dance. The ticket guy winked at Isaac and naughtily flashed the metal bolt in his tongue. "Well, aren't you adorable," he said as he took the twenty, pulled a ten-dollar bill out of his drawer, and slid it across the counter toward Isaac.

Isaac smiled and pushed the ten-dollar bill back at him. "I'm paying for both of us." He pulled me out from behind him.

The ticket guy took one look at me and hissed, "Oh, my God. What in fuck's name are *you* doing here?"

"I'm sorry, what?" I glanced around at the people next to me.

He shook a black lacquered fingernail at me. "I'm talking to *you*, you damned traitor."

"Hey—" I said.

Slamming a *Back in a Moment* sign onto the counter, he hopped off his stool and ran to the back of the room to speak to an older bald man in a black suit, whom I recognized as William Chan, the owner of the restaurant.

Loud groans and complaints drifted up from the crowd behind us.

"What's that about?" Isaac asked.

"I'm not sure." I peered through the ticket window at Chan and the ticket guy, who were having a heated exchange. "This may have something to do with the case I told you about. The one with the three straight women. It's been all over the news lately, thanks to Ed."

The ticket guy gestured wildly at Chan and pointed in our direction. Chan stooped and peered at us.

"That's the owner, isn't it?" Isaac said.

I nodded.

"Maybe we should go."

Chan said something to the ticket guy and then advanced toward us, the young man trailing close behind.

"It doesn't look like we're going to have much choice in the matter," I said.

Chan came out the side door and approached me. "Excuse me, may I have a word with you, please? Out here." He indicated the sidewalk with a sweep of his hand.

The ticket guy resumed his place on the stool. "Next!" he called out, waving forward the people who'd been waiting behind us as Isaac and I moved a few yards down the sidewalk with Chan.

"What's the problem here?" Isaac said to Chan.

Chan gave his back to Isaac and turned to me. "I understand you're the lawyer representing those women against Saint-Cloud."

"What about it?" I asked.

"I'm sorry," Chan said, "but we can't admit people like you in our club. It's not good for business."

"What do you mean, people like him?" Isaac said.

I put my hand on Isaac's shoulder, and he shook it off. "This is bullshit," he said.

One of the bouncers edged toward us. Chan shook his head at him.

"Mr. Chan," I tried, "with respect, I'm gay myself, and—"

"That's neither here nor there. Some people in this community see you and your firm as taking sides against us. The fact you're gay makes it even worse. It makes you seem like a turncoat. If I let you in tonight, knowing who you are, it's likely to get out. The last thing I need is a boycott of my club."

"But I'm *not* a turncoat."

Chan turned away and walked back toward the club.

"Jesus Christ!" I kicked a beer bottle into the gutter. "What the hell is wrong with you people?"

Chan halted and waved over the bouncer. Then he returned and faced off with me. The light from a streetlamp cut across his face at a harsh angle, leaving half of it in shadow.

"Leave the premises immediately, before things get ugly," he said through clenched teeth.

The bouncer fell in alongside him. I glanced in the direction of the crowd outside the club, noting we were in full view of everyone.

Isaac pulled my arm. "Come on, Marc. The guy's a moron. Let's get the fuck out of here."

Something inside me collapsed in that moment. I lowered my head and allowed Isaac to pull me along by the arm. The sound of jeers, whistles, and catcalls echoed in my head, and somewhere close to us I heard the crash of a bottle breaking.

We ended up at Mecca on Market, a high-priced restaurant for ambiguous young professionals of all persuasions. We made it safely past the doorman, checked our coats, and took refuge on the last two of the plush stools encircling the massive saucer-shaped bar occupying the center of the room. The place was crammed wall-to-counter with beautiful people out on the prowl in the dim light, and the ear-splitting music all but drowned out any attempts at normal human conversation. People mostly communicated by sense of touch.

One of the shirtless, glitter-spackled barboys skidded across the slick concrete and pushed his shorn head over the bar at us. "What'll it be, boys?" he shouted in our ears.

"One cosmo, and keep them coming," Isaac shouted back with an exaggerated wink.

The barboy gave him a thumbs-up. "What about you, handsome?" he said to me with a rakish smile.

"I'll have a Perrier with a twist of lime, thanks."

"Sure thing!" He poured my drink, then snatched up a cocktail shaker and martini glass and got to work on Isaac's cocktail.

Isaac settled back to check out the maelstrom of beautiful people undulating around us. He was smiling and looking more relaxed than I'd seen him in weeks. I, on the other hand, was still furious about being eighty-sixed from the last place.

"One cosmo!" shouted the barboy as he slid the cherry-red

drink at Isaac.

Isaac tossed him a credit card. "Keep it open!"

The barboy nodded and slid away from us with the credit card in his hand.

Isaac took a long, slow sip of his drink and closed his eyes. After a moment, he glanced at me out of the corner of his eye. "Sorry," he said.

I raised my glass of water and eyed his drink, overcome by a sudden craving.

"What's the matter?" Isaac asked. "Should we leave?"

"It's nothing." I drained my glass and set it down hard against the counter, signaling the barboy for another.

Isaac searched my face, and I averted my eyes.

"You're not still pissed about what happened back there, are you?" he asked, sliding away his half-empty glass.

"Yeah, I am." I closed my eyes and pushed back against my mounting frustration. "I don't know whether I'm angrier at Chan for calling me a turncoat or at Ed for forcing that goddamned Saint-Cloud case on me in the first place."

"I vote for Ed. From what you tell me, he can be a real prick." Isaac waved at the barboy, pointed at my glass, and held up two fingers for two more waters.

"He's not that bad. The truth is I'm as much to blame for this whole fiasco as he is. At the end of the day, I could have stood on principle and refused the case."

"Here you go, boys," said the barboy, dropping two glasses of sparkling water on the counter in front of us. "More of the hard stuff."

Isaac waved him off and turned back to me. "I think you should let it go for now, Marc. Try and have a good time tonight, all right? For my sake." He cocked his head to one side and kissed me on the nose. "Hey, I'm talking to you."

"I'll be all right. Sorry about spoiling your evening."

He stretched luxuriantly and took a sip of his sparkling water.

"Nothing could spoil my evening tonight. Not after finding out this whole immigration thing could stretch out another ten years. That's great, isn't it?"

"Well, yeah, things could be worse," I said.

"And it was so nice of Phoebe to come over, wasn't it?"

I nodded. "I wouldn't have done it."

Isaac laughed. "That's because you're so conventional. For a gay lawyer, that is. But she's different. It's like she knows things, you know?"

I shook my head. "What do you mean?"

Isaac shrugged. "I don't know, exactly," he said. "She's great, that's all."

"What did you guys talk about for all that time, by the way?"

Isaac looked at me, all expression draining from his face. "My case and other things."

"What other things?"

He looked away for a moment and pursed his lips. The volume of the music increased as Madonna's latest hit throbbed out of the speakers. Isaac looked back at me and leaned forward. "We talked about personal things."

"Personal things?" My head began to hurt. "There are no personal things when it comes to you and me. You know that."

Isaac edged closer and put his chin on my shoulder. "Let's leave it at that for the moment. I'll tell you eventually, but I don't want to jinx things right now."

"Oh."

"Put it this way, if it weren't for what Phoebe and I talked about tonight, we wouldn't be here right now. You get that, don't you?"

The only thing I *got* at that moment was a splitting headache. But I smiled at Isaac anyway and dutifully nodded, which appeared to satisfy him. When the moment felt right, I excused myself and wandered away from my barstool to collect myself. I ended up pressed into a corner near the restrooms, where I worked hard to process everything happening in my life, sorting it all into little mental boxes.

At that point, an excruciatingly handsome Middle Eastern guy with slicked-back hair bumped into me and spilled his whiskey sour on my new shirt. The whole thing. The sting of alcohol went straight to my brain, and an electric jolt of fear shot through me. You would have thought I'd been doused in napalm. The half-drunk Middle Eastern guy followed me into the restroom, falling over himself apologizing. I stripped off my shirt and ran water over it in the sink, certain I was ruining it, while he hovered in the background. When I finished, he grabbed a handful of paper towels and helped me dry off, then he slipped his phone number into my pocket, insisting I call him in case the shirt needed professional cleaning.

As I made my way back to the bar, still stinking of alcohol, I spotted a highball glass sitting forlorn in the corner on one of the club's speakers. Changing course, I pressed toward it and found it was still half full of straight vodka and ice. I made sure no one was looking, hesitated a moment, then drained it in one gulp. Hating myself, I wiped my mouth, took a deep breath, and staggered back to the bar, where I found Isaac engaged in an animated discussion with two women. The more talkative of the two was a tall, stocky albino blonde with freckles in a white dress shirt and a pair of hip-hugger jeans. The other was lovely and demure, a brunette with almond-shaped green eyes and a creamy, pale complexion, draped in a little black dress.

As I approached them, Isaac put his arm around my shoulders and drew me near. "This is my partner, Marc. Marc, meet Ingrid—" he indicated the blonde woman, "—and Christianne." He nodded at the brunette.

I forced a smile and extended my free hand at Ingrid. She quickly scanned me before taking my hand and giving it a firm squeeze. Christianne averted her eyes and shifted closer to Ingrid.

"They're visiting from Canada," Isaac explained, studying my face. He lowered his head to my ear and whispered, "Have you been drinking?"

I shook my head and turned to the women. "Canada, really?" I glanced between the two of them. "Which part?"

Ingrid and Christianne exchanged a look. "Do you know Canada?" Ingrid asked.

"I've never been there, but I know the main cities . . . Vancouver, Toronto, Montreal, Ottawa. Are you from any of them?"

"They're from Toronto," Isaac confirmed. "And they're here for a few more days."

"That's nice," I said, searching the bar for my water glass.

"Excuse us a moment," Isaac said. The women nodded and huddled together. Isaac turned to me and moved in close. "Are you sure you haven't been drinking? You smell of alcohol."

"Some drunk guy spilled his drink on me. It's no big deal. I'm okay."

He stared at me, scrutinizing my face. "Are you sure?"

"Yeah, I'm positive. All good."

Isaac nodded slowly. "Okay. Well, anyway, you'll never believe what we've been talking about, these women and me."

I looked over his shoulder at them and shrugged. "Nothing too interesting, I would guess."

Isaac smirked. "Don't be so sure about that, Mr. Elitist."

"Oh, please. The suspense is putting me to sleep."

"All right, well, maybe this will wake you up." He glanced back at them for a moment. "Those women just propositioned me."

It took a few seconds for his statement to penetrate the fog and reach my brain. "What?" I looked over at the women, who were engaged in an intense conversation.

"They told me I have an exotic look. They like my skin color, the texture of my hair, my high cheekbones."

"They want to sleep with you because of your high cheekbones?"

Isaac grinned. "I never said they wanted to sleep with me."

"You said they propositioned you."

"Shut up for a second, please." Isaac cupped his hand over my mouth. "In a nutshell, they want my sperm. For Christianne, the pretty one. They've been looking around for a sperm donor, and they asked me if I was interested."

I moved away from his hand and leaned against the bar. The floor was starting to whirl under my feet. "What did you tell them?"

"I told them I'd think about it." He held up a slip of paper. "We exchanged phone numbers."

I tried to zero in on the piece of paper but was seeing double. My stomach was starting to complain. "Let's go home. I'm feeling sick."

The corners of Isaac's mouth turned down. "You're upset, aren't you?"

I shook my head and leaned heavily against him. "It's too much right now, sorry. Let's just go, please."

Things got blurry at that point. Isaac said something or other to the women, who stared at me with worried faces. The next and only other thing I recall was being violently ill in the back of a cab.

Chapter 15

I woke to the rough tongue of Nilo as he licked my face. I couldn't open my eyes yet, but I could sense through my swollen lids that the sun was up and streaming into the room through the open blinds. I hadn't felt this bad since my last and most memorable hangover in a Mexican hotel room eight years earlier.

The smell of fried beans and cardamom coffee wafted into the room from the kitchen, and I could make out the voice of a CNN news presenter. I forced open one eye and groggily squinted at Nilo for a few seconds before picking him up and dropping him onto the floor. He crept under the bed, his tail still visible and twitching side-to-side, and purred loudly.

The bedroom door creaked open, and Isaac's head appeared in the doorway. I raised my hand at him and returned to my pillow with a loud groan.

"Feel like some juice?" he asked.

"What time is it?"

He pushed open the door the rest of the way and came in, carrying a glass of orange juice.

"It's ten o'clock in the morning, and you're late for work." He placed the juice and two aspirin on the nightstand.

I sat up and washed down the tablets. Isaac tousled my tangled hair and shook his head.

"Is it my imagination," I said, "or did I really throw up in the back of a taxi last night?"

"It was this morning. Finish your juice and come out for breakfast."

I applied pressure to my temples, which sometimes helped with a headache. "I've got a deposition at the office at one o'clock for that fucking Saint-Cloud case," I said, glancing at the digital clock on the nightstand. I finished the juice and handed him the glass. "How did I make it into bed? I can't remember a thing."

"Mostly by yourself, with some help from me." He rubbed his eyes with the back of his hand. They looked tired and bloodshot. "You were totally out of it, though. I thought the cab driver was going to kill you when you got sick. You must have thrown up around five or six times. It was awful. What happened?"

"I have no idea." I pried myself off the bed and got to my unsteady feet.

"Maybe you should see a doctor."

"I don't need to see a doctor. I'm all right." I raked my fingers through my hair and inclined my head at the doorway. "I just need to get some breakfast in me."

"You're *all right*?" His voice took on an edge.

"Yeah, I think so."

Isaac looked at the floor for a beat, then looked up at me. "Who's Amir?"

"Who?"

He produced a slip of paper from his pocket and held it out at me. "I found this in your trousers."

I took it out of his hand and examined it. "Oh, right. It's the guy who spilled his drink on me."

"Why do you have his number?"

"He offered to have my shirt dry-cleaned and gave me his number. Honestly, it's nothing."

"It's nothing?"

"Yeah." I crumpled up the paper and tossed it into the wastepaper can. "Nothing."

"It's nothing that you disappeared for an hour and then came back stinking of alcohol?"

"He spilled—"

"It's *nothing* you got batshit sick and woke up with a hangover with another guy's phone number in your pocket? What the fuck, Marc?"

I flushed hot as the blood rushed to my head. "I know it looks bad—"

"Are you drinking again? Seeing someone? Whoring around?"

"No! Absolutely not!"

"Then what?"

"I told you! I went for a walk, a guy spilled his drink on me, and he gave me his goddamn number. That's it! Now drop it, please."

Isaac fell silent.

"Isaac, I'm trying my best to hold it together here. The pressure of everything is getting to me; there's no question about that. But I have *not* been drinking, and I'm definitely not seeing anyone. I'm managing, I swear it to you."

Isaac nodded.

"And I'm sorry for worrying you," I said.

"That's okay. I get it."

"That said, I probably do need to do something before I blow my stack."

He looked up at me.

"I was thinking I might look for a program or something," I said. "Or maybe a counselor. I don't know . . ."

"Maybe we could go together, you know, as a couple."

"Sure, why not?" I pulled him into a hug and held him. "I'll look into it."

As I rose from the bed, I flashed again on the taxi. "Wait, why were we in a cab last night? What happened to the car?"

Isaac cringed. "You're not going to like this."

"Oh, fuck me." My heart fluttered hard in my chest.

"Someone pried open the fuel door and poured something nasty into the gas tank," he said, looking like someone ready to take cover from a grenade explosion. "I think it ruined the transmission. It wouldn't start. I've made arrangements to have it towed to the dealership."

"Goddamnit!" I roared. "That's it! I've had enough of this shit." I dropped back onto the bed and screamed into my pillow.

Isaac sat next to me and rubbed my back, trying his best to calm me down. After a couple of minutes, he eased my face away from the pillow and drew me into his arms, where I sobbed myself dry.

I arrived at the office with five minutes to spare. The manager of Saint-Cloud, his lawyer, and the court reporter were in the boardroom, and the plaintiffs were gathered in the waiting room. Ignoring them all, I flew past Susan and pounded up the stairs to Ed's office. He was just hanging up the telephone.

"What is it, Marc?" He stared hard at me. "Shouldn't you be downstairs?"

I dropped a sheaf of papers on his desk. "These are my notes for the deposition. The same ones we went over yesterday morning."

Ed stood up and glanced at the notes, then at me. "You can't be serious—"

"Ed, I can't continue as lead attorney on this case. I warned you it was bad news, and it is. Last night I was eighty-sixed from a nightclub. They called me a turncoat. And you know what? I am. So I'm afraid you're going to have to take over from here; that is, if you still want the firm to represent those women."

He blinked at my notes and flipped through the pages. The clock on his wall chimed one o'clock. He raised his eyes. "Did they actually say it was because of this case?"

"Yes, they did. And after that, someone fucked up my car. I'm sorry, Ed, but I shouldn't have let you bully me into going forward with it."

Ed nodded and squeezed the bridge of his nose. "We can't just drop the case."

The door opened, and Vlad stuck his head in the room. "Sorry to interrupt, but the natives are getting restless downstairs."

"Offer them coffee and croissants, Vlad," Ed said. "I'll be right down."

Vlad raised his eyebrows. "All right, but I don't think that's going to hold them for long."

Ed waved him off, then moved to the window and looked out at the street. He frowned and called me over. Around two dozen angry people were amassing in front of the building, armed with placards and signs.

"There you go," I chided him.

"This gives me an idea," he said. "Follow me."

I trailed behind him down the stairs and into the waiting room. The protestors caught sight of us through the front window. They booed and hissed and shook their signs menacingly at the building. Millicent Hudson rose from a sofa, her eyes wide and terrified.

"Mr. Haddad, who are those awful people?"

"Apparently, Ms. Hudson, they're protesting our deposition of Mr. Hart," Ed responded. "It may be dangerous to continue today. I'm going to speak to the lawyer for Saint-Cloud to see if we can reschedule the deposition in a more secure venue."

Millicent glanced back at the other women who were huddled together on another of the sofas. "I'm sure that won't be a problem for us," she said. The others nodded their agreement.

Vlad entered the room and pointed at the telephone. Someone had called the cops.

"Please wait in the back of the building," Ed said to the

women. "There's a lounge where you'll be out of sight of the protesters. Vlad will show you the way."

The women followed Vlad past the receptionist and disappeared around the corner into the breakout lounge.

Ed turned to me. "I'll talk to the police. See if you can get things under control in the boardroom."

Saint-Cloud's lawyer, Robert Boatswain, rose to his feet as I walked into the room. He was an elegant, well-groomed man with close-cropped gray hair and a firm handshake. Brent Hart, the salon's manager, was equally dapper, with short auburn hair and a diamond stud in one ear. Boatswain had been opposing counsel in a weight discrimination case the firm had tackled a year before. He and I had managed to maintain respectful, cordial relations throughout the proceedings.

"Marc," Boatswain greeted me, "how are you?"

I quickly acknowledged Hart and the court reporter and pulled Boatswain aside.

"Bob, we've got a problem developing outside with some protestors. We think it's best if we postpone the deposition and schedule it at a more secure location."

Boatswain eyed me suspiciously. "If they're outside, then how can they affect the deposition?"

"My clients are terrified, Bob. This is not going forward today. That's aside from the issue of the costs we'll need to recover."

"Excuse me?"

"How do you suppose those people outside knew about the deposition? Date, time, place." I nodded in Hart's direction.

"What's the problem?" Hart asked.

"It appears, Mr. Hart," I explained, "that some of your supporters have gathered in front of the building and are threatening to dismantle it brick by brick. You wouldn't, by any chance, know how they found out about this deposition, would you?"

Hart leaped to his feet. "What exactly are you implying?"

Boatswain moved to Hart's side. "Mr. Mendes was suggesting we postpone the deposition so it can go forward somewhere else, somewhere more neutral."

Hart tossed up his hands. "More delays? That's just fantastic!" He beamed a death stare at me. "When is this case, this persecution, ever going to end?"

"You can discuss that with your lawyer." I turned to Boatswain. "Our firm will urge prosecution of anyone directly or indirectly responsible for acts of vandalism or violent protest directed at my clients or at any of the people who work here. Please make sure your client understands this, Mr. Boatswain."

We settled on a series of dates in early November, right before the start of the holidays. The depositions would be held either at Boatswain's office or at one of the conference rooms in the courthouse; the details could be agreed on later.

I shook hands with Boatswain, and Hart tornadoed out of the boardroom. A cheer exploded from the crowd outside as he pushed onto the sidewalk. Boatswain frowned and shook his head.

"Give me a call on Monday." He hefted his alligator-skin briefcase. "Maybe we can put this one to sleep before it gets too complicated for all of us."

I thanked him and told him Ed would be the one calling him. The court reporter followed him out of the room and handed me a piece of paper as she walked past. It was a bill for her abbreviated services.

Setting aside the bill, I closed the door and lowered my head to the conference table, grateful for the momentary reprieve. A knock at the door brought me back. After a moment, Ed stepped into the room, closed the door behind him, and joined me at the table.

"The police are going to want a statement from you," he said, handing me a sheet from a memo pad. "This is the detective's number. Call him when you have a minute."

I stared at the number and pocketed it. I held back any comment for fear of saying something I was going to regret, wishing he would just go away.

"One more thing," Ed said. "I want to apologize to you about the Saint-Cloud case. You were right about it being a liability for the firm. I'll find a way to make it go away."

I blinked at him. "We should consult more closely with each other before we commit ourselves to controversial cases like that."

"I agree."

Ed held out his hand in a gesture of apology. After a moment of hesitation, I clasped it with mine. The warm contact of his skin reminded me of the happier days when I'd first joined the firm. As my anger subsided, the tension in my neck and shoulders eased. But I was still smarting from everything that had gone on before, and Ed's apology wasn't going to erase it all. I let go of his hand and left the room.

When I got to my office, Silva was holding on the line.

"Can we meet tonight?" he asked with an excited edge to his voice. "I have some news to share with you."

I stared at Isaac's photograph for a moment, then averted my eyes. Things were way too heavy, at home, at work. I reflected on my dinner with Silva, on how normal and relaxed I'd felt with him. Even his playful gesture in the restroom, strange as it had been, had a naughty quality that intrigued and excited me. I hadn't felt anything like that in years. At that moment, an outing with Silva was just the distraction I needed.

"I can't do dinner tonight, Alejandro. But I'm happy to meet you after work for an hour or so."

We agreed on the cigar bar across the street at six in the evening. As I ended the call, Vlad poked his head into my office.

"Your partner's holding on line three," he said.

I suddenly became aware of the pounding of my heart. Grabbing the receiver in my moist hand, I determined to tell Isaac the truth this time.

"How did it go?" he asked.

"I'm off the case, thank God."

"That's great," he said quietly. "Feel better now?"

"Relieved, yes. Now I've just got to figure out what to do about the rest of the shit that's going on in my life."

"Phoebe called, Marc," he said after a long pause. "She filed the papers today and was able to convince the court to give us a two-hour block on the tenth of October, at ten in the morning. She wants us to start rounding up character witnesses, affidavits of recommendation, copies of all my past tax returns, and a bunch of other things. I wrote it all down for us to review tonight."

"October, really?" For an instant, my vision blurred. I closed my eyes to steady myself. Everything was moving much too fast.

"I'll be home at around eight," I ventured, preparing for a bad reaction.

There was a silence at the other end of the line. Then I heard Isaac breathing.

"Hello?"

"Working late again?" he asked.

"Only until six. But I've got to meet a former client after work."

"A former client? Where? And since when?"

"We recently settled a difficult case that's taken an emotional toll on him. He wants to fill me in about how he's doing post-case. Ed doesn't want us meeting in the office."

"What's his name? And why doesn't Ed want you to meet him at the office? How do I know it's not just some guy you met? Like that Amir character."

"Isaac, I swear, it's a former client. I'll be home at eight, or before, okay? I promise, I'll tell you all about it later."

Isaac was no longer on the line. I wasn't sure whether he'd hung up on me or whether the connection had been lost. I punched in my home number and listened to it ring a dozen times before giving up. Throughout the day, I called home every so often, but Isaac wasn't answering.

Chapter 16

The cavernous Cigar Bar on Montgomery Street was one of the only indoor venues left in the city where one could still smoke, which meant it was usually packed and murky with fumes. At prime time, which was around eight o'clock in the evening, the concentration of cigar smoke made it impossible to see from one end of the bar to the other. When I arrived at six in the evening, though, the crowds had yet to arrive, so the main room was mercifully smoke-free. I'd chosen it for my rendezvous with Silva because it was near my office and had lots of dark niches—perfect for a clandestine meeting.

I found Silva sitting in a booth set into a dark spot at the rear of the club, smoking an expensive cigar and cradling a highball glass in his other hand. When he saw me approaching, he set the cigar in a marble ashtray and received me with a warm hug. He was dressed in a dark blue collarless shirt, white linen trousers, and black leather moccasins.

Stepping back, I took him in. "Money agrees with you, Alejandro. You look better each time I see you."

He grinned at that and pulled me into the booth, comfortably spreading out his arms and legs. "This place is great!" He picked up the cigar, took a puff, and blew the smoke out the side of his mouth.

I gestured at his drink. "Have you been here long?"

"About thirty minutes." He set aside the cigar. "What can I get you?"

"It's on me this time, remember."

"I'll get the first round," he said, scooting out of the booth.

"Fine. I'll have a Perrier with a lime and some ice."

As he walked to the bar, I admired the rear view. There was a new swagger to his walk that suggested he was conscious I was watching. He briefly flirted with the bartender, a Spanish-looking woman with long black hair, a knit halter top, and skinny jeans, and was soon back at the table, sliding a tall ice-filled glass to me.

I took a sip and nearly spit out what hit my tongue.

"What is this?"

"It's a G and T." Silva smirked and took a sip of his whiskey.

"I asked for a Perrier," I snapped, my hand still on the glass. I was dying to take another sip, which made me all the angrier. "I told you I don't drink."

"Come on, Mark," he teased. "One drink won't hurt." He tapped the glass. "Live a little."

"One drink will *definitely* hurt." I moved the glass across the table and shook my head at Silva. "Don't ever do that again, please."

"Sorry," he said, looking suddenly sheepish. "I didn't mean anything bad. I just thought . . ." He took the glass back to the bar and returned with a large bottle of Perrier, a bucket of ice, and an empty glass. "They didn't have lime."

"No worries," I said as I filled my glass with ice. "So what's your big news?"

Silva's face lit up, and he moved closer to me. "I've got an interview tomorrow at Mercedes-Benz. That guy I know put in a good word for me. They have an opening!"

"That's fantastic, Alejandro. Congratulations!"

Silva smiled and took a sip of his whiskey. "I don't have it yet. But an interview's something, right?"

"Definitely, yes. I'm happy for you."

The volume of noise in the club was building as more people arrived. Silva edged even closer and lowered his voice. "The other news I had was that I paid Peter everything I owed him. Every penny."

His mention of his former roommate caught me off guard. I flashed on my meeting with the elderly man and recalled his poisoned opinion of Silva.

"You went to see him?"

Silva nodded. "Yesterday afternoon with my parole officer. I wanted to apologize to him for everything and to make things right. He agreed to see me."

"How did that go?"

Silva looked down at the table for a beat, then he looked up at me. "It went all right. It felt good to close the book on that one."

"I'm glad to hear that." I sipped some water and took a moment to consider what he'd just told me. "Alejandro, there's something I've been meaning to ask you."

He drained what was left of his whiskey and pushed away the glass. His eyes shone in the dim light. "Ask away."

"Those men, Peter Miller, Charlie Stewart, they were both quite a lot older than you. How did you end up rooming with them?"

Silva stared at me for a moment, then crushed out his cigar, which was smoldering forlornly in the ashtray. "I grew up without a father." He shrugged. "And I was raised by my grandfather. What can I say? I've always gotten on well with older guys. They make me feel, I don't know, protected maybe."

"I see." I refilled my glass and took a sip to relieve my parched mouth. "Is that what I am to you? Another older guy?"

Silva chuckled. "No, Marc. That's not it." He edged closer until our legs were touching. "Those other guys were interesting and nice. But they were faggy and much older than you. You don't even look gay. I see you more like a big brother, someone I can talk to, someone who really gets me. I've never met anyone like you before." He placed his hand on my thigh.

"Alejandro, why are you touching my leg?" I pushed back against the arousal provoked by his warm hand, poised inches from my crotch.

He leaned closer. "Because you're letting me."

For a moment, I felt paralyzed, unable to think, powerless to act as Silva's hand crept higher on my leg. With the greatest of effort, I placed my hand on his and halted his progress.

"I told you, Alejandro, I have a partner."

He slid back his hand. "Then what are you doing here with *me*?"

The club was now full of people engaged in loud conversation. Sweet-smelling smoke drifted in bluish clouds across the room.

"We should leave," I said, sidestepping his question. "It's getting rancid in here."

"Where do you want to go?"

"Anywhere. I need air."

I stepped outside without waiting for Silva and walked north up Montgomery, my confused head gyrating. It was already dark, and the neon lights of the Broadway strip joints loomed ahead.

A busty Asian woman in a red thong bikini stepped in my way as I rounded the corner in front of the Centerfolds Gentlemen's Club at Broadway. "Hi there, gorgeous! We've got a special show tonight."

I tried to go around her, but she moved in front of me, blocking my path. Silva came up from behind and led me around her by the arm.

"Hang on a sec, boys," the woman tried. "We've got fully nude lap dancers and private shows. And it's two for one tonight."

"No thanks," Silva said as we pulled away.

The young woman spat an angry epithet at us. The wrong one. Silva released my arm and walked over to her.

"What did you say?" he asked in a voice that was much too calm for the occasion.

"Faggots!" she repeated. She backed away and waved at the door of the strip club. A massive Samoan bouncer wearing a pair of black horn-rimmed glasses swaggered out and stood behind her. Now that she had reinforcements, she stepped up to Silva, jutting out her chin at him. "You got a problem with that?"

"Yes, I do." Silva's voice was level, but his eyes were ablaze. "I'm not a faggot, and I recommend you take that back, fast."

I watched in fascination as the young woman wilted under the heat of Silva's hate-filled gaze.

"What if I don't? What are you going to do about it?" All conviction had gone out of her voice.

Silva lowered his head, and I moved closer to hear what he was going to say. After a well-considered pause, he spoke again, softly: "I know who you are, where you work, and what time this place closes."

The young woman flinched. Silva held his ground and continued to stare her down. After a moment, she began to giggle nervously. "Ah, come on, guy!" She doubled over in a fit of laughter. "Can't you take a joke?"

"Take it back," Silva repeated.

"Sure, okay, I take it back." The young woman's eyes darted between the two of us, and she held up her hands. "Are we cool here?"

Silva regarded her with an expression usually reserved for those occasions when one inadvertently steps on a shit-filled disposable diaper. I took hold of him by the crook of his arm and led him away from the woman.

"Come back and see us anytime, boys," she called out, retreating into the club with the bouncer.

Silva stared back at the club entrance, then turned his head and looked at me with a bewildered expression.

"What the hell was that all about?" I asked.

"She called me a faggot."

"She called us both faggots. But did you happen to notice I didn't feel the need to threaten her?"

I waited for a response from Silva. Realizing none was forthcoming, I continued my walk down Broadway toward the Embarcadero, with Silva matching my stride.

"I'm not gay!" he said.

I halted and turned on him. "Maybe you don't get what I'm saying, Alejandro. You threatened that woman. That was wrong."

Silva looked close to tears. "You're angry. I'm sorry, Marc. I didn't mean anything bad. I only wanted her to know she couldn't get away with calling people nasty names."

I continued down the hill, with Silva trailing behind. I avoided looking back at him and discouraged his attempts at conversation with short, monosyllabic replies.

As we reached the T-intersection of Broadway at the Embarcadero and waited for the crosswalk signal, the lights of Pier 7 caught my attention. It had been a long time since I'd walked on the old wooden pier.

When the signal changed, I crossed the street and headed to the far end of the pier, which was spottily illuminated by some old-fashioned streetlamps. It was peaceful there, the stillness broken only by the gentle lapping of water against the pilings and the distant hum of traffic.

I leaned against the black wrought iron railing and gazed across the water at Yerba Buena Island, a large heap of rocks and trees looming in the dark with the glittering San Francisco span of the Bay Bridge thrust into it. I lost myself in the view, blocking out all extraneous sights, sounds, and thoughts.

As I watched the waters of the bay splash against the rocks and relished the cool, salty breeze rustling my hair, I felt the elusive sensation of absolute calm. And then I heard Silva sigh. I turned to face him.

His skin was glistening and radiated a heady mix of Santos

de Cartier and pheromones. "Why didn't you wait for me back at the club?"

"I told you, I needed air. There was too much smoke."

"No, that's not it." His arm brushed mine. "You were scared of me, I think."

"Yes, actually, I *am* scared of you. Or maybe I'm scared of myself. I don't know."

"You don't have to be. I'm not going to hurt you if that's what you're worried about."

"Alejandro, can I ask you something? Something personal."

Silva lifted his shoulders. "Sure, why not?"

"Explain to me again about what happened between you and Charlie Stewart."

Silva dropped his gaze. "I don't like to talk about that."

"Try," I insisted. "It's important."

"Why is it important? I made a mistake. I overreacted, and I paid for it. Why do you have to dredge all that up?"

"Because I don't get it, Alejandro. How was Charlie Stewart any different from Peter Miller?"

Silva's head jerked up at that.

"Peter told me he took liberties with you. Why did you overreact with Charlie but not with Peter? I don't understand."

"I don't understand either! I hate even thinking about it. A man is dead because of *me*. It's like a horrible video playing over and over and over again in my head. It makes me crazy. Sometimes I wish I could stick my head under a steamroller and have it all squeezed out of my skull just to have a moment's peace." Silva laid his hand on my arm. "But sometimes, Marc, sometimes I'm able to forget, if only for a while. Like the times when I'm with you, and we're talking and enjoying each other's company. Tonight, for instance. When we were at the cigar club, I was able to forget."

I didn't know what to say. Silva's explanation just didn't add up for me. But it was already a quarter to eight, and I was exhausted and hungry. So I nodded as if I understood and gave up on my probing.

Lowering my head into my hands, I massaged my temples. Silva moved around behind me and rubbed my shoulders with his powerful hands. The pressure felt good, and I flexed my neck muscles to meet his fingers, his thumbs, the heels of his hands. I loosened my tie and unbuttoned the top button of my shirt.

"You've got this big knot right here," he said, focusing on one spot on the lower left of my neck and applying steady pressure with his thumbs. "I can work it out."

"I think I need to see a chiropractor."

"You don't need a chiropractor. You've got me now."

He continued to knead my shoulders for a few minutes. And then he stopped. Pulling down my shirt collar, he lowered his face to my neck, his warm, humid breath making moist contact with my skin, and gently kissed me. And I let him. He stopped for a moment and tugged on the platinum chain around my neck.

"This is nice," he said, a note of wonder in his voice.

"Thanks."

"Where did you get it?"

"It was a gift."

"Who from?"

"From my partner," I muttered, readjusting it.

Silva shrugged and kissed me again, this time with more feeling. One of his hands reached around and slowly worked my shirt out of my trousers. Then he slipped both hands inside my undershirt and slid his palms up to my chest. I turned around and found myself pinned against the railing by his arms. It was a struggle not to return the kiss he planted on my mouth, but I pushed him away by the shoulders and stared at him.

"What's wrong?" he asked. "You don't like it?"

"Alejandro, didn't you just tell me you weren't gay?"

"I'm not."

"Then, what are you doing?"

"What do you mean? *You're* gay, aren't you?"

An alarm sounded in my head, and my lawyer instincts engaged. "Hang on a second. Define the word *gay*."

"Define it?"

"Yes. Tell me what comes to your mind when you hear the word *gay*."

Silva blinked at me. "I don't want to say something vulgar or anything."

"Don't worry about that. Just tell me."

"Is it important?"

"It's important to me. So, please, by all means, feel free to be as vulgar as you need to explain it to me."

"All right." He drew a breath and closed his eyes. "A gay person likes . . . no, a gay person *enjoys* having a man's penis inside of him."

"A *man's* penis?"

Silva opened his eyes. "Yes."

"You don't happen to mean a *straight man's penis*, do you?"

"Yes."

"So that's your distinction? The guy who gets it up the ass is the gay one, and the one who sticks it to him is straight?"

"Of course."

"What do you mean 'of course'? What if the straight guy also likes to get fucked every once in a while? What does that make him?"

"It makes him gay."

"Alejandro, where did you get this shit?"

"Hey! Why are you talking to me that way?"

"Because it's shit, that's why! Because I don't understand what the hell you're talking about. I mean, I'm not much into labels either. But for God's sake, Alejandro, all of these hypothetical people we're discussing, they're all men having sex with men, aren't they?"

172

"In Mexico, only the guys who like having a penis inside them are *gay*. All the others are straight like me."

"In Mexico? That's where you heard this?"

"Yes."

I stepped back and indicated the skyline with a sweep of my hand. "This isn't Mexico. Here, any man who sleeps with another man is either gay or bisexual. Straight guys only sleep with women. And speaking of women, when was the last time you slept with a woman, Alejandro?"

Silva looked down at his feet. "You're saying I'm gay, aren't you?"

"Answer my question, please. When was the last time you slept with a woman?"

He looked up at me defiantly. "I've never slept with a woman."

"Thank you, Alejandro. Thank you for that."

"So you *are* saying I'm gay."

"I didn't say that. I'm only confirming that you, Alejandro Silva, enjoy having sex, as an active partner, with other men. You may call someone like that *straight* in Mexico, fine. But here in San Francisco, we call a person like that a *top*, and most people here would consider such a person to be *gay*. It's a difference in terms to describe the same thing. Do you understand?"

"A difference in terms?" Silva's voice cracked with emotion.

"Yes. The same as how in Spanish you say *hombre*, whereas, in English, we use the word *man*. Both terms describe the same object."

Silva shook his head. "I still don't want to be treated as if I'm that way. It makes me really angry."

"Then you seriously need some help. You've already hurt someone because of that anger. And tonight you threatened someone else because she called you a similar name. That's not normal."

"I know, I know." Silva closed his eyes and shook his head.

"But what can I do about it?" he whispered. "It's how I feel."

I stared at him, surprised by the appearance of tears dampening his cheeks, shining in the reflected lights of the streetlamps. "If I can put you in touch with a counselor, will you go?"

"I don't know," he said in a low voice. "Maybe."

"You said you trusted me."

I reached out and caressed his arm, intending to reassure him. But as my fingers made contact with his bicep, I felt a stirring in the pit of my stomach and drew my hand back.

Silva opened his eyes and glanced down at my hand. "I do trust you."

"Then, trust me on this. If you want us to stay friends, then you must follow my advice on this."

"I want to be more than friends with you, Marc. I really like you. You understand that, don't you?" He moved closer, his gaze drifting down to my lips, inviting another kiss.

"Yes, I understand that. But we can't." I dropped back a step to regain control of myself. "I'm happy to be your friend. But I'm not looking for a romantic or sexual relationship."

"Are you sure about that?" He studied my face in the semi-darkness.

"Yes, I'm sure," I answered, my voice barely audible.

"Then what are you doing here with me, Marc, letting me hold you, letting me kiss you?" He tried to take my hand, but I moved it out of his reach.

"I don't know, Alejandro. I'm sorry. I haven't been myself lately. I didn't intend for this to happen. Maybe we should cool things off for a while."

I glanced at my watch. It was a quarter past eight. "I'm expected at home for dinner. I'm already late."

"Wait! Where does that leave us? When can I see you again?" he asked, his face crumpling. I felt terrible to leave him there like that. But I was desperate to end the potential disaster

I'd set in motion and rush back home to Isaac.

"We can talk about that another time, all right? I promise. But right now, I've got to run."

I gave Silva a quick hug and jogged all the way to the Embarcadero. As I reached the sidewalk, I turned and looked back toward the end of the pier. I could just make out Silva, still standing where I'd left him. He appeared to be facing the island, but I couldn't be sure. Perhaps he was watching me as I moved toward Fisherman's Wharf in the direction of my apartment building.

Chapter 17

I arrived home past nine to an empty apartment. After searching the bedroom, the bathroom, and the closets, I resigned myself to the reality that Isaac was royally pissed off at me and had left. It was his typical MO, a form of passive revenge he inflicted whenever he felt slighted. But he always came back. This time, I was determined to explain everything to him regardless of how much it hurt.

After finishing an improvised meal of warmed-up rice, black beans, and stir-fried seitan, I padded to the living room and drew open the curtains to reveal our nighttime view of the Golden Gate Bridge. Then I settled into a recliner armed with a tattered copy of Fitzgerald's *The Beautiful and the Damned* and a mug of decaf. Sensing my anxiety, Nilo crept onto my lap and curled into a ball of vibrating fur.

After a few minutes of restless reading, I set down the novel and stroked Nilo's head, forcefully suppressing any thoughts of Alejandro Silva. I must have dozed off because the next thing I became aware of was Isaac standing over me. He was staring at me with an unfathomable look on his face, an expression devoid of emotion.

"Isaac," I said, rubbing my eyes. "What time is it?" Nilo raised his head and jumped off my lap.

"What's his name?" Isaac asked.

"Whose name?"

"The guy you went out with tonight."

I drew myself up. "Remember that sexual harassment case I told you about a few months ago, the one that turned crazy?"

Isaac thought for a moment. "You mean the one where your client went to prison?"

"That's the one."

He pulled up a chair and slumped into it. "What about it?"

"It settled a while back, shortly after your mother passed. The plaintiff's name was Alejandro Silva, the guy I met tonight. He swung by the office a few days ago to thank everyone. He also invited me out to dinner and gave me this."

I handed Isaac the gift box, which he opened. He stared inside for a few seconds, then handed it back to me.

"That was a couple of days ago?" he asked.

"The day I went to see Phoebe. The day you locked yourself in the bathroom."

Isaac sat straight up and looked at me sharply. "You told me you were driving around the city that night."

"I'm sorry, I lied. We'd just had that argument, and I was still sore at you. I thought it would just make things worse if I told you the truth."

"What about tonight?"

"He wanted to share some news with me. So I agreed to meet him after work. That was before you called me."

"Where did you go with him?"

"To the cigar club across the street from the office. Why?"

Isaac nodded. "I followed you after you got off from work. I was waiting around the corner and saw you cross the street and go into the club."

"Well, then you know I'm telling you the truth." I didn't like that Isaac had been spying on me as it didn't say much about the state of our relationship. But considering the circumstances, I left the issue alone.

"I went inside and saw the two of you sitting together in a corner."

"You did? Where were you?"

"I was sitting on the other side of the bar. I stayed long enough to get a look at the guy you were with and then left."

"Why?"

"Because I was angry and afraid. I still am. You're not acting normal, Marc. You're lying and keeping secrets from me."

"I'm not—"

"I know that I haven't been myself for a long time and that most of this is my fault. I'm sorry. But I *need* for us to go back to the way we were before. That starts with you coming clean with me."

I nodded. Isaac deserved to know everything. We both deserved it if we were going to survive as a couple. "He reminds me of Simon," I ventured after a long pause.

As my words sunk in, Isaac shook his head slowly. "What do you mean?"

"Alejandro Silva . . . he reminds me of Simon. I can't put my finger on it exactly, something about his physical appearance, his manner, I don't know."

"And that's supposed to be a good thing?"

I shrugged. "It just is," I said. "I think I've sensed it from the beginning. But it wasn't until he came to the office the other day that it really hit me."

Isaac stood and paced the room. "That should have you running the other way, Marc. Simon was the one that messed you up!"

"Yes, but regardless of that, he was my first. Besides, I've always felt somehow responsible for what happened to him. So maybe—"

"You told me that was an accident!" Isaac yelled. "How could you possibly be responsible?"

"I know that in my head, Isaac," I said, close to tears. "But when I saw Silva the other day, looking so much like Simon, I felt like the universe was giving me the opportunity to finally get some closure—in here." I touched my chest.

"And how did *tha*t go?" Isaac snapped.

I looked down a moment. "Not very well," I said. "It seems Mr. Silva misunderstood my intentions, or maybe I gave off mixed signals."

Isaac stopped his pacing and stared at me, waiting.

"I told him I had a partner," I continued. "But that didn't put him off." I met Isaac's gaze and felt the heat of his anger. "He kissed me. I told him I couldn't meet him again, and that was it. I came home."

"You should have told me about this from the beginning, Marc," he said. "I would've been able to help you figure out what to do."

"I know; I'm sorry, but I thought I could control things. I guess I only made matters more complicated."

"Yes, I'd agree that you *have* made matters more complicated. And now that you've kissed him—"

"I didn't kiss him. He kissed me."

"Not a big difference in my book. Anyway, now that he's kissed you, and you let him, he's probably making plans for the wedding."

"Very funny. The question is, what do I do now?"

"You don't do anything. You already told him you couldn't see him again. So don't see him again. Simple as that."

"I'm not sure he'll stay away."

Isaac snatched my empty mug from the coffee table. "Fine, then go ahead and see him again. Be weak with him like you are with everyone else in your life, your parents, your boss, me." He walked into the kitchen.

His accusation cut me to the quick, worse than if he'd taken an ice pick to my heart.

"What do you mean I'm weak?" I asked, following him

into the kitchen.

He looked at me, his hands submerged in suds as he washed my dinner plate. "You're afraid to tell people the truth. You couldn't talk to your parents for years about your sexuality. That was weak. You let Ed pressure you into working on those cases you didn't feel right about taking. That was weak. And now this . . ." He turned back to the dishes and rinsed them.

"What about with you?" I asked. "You said I was weak with you . . ."

Isaac shook his head and continued rinsing.

"When was I weak with you?" I repeated.

"You mean *besides* lying to me about having dinner with this Silva character?" He turned off the faucet and dried his hands. "Marc, you let me stay in this apartment for two months without saying anything, without encouraging me to go out."

"That's completely untrue! You're the one who holed up all that time in our bedroom, refusing to lift a finger to do anything for yourself except shit, shower, and eat the food I prepared for you. You deflected *all* of my attempts to help you."

"You let two entire months go by before you even opened your mouth. That was weak. What were you afraid of?"

"I wasn't afraid. I just thought you needed *space*, time to mourn your mother."

"Wrong. I needed encouragement, someone to help me snap out of my depression—someone like Phoebe."

He pushed past me into the living room and claimed my recliner. "Anyway, now it's my turn. I have a couple of important things to tell you."

"What?" I asked anxiously, sitting on the floor in front of him.

"First, I got a call from the HR manager at Landis, Murray this afternoon. They're willing to take me back on a probationary basis. I start on Monday."

"That's great news, Isaac."

"Second, after I saw you at the cigar place, I called Ingrid and Christianne and booked a lunch date with them for tomorrow."

"Why would you do that?"

"I want to talk to them about their offer, of course."

"What does that have to do with my going to the cigar bar?"

Isaac shrugged. "If you can act unilaterally, I can too."

"You're not really going to take them up on that sperm donation thing, are you?"

Isaac pulled a face. "I don't know. I want to hear them out."

"You're prepared to make a life-changing decision without me?"

He leaned forward and looked at me closely. "I want you to come, too. So we can make a decision about it together."

I had no desire to participate in Isaac's sperm project when we had so many more pressing issues to consider.

"It's that important to you?" I asked.

"Yes."

I drew a deep breath, rocked onto my knees, and took Isaac's hands in mine. "Isaac, after everything we've talked about tonight, I don't want to be weak and not tell you exactly how I feel about this."

Isaac nodded his head slowly and waited.

"I don't want to go to lunch with those women."

Isaac pulled away from me. "But—"

I held up my hand. "*But* considering how strongly you feel about it, I'll agree to meet with them just this once to hear them out."

Isaac looked away and nodded. "I suppose that's fair."

"Now, can we please go to bed? I'm exhausted."

Chapter 18

The moment I stepped through the door of my office the following day, I sensed something was wrong. The signs were unmistakable: the quieter than usual staff, the furtive glances, the averted eyes, a vague warning from Vlad that trouble was brewing, and, finally, the sticky note taped to my computer screen.

Please see me as soon as you come in! Ed.

Sitting down at my desk, I yanked the sticky off the display and booted up my computer.

"What the hell are you doing?"

I looked up and found Ed standing in my doorway looking very un-Ed-like, glowering, nostrils flaring.

"I beg your pardon?" I looked through him, channeling calm.

"Didn't you see the damned note I left on your screen?"

"Close the door, Ed, and stop swearing at me, please. It doesn't become you."

He pushed the door closed, pulled out a client chair, and dropped into it. "What's going on between you and Silva?"

"Nothing, why?"

"You were spotted with him yesterday evening at the cigar club across the road, sitting snug as two bugs."

"What about it?"

"I warned you to stay away from him."

"He's a *former* client, Ed. I can meet with him if I want."

"As senior partner of this firm, *I'll* decide that."

I stared at my computer screen, sorting out my feelings and, more importantly, buying myself some time to formulate a response.

"So, I'll ask again, what's going on between you two?" he asked. "More importantly, when did it start?"

"Ed, I'd appreciate it if you'd butt out of my private life."

"I don't give a rat's ass about your private life. What I want to know is whether or not this firm should expect to answer an ethics complaint from the state bar."

"Based on what?"

"Based on what I saw the other afternoon in our boardroom! You. Silva. The gift. And then again yesterday. I don't know! That's why I'm asking. You're the one who should know the answer to that." Ed rose and paced the room.

I got up from my desk, stepped past him, and opened the door. "Let me handle Silva."

Ed frowned at the open door. "I can't believe you're not going to fill me in."

"Believe it and get over it. Now, if you'll excuse me, I have to work on some interrogatories. They're due tomorrow."

He stepped up to me, exasperation marring his face. "Marc, you have no idea the pains I'm taking to restrain myself."

"Restrain yourself from what?"

"From suggesting that we . . ."

"Do you want to dissolve the partnership, Ed?" I asked, interrupting him. "Is that what you're trying to say? If so, just tell me."

"Is that what you want?"

"I don't, but if *you* do, then I guess we'd better talk about it—some other time." I stepped away from the door, giving him clear passage into the hallway.

Ed shook his head and walked out of my office, slamming the door shut as he left. I'd never seen him that angry in my entire association with him: not with opposing counsel, not with temperamental judges, not with problematic clients, and never with me.

I returned to my desk, turned off my telephone, and lost myself in the interrogatories, coming up for air when nature demanded, and then only with the greatest reluctance. I wanted no interruptions, so it was with a gargantuan effort that I wrenched my head toward my doorway at the sound of Vlad's insistent voice.

"I've been knocking for a couple of minutes. Are you all right?" he asked, craning his neck around my door.

"I'm fine, Vlad. What do you need?"

"You've got a visitor." He indicated the person was behind him in the hallway.

"Who is it?" I mouthed.

Vlad stepped further into the room and whispered, "It's your partner."

I looked at my watch and was astonished to see it was already half past noon. "Tell him to come in."

Vlad withdrew, and a moment later Isaac stepped into the office with a questioning look. "I've been waiting for over a half hour. Ingrid and Christianne must be wondering what happened to us."

I pushed away from my desk and grabbed my coat. "Sorry, sorry, I lost track of time. Let's go."

I kissed him on the cheek and pulled him out the door. We bounded down the stairs, raced past the receptionist, and collided with Alejandro Silva, who was, at that moment, walking through the front door of the building, impeccably dressed in a white silk shirt and black linen trousers.

"Marc," he said, his smile evaporating as he took in the sight of Isaac and me holding hands.

I glanced at Isaac. He was scanning Silva, from the expensive haircut all the way down to his Versace sandals.

It was almost hilarious—Isaac and Alejandro standing there, each sizing up the other. Almost hilarious, but not quite. I herded the two of them out of the building and onto the sidewalk.

"Um, Alejandro," I said. "This is Isaac, my partner."

Silva stared vacantly, first at Isaac, then at me. When he spoke again, his voice was studiously controlled. "I know who he is."

"You do?" Isaac asked. "How?"

Silva turned his back on Isaac and focused on me. "I wanted to tell you about my interview this morning, Marc." He held out an envelope bearing a Mercedes-Benz logo. "I got the job."

"Congratulations, Alejandro, I'm happy for you. But, remember, I told you yesterday we had to cool things off. I'm with Isaac."

Silva glanced at Isaac. "I've been asking around. Nobody's seen him for months. I figured it was over, or will be soon enough."

Isaac grabbed my hand and dug in his nails. "Well, you figured wrong, amigo."

At that moment, the front door swung open, and Ed stepped outside, taking in the sight of us. "Well, isn't this a pretty picture?"

Isaac greeted Ed, who gestured toward Silva. "I see you've met our *former* client, Mr. Silva."

"Hello, Mr. Haddad," Silva said with a nervous smile. "I hope you liked my gift."

"We're all still enjoying it, Mr. Silva," Ed responded. "Isn't that right, Mendes?" He raised an eyebrow at me. "I'm off to lunch," he said, *sotto voce*. "Good luck fixing this mess." Then, spinning away, he vanished around the corner.

An awkward silence followed.

"I think I'd better let the two of you sort this out," Isaac said. "I'll be at Gaylord's with *our guests*, Marc, when you're finished here." He glared at me before stomping off down the sidewalk.

I waited for Isaac to recede in the distance before pivoting back to Silva. He was staring at me with the eyes of an injured animal.

"He hasn't been much of a partner to you from what I've heard," he said. "I don't know why you're still with him."

"Not that it's any of your business," I said, controlling myself as best I could. "But his mother passed a couple of months back. That's why he hasn't been around."

"Okay, fine. So you're still together. That doesn't mean that you and I can't still see each other as friends. You can have friends, can't you?"

I put my hand on his shoulder. "Not after what happened last night, Alejandro. I'm sorry, but we can't meet again."

Silva blinked, then shook me off. "What do you mean? Of course, we can meet again!"

"No, we—"

"Work it out with your so-called partner, or don't; I don't care," Silva growled. "But you and I are just getting started."

Turning on his heels, he hiked up Montgomery Street. When he reached Pacific, he looked back at me. Our eyes met for one brief confused moment. Then, shaking his head, he turned the corner and was gone.

I arrived at Gaylord's just as Isaac and the Canadian women, Ingrid and Christianne, joined the buffet line for a second helping of Indian food. Stepping in behind them, I grabbed a plate and picked at the selection of curries.

Isaac leaned into me and whispered, "What happened?"

I ladled a spoonful of yellow daal onto my rice. "I'll tell

you after lunch."

He pulled me away from the buffet line. "Is it over, or isn't it?"

"I told him it was."

"What did he say?"

"He said it wasn't." I grabbed a napkin and dabbed my forehead. "It's probably just bluster."

"It'd better be." Isaac released my arm and rejoined the women.

The lunch crowd was clearing out when we got to the booth. As we ate, the Canadian women spoke enthusiastically about their baby plans. I poked at my food and listened without much interest, prepared to shoot down the project once they finished their presentation. Silva's last words were playing a repeating loop in my head. Every few minutes, Isaac nudged me under the table to jar me out of my daze. The third time he nudged, I pushed back hard and glowered at him. He was staring across the room. Following his line of sight, I saw Silva standing at the cashier, counting out a wad of cash to pay for a tray of food.

The women stopped speaking, and they both turned to see what we were looking at. Silva swaggered into the dining room, escorted by a waiter who led him to an empty table a few feet away. He nodded at us, snapped open his napkin, and tucked into his food.

"Oh, he's gorgeous," Christianne remarked, unabashedly staring at him.

"Friend of yours?" Ingrid asked.

"He's a friend of Marc's," Isaac said tersely.

"Why? Do you want his sperm, too?" I quipped, trying to lighten the mood.

"Hey!" Ingrid shot back. "The more, the merrier."

I watched in horror as she waved Silva over to our booth. He left his tray and crossed the room to us, beaming a wide smile.

"You're welcome to join us," Ingrid said to him. "There's enough room for you to squeeze in here next to my girlfriend."

Christianne scooted in, and Silva shrugged and slid onto the bench.

"My name's Ingrid, and this here is Christianne." Ingrid draped her arm around Christianne and pulled her close. "We're visiting from Canada." She waved her free hand at us. "I think you know these boys?"

"I know Marc," Silva answered. "The other guy I met earlier today."

Isaac's eyes blazed, and he grabbed a handful of my thigh. Noticing this, the slightest hint of a smile animated Silva's lips. He turned to Ingrid.

"I'm Alejandro, by the way."

"Hi, Alejandro. We were just explaining our proposal to Isaac and Marc—"

I shot up from the table and waved my hand as if the force of the motion could brush the interaction away.

"I've got this, thanks." Taking Silva by the arm, I led him back to his table.

"What in God's name are you doing?" I spat through gritted teeth.

"What proposal are they talking about?" he asked, glancing curiously back at the table, then at me.

"Never mind that. Why are you here?"

"I'm sorry about earlier. I was upset. But I really need to talk to you. There's something super important I never got a chance to tell you, besides about my new job. That's why I went to your office earlier today."

"Alejandro, I told you. I'm not available. We can't meet anymore."

"It's not about me and you!" Tears pooled in his eyes. "It's something *way* beyond that. I really need to talk to you about it."

I looked over at Isaac and the women. They were engaged in what looked like a heated exchange. "Tell me now."

"I can't tell you now. It's super private. Nobody can be around when I tell you. Meet me later, please."

"Alejandro—"

"Seriously, it's a matter of life and death."

"Alejandro, please—"

"It's about that other case."

"Which other case? You mean Charlie Stewart?"

Alejandro cast about the restaurant, then looked at me and nodded. "I can't say any more here, Marc. Please meet me later." Silva's hands were trembling. He clasped them and slid them off the table onto his lap.

I looked back at Isaac, who was shaking his head at me. I flashed him a discreet look of exasperation and turned back to Silva.

"When and where?" I asked.

"Tonight. At ten. In the lobby of my hotel."

I gave him a reproachful look. "I'm not going to your room, Alejandro."

"Not in my room. We'll meet in the lobby; then we'll go somewhere neutral, maybe the lounge right off the lobby. Don't worry."

I stood and looked down at him. "You honestly think I'd agree to meet you at your hotel? After what happened last night?"

"I know it seems suspicious, Marc. But I wouldn't ask you if it weren't important. Please trust me, like I trusted you; let me confide in you one last time."

I felt the arrow hit its mark and lodge deep inside my conscience. "We'll see," I said in a low voice. I nodded at the booth where Isaac and the women had fallen silent. "I've got to get back to our guests."

Silva slipped out from his table and followed me as I returned to the booth, which was now clear of dishes.

"It was nice meeting you," he said to Ingrid and Christianne, lifting his manicured hand. "I'm leaving now."

Ingrid whipped out a slip of paper and held it out to Silva.

"Call us. We're here for a couple more days."

Silva took the piece of paper, glanced at it, then carefully folded it, slid it into his breast pocket, and walked out of the restaurant.

"So what did I miss?" I asked, breaking the silence that had descended over the table.

"We've reached an unfortunate impasse," Ingrid said.

"They want me to father a baby and then sign away all parental rights. I'm not okay with that," Isaac explained.

Ingrid crossed her arms and held them tight.

"I'm sure they'd let you at least visit the child." I laid my hand on Isaac's clenched fist and looked back and forth between Ingrid and Christianne. "Right?"

"That's not the arrangement we're looking for," Ingrid said as Christianne examined her fingernails. "We'd want the donor to sign a legally enforceable written promise never to contact the child. We'd pay him, of course."

"In your dreams," Isaac muttered.

"That's fine," Ingrid responded, gathering up her things. "If it doesn't work for you, I'm sure we'll find someone else who it *does* work for."

After a terse good-bye in which Isaac and the women shook hands and promised not to harbor any hard feelings, he and I were left alone at the table to nurse our cups of lukewarm tea.

"Well, that was disappointing," Isaac reflected, breathing in the steam.

"If you want a child that badly, we could always look into adopting."

He stared into his cup and nodded.

"Once this immigration thing is behind us, of course," I added.

Isaac blinked and regarded me out of the corner of his eye. "So, changing subjects, what happened with Mr. Charming?" He nodded at the table where Silva had been sitting. "Is he finally out of our lives?"

"He wants to meet one last time. Says it's a matter of life and death. Something to do with his other case."

Isaac swung around and faced me. "The criminal case?"

"Something like that. It's extremely confidential, apparently. He couldn't go into detail about it here."

A bitter laugh escaped Isaac's lips. "Tell him to talk to someone else about it. There are hundreds of lawyers in this city, if not thousands."

I shrugged. "I think I should hear him out, this one final time."

"He's manipulating you, Marc."

"I don't think he is. He seemed genuinely scared. Anyway, he wants me to meet him tonight."

"When?"

"At ten." I steadied myself for the next part. "In the lobby of his hotel. He's staying at the Headlands on Lombard."

Isaac pushed aside his teacup. "That's crazy! You didn't agree to meet him, did you?"

"I didn't promise one way or the other. But I think I'm going to go. Something tells me I should. More for me than for him, I think."

"Then I'm going with you."

"That would defeat the purpose, Isaac."

"I disagree! You can't go gallivanting out to see some guy at his hotel at ten o'clock at night! Especially not that guy. He's crazy obsessed with you. Plus, you've already kissed him. Tell him no."

"Isaac, listen—"

"No!" Isaac shrunk away from me, his eyes wide and angry.

"Hear me out, please."

He pressed his eyes shut and counted to ten under his breath, then he opened them and gifted me the blackest of looks. "It had better be good."

"There's a diner directly across the street from the hotel. It's that retro one with all the neon. We'll go together, and you can wait for me there while I meet with him in the lounge off the lobby. I already told him I wouldn't go up to his room."

"Just how I want to spend my evening."

"I'll be done in no time, I promise. I just need to assess what's going on, for him, for us. If there's anything that needs intervention, I'll make it happen. If he's playing games, I'll set him straight. Either way, we'll be done with him."

"You'd better be right, Marc." Isaac raked both hands through his hair and held tight. "There isn't room in our lives for more of this shit."

I arrived home at around six in the evening and found Isaac and Phoebe sitting in the living room. They both looked up as I entered.

"What's this?" I asked.

"Good evening, Mr. Mendes," Phoebe said, holding out her hand, inviting a handshake.

"I asked Phoebe to come over," Isaac explained. "I needed to talk to someone. I didn't know who else to call."

I shook Phoebe's hand and plopped onto the sofa next to Isaac. "What are we talking about exactly?"

"Isaac, dear," Phoebe said. "I'd like to speak with Marc alone if that's all right."

"No problem." Isaac kissed me on the cheek and left Phoebe and me alone in the room.

Once she was sure he was out of earshot, Phoebe turned to me. "That boy is devoted to you, heart and soul, Mr. Mendes. I hope you know that."

"I do."

"He would do anything for you. Absolutely *anything*."

Exhausted from the day, I rubbed my face with both hands. "I know all that."

"I assume you care for him as well?"

"Of course, I care for him. I love him! I'm ready to follow him to the ends of the Earth if that's what it takes."

"Then why are you allowing this Alejandro character to interfere with that?" Phoebe asked, her face etched with concern.

I stood up. "Why would Isaac tell you about that?"

"Please sit, Mr. Mendes. Isaac needed to talk to someone. Who better than his lawyer?"

I closed my eyes and took a breath, then sat down. "It's a complicated situation, one with very deep roots."

"Do you have any idea how all of this is impacting poor Isaac? To be frank, Mr. Mendes, I fear for him, for both of you."

I looked away, choking back a surge of sadness.

"I understand the young man in question was your client."

"Things got out of control," I rasped. "I don't even know how it happened, to be honest. But it couldn't have come at a worse time, what with us in the middle of Isaac's immigration case, his mother passing away, the stresses at work." I looked at Phoebe through tears that had welled up in my eyes and swiped them away. "I'm struggling with all of this, barely able to tread water. I should be able to handle it. The idea that I can't kills me. After all, I've spent my whole working life helping other people sort out their messes. Why am I still wrestling with my own?"

"You're human."

"Whatever. All I know is I have to fix this thing with Alejandro Silva, with everything that he symbolizes for me, once and for all. Then I can at least close that chapter, and Isaac and I can move on."

Phoebe shook her head.

"What?" I asked.

"May I offer you some advice?"

"Yes, please."

"Work out your issues on a psychiatrist's couch, Mr. Mendes. As for Mr. Silva, run as fast and as far from him as you can. Don't meet him; don't take his calls. Nothing. That's the only thing that will work in a case like this. If necessary, file a restraining order against him. If he violates it, he'll land back in prison."

My head snapped up at that.

"Yes, Isaac told me. The man's a convicted felon."

"I'm meeting with him tonight."

"Don't go."

"It'll be the last time. He has something important to tell me."

"It's a lie. Trust me, I know this kind of person."

"Do you mind if I join you now?" Isaac chimed in, leaning through the doorway.

Phoebe waved him into the room, and he sat next to me.

"Phoebe was saying I should break all communication with Silva."

"You should!" Isaac said.

"I agree. Once I break it off with him, it might be a good idea for us to get out of the city for a few days while it blows over."

"That seems sensible," Phoebe agreed, glancing at Isaac.

Isaac shook his head. "You said, *once* you break it off. You mean you're going to see him tonight."

"This will be the very last time. I'll hear him out, and then I'll make him understand that we won't see each other ever again."

Phoebe and Isaac traded a look, then focused on me.

"I can do this," I said, squeezing Isaac's hand. "Then tomorrow, we'll pack up and have ourselves a road trip. We can drive south along the coast and maybe stop in Los Angeles to visit my parents. It'll be good for us."

After a moment, Isaac turned to me.

"I'm going to trust you on this, Marc, against my better judgment. What's more, you can go alone. I'm not going to tag along like we planned."

"Are you sure?" I asked.

"No, I'm *not* sure. But as long as I have your word this will be the absolute last time you see him—and Phoebe here is our witness—then I'll agree."

"I swear it. This will be the last time."

"And afterward," Phoebe said, "when the two of you return from your trip, we must focus all our efforts on preparing Isaac's asylum claim. His hearing is weeks away, and we cannot afford to have any distractions."

Chapter 19

My cab pulled up in front of the Headlands Hotel at five minutes past ten. As I counted out the cash to pay the driver, Silva pushed out of the revolving doors and approached the cab—black tank top, tight blue jeans. No underwear.

"God, help me," I whispered to myself.

Silva pulled open the door and slid into the vehicle next to me. He pulled back my hand and slipped the driver a one-hundred-dollar bill. "Otis and Van Ness, please."

"What are you doing?" I said to him as the driver pulled away from the curb and executed a U-turn in the middle of the street.

He leaned against me and spoke in a low voice, "We're going someplace neutral like I told you." I could smell his hair.

"You said the lounge off the lobby of your hotel."

"No, I said *maybe* the lounge. But that was no good. There were too many people there. Where we're going is better."

"Otis and Van Ness is not better. That's the Transformer Club!"

"Not *in* the club itself. In the office on the third floor. It's totally safe. The guy I know there lets me use it after hours."

"Why are you taking me to a sex club, Alejandro?"

"I know it seems weird, Marc. But I wouldn't ask you if it weren't important. It'll be okay. Trust me. The office is tucked away, so we can talk in private."

"I have an office! Why not go there instead?"

"Your office isn't neutral, is it?" he said, searching my face.

I reached for the door handle, preparing to jump out of the cab at the next stoplight. Silva reached across my chest and gently pulled back my hand, his warm thigh pressed against mine.

"Don't be so nervous, Marc," he said, his strong teeth shining electric white in the dark cab interior. "Everything will be fine."

I flashed on the first time I'd crossed the threshold of a sex club. It had been years ago with Simon on one of our drug-fueled adventures. The memory of it provoked a nervous excitement that reverberated through my psyche. *You're coming full circle now*, I thought.

The cab jerked to a stop in front of the nondescript building. The only indication anything was going on inside was the license plate-sized red neon sign flashing above the open door and a boisterous lineup of guys snaking around the corner.

Silva grabbed my hand and led me at a fast clip past the line and past the bouncers, who stepped back to give us room to pass. As we pushed into the building and bounded up the exit stairs toward the second floor, the dizzying smell of pot slammed me. The place reeked of it. I grabbed for the handrail and held tight. My knees were buckling, and I felt a gnawing in my gut.

"What's wrong?" Silva passed his hand over my damp forehead. "You look terrible."

"I can't go in there, Alejandro. Sorry."

I turned away from him and made my way back down to the street. Silva pattered down the stairs and stood between me and the door. The patrons on the other side of the railing glanced in our direction, and I turned to hide my face.

"Are you sick?" He squeezed my hand.

"It's this place, Alejandro. There are too many people. Someone's bound to recognize me. If word of this gets back to Isaac—"

Silva put his arm around my shoulders and pulled me tight. "It will be fine, Marc."

I let him lead me back up the stairs, focusing on the sweet scent of his skin—patchouli, sandalwood, musk—and trying my best to block out the heady smell of marijuana.

I was ravenous for something strong by the time we reached the dimly lit enclosed office on the third floor. It was a sweltering narrow rectangle of a room with a natty burgundy velour sofa running along one wall and a small desk with a computer in the far corner. A full-size refrigerator, tattered party posters, and a candy jar filled with condoms made up the rest of the décor, along with a flat-screen showing hardcore porn with the volume turned down low. Considering how busy it was in the club, it was surprisingly quiet in the office, save for the soft moaning coming from the screen. Silva locked the door, grabbed a beer from the refrigerator, and held it out to me.

"Just water, thanks," I said, glancing around the room. Sweat streamed down the sides of my face.

He shrugged and fished around in the refrigerator. A moment later, he held out a bottle of San Pellegrino, which I twisted open and chugged. He rolled the beer bottle against his forehead to cool himself.

"Sure you wouldn't rather have one of these?" he asked. He held out the bottle again and flashed his teeth. "I noticed you sneaked a sip of champagne the other night at the restaurant when you thought I wasn't looking."

I felt myself redden.

"It's not a problem for me, Marc," he said, waving the bottle. "You don't need to pretend here. You can be who you really want to be. If you want a beer, have a beer. Or whatever. You'll get no judgments from me. Nothing leaves this room."

I shook my head and glanced at the video, which had segued to a poolside orgy of sinewy twenty-something blond guys. Silva followed my line of sight and chuckled. Then he slid a tiny blue and silver bottle out of his pocket, popped the cap, and drew in a long sniff. Though it had been years since I'd been around poppers, I immediately recognized the unmistakable musty-sweet smell—the smell of sex. Silva held the bottle out at me.

"Here, have some. It'll help you relax."

"No, thanks. I'm fine." I pushed the bottle away.

"Been a while, eh?"

I pointed at a small window set high above the desk. "Can you crack that open, please?"

"It's just for light," he said, dropping onto the sofa and drawing up his legs. "Come on, sit!" He slapped the cushion next to him.

I settled on the sofa and nestled against the armrest to establish a physical distance, glancing nervously at the video screen again.

"That's a good one." Silva nodded at the screen. "Especially this next part."

"Turn it off, please," I said, trying my best to keep my voice steady.

"Don't know how, sorry." He reached into the pocket of his jeans and drew out a rolled-up sandwich baggie. Snapping it open, he extracted a crumpled joint and a zippo. "It's always on."

I watched in horrified fascination as he fired up and took his first drag. I wanted desperately to run out of there; I was thirsting to take a drag.

"You don't look so good, Marc," he said once he'd released the smoke, blowing it toward the screen. "Here, have some." He held out the joint. "Believe me, you'll feel a lot better."

I put up my hand. "No, I'm okay. Just please, tell me what you wanted to tell me. I don't have all night."

"Come closer." He pounded the cushion next to him again.

"I can hear you perfectly well from here, Alejandro."

He shrugged and scooted closer until one of his knees was touching mine. "If the mountain won't come to Mohammed . . ."

"Very cute."

"You're the mountain," he said, taking another drag.

"If you say so."

He blew the smoke out of the side of his mouth and peeled off his tank top, exposing his muscular chest, dusted with dark hair. "I'm Mohammed."

"No, you're Mrs. Robinson."

Silva narrowed his eyes at me. "I don't know what that means." He folded his tank top into a neat square and set it aside.

"It's from a movie. It means you're trying to seduce me."

"I know where it's from. I just don't know what *you* mean. Mrs. Robinson was married. I'm not. In this instance, I'm available, and supposedly you're not. And yet, here you are."

He held the joint under my nose, and I froze as wisps of the pungent smoke drifted into my nostrils. "Just one hit," he murmured.

I stared into his eyes, teetering at the edge of a precipice. I was back in Israel again, in Mitzpe Ramon, standing on the lip of the makhtesh five hundred meters above the desert floor, with Simon at my side, both of us high as eagles, fucked up on acid and pot, daring each other to jump.

I closed my eyes, and Silva pressed the joint against my lips as tears streamed down my cheeks. "Open your mouth, Marc," he said. "You know you want to."

Holding out my arms to either side, I surrendered to gravity and let myself drop over the edge. Battered by the searing *khamsin*, we plummeted to the desert floor, Simon and me, in our insane bid for immortality. Just before the moment of impact, I opened my eyes and found Silva staring at me, waiting. I parted my lips, and he inserted the joint, and I took in a deep lungful of smoke.

"That's my boy!" he said, brushing my cheek with the tip of his index finger.

After a couple of moments, I let out the smoke. I took another long drag and relaxed into the high, jettisoning the tension of self-control I'd endured for a decade. When I finally released the second lungful, I grabbed a beer and chugged half the bottle in one go.

"Easy, there," Silva said, taking the bottle out of my hand. "Pace yourself."

I nodded and set aside the joint, feeling like a man waking up from a coma to a new world. Silva produced another little bottle and jiggled it.

"What's that?" I reached for it, and he pulled it back.

"GHB, liquid ecstasy," he said with a broad smile. "Ever tried it?"

"It's a little after my time," I said. "Quaaludes and coke were my drugs of choice. But I know what it is."

He opened the bottle, which had a dropper attached to the cap, and squeezed a single drop into my beer. "A little Gina goes a long way," he said, swirling around the beer in the bottle and setting it on the table. "You don't have to if you don't want to. But it's there if you want to give it a try. One sip is enough."

I shook my head. A couple of hits of pot and some beer was one thing. But I wasn't sure I was ready to open the door to anything harder.

"What was the life-or-death thing you wanted to tell me?" I said, wrenching my gaze away from the G-laced beer to focus on Silva's birthmark.

A dark frown drifted across his face, and he pinched the hot end of the joint we'd been sharing to extinguish it. Then he drew a measured breath and lowered his eyes.

"Charlie was dealing," he said after a long silence. "He screwed up. More than once. His suppliers were a skinny white dude from Oakland and his ape of a Brazilian sidekick." He looked up. "Basically, they killed him and framed me."

I grasped his arm. "What?"

201

"They forced me to say what I told the police and threatened to make me disappear if I told anyone the truth."

I stared at him open-mouthed, trying to make sense of what he was saying and working out how to respond.

"You can't say anything, Marc."

"Did you at least tell your public defender?"

"No! Of course not! I'm not suicidal! I haven't told anyone until now. And you're not going to say anything either."

"But, Alejandro—"

"I know the rules, Marc. You have to keep anything I say confidential."

"Yes, of course. It's all confidential. But why are you telling me this if you don't want my advice?"

Alejandro frowned at me. "There's *nothing* I can do! If they find out I breathed a word about it to anyone—even to my lawyer—I'm dead. I only told you because I wanted you to know I'm not some violent psycho like you've been thinking and also to demonstrate how much I trust you. I'm a victim, not a criminal." He touched my leg. "Do you understand now?"

I looked down at his hand and back up at him. "Do I understand what?"

"That you don't have to be afraid of me anymore." He moved his hand up my thigh. "I have what you're missing, Marc." He moved in and unfastened the top two buttons of my shirt.

"I'm . . . I'm not missing anything," I stammered, now fully aroused.

Grabbing the beer bottle off the table, he took a sip and grinned. "You're missing excitement in your life, passion, a hint of danger. It's so obvious." He kissed my neck and nipped at my earlobe, then pulled back and gazed deeply into my eyes. "I can offer you that and more. That other guy, Mr. Uptight Paralegal, the guy who wants to bring a fucking baby into your life, all he offers you is boring stability."

"You don't even know him. He's good for me."

"I know the type. All he can give you is vanilla sex and sparkling water. *I'll* drag you to hell and back. I'll fuck your brains out in ways you never imagined and have you begging me for more."

"I love him. He's my rock . . ."

"And yet," Silva said, removing my shirt and tossing it onto the chair, "here we are."

He pressed the bottle to my lips, and I took a quick sip, flashing on the salty aftertaste of the drink I'd snuck the other night at Mecca. Then he pulled my neck toward him and kissed me on the mouth, a deep, lingering, passion-filled kiss that went on and on. We hung suspended in that moment until, finally, I felt a rush to the lower half of my body as the G kicked in. The weight of Silva's body against mine, the touch of his hands, the slick of his tongue, the press of his groin; skin on skin; mouth on mouth.

I dug a condom out of the candy jar and pressed it into his hand. He grinned at it. "This is for later," he said, setting it aside and absently fingering my Star of David pendant, his eyes gleaming in the dim light. He kissed me again, then slipped out of his jeans and shepherded my head into his lap and held me close.

"*Gam ki elech b'gei tzalmavet,*
I will fear no evil; I will fear no evil . . .

"*Gam ki elech b'gei tzalmavet,*
I will fear no evil; I will fear no evil!"

"Will you *please* stop that wailing and get back in here?"

I fell silent and blinked in the darkness: at our tent pitched at the edge of a spring; at the ruins of the caravanserai on the rocky outcrop—neonesque and eerie in the waning glow of a full moon. I dropped to one knee, fighting back the shaking that had gripped me, the knife's edge of panic and paranoia, the feeling that I was going mad. I cried out again:

"Gam ki elech b'gei tzalmavet,
I will fear no evil; I will fear no evil!"

Simon's head shot out of the tent. "What the fuck is wrong with you?" he growled. "Come in here and get some sleep." He pulled back a curtain of hair that had fallen across his face as he watched me pitch over onto my side in the dirt.

"I'm sorry, Simon," I whimpered, curling into a tight fetal coil. "I'm too coked up. I fucking need to do something, or I'm going to jump out of my skin."

He crawled out of the tent in nothing but a pair of khaki underpants and drew me close, kissing me and raking his fingers through my hair. "Relax, man. I've got a 'lude in the tent that'll help bring you down. Now come on; get back inside."

I yanked away from him and dragged myself in the direction of the hill. The moon had set, and the landscape was plunged into near darkness. Everything around me was now dappled in a phosphorescence emanating from the canopy of throbbing stars overhead. I feared that any minute they'd fall to the earth and pierce me through—a scattershot of white-hot shrapnel. Feeling a sudden surge of adrenaline, I jumped to my feet and sprinted toward the caravanserai on the hill, fighting my way through the acacias, protecting my face from the thorns with my arms.

"Where are you going?" Simon shouted. "Marc, wait!" He dashed after me, the sand and stones thrashing his bare feet, the acacias flaying the skin on his arms, his chest—my dear Simon's beautiful chest—but I was faster. I made it to the switchback trail and sped up the hill, screaming out to God to save me.

"Lo irah rah!!! Lo irah rahhhhhhhh!"

"Stop! Marc!" Simon screamed. "Marc, wait! Marc!!!"

"Marc! Marc! Wake up!"

I jolted back to consciousness and took in the dark blur of my funky-smelling surroundings, working hard to establish my bearings. I had no idea *where* I was or *when* I was: the Negev in Israel, a Los Angeles bathhouse, some fucked-up nightmare, a combination of all three?

"Marc! Are you all right? Marc, say something."

I focused on the bleary silhouette of the person calling to me. After God knows how long, the blur resolved into the image of Isaac—dressed in a white button-down shirt and jeans.

"Isaac," I tried to say. But my throat was parched, and all that came out was a hiss. I swallowed hard and tried again. "Get me some water, please," I rasped.

Isaac produced a water bottle, and I took a few halting sips then handed it back to him, painfully aware of a pulsing in my head. I cast about and realized I was sitting inside some kind of tent, reclined against a bundle of clothes. Someone was passed out in a dark corner, a black guy in a red tracksuit. Looking down at myself, I saw I was wearing only a T-shirt and a pair of boxer shorts. In that moment, the memory of what had happened came crashing through the fog of my consciousness. I scuttled away from Isaac, grabbed for something to drape over myself, and buried my face in my hands. Isaac yanked down my arms and thrust a pair of sweatpants and a hoodie into them.

"Get dressed," he instructed. "Now!"

"Isaac, I'm—"

"Never mind that," he shot back. "I need to get you out of here *now*. Just put those things on, and let's go."

I fumbled on the sweats with trembling hands, and Isaac helped thread the hoodie over my head. Then he grasped my hand and eased me out of my corner onto my knees. In that instant, Silva stuck his head through the tent opening.

"Well, well," he said with a snigger. "If it isn't Mr. Straight-Laced Paralegal. You're not here to join us, are you?"

Isaac spun around. "You stay the fuck away from Marc!" he shouted.

Silva put up his hands. "Seriously, dude. You're more than welcome to join us—the more, the merrier. Last night we had ourselves a nice little choo choo train in here; five guys in all. Isn't that right, Marc?"

Isaac let out a roar and lunged at Silva, pushing him out of the tent. I crawled out after them and found Isaac straddling Silva on the concrete floor with his hands around his throat. Three security guys dashed toward them, slaloming through the surrounding tents and smatter of inebriated patrons, and tore Isaac off Silva. Silva jumped up and brushed himself off, raising his head at Isaac, who struggled to break free from the security guys.

"Come on, office boy," Silva chided, waving Isaac forward. "Let's have it out once and for all."

"Leave us alone!" Isaac bellowed. "Just leave us the fuck alone!"

"Hey, don't try and pin this on me," Silva said. "Marc's here because he *wants* to be here."

I shook my head to clear the fog drifting across my brain as the guards dragged Isaac the length of the club toward the exit.

"Good riddance," Silva muttered. He tried to draw me into a hug, but I pulled away from him and ran to catch up with Isaac. We exited the club together, shoved onto the sidewalk by the security staff, who warned us never to return.

I followed Isaac to his double-parked black Saturn near the club entrance. We rode back home in the advancing dawn, with him refusing even to glance in my direction. As we drove up to our apartment building, I caught sight of the Golden Gate

Bridge in the distance, spanning the sparkling waters of the bay, and I held my breath. That familiar landmark, ever popular with jumpers, never looked so tempting to me as it did in that moment.

The apartment was dark when we stepped inside. I took a detour to the kitchen to pour myself a glass of water and crept into the living room, terrified of what was coming next. I nearly spilled the water as I rounded the corner into the room and found Isaac occupying my chair in the half-light.

"Go take a shower," he said in a low voice.

"Isaac, I—"

His hand shot up. "Don't say another word, Marc."

"But—"

"I don't want to hear anything yet!" He pointed in the direction of our bedroom. "Just, please . . . Go take a shower, change into something clean, then grab our bags and meet me at my car. I've packed everything—for our trip."

Feeling disoriented, I glanced around the room at I don't know what, eventually meeting his eyes again. There was a fire in them that told me he was beyond angry, furious in fact, which clashed terrifyingly with his ice-calm demeanor.

"I can't just take off like that," I blurted out. "I have a deposition to conduct."

"A deposition. Right."

"It's scheduled for ten—"

"You're in no condition to conduct a goddamn deposition, Marc. I spoke with Ed last night. Everything's arranged."

"You called him?"

"Yes, I did. And Phoebe agreed to drop by every other day to look in on Nilo." He rose from the chair and brushed past me. "Now, please shut up and do as I say."

We drove south on the 101, Isaac in the driver's seat of his car, stone-faced, and me staring out the window through raw eyes at the passing water and hills. The eastern sky was lightening over the bay, minute by minute sharpening everything into a painful bas-relief. I put on a pair of dark sunglasses to deflect the glare and closed my eyes. We rode in near silence, broken only by the sound of the radio tuned to some random, staticky twenty-four-hour news station. We spoke only when necessary, when we stopped for gas or when Isaac asked for a bottle of water or something to eat.

As we sped past San Jose, I gave in to an incongruous urge to run my fingers through his hair. He jerked away the moment my fingers touched his head. I withdrew my hand and settled for studying him, focusing for the first time in ages on his masculine, Asian good looks.

I was overcome by a sudden stirring of sadness and guilt. How could I have allowed myself to get so badly sidetracked when the government was threatening to send away my beloved longtime companion, to ban him from his home, his lover, and the life he'd been building for over a decade?

As if reading my thoughts, Isaac glanced at me. His gaze froze at my neck, and he pulled the car onto the shoulder. "Where's the pendant?" he asked.

I felt for the chain, and my heart halted for an instant. It was gone. "He must have slipped it off without my noticing."

Isaac slapped the steering wheel. "That motherfucker!" He spun on me. "How could you let that happen, Marc?"

"I'm sorry." I lowered my head into my hands and sobbed. "I'm so sorry! I'm such a fucking idiot."

I remained in that position, unable to move, crying myself into exhaustion. At one point, I heard the door open, but I didn't dare look up for fear that Isaac had abandoned the car and left me alone by the side of the freeway with rush hour traffic whizzing by. But the door slammed shut again a few minutes later, and I risked a glance in its direction. Isaac had grabbed a sweater out of the trunk and was staring straight ahead, unblinking.

"Are you done?" he asked.

I nodded. "I'm sorry."

Isaac shifted in my direction and stared hard at me. He'd been crying, too. "Do you want to fix this, Marc?"

"I do," I responded, my voice barely audible.

"Then you have to fix yourself. *And* we have to fix us. That fucker is just the symptom of what's gone wrong, with you, with us."

"More with me."

Isaac waved away my comment. "We've *both* been under a lot of pressure for a few months now. You with work. Me with this whole immigration thing and with my mother's passing." He swiped away the tears that now streamed down his cheeks. "Before all of that, everything was fine . . ."

I grabbed his hand. "I'm really sorry, Isaac, for all the pain my stupidity has caused you."

"Me too," he said.

His tone frightened me. There was no denying we were in two separate boats on a calm and airless sea, slowly drifting away from each other. I loved Isaac. Despite all that had happened, I loved him and was sure he felt the same.

Isaac drew back his hand. "It may sound strange and maybe even sort of silly and dysfunctional, Marc, but you're my life. You've been everything for me for the last six years. Even when my mother lived with us, no matter how close I was to her, it was always *you* I looked forward to seeing at the end of each day. Her too, of course. I adored her; you know that. But you're my partner, my lover—for life. I decided that a long time ago. Even after everything that has happened, and even if you are an ass sometimes, you're still the man I love and always will love. That's why this trip is important. Let's focus on ourselves first. After that, once we're both in a better mental space, we'll deal with that other thing—and with getting you sober again."

Chapter 20

We stopped for breakfast in Monterey and wordlessly strolled touristy Cannery Row. From there, we navigated the 17-Mile Drive along the coast through gnarled pines and California oaks into the beach city of Carmel-by-the-Sea, with its gingerbread cottages and art galleries.

After a quick picnic lunch eaten in morose silence, we continued on to Mission San Carlos Borromeo de Carmelo, where Father Junipero Serra, the founder of California's Spanish missions, is buried. Isaac drifted from my side and distracted himself, snapping picture after picture of the mission and its museum-style displays of eighteenth-century mission life. I waited for him in the cool of the mission cemetery, struggling against the recollection of the night before—feeling Silva all over me, inside me. I could still smell the scent of him on my skin. He had promised me sex like I'd never had before, and, true to his word, he'd more than delivered. The memory of it all aroused me, there among the beautifully maintained rosebushes, the fragrant honeysuckle, the dive-bombing swallows, and the ghosts of centuries' worth of Franciscan monks. Dipping into the restroom, I sought out a stall and took care of myself, immediately feeling like shit afterward and craving something potent to deaden the pain. I found Isaac leaning against the sink when I'd finished, his arms crossed tightly.

"Are you all right?" he asked as I soaped up my hands.

"Not really."

He shook his head. "Don't disappear like that, please." He tore a piece of paper towel from the dispenser and handed it to me. "You had me worried."

"Worried about what?"

"Please, Marc, let me know if you're going to move away from where I leave you. This isn't a good time for disappearing acts."

"You're right. Sorry." I tossed the used paper towel at the overflowing trash receptacle. "How did you find me, anyway?"

"When?"

"Last night?"

"I was worried, and I went looking for you. You weren't at the hotel, so I called our cab company."

I nodded and exited the building with Isaac in tow.

I hoped this wasn't how it was going to be, with me pining after Silva and Isaac policing my every movement. But it was still early days. Silva was like any other addiction; the drug had been removed, and I needed time and space to recover and seek some professional intervention. I'd been here before.

We reached Big Sur just as the sun dipped below the horizon, and twilight tortured the sky from blue to orange to blood red and black, and, ultimately, to a lingering electric blue. Overwhelmed by the beauty of the fading day, Isaac and I called a truce and joined arms at the edge of a precipice, waiting for the stars to come out. I pulled him close and savored the sensation of his body against mine in that moment of calm, under the infinity of the darkening sky, contemplating the vast, wave-spackled Pacific. Isaac rested his head against my shoulder. He was crying.

Twilight gave way to the star-splashed black of a moonless

night, and the evening turned cold. Isaac was on the point of collapsing from heartache and lack of sleep, and I was still strung out from the night before. We were both in desperate need of a comfortable bed into which we could sink and surrender our consciousness. Tearing ourselves away from that idyllic setting, we trudged back to Isaac's car.

Not five minutes later, we came across a collection of chic cottages nestled in a large stand of coastal redwoods off the main highway. Isaac dozed in the car while I went into the office and negotiated for the single remaining vacancy—an overpriced two-bedroom chalet with a private hot tub. Forced to settle at nine hundred seventy-five a night, I exited the office, key in hand, and knocked on the passenger side window. Isaac opened one eye and regarded me for a beat, then popped out of the car on wobbly legs and followed me, his eyes half closed, up the stone path and into the cottage. Inside, it looked more like a rustic bungalow than anything worth a grand. I went into the bathroom to inspect the so-called hot tub and when I returned, I found Isaac on the still-made king-size bed, fully clothed and snoring.

I sighed, slipped out of my clothes, and retired to the tub to float in the almost-too-hot water. After a few relaxing minutes, the image of Silva seeped back into my mind, provoked by the lapping of the water against my bare skin. Before it could take hold, I called up the memory of a late autumn hike in the Arava desert with Simon, of our stumbling across an isolated oasis where we stripped naked, bathed in a cold spring, fantasized about the future, and made love for hours. It was one of the happiest days of my life. In the face of that memory, Silva's image dissipated like a fading mirage, and my heart rate returned to near normal.

Right about the time my fingers were pruning up, I lifted myself out of the tub, toweled off, and wandered back to the bedroom where Isaac was sleeping. He was spread-eagled vertically across the entire bed and still snoring. I kissed him on the cheek, padded over to the second bedroom, and slipped under the covers, passing out the moment I felt the soft feather pillow against my face.

A hot slash of sunlight across my face awakened me the following morning as it streamed in through the parted wooden blinds. Pulling the pillow over my head, I buried my face in the mattress. I remained that way for a few minutes and must have fallen asleep because the next thing I was aware of was the sensation of a new weight on the bed as it sunk to the right. I peeked out from under the pillow and found Isaac gazing at me, expressionless. He was wearing one of the suite's complimentary velour bathrobes and clasping a cup of tea with both hands.

"Good morning," I croaked. "How'd you sleep?"

"Like the dead." He squinted up at the exposed wood beam ceiling. "This place is wild. How much did it cost?"

I sat up and took a sip of his tea, holding it in my mouth a couple seconds before swallowing it. "You don't want to know."

"No, really, how much? And why did we have to get such a big place?"

As I opened my mouth to respond, my cell phone started to chirp on the dresser.

"Don't answer that," Isaac said as I reached for it.

My hand hovered in the air. "He doesn't have my number."

"I didn't say he did."

"It might be the office."

"I told you I took care of that. Just leave it. You're not available."

I eyed the phone as it chirped a few more times before falling silent, then I switched it off and tossed it in the drawer. After a couple of beats, I turned back to Isaac. "This cottage was all they had, and I didn't feel like driving around aimlessly in the dark."

Isaac nodded. "Want some tea?"

"Coffee, please."

Once I finished my coffee, Isaac grudgingly allowed me to lead him into the bathroom, where we showered together for the first time in ages. I'd forgotten how enjoyable it was to have my body soaped up and scrubbed by somebody else. I returned the favor, and Isaac soon warmed up to the gesture. We scrubbed clean every inch of exposed and semi-exposed flesh, then spent the rest of the time making out like a couple of high school kids underneath the steady, intense water pressure.

But the moment of forced romance was short-lived. Isaac gave me his back as he toweled off, and we dressed in silence, in opposite corners of the room. His aloofness was all the more painful so soon after the intimacy of our shower. I was desperate to try anything to salvage whatever could be salvaged. So I took a gamble; I cleared my throat, preparing to speak, and Isaac glanced at me.

"What is it?" he asked. The sharpness in his voice sliced into me.

"Phoebe wanted me to talk to you about something."

He shot me a questioning look. "When did you talk to Phoebe?"

"I mean that first night she came over."

Isaac arched an eyebrow and bent over to lace up his shoes.

"Do you remember when I stepped into the hallway with her?" I asked.

"Yeah, I do." He straightened up and shouldered his bag, readying himself to go. "What about it?"

"She thinks we should explore the possibility of emigrating to another country."

Isaac's face twisted in exasperation. "Marc, this isn't the time to be talking about that. You're fucking *using* again; I only *just* rescued you from some kind of chemsex orgy organized by your new fuck buddy! In what world do you think it's okay for us to be planning for the future?"

"Isaac, please! I don't blame you for being angry. But it doesn't help to have you rubbing my face in it. I'll get help with the addiction stuff as soon as we get to LA, I *promise*. It was just a stupid lapse, and it won't ever happen again, I swear it. But we can't afford to put off dealing with our immigration issue because of what happened last night. Time is passing, and we have decisions to make—together."

Isaac shook his head and let his bag drop to the floor. "What exactly do you mean you'll get help with the addiction stuff?"

"I'll call NA and find out where I can go for a meeting."

"No meetings, Marc. You've just had a major relapse! You're going back to rehab."

"I don't need rehab, Isaac. I've got this. I've just got to go back to the meetings and work through the steps again."

"But—"

"I'm absolutely not going back to rehab, Isaac!"

"Fine, but you're not waiting until we get to LA to deal with this." He dug his cell phone out of his pocket and tossed it at me. "Call NA *now* and find out when and where you can go to a meeting once we get to the city. The sooner, the better. And I'm going with you this time."

"Okay, okay, you can come with," I said. "But *first*, about what Phoebe said . . ."

Isaac crossed his arms. "She told me the same thing—about us leaving the United States."

"She did? When?"

"The same night she told you. And again on the telephone a couple of times."

"Why didn't you say anything?" I asked.

"Because I didn't think you'd be interested in leaving."

"You mean *you* are?"

Isaac turned away for a moment and swallowed hard. "Not

by myself. I mean, I might have considered it *if* we were going together. But that was all pre-*that guy*." He looked back at me with hard eyes. "Things are different now."

"Forget him! Of course, we'd go together. I told you I was willing to go with you to El Salvador if it was necessary, didn't I?"

"Marc, be serious. Would you really want to leave the country where you were born, where your career and your friends and family are?"

"It's not that I'd necessarily *want* to. But—"

He shook his head and frowned. "Fine, then I guess we'll just fight the case all the way up to the goddamn fucking US Supreme Court if we have to, and then see what happens."

"I don't want to wait ten years only to find out we have to leave."

"So then, what?"

"We should explore all our options, including leaving the country if we have to, while we're still young enough to make a new life elsewhere."

Isaac lowered himself onto a chair. "Are you sure you want to do that?"

"It won't hurt to make inquiries. I'd like to talk to my father about it, too. I'd like his opinion if that's all right with you."

"Sure, why not? We'll *both* talk to him."

"Good, so then we're agreed," I said, feeling a bit lighter. "I was thinking we might check out England or Australia."

Isaac shook his head. "I think we should go to Canada."

"Why Canada?"

"Lots of reasons. I know some people from back home who moved there during the civil war; they love it. Also, it's a socially progressive country—"

"I don't know. I've always thought of it as cold and boring."

"You've never been there, so—"

"No, but—" I interjected.

"So how could you know?"

"No, you're right, but don't you think England, or Australia, or even New Zealand would be more interesting places to live?"

"Australia and New Zealand are too far away from everything. And as for England, I don't know. I don't want to have to learn a whole other way of speaking English. But I guess we could check it out."

"So we'll check it out. But you've got to keep an open mind."

Isaac stood up. "So do you."

"I will."

"Good! Now stop stalling and make that call."

Chapter 21

After a quick breakfast, we roared back onto the highway and drove six hours nonstop down the coast and into Los Angeles, which was in the throes of an autumn heat wave. At three in the afternoon, we pulled onto my parents' street. The neighborhood looked as lifeless as a studio backlot as it baked under the cruel Southern California sun, flaring high in a cloudless expanse.

The sprinklers in the front yard were turned on, full strength, and a muddy stream of runoff flowed into the parched gutter and down the street on its way to the ocean, which I found odd. We got out of the car and navigated our way up the walkway. Trying to reach the front door without getting wet was like running an obstacle course. Isaac sprinted past me and accidentally knocked me onto the soggy lawn as he hopped onto the front porch.

"Hey, watch it," I said as I reached the porch and shook the water out of my hair.

He jammed his finger into the doorbell.

"Hang on a second! I want to surprise them." I held up the key.

The front door swung open to reveal my mother in a cornflower blue housedress and headscarf, looking paler and thinner than the last time I'd seen her. She stood behind the screen door in the darkened foyer and blinked at us in the glare of the afternoon sun.

"May I help you?" she asked.

"Ima, it's me," I said.

She squinted at me through the screen. "Marc?"

"Yes, Ima." I traded a look with Isaac. "Isaac's here, too."

"Hello, Mrs. Mendes." Isaac raised his hand, his face crinkled with concern.

"I'm sorry, boys. I'm a little under the weather today." She unlocked the screen door and let us into the air-conditioned house.

Draping my arm around her shoulders, I shepherded her down the long hallway to the family room. We sat next to each other on the sofa. Isaac remained standing to one side, nervously looking around the room.

"Isaac, dear, please sit," my mother said, indicating a side chair.

Isaac nodded and lowered himself into the chair and stared at us.

"Ima, what's wrong?" I asked, gently stroking her arm.

"I'm just feeling a little low, *hijo*. Nothing to worry about." She brushed my face with the back of her hand. Then, as if suddenly remembering something, she asked. "Why are you here, Marc? We weren't expecting you, were we?"

"It's nothing important, Mrs. Mendes," Isaac interjected. "We were just passing through."

"No, Isaac," I said. "Ima, Isaac and I have something we need to discuss with Abba." I nodded at Isaac, and he frowned at me.

"Your father's at the *esnoga*," she said. "He should be home soon." She paused a moment and gazed at my face, looking first at my eyes, moving up to my forehead, then back down to my mouth, as if she were looking at me through a smoky haze.

"What is it, Ima?"

"What's happened, Marc?" she asked softly.

"Nothing, Ima. We just need to speak with Abba."

She shook her head and looked at Isaac. "I know my son.

Something's not right. I can see it in his eyes." She took my hand and looked back at me.

"Marc's using again, Mrs. Mendes," Isaac said flatly.

"Isaac!" I shouted.

"I'm not carrying this alone, Marc!" he said, crossing his arms. "Your family needs to know, too."

My mother pulled back her hands and stood up, a frightened look clouding her face. I jumped to my feet and reached for her, but she backed away.

"Ima, please . . ."

We were startled by the sound of the front door closing, followed by heavy footsteps moving in our direction. A moment later, my father appeared at the entrance to the family room. He regarded each of us in turn with a stern expression.

"Hannah," he said to my mother, "what is this?"

"Hello, Rabbi," Isaac said, rising out of the side chair.

"Abba." I moved toward him and was stopped in my tracks by his upheld hand.

"Hannah," he repeated, "what's happened?"

"Your son is using drugs again," she said, her voice edged with disappointment and anger. "Isaac just told me."

My father stared hard at me for a beat. "Is this true, Marc?"

"Abba, I . . ." I shook my head and dropped my gaze.

"Look at me, please," he said.

I looked back up at him; Isaac moved to my side and put his hand on my shoulder. I resisted the urge to shake him off.

"It was just a slip, Abba, a couple of nights ago. But I'm going to be getting help." I prayed Isaac wouldn't dare mention anything to my parents about Silva or the Transformer Club.

"We'll be attending some NA meetings while we're here, Rabbi," Isaac said. "I'll make sure he keeps up with them when we get back to San Francisco."

My father nodded. He looked at Isaac as if for the first time. "Hello, Isaac."

"I'm glad to see you again, sir," Isaac replied.

My father offered him a polite smile, then turned to me and became serious again. "Marc, please go to my study. I'd like to speak with you alone." He approached my mother and kissed her. "Why don't you rest awhile, Hannah."

"I've been resting the whole day," she snapped. "I've got things to look at in the kitchen. Isaac can help me if he wishes."

"Of course, Mrs. Mendes," Isaac said.

As they moved past, I squeezed my mother's arm. She kept walking without acknowledging my touch. Noting her indifference, my father raised his eyebrows at me and pointed in the direction of his study.

"What's wrong with Ima, Abba?" I asked once we were behind the closed doors of his study.

He pointed at one of the two guest chairs in front of his desk and sat in the other.

I stared at my chair for a moment, preparing for one of his interrogations, then lowered myself into it, determined to maintain control.

"Your mother's been feeling deeply nostalgic about Cuba," he said quietly. "I'm sure it will pass."

"I'm sorry, Abba; we didn't know."

"No, of course. How could you know?" There was a hint of reproach in his voice. "I'm sure her state of mind wasn't helped by your unexpected and unpleasant disclosure."

"Isaac had no right to alarm Ima," I retorted. "It surprised me as much as it did her."

He pulled on his beard and studied me with a serene expression. "Why would your partner tell your mother about your relapse without your consent?"

"There's a lot going on between Isaac and me right now, Abba. Things of a personal nature. To be honest, we're struggling as a couple. To make matters worse, I'm being pressed to my limits at work. I'm this close to calling it quits. It's a miracle

I didn't start using again before this. But, God willing, I'll get things back under control, I promise."

My father searched my face, trying to make sense of what I'd told him. After a moment, he leaned forward and snatched up my hands. "Let's take this one thing at a time, shall we?"

"Yes, Abba, fine. Whatever you want."

"You can start by telling me why the two of you are here in Los Angeles unannounced in the middle of the week at four in the afternoon."

We were interrupted by a soft rapping at the door. "Come in," my father said, without taking his eyes off me.

The door creaked open, and Isaac stuck his head into the room. "Is everything all right?" He looked first at my father, then at me.

My father offered him a warm but guarded smile. "Come in, Isaac, please join us." He moved behind his desk and offered Isaac the chair next to me.

Isaac thanked him and sat down.

"Marc and I were discussing the reason for your visit today," my father said.

Isaac frowned at me. "You told him about Canada?"

What came to my mind was: *Oh, shit!* What I actually said was: "No!"

"Canada?" my father said. His heavy eyebrows crashed into each other at the bridge of his nose.

"Yes, we—" Isaac started.

"No, wait." I held up my hand. Isaac moved my arm aside and shook his head.

"What's going on here?" my father asked. "Isaac says Canada, you say no . . .?"

"Abba," I tossed a sidelong glance at Isaac, "it looks as if Isaac and I may not be able to remain in the United States. Where we'll end up, only God knows. But it seems his immigration status here is in danger of being revoked. That's what we came to talk to you about."

My father slowly pushed away from his desk and regarded the two of us as if from a distance. "Why is his status in danger of being revoked?" He turned to Isaac. "Are you in trouble with the law?"

"No, sir. I mean, I haven't committed a crime or anything like that."

"Then what is the issue?"

Stepping in, I spent the next few minutes explaining Isaac's immigration issues to my father. He listened quietly, stopping me every now and then when he needed clarification. When I got to the part about the lengthy appeal process, he raised his palm, nodded, and closed his eyes. He remained that way for a couple of minutes, rocking back and forth in his chair ever so slightly. I wasn't sure whether he was dozing or praying.

I looked over at Isaac. He was watching my father with a curious, expectant expression. After a moment, he looked at me and cocked his head in my father's direction with a look that clearly meant: *What's wrong with him?* I shrugged, closed my own eyes, and waited. Then I felt Isaac tap the back of my hand with warm fingers. I opened my eyes to find my father staring at me from across his desk, a troubled expression spoiling his face. He shook his head sadly. "I understand," he said. "It begins all over again."

"What does, Abba?"

"The leaving, the fleeing. When will it end?" His eyes glistened with emotion. "Do you realize," he said, looking now at Isaac, "that in all its recorded history, this family has never been able to successfully settle anywhere?"

"Yes," Isaac nodded, "but because of religious persecution, right?"

"Religious, racial, political; if it isn't one reason, it's another. My point is it never ends: our ancestors, my grandfather, my father, me, and now my son."

224

"Abba," I said, "we *could* try to fight it all the way up the appellate ladder. That would at least buy us a few years. Maybe by then, the law will have changed."

"Given the circumstances," my father said, after another thoughtful pause, "I suppose you must go. It doesn't make sense to sit around for years, hoping for a positive result when you could be starting again somewhere else where you're more welcome. It certainly wouldn't be the first time someone in our family was forced to emigrate. I don't expect it will be the last."

We all sat quietly for a while. I could hear a faint stirring in the foyer beyond the door and wondered whether I should call my mother into the room.

"You mentioned Canada," my father said after a moment.

"I'm interested in Canada," Isaac confirmed. "Marc's in favor of England or Australia."

"Or Spain," I added.

"Spain, right," Isaac said, rolling his eyes.

"There's a thriving Sephardi community in Montreal," my father offered. "Do you remember Daniel Abecassis and his family? They moved to Montreal."

I paused for a moment. "I remember them, yes."

"I could put you in touch with them."

"We want to keep our options open at this point, Abba." I shifted position in my chair. "After all, we're still kicking around ideas. We don't know which countries would even accept us, if any."

My father sat back and nodded. Isaac shrugged and glanced at his watch.

"Will you tell Ima?" I asked. My stomach was starting to growl.

"No, you will." My father stood and stretched. He looked tired and a little sad. "Stay for dinner. I'll call your brother."

"Thank you, Abba." I looked at Isaac; he smiled noncommittally. "I'll call Jacob if that's all right."

My father came around the desk and kissed my forehead. "It seems you forgot something." He drew a black felt kipa from his coat pocket and placed it on my head.

"I'll take one too, please." Isaac held out his hand, his face serious, holding his emotions in check.

My father smiled and produced another kipa and pressed it into Isaac's hand. "Thank you, young man."

I could sense genuine affection emanating from my father toward Isaac. It was a wonder to me how he'd managed to win over my family in such a short time. I was still contemplating this as my father opened the door and revealed my mother sitting on the staircase outside the study. Her face was impassive.

"Hannah . . ." my father said, placing his hand on her shoulder.

"I think they should go to Canada," she stated, in a tone calculated to carry into the study.

"There, you see," Isaac said, a bit too cheerily for my liking. "Now we're all agreed."

Alarmed at how quickly critical decisions were being made, I sped to the doorway. "Ima, I—"

"Spare yourself the explanations, dear," she said. "I heard it all. I agree with your father. You should call Daniel Abecassis. You remember his eldest daughter Noga, don't you? She also went into law. She graduated from McGill University two years ago. *Summa cum laude*, her mother tells me. Now she's working in Ottawa for the federal government."

"I'm happy to hear it."

"I'm sure Noga would love to show you around Montreal and Ottawa. You two have so much in common."

I suppressed any further comment. It wasn't worth an argument with my poor parents, who were shocked enough by the news their addict son was using again and might have to leave the country. They were just doing their best to cope with the situation in their way.

"In any case," my father said, breaking the tension, "while you contemplate that, please bring in your things from the car. You'll sleep in your old room, and we'll prepare the guest room for Isaac."

Chapter 22

A loud pounding on my bedroom door shocked me out of a deep, dreamless sleep. Instinctively, I flung my arm over to Isaac's side of the bed and was startled to find it empty. The knocking continued.

"Yes? What is it?" I rubbed my eyes and cast about the room, trying to score my bearings.

"Someone from your office is calling," came my mother's muffled voice.

I shook my head to clear it, then wrapped a sheet around myself, plodded up to the door, and opened it a crack.

"I'm sorry, what?"

"He said it's urgent." My mother pointed at the telephone on the nightstand.

"Who's *he*, Ima?"

She shook her head. "I didn't get his name. But it sounds important. Come down for dinner afterward. Your brother and Margalit are here already."

I rubbed my eyes and suppressed a yawn with the back of my hand. "What time is it?"

"You've been napping for three hours. Now, please hurry. We're all waiting for you."

I shut the door, dragged myself over to the nightstand, and picked up the phone.

"Hello . . . Marc?" Alejandro Silva's voice pulsed out of the receiver and electrified me into full consciousness.

I could hear someone breathing on the extension. "I've got it, Ima," I said, sitting bolt upright. A moment later, the phone went *click*.

"Hello?" Silva repeated.

"How did you get this number, Alejandro?" I asked, preparing for a confrontation. "Why did you say you were calling from my office?"

"Don't be angry, Marc. I was worried! They hadn't seen you for a couple of days at your work. And your cell phone is disconnected. Is everything okay?"

"Who gave you this number?" I growled.

In that instant, the bedroom door groaned open, and Isaac looked inside. He raised his head at me. I covered the receiver and mouthed, "It's Silva."

Isaac's eyes sprung wide. "What the fuck?" he whispered, pushing the door closed. He sat next to me and put his ear to the receiver.

"Who gave you this number?" I repeated.

"I asked around," Silva said. "When are you coming back?"

"Don't call here again." I was trying my best to control my shaking voice.

"But I need to talk to you!"

"Find someone else to talk to, Alejandro. I'm *not* available."

"You were available the other night," he snapped, a note of anger creeping into his voice.

I glanced at Isaac and shook my head.

"Have you told *him* yet?" Alejandro asked as if sensing Isaac's presence. "Have you told your boyfriend everything I did to you? How you couldn't get enough?"

Isaac pulled away, his eyes aflame, his fists clenched tight.

"I've told him everything," I said, locking eyes with Isaac.

"And he's okay with that?" Silva spat out. "What a fucking

pendejo! I wouldn't be!"

"Alejandro, for God's sake, I'm at my parents' house. Have some respect, please! We'll be back in San Francisco in a week or two. Whatever you have to say can wait until then."

There was a loud crash at the other end of the line, and it went dead. I hung up and looked at Isaac, who was stomping about the room.

"The guy's totally obsessed," I muttered.

"Why did you tell him when we'd be back?" he said, swinging on me. "You left the door open!"

"It was the only way to end the conversation without an escalation, sorry. I don't want him showing up here and making a scene in front of my parents. I wouldn't be able to bear that."

"How did he know you were here?"

"I have no idea," I said, slipping into my clothes. "But I'm sure as hell going to find out."

As we descended the stairs, Jacob was walking through the front door in a black T-shirt, blue jeans, and flip flops, carrying a ceramic bowl covered in foil.

When I greeted him, he held the bowl out to me, avoiding eye contact. "Take this into the kitchen, please. I've got to bring in a couple more things from the car."

"What is it?" I took the bowl and dropped it on the console with a gasp. "This is hot!"

"Margalit whipped up some black beans. I've got the rice maker out in the car. Be right back." He turned to run back out the door.

"Hang on a second, Jake," I called.

He halted and turned around, his strained smile melting away. He glanced at Isaac, then back at me. "Come outside."

Isaac grabbed the bowl off the console. "I'll take the beans into the kitchen. You guys can have your privacy." His voice was bitter; he was obviously still smarting from my telephone call with Silva.

Jacob waited until Isaac had vanished down the hallway, then pulled me onto the porch and closed the front door.

"How long has this deportation thing been going on?" he asked. "And when were you planning on telling me?"

"We received the notice in April."

"That's nearly four months ago, and you're only now saying anything?"

I shook my head in frustration. "I'm sorry, Jake, but I was handling it."

"What do you mean you were handling it? We're talking about a potentially transformative event, and yet you waited four months to mention it to anyone in your own family?"

"I didn't want to disappoint Abba! You know how difficult it was for him to leave his own country and start all over again here. And now that he's settled, can you imagine him being told his son might have to expatriate . . . for the love of another man?"

Jacob shook his head. "You talk about him as if he were a child. He's used to these things. People move away. *He* did it, leaving a whole slew of relatives behind. He can't even visit the graves of his own parents now."

"I don't know what else to say, Jake. I'm doing my best. The last thing I need is to have you mad at me, too."

I sank onto the top step and lowered my head to my knees. After a moment, he sat next to me.

"Hey, I'm sorry," he said, rubbing my back. "I didn't mean to sound so harsh. I was just shocked to find out about it from Abba and Ima instead of from you."

I straightened up and stared into the darkness. "No, you're right," I said, "I *should've* told you. I didn't mean to shut you out."

I could feel him closely reading my face in the amber glow of the porch light. "How are *you* holding up these days?" he asked after a long pause. "Besides Isaac's immigration thing?"

"Not great, to be honest."

"You haven't fallen off the wagon, have you?"

I shifted my gaze evasively. I wasn't ready to own it with him. Not yet.

"Hey," he said gently, "It's just you and me here. Open up."

"I don't know . . ." I lowered my eyes. "Maybe . . ."

"Maybe *no* or maybe *yes*?"

I glanced at the front door and back at him. "Yes, a couple of nights ago. Isaac told Ima and Abba."

"Oh, fuck," he whispered. "Why would he do that?"

I shrugged. "Just some trouble in paradise, that's all. We talked it out with Abba. We'll be dealing with it together, Isaac and me. Everything's under control."

He touched my knee, which was an unusually intimate gesture for him. "Are you sure?"

"Yes, one hundred percent. We'll be okay."

Jacob drew back his hand, and we fell silent again. The sound of heavy cross traffic two blocks away on Third Street wafted over the neighborhood.

"He seems good for you, you know," he said. "Isaac, I mean. Despite all your ups and downs as a couple."

"He is," I replied, a lump forming in my throat as I said it.

Sensing the weight of the emotion behind my words, Jacob placed his hand on my knee again.

"I haven't seen you so yourself around *anyone* since . . . well, since Simon Perelis."

His words brought with them a wave of nausea. It was ages since I'd heard *that name* outside of my dreams and lost moments; nobody within the family had dared speak about him in my presence in over fifteen years.

"What?" I gasped, the question barely escaping my lips.

"Well, they're nothing alike, obviously. Plus, Isaac's more than a friend, I get that. But I remember how happy you always seemed when you were in Simon's company." He paused awkwardly when he saw my face crumple. "Sorry, I . . . I didn't mean to bring him up. It's just that I know you two were close before . . . You know—before what happened in Israel."

"Stop . . . Jake, please . . ." It was all I could get out before I broke into tears. I pivoted away and struggled to pull myself together.

He pulled me close and hung an arm over my shoulder. "Hey, hey, I'm sorry . . . I didn't . . ."

Despite myself, I buried my face in his neck and held him tight. We sat like that for a few moments until I regained my composure and finally let go.

"I'm sorry," I said, my voice hoarse with emotion. "It was just a shock—your mentioning him out of the blue."

Jacob studied me in the silence that followed. Then, tilting his head to one side, he opened his mouth to say something but thought the better of it.

"What?" I asked.

"Nothing . . . I just . . ." He held my gaze the way only he knew how. "I mean, we don't have to talk about it if you don't want, but . . . was there something . . . you know . . . something sexual going on between you two?"

His question hung in the air a moment. I looked down at my feet. There was no sense in hiding the fact anymore. "Yeah. There was."

"Right." Jacob tugged at his beard. "That would explain why you followed him to Israel . . ."

"I didn't follow him!" I corrected. "If you remember, I was going there anyway. It was Ima and Simon's mom who came up with the idea that Lisa and I should go to the same kibbutz he was at."

Jacob squinted into the darkness, puzzling out the details, making connections.

"So . . . did it start over there . . . or before?"

I shook my head and looked away, confirming his suspicions with my silence.

"Right . . ." he said to himself. "So, all those times you went to the Perelises to visit Lisa, to do homework, to run errands for Ima, you were really just getting together with him?"

I remained silent, wishing I could sink into the doorstep.

"But . . . you couldn't have been much more than fourteen. Simon was—"

"I was thirteen when it started, Jake," I admitted, wishing he would stop with the questions. "It lasted a couple of years, then he took off to Israel. End of story."

"Thirteen . . .?" Jacob cocked his head to one side. "And did you get back together with him when you went to Israel?"

I crossed my arms and held myself tight. "I don't want to talk about this, Jake."

Jacob nodded and looked away, processing what I'd just confessed. After a beat, he turned back and stared me down. "What really happened in Israel, Marc?" he pressed in a low voice.

"You *know* what happened," I whispered.

"I mean *before* the accident. More of the same?"

"Yes, Jake, flipping more of the same. We hooked up again, and the rest is history: Israel, him, the desert, the accident—all of it made me the mess I am today."

He nodded pensively. "It all makes sense now. I remember when Abba brought you back. You were—you'd changed."

"I'm serious, Jake; can we move on, please? My present and future are complicated enough. Dredging up ancient history, especially that history, doesn't help things."

Jacob held up his hand. "Okay, all right, I get it."

"And I'd prefer if we never talked about those things again if that's all right."

"Fine, we won't talk about them again." He put his hand on my shoulder. "I'm sorry for prying, Marc. You know I'm not that way normally."

He squeezed my arm, and we fell silent. After a long pause, he glanced at his watch. "We'd better get back in there before Ima kills us." He stood and pulled me up by the hand, and I drew him close and hugged him.

Isaac and I spent a few more days with my parents. Those were days brimming with Mendes family dynamics: the endless cycle of discussions, debates, and pregnant silences—days lacking in any kind of privacy for Isaac and me, save for the couple of hours each day when we broke away to attend NA meetings. The saving grace of all this activity was that the subject of Silva faded into the background, which afforded Isaac and me time to recover some semblance of normality.

At the end of it all, I was thoroughly wrung out, as was everyone else. So it was a great relief, when the day finally arrived, to hug them all good-bye and get back on the road again—just Isaac and me. It was my turn to drive.

We headed for the great Anza-Borrego desert on our way to a star party Isaac had always wanted us to attend. The annual event was held in Borrego Springs, four hours southeast of Los Angeles. Hundreds of stargazers and their telescopes descended on the small town, which was well situated for a clear, unobstructed view of the night sky. It was meant to be a final distraction before we headed back to what awaited us in San Francisco.

We drove for a couple of hours before either of us made a sound any more significant than a monosyllabic grunt, both of us adrift in our thoughts. Isaac hardly blinked as he gazed out the window at the passing landscape.

As we rode past San Onofre, he turned to me and said, "Let's skip the star party."

"You don't want to go?" I asked.

"Let's still go to the desert, but we can have our own star party." He was looking in my direction, but his eyes were seeing past me. "I don't feel like being around crowds of people right now. Why not just us and the stars? Like that time in Napa."

"Sure. Any place in particular you want to go?"

"Keep driving to Anza, but when we reach Borrego Springs, keep right on going for about another half hour. Then we'll stop, right smack in the middle of nowhere." He flashed a sober grin.

I wasn't a fan of the deep desert at night; in fact, it terrified me. But this was his gig, and I didn't want to be the cause of any more disappointment.

"Anza it is," I said, stepping on the gas.

The sun was reddening the cliffs as we rounded the Yaqui Pass and began our descent to the desert floor. We drove with the windows rolled all the way down and bathed in the accumulated heat of the day, radiating off the ochre and black volcanic rocks. By the time we reached Borrego Springs, the desert had been plunged into the total darkness of a moonless night, and I broke into a hot sweat.

We gassed up at a service station and bought a couple of gallon jugs of water, some fruit, and a few granola bars. Ten minutes later, we shoved off again into the dark open desert, leaving the security of the town behind us.

After fifteen minutes of straight driving, the distance and the darkness absorbed and obliterated the town lights behind us. The only thing visible was the glow of our headlights as they splashed out on the empty black road ahead.

As we drove on, I was gripped by the familiar pangs of terror I'd first encountered deep in the Negev desert. I glanced over at Isaac, his face softly illuminated by the blue-green glow of the dashboard. He was peering into the blackness, his eyes a pair of dark horizontal slits.

"Pull over," he said, his voice pregnant with wonder.

"Are we there yet?" I croaked.

"Just pull over, please."

I checked my mirrors and guided the car onto the shoulder, narrowly avoiding a side-slide into the sand.

"Turn off the headlights," he instructed.

"Why? It's dark out there."

He shifted around in his seat to look at me; I was startled by the excitement pulsating on his face.

"There's more light out there than you think," he said.

I sat without moving, torn between my increasing dread and the urge to comply. Isaac released an exasperated sigh, reached across my body, and snapped off the headlights. The instant the lights went out, I squeezed my eyes shut against the dark, in danger of hyperventilating. At the same time, I felt the passenger door spring open. A rush of cool air rustled my hair.

"Oh, Jesus!" came Isaac's voice from outside. "This is freaking amazing."

Still clutching the steering wheel, I opened one eye and gave myself a few seconds to adjust to the low light before opening the other one. Just as my heartbeat was settling, Isaac flew past the hood, leaping and dancing, illuminated by a delicate silver glow bathing the landscape.

"What are you doing?" I called out.

"Come out, Marc." A moment later, he disappeared from view. My heart missed a couple of beats as I shot across the seat to the passenger door. Isaac was lying on his back in the sand, his teeth glowing white in a wide grin. "Come out here." He pointed at the sky. "It's beautiful."

I looked up at the canopy of cold, hard stars stretched out overhead and looked back at Isaac. "I've seen it before."

"Not like this, you haven't."

"Exactly like this. In Israel. Hey, get off the ground, will you? You're liable to get stung by a scorpion."

He sat up and crossed his legs. "Why won't you come out here with me?"

"Because it makes me nervous."

Isaac stared at me for a moment and got to his feet. "I thought you loved the desert."

"I do love it, just not in the dead of night. Now come back inside!" I slid across the seat to the driver's side. Isaac climbed in and shut the door with a sigh.

"You told me you lived in the desert," he said.

"I lived on a kibbutz near the *edge* of the desert with other people. Not out in the goddamn empty wilderness like a fricking nomad."

"What do you mean? That's the best part, getting away from it all, breathing fresh air, treating your eyes to unobstructed views of the cosmos! Connecting with your inner self."

"Not for me, sorry."

"But why?" Isaac asked, frustration seeping into his voice.

I shook my head.

"Tell me," he insisted.

"I can't."

"Marc . . . if you can't tell me, then I don't know what we're doing here. I'm supposed to be your partner. We're not meant to keep secrets from each other. Otherwise, what's the point?"

I nodded. "I know, I know . . . It's just . . . it's so difficult . . ."

"Just say it!"

"Okay, fine! But, remember, you asked for it."

Isaac gripped my hand and waited.

I peered into the dark for a beat, then looked back at him. "I do love the desert. But some horrible shit happened to me there, too, Isaac—in Israel. I've never told *anyone*. I can't even bring myself to think about it. But just now, as we were driving, it all came flooding back. And it terrified me."

Isaac searched my face with a slight air of suspicion. "If it was as bad as that, you should have said something before, instead of letting me drag you all the way out here, don't you think?"

"I thought we were going to a star party surrounded by a

bunch of other people. You know, safety in numbers and all that. But when you changed your mind, I decided to try and tough it out."

Isaac rolled his eyes and ran a hand through his hair. "You give in to things too easily, Marc. It's why you're in the mess you're in."

I considered that for a moment. "I thought it was *our* mess."

Isaac shook his head and stared out at the landscape, lost in thought.

"Anyway," I said, switching the engine back on, "I'm feeling better now. Shall we continue?"

"It's up to you," Isaac muttered. "If you want to turn back, I won't complain."

"You had someplace in mind, right?"

"Yes, of course. It's farther down the road."

I switched on the headlights and coaxed the car back onto the highway. We covered several miles more of ruler-straight asphalt in total silence. The panicky feeling was coming on again, but I resolved to push it back as best as possible and keep driving. Just when I thought I was about to lose my mind, Isaac spoke up.

"Slow down; it's coming up on the left."

"How can you even tell where we are?"

"There it is!" He pointed left. "Turn off onto that dirt road."

I brought the car to a rolling stop and studied his face. "You're kidding, right?"

"No, really, turn off here."

I put the car in gear and swung it around to face down the dirt road he was pointing at. The headlights shone a few yards ahead, and all I could see was sand and scrub. I kicked on the high beams and saw more of the same.

"Go on," Isaac said, "drive."

"Please tell me where we're going, Isaac, or else I'm turning this car around."

"All right, it was meant to be a surprise, but I guess you're not going to let that happen. There are some caves about ten miles down the road."

"Some caves?"

"Yes. They're what's left of an old shale mining outfit. It's perfect. Far enough away from the road that we won't be disturbed by cars, and there's loads of level ground to set up my telescope and make ourselves a campfire. And in case we get a windstorm, we can sleep inside one of the caves. They're warm."

I blinked at him. "You're nuts, you know that?"

"It's a great place to search the skies. Don't be such a coward, Marc!"

I opened my mouth to protest, then thought the better of it, embarrassed into silence. Isaac was right; I *was* a coward. No one knew that better than him. But being something of a trained expert in faking confidence, I was determined to prove him wrong. So, taking a deep breath, I eased the car onto the dirt and inched ahead.

The road ended at a wall of rock. I turned off the engine and cut the headlights at Isaac's direction. He unloaded our gear, lugged it to a dark opening in the rock, and disappeared inside. I instinctively rolled up the windows and locked the doors. A moment later, a beam of light shot out of the opening, and Isaac emerged wielding a high-power flashlight. He crunched up to the side of the car and knocked on the window.

"You can come out now, scaredy-cat," came his muffled voice from the other side of the glass.

I opened the door and stepped outside. A cool, dry breeze blew across the level area in front of the caves, carrying with it the scent of sage and toasted grass.

"See," he said, "nothing to be afraid of. It's just us. I'm going to set up the telescope. You spread out the sleeping bags and build us a fire in that ring of stones over there."

"With what?"

"Never mind," Isaac said, a tint of exasperation coloring his voice. He finished extending the legs of his refractor and made a couple of adjustments in the viewfinder. "I'll build the fire; you set up the sleeping bags."

A few minutes later, we were huddled next to a crackling campfire, gazing into it, warming our hands. The telescope was sitting to one side, forlorn. Isaac had fallen silent, having lost his enthusiasm for stargazing. Every so often, the desert silence was broken by a distant howl or the unnerving hoot of an owl or something weird and nocturnal. A nearby screech drove me into Isaac's arms, and I held him tight as if my life depended on it. Startled, he pulled back a bit and crinkled his nose at me, his face reflecting the flickering light of the campfire.

"So tell me," he said finally. "What exactly happened to you in Israel?"

I should have expected the question, but it threw me nonetheless. Letting go of him, I wrapped my arms around myself and steadied my emotions.

"You've never talked about it with anyone?" he added in a gentler tone. "Not even with a therapist?"

"Not with anyone."

He moved closer and stroked my back. "Maybe it's time you let it out, whatever it is. It's obviously been eating you up inside." He picked a long stick out of the kindling. "There!" He pointed it at the flames. "Focus on the glowing center of the fire. Speak to *it*, not to me. Imagine it's the burning bush in the wilderness like in the Bible. That's God there. Tell him what happened."

"Very funny."

"You still believe in God, don't you?"

I shrugged. "We haven't been on speaking terms lately."

"All of that changes tonight." He jutted the stick at the fire. "Now, stop stalling, focus on the flames, and start talking."

I arched an eyebrow at him and examined his face, which was moist and glowing red.

"Just do it, Marc," he urged. "I guarantee you'll feel better."

A loud crackling erupted from the pit as the sticks and logs Isaac had used to build the campfire fell in on each other and sprayed sparks into the air. Taking that as my cue, I faced the flames while Isaac stoked the fire with a few more kindling sticks.

"Hello again, God," I said, half joking. "It's been a while."

Isaac faded back into the dark and, suddenly, it was just me and the flames.

"It's about Simon . . ." I drew out the name slowly, painfully. I clasped my trembling hands, took a calming breath, and tried it again. "Simon Perelis."

"Simon again?" Isaac said behind me. "Haven't we exhausted that subject?"

"I haven't told you everything," I said.

The flames sputtered and sparked, then settled into a steady crackle. I closed my eyes and plumbed deep.

"God, he was beautiful . . . black hair, hazel eyes, built like a brick shithouse, even as a teenager. I was completely infatuated with him, and he knew it . . ."

I opened my eyes and stared hard into the center of the flames.

"We were visiting his family for one of the Jewish festivals the day everything started. He lured me into the basement of their house. Nothing heavy at first, just kid's stuff. After that, it became a regular thing. For two whole years. When he turned eighteen, he left for Israel and never came back. That killed me."

I paused and watched a random spark rise skyward in a trail of smoke. It lingered there for a moment and vanished. Then I lowered my gaze again.

"It wasn't until Simon was gone that I realized I actually loved him, which was confusing for me at that age. I pined for him, miserably suffering, longing for the day I could see him again.

"When I graduated high school, I signed up to work on the

kibbutz where Simon lived. Kfar Kerem in the Negev Highlands. I ran into him the day of our orientation. The three years of our separation had agreed with him. There was a calm maturity that belied his twenty-one years, and I found myself more attracted to him than ever.

"At first, he was cold with me, unwilling to acknowledge the bond we'd shared and suspicious of my motivation for choosing his kibbutz. He warned me to keep my distance, but I kept seeking him out. I don't know . . . somehow, I felt he'd eventually give in or let down his guard . . . anything. But each time, he'd rebuff me, sometimes angrily, sometimes not. Just when I was about to give up hope, quit the kibbutz, and fuck off to some other part of the country, he found me, hunkered down alone one night in the community's baseball dugout . . ."

"Here you are," he said, sliding in next to me on the bench. I watched in disbelief as he kicked his feet onto the rail and leaned back, resting his head against his strong arms. He was dressed in a pair of tight blue jeans and an even tighter faded red T-shirt. There was a healthy glow about him that made me ache for him all the more.

Suspicious of his intentions and protective of my battered feelings, I tossed him a side glance and muttered, "I'm always here. What about it?"

Simon sat up and let out a chuckle. A lock of his neck-length hair fell across his right eye, and he flipped it back with a flick of his hand. "Lighten up, man. I'm trying to bury the hatchet with you." He scooted closer and reclined against me.

I slid away, glaring at him. "It's too late for that."

His smile faded, his face suddenly serious. "Come on, Marc."

"Come on, what?"

"This hasn't been easy for me either." He glanced around and lowered his voice. "Your showing up here took me by surprise, that's all." He reached over and tousled my hair, and I held steady. The touch of his hand was electric. "It's just taken me a while to get used to your being back in my life."

I raised my eyes and held his gaze for a few dizzying seconds; then, against my better inclinations, I slid toward him and allowed him to pull me into a long embrace. I breathed in the familiar scent of him—the warm smell of his skin, that heady mix of sandalwood and bergamot, a hint of tobacco. I held tight, feeling his warm breath on my neck, the press of his chest against mine. When he finally released me, I saw that his eyes were wet. He drew a breath and fixed me with his gaze. "I'm *really* sorry, man," he said, his voice hoarse with emotion. "For avoiding you. I can be a royal asshole sometimes."

I blinked at him, unable to formulate a response. I was still shocked by his sudden change. He responded by planting a lingering kiss on my mouth.

I pulled away from him. "What are you doing?"

Simon cocked his head. "That's what you wanted, wasn't it?"

"Yes, but—" I placed my hands on his shoulders and looked him in the eye, "—I don't get this 180-degree turn of yours. Yesterday you hated me; today, you're ready to get back together with me? It's freaky."

"I'm sorry for being such a dick. Seeing you again after so long . . . it was . . . I don't know. I thought I'd put all that shit behind me."

"Gee, thanks."

"It wasn't just about you, Marc. It was everything! Los Angeles, my parents, a bunch of serious crap you're not even aware of. I have my own story, you know." He pushed back against the bench, put up his legs again, and closed his eyes. "Being away from all that gave me the space to reinvent myself." He glanced at me. "Or so I thought."

"What do you mean *reinvent yourself*?"

Simon shook his head and stared into the blackness of the baseball field. "I thought maybe if I hung around with normal people and slept with a girl or two, I might forget I was ever into guys."

"Oh," I said, feeling suddenly nauseous at Simon's use of the word *normal* and at the thought of him with a woman. "How did *that* work out for you?"

Simon let out a humorless chuckle; then his face darkened. "Not very well. A few dates here and there, some random sex stuff. But nothing ever really changed inside. Still, though, I never gave up hope." He sat up, fished a joint out of his jeans, and sparked it, which caught me off guard. "And then you showed up." He took a long drag and held the joint out to me.

I pushed away his hand. "No, thanks. I don't do that. And neither did you, from what I recall."

He let out the smoke he was holding and pushed his hand at me. "Try it."

I shook my head.

"Go on," he said. "Trust me. It's quality stuff. It'll make you good and mellow. I can see you need it right now."

I crinkled my nose at the joint, then took it and tried a puff.

"Not like that!" He took it from me. "Draw the smoke deep into your lungs and hold it a few seconds, then let it out. Like this." He took another drag, then handed the joint back to me.

I mimicked him, spluttered a bit, then tried it again, managing to hold in the smoke for a longer spell the second time.

Simon took the joint out of my hand and pinched the end to extinguish it. "That's enough for your first time."

"I don't feel anything," I said.

"You will. Give it five minutes or so." He scooted closer, draping his leg over mine. "So, as I was saying, when you got here, all the old feelings came back. At first, I was shocked; then I got angry, at myself more than anything. *Nothing* had changed.

I'd just buried it all deep inside, and seeing you made it bubble to the surface."

"That's why you've been so mean to me?"

"I shouldn't have taken it out on you. You didn't deserve that." He stroked my hair. "I promise to make it up to you."

Just then, a euphoric rush hit me as the marijuana kicked in, and I reached up to kiss him. He drew me close, and our mouths merged. We kissed deeply, then more passionately, fumbling our shirts off at the same time, pressing our bare chests against each other. It went on and on for what felt like hours.

When we were finished, we sat naked in the dugout for a few minutes, catching our breath and exchanging embarrassed glances. Finally, we got back into our clothes and leaned against each other, neither of us eager to get back to our bunkhouses.

After a few minutes of silence, he sat up, readying himself to go. "Now that we've gotten *that* out of the way," he said with a smirk, "what do you say we go for a drive this weekend to get away from it all, just you and me? I know a few places in the desert where we can spend some good alone time together. It'll give us a chance to reconnect properly—no holds barred."

Of course, I agreed right away. I'd never been a big fan of roughing it. But now that·Simon had come around, I wasn't about to deny him anything.

Our first drive from Kfar Kerem to the Mitzpe Ramon outpost in a jeep Simon borrowed from the kibbutz took a couple of hours. It gave us time to chitchat about the family back home, listen to a few cassettes, and have some easy laughs. I felt alive for the first time in years, relishing the experience of sharing with Simon, both of us adults now, able to be ourselves at last. It was the beginning of a new life for me.

At around three in the afternoon, we descended into the

massive Ramon crater and navigated a snaking highway deep into the chasm. The sun was dropping into the west when we turned off on a dirt road and four-wheeled it through a forest of scrub brush and acacias. We halted in an unexpected patch of green next to a bubbling creek—a little oasis in the middle of the wilderness. The ruins of an ancient Ottoman caravanserai perched on a low hill overlooked the clearing. Simon cleared away some stones, laid out a wicker mat for us, then hauled a cooler out of the back of the jeep. He cracked it open, pulled out a cold bottle of *arak*, and slapped the mat.

"Sit!" He flashed a wide grin and poured us a couple of shots.

Six shots later, out came the joints. We smoked until the sun went down and the stars came out. Once I was mellowed out, he convinced me to try a tab of acid. Mind you, I'd never done drugs before, let alone psychedelics, so when the acid hit, I was blindsided.

Simon pulled off my shirt and helped me out of my jeans. Then he stripped naked and made love to me, both of us hallucinating God knows what, doing things to each other I never imagined possible. This went on weekend after weekend, our drug-fueled trips to the desert. Little by little, he opened me up mentally, emotionally, sexually—Simon, the master; me, the neophyte. If I was in love with him before in Los Angeles, I came to adore him in Israel, to crave his presence, to depend on him for my very existence. I'd have done anything for him. Absolutely anything.

And then it happened . . .

I froze for a beat, struggling hard against a reluctance to speak, to relive what I'd suppressed for so long. Tears pooled in my stinging eyes and spilled onto my cheeks. Swiping them away, I gritted my teeth and, still addressing the fire, pressed on.

After a few months, we returned to the clearing in the crater where it all started, the one with the ruins on the hill. We'd set up a tent and planned on spending the whole weekend there. It was the middle of the night. The moon had gone down, and the sky was full of stars. Simon and I had exhausted ourselves after hours of sex out in the open, and he'd crawled back into the tent. But I'd snorted way too much coke. I was shaking. My heart was pounding, and my chest felt like it was caving in. And I started to freak out. Big time. Simon tried to coax me back into the tent. But I couldn't. It was too enclosed, and I was terrified I'd lose my mind. So I took off, running up the hill, screaming out to God.

When I reached the ruins, I found the opening to a still-intact watchtower and sped up the stone steps to the top of the crumbling turret. I climbed onto the ledge and gazed out over the landscape, ready to jump, asking God to help me fly. Just then, Simon appeared at the opening. He was in his underwear, breathless and frightened, his chest and arms torn by the acacia bushes he'd plowed through chasing after me, his bare feet a bloody mess.

"Marc, come down from there," he called, holding out his hands to me.

I spun around, losing my balance for a moment, then, miraculously, recovering it. "This is all your fault," I screamed at him, tears streaming down my face. "I'd have never taken any of that shit if it hadn't been for you! Now, look at me."

He crept toward me, waving me forward. "You snorted a little too much, that's all. I'm sorry. I should have been monitoring you more closely. Now, come on. Get down from there."

"No!" I screamed. "Get away from me."

He edged closer until he was touching the wall, then he climbed onto the ledge.

"Leave me alone, Simon. Please!" I blubbered.

"Come down, Marc," he pleaded, moving closer, reaching out to me. "Just there if you want." He cocked his head at the dusty platform below. "It's too dangerous up here."

I glanced down at the platform for a moment, and in that moment, Simon lunged forward and grabbed my arm, which startled me. I pulled away from him . . . he lost his balance . . .

I choked back tears as I recalled that moment. *The* moment. Swallowing hard, I squeezed my eyes shut, drew in a deep breath and . . .

I almost jumped after him as he went over the edge. I should have, but I didn't. Something stopped me. Instead, I crept off the ledge, felt my way back down the stone steps, emerged from the watchtower, and, after a few minutes, found Simon's twisted body a few feet away down a ravine. His head had struck a boulder. The impact had shattered his skull. It was horrible! My Simon, beautiful Simon, dead in a ditch. And it was all my fault. If only I'd done as he'd asked, he'd still be alive. It was as if I'd lured him onto the ledge and pushed him off. I was no better than a murderer. And like the murderer I was, I left him there in that ditch and made my way back to our camp. I spent what was left of the night huddled against an outcrop of rocks, bruised and terrified . . .

Once the sun came up, I felt more in control of myself and the situation. I got dressed, got rid of the drugs, washed down an energy bar with some water, climbed another hill, and spotted a group of people hiking in the distance. They were from some kooky messianic commune a few miles away. I waved them down and reported Simon missing; I told them he'd wandered away from the camp at night and hadn't come back. They took me to their village, fed me, tended my wounds, and called the authorities. After a couple of hours of searching the area, they found Simon's body and, after questioning me for a while, concluded he had either fallen or jumped from the top of the caravanserai.

The whole experience shattered me: losing the love of my life, feeling responsible for his death, and burying the truth of what happened to him deep inside. I ended up suffering a breakdown. My father had to fly to Israel to bring me back to Los Angeles. It was so painful and humiliating. . . for me, for my whole family . . . for Simon's family . . . not to mention it was an enormous tragedy in our community, as you can imagine. Simon's poor parents tried their best not to blame me, but . . .

I closed my eyes and fell silent, having run out of energy to speak another word. But it was out now. Talking about it hadn't been as awful as I'd expected. Painful, yes, but nothing like actually reliving the experience, which was what I'd always dreaded— why I'd suppressed the memory of it for decades. I opened my eyes and looked over at Isaac. He was staring at me, his mouth slightly open.

"That's horrible," he said.

I nodded. "You were right. It helped to get it out."

"No, I mean, it's horrible what you did!" He stood up and looked down at me. "How could you leave him there? How could you let people think he jumped? I'm sorry, but what kind of a person does that?"

"I told you, I wasn't thinking straight! I was under the influence, and I panicked. I was afraid they'd blame me."

250

"Okay, I get that. But you're not under the influence now, are you?"

"Obviously not."

"So then, now that you've gotten it all out, what are you going to do about it?"

"What do you mean? What could I possibly do about it?" I asked.

"Well, for starters, you could face Simon's parents like a man and tell them what happened to their son. I'm sure they'd want to know he didn't kill himself—don't you think?"

The idea of coming clean to Simon's parents had always dogged my conscience, but I'd always found some reason to put it off. After a few years of dithering, any urgency I'd felt faded into the background of my messy life.

"Yes, I'm sure they'd want to know that," I said in a low voice.

"In fact," Isaac continued, "if things played out the way you described, setting aside the issue of the drugs, Simon died trying to save *you* from killing yourself. In my book, that makes him a hero."

"What do you mean, *if* things played out how I described?"

Isaac pitched a stone across the clearing and struck a Joshua tree dead-on, startling a couple of night birds nesting in its branches. "I mean, your version of things isn't always reliable, is it?"

"We're changing subjects now, are we?"

"*Are* we?"

I shook my head and swallowed hard against the urge to shoot back an angry retort.

"You said that Silva reminds you of Simon," Isaac said.

I picked up a stick and snapped it in half. "In a way, he does."

"Maybe that's the sort of guy you need, Marc. Edgy and reckless, even a little dangerous. I can't compete with that. It's not who I am."

251

"I'm not going to deny I've made bad choices, Isaac. And, yes, maybe something inside me hungers for that. But I made a conscious decision long ago to choose better. I chose sobriety, and I chose you. You're the best thing that's happened to me. I'm a better person because of you. I don't want to lose—"

Isaac thrust out his palm. "Enough, Marc. Enough!" He lowered his hand, his eyes glistening in the flames.. "Now that your tongue is good and loose, I think it's time you told me *everything* that happened between you and Silva that night. At the Transformer Club. *The truth*."

I glanced back at the fire and drew a breath. "He wanted to meet me privately to tell me he'd been framed. For the killing. He said it was his roommate's drug deal gone wrong. The guy's suppliers murdered him, and they made Silva take the rap. They threatened to kill him if he ever told anyone. But he wanted me to know the truth—that he was a victim, not a criminal."

Isaac shook his head. "That's manipulative bullshit! What I want to know is why the two of you went from his hotel to the Transformer Club. Or had you planned to go there with him all along?"

"No! When I showed up at his hotel, he hopped into the cab, said it was too busy in the lobby, and took us to the club."

"And you went with him."

"Yes, I know, it was totally stupid. But anyway, I did. The place was reeking of pot. He took me up to an office, sparked a joint, and told me his story about the frame-up. Then he lit up another."

"You're stalling, Marc. Get to the point."

"One thing led to another. We shared a joint, drank some beer he'd laced with ecstasy, and . . . I ended up having sex with him . . . and a few other guys. I was tired, weak, high, whatever. I'm not making excuses. I'm just telling you how it was. I regret it, and I'm sorry. It won't happen again. I swear it."

Isaac's face was a study in stoicism. He crossed his arms and stared into the darkness. When I reached out to touch him, he rose to his feet, and my hand touched air. He crunched over to his telescope and packed it away. Then he fed the fire, brought out his sleeping bag, and wriggled into it.

I remained sitting, watching him resting his head on his arms. Every so often, he cleared his throat as if he were about to speak, but he always fell silent.

"So where does that leave us?" I asked after a few minutes.

Isaac opened his eyes and stared at me for a moment; then he sat up.

"I knew you were damaged goods when we met, Marc," he said. "I'm sorry if it sounds harsh, but it's true. You warned me as much."

"We're all damaged."

Isaac brushed off my comment with a wave of his hand. "Sorry, but you were more damaged than most. More than I imagined, it turns out, considering what happened with Simon especially. But I took a chance on you, and it's been good. You've done really well. I don't regret a single day we've spent together. Now, though, it seems you're at a crossroads." He breathed a painful sigh.

"Maybe I'm not right for you anymore, Marc. If Silva's not the criminal you thought he was, if he's more compatible with you than I am, then maybe you should pursue a relationship with him. You've already started anyway. I'm not going to stop you if that's what you want."

"But that's not what I want. I don't want him. I want you, Isaac. I love you! You know that!"

"You love me?"

"Yes! That's what I've been saying. I don't want to lose you."

"If you love me, you're going to have to win me back, Marc. Because you've already lost me." Isaac slipped back into his sleeping bag and turned away from me.

"I don't get it. You asked me to unload my conscience, and

I did. You asked me to tell you the truth about what happened with Silva, and I did. I don't know what more you want me to do."

Isaac sat up in his sleeping bag. "You can start by going to rehab like I asked you to, Marc, just as soon as we get back to San Francisco."

"Yes, okay, if it means that much to you, I'll go to rehab."

"You'll also need to unload your conscience, as you put it, to a professional, so that you can start dealing with the guilt you've been carrying nearly half your life. Once you've done those two things, we'll see what's left to salvage from of relationship."

Chapter 23

Sixteen hours later, Isaac and I blew into San Francisco on a fog-choked Sunday evening after a day of anxious, nonstop driving. The morning after our campfire experience, as dawn broke, Isaac had received a call from Phoebe on his cell phone with the bad news that we'd suffered a break-in at our apartment and Nilo was missing. Naturally I suspected Silva. I'd never told him where I lived, but I didn't doubt he could have discovered my address. Isaac kept a stony silence on the subject and gunned it while I arranged things with Phoebe.

I gave our consent for the police to process the apartment in our absence and for Phoebe to stand in for us while they did. When we pulled up to the building, she was waiting for us with a sharp-eyed female police detective in her mid-thirties, flawlessly dressed in a blue-gray pantsuit and matching pumps. Phoebe gave Isaac a quick hug and introduced us to the detective, whose name was Bey.

"Whoever it was knew how to cover their tracks," Detective Bey said to me. She glanced at Isaac and Phoebe, who had retreated a bit. "Somehow, they managed to slip past the porter without being noticed."

"It must have happened in the wee hours," Phoebe offered. "I was here last night, and everything was fine. This morning I dropped in to bring some more litter, as you were running low.

That's when I noticed Nilo was missing."

"How did they get into the apartment?" I asked. "We have a deadbolt."

"The deadbolt was engaged when I arrived this morning," Phoebe said.

"Whoever did this was as skilled as a locksmith," Bey said. "Either that or they climbed up the side of the building with a rope like Batman. In any case, the unit is negative for prints, and everything is in its place, according to Ms. Thistlewig here."

"Wait," I said, nervously grasping a handful of my hair, "you mean the place is locked, nothing is missing, and there aren't any prints? How do you even know anyone was there?"

"Nilo!" Phoebe and Isaac shouted at the same time.

Bey nodded. "That's right; all that seems to be missing is the cat. Have a look yourselves and call me tomorrow if you notice anything else missing or anything strange." She handed me her business card. "I'll wait until then to finalize my report."

"That's it?" I asked.

Detective Bey shrugged, readjusting a lock of her chestnut hair that had blown across her face in the stiff breeze. "It's a lot of trouble to go through just to steal a cat."

"Someone named Alejandro Silva did this, I'm sure of it," I blurted out, catching Phoebe's stern gaze. "He's a disgruntled former client. He's obviously trying to send a message."

"To be honest, Mr. Mendes, if your lawyer hadn't reported this as a break-in, we wouldn't have been able to tell anything happened here at all from the looks of things. Other than the missing cat, which, for all we know, slipped out of the apartment while the door was open, it all looks normal."

"I can assure you, detective, that didn't happen," Phoebe inserted.

The detective shrugged again and shut her steno pad, lodging her pen into the spiral wire.

"Could you at least go and speak with him? With Silva?" I

said. "He's staying at the Headlands on Lombard, no more than a mile from here."

Phoebe exchanged a look with the detective, who reopened her steno pad and took down the information. She promised to swing by the Headlands in the next couple of days to see what Silva had to say before finalizing her report.

"Why didn't you tell her Silva's on parole?" Isaac asked as we rode up to the apartment in the elevator with Phoebe.

"I don't know," I muttered. "It didn't come to mind—sorry. I'll call the detective tomorrow."

Phoebe observed us silently from the corner of the elevator, her satchel dangling from one hand, and waited until we'd exited before following us to the apartment. As she'd reported, nothing was missing other than poor Nilo. Everything was undisturbed, except for, maybe, a couple of drawers in my office where I kept important papers, including, significantly, the paperwork related to Isaac's immigration case.

Isaac retreated to the living room and broke down in tears over Nilo, who, after all, had been his mother's cat. Phoebe did her best to comfort him while I stood by, feeling helpless and guilty at the same time.

I rolled our suitcases into the bedroom and unpacked them, then returned to the living room. I found Isaac and Phoebe sitting next to each other on the sofa, sipping tea. Isaac's eyes were rimmed in red, but he had recovered his composure and was attending to something Phoebe was saying to him. They both looked up as I walked into the room. Phoebe held her hand open at the chair opposite them.

"Please join us, Marc," she said.

I lowered myself into the chair and searched Isaac's face. He was avoiding direct eye contact with me.

"Distressing as this evening has been," Phoebe began, "we have little time to lose. We cannot allow this, or anything else really, to distract us from preparing Isaac's case. His hearing is speedily approaching. If we fail to hammer out our strategy, the hearing is as good as lost."

Isaac nodded, and Phoebe dug around in her satchel for her notebook.

"I realize it's been a long, trying day for the both of you," she continued, speaking into the satchel. "But if you don't mind, I'd like to make a start now."

"Now?" I said, looking at Isaac. "That's a little abrupt, isn't it? I'm still processing the break-in."

Phoebe's head snapped up. "You have something better to do?"

"It's fine, Marc," Isaac said, still unable or unwilling to look at me.

"Okay, yes." I held up my hands in surrender. "Let's do it."

"Excellent," Phoebe said, settling herself. She flipped open her notebook, pen in hand. "Now, Marc, before the two of you left so suddenly on your trip, Isaac and I spent quite a bit of time reviewing his testimony for the hearing. So, as far as that goes, we've got everything under control. However, we also discussed the need to impress the judge with the amount and quality of community support Isaac enjoys."

"Phoebe thinks we should recruit as many character witnesses as possible," Isaac explained.

"More than that, dear," Phoebe said, "I'd like for us to fill the courtroom to the rafters with your friends and supporters."

"That courtroom holds around seventy-five people," I said. "There can't possibly be enough time to hear from that many witnesses."

"That won't be necessary," Phoebe said, a smile creeping onto her face. "The mere presence of so many souls supporting Isaac will speak volumes to the judge. Testimony from two or three character witnesses will serve our purposes."

Phoebe's strategy appeared sound, and Isaac's mood lifted at the prospect of jamming the courtroom with a crowd of well-wishers. His face glowed with excitement. If he had to go down for the count, he said, he wanted to go down fighting with everything he had. We spent the rest of the evening drawing up a list of people to call and came up with forty-eight names off the top of our heads; we resolved to work on beefing up the list over the coming days.

Once we were done with that, Phoebe pulled a sheaf of papers and brochures out of her satchel and held them high. "Now then, on a related subject, I've taken the liberty of bringing along some consular materials I collected whilst you were away, which we should also go over—in relation to your possible relocation."

Isaac shot me a look.

"Why would we do that before we know the outcome of the hearing?" I asked.

Phoebe dropped the papers on the coffee table. "These applications take time to process, Marc, months, sometimes, even years. It's best if we run the two processes in tandem. Yes?"

Isaac took a considered sip of tea. "That's fine," he said.

Phoebe took her time methodically arranging it all on the coffee table in little stacks. "These are the materials I collected from the various and sundry consulates general, including those of the United Kingdom, Spain, Australia, New Zealand, and Canada." She indicated the papers with a sweep of her hand. "I've arranged them in order of flexibility of immigration laws."

We took an hour or so to review the immigration rules for all five countries, and another two to debate which of them best suited our situation. In a nutshell, the UK required each of us to invest three hundred thousand in a business; Spain required one hundred thousand each; Australia, New Zealand, and Canada had merits-based immigration programs where one's education, experience, and language abilities were taken into account. So we could either buy our way into England and Spain, or we could apply to Australia, New Zealand, or Canada on the strength of who we were, what we'd accomplished in our lives, and what we could offer each country.

Our next task was to narrow down our choices from five to one. Isaac refused to consider the investment route, which left three. He then objected to the distance of Australia and New Zealand compared with Canada. I pointed out New Zealand's progressive laws, which offered recognition to same-sex couples equal to that offered to heterosexual couples. Australia's abundance of job opportunities, along with its progressive and open society, also attracted me.

Phoebe argued that Canada was also open and progressive and likewise entertained same-sex applications on what she called humanitarian and compassionate grounds. She pressed home how Canada was a North American society, similar in many ways to the United States. As such, it would require much less adaptation than any of the other places we'd considered.

"Besides, Marc," Isaac tossed in, "don't you ever want to see your parents again?"

"Yes, of course, I do," I answered.

"Then Canada is the ideal choice," he said, settling the issue. "A couple of hours on a plane, and there they are, or here you are. It would be like flying to any other city in America."

Phoebe smiled at me. I detected a note of muted victory in her expression. "I've handled a number of these cases," she said. "So I'd be happy to act as your lawyer and file all the necessary documents."

"That would be great; thank you, Phoebe," Isaac said.

I flipped through the application package and browsed the instructions and procedures. "It looks pretty straightforward to me," I said after a moment. "Maybe we don't even need a lawyer for this."

Phoebe arched an eyebrow. "It's not like you don't have any issues associated with the application."

"What issues? Isaac and I surely have enough points to

qualify individually for independent immigration, let alone as a couple."

"To clarify," Phoebe said, "there is *no* application as a couple available at this point. Not for a same-sex relationship. As such, the applications will indeed need to be filed as independent cases. But they should *also* be filed, in the alternative, as humanitarian cases, to cover your long-term relationship—just in case."

"Just in case what?" Isaac asked.

"In case one or the other of you is refused, of course. It's an extra bit of insurance. Again, if you were a heterosexual couple, then the dependent spouse, so to speak, would automatically be admitted based on acceptance of the principal applicant. But since you are, essentially, two separate individuals, albeit in a common-law relationship, acceptance of one does not guarantee acceptance of the other. Hence, it's best to file an alternative humanitarian and compassionate application. And for *that*, you should be represented by a competent lawyer."

"Makes perfect sense to me," Isaac said. "I agree you should act as my lawyer in this as well."

I continued to silently read through the materials for a few minutes while Phoebe and Isaac stared at me, waiting for a reaction.

"I don't know," I said, as tactfully as possible. "If this were a court case, like Isaac's removal hearing, I wouldn't dream of handling it on my own. But this is a straightforward application. I don't see the need to bother you with this, Phoebe."

"Hang on a second," Isaac countered, standing up. "This is *my* case we're talking about."

"It's your case *principally*, I would say," Phoebe offered, with a quick glance in my direction.

"No, Phoebe," Isaac said. "I'm sorry I didn't say something before. Things have changed. Now it's my case completely, and I want you to handle it for me. If Marc wants to accompany me, he can file his own application."

"What are you talking about?" I asked. "We're going together."

"What's going on here, please?" Phoebe interjected.

"No offense, Marc," Isaac said, ignoring her question, "but I don't want anything to go wrong with my application. I can't afford it. And I want Phoebe as my lawyer. You can handle your own case if you want."

Phoebe shook her head at Isaac and gestured at a spot next to her on the sofa. Isaac stared at her finger for a moment, then sat down.

"Now, Isaac," she said, "if there is *any* chance you're going together, then the applications should be filed as one package. That way, you can have your interviews at the same time."

"There's an interview?" Isaac asked, looking first at Phoebe then at me.

"Yes, there is. It says so here." I pointed out the relevant paragraph in the informational booklet. "At the Canadian consulate. It's where they make the final decision."

"Well, not exactly," Phoebe corrected. "There *is* an appeal process."

"But only if we're refused," I noted.

My words were met by silence as Isaac and Phoebe shared a moment of voiceless communication. After a moment, Phoebe nodded and gathered up the papers.

"Gentlemen, why don't the two of you discuss this between yourselves and then let me know how you would like to proceed. Mind you, you should make your decision as soon as possible and get your applications filed at speed. Even in the best of circumstances, the process could take as long as two years."

"We'll discuss it tonight and let you know by tomorrow. Is that fair, Isaac?"

Isaac met my question with a frown.

It was eleven thirty by the time we called it a night and saw Phoebe to the elevator. No sooner had the doors slid shut than

Isaac turned on me and poked my chest with his index finger.

"You're not going to prepare my application."

I moved his finger aside. "You don't trust me?" I rubbed the sore spot on my chest where his finger had struck.

Isaac walked back into the apartment and fell onto the sofa with a thud. I followed him and stood over him.

"And what's this about you going alone? Why did you tell Phoebe it was your case completely?"

"I told you we were finished, didn't I? Besides, Phoebe's my lawyer! I get to tell her anything I want."

"But we're *not* finished. I agreed to go into rehab, didn't I?" I sat next to him and touched his leg. Isaac stared at my hand and shook his head.

"This is *my* life we're talking about here, Marc. My life! You should have considered *me*, your life partner, before you let that guy into our world—whatever your reasons. Now, look at where I'm at! You fucked around on me, the guy you picked is stalking us, and now the fucker has invaded what was supposed to be our sacred space, our home, and stolen *my* little Nilo, the only thing that connected me with my mom. Thank you very much."

"I'm sorry about all that. I'll fix it if I can, I promise. Either way, I'm at your side, come what may, whether you want me as your partner or not."

"You can do what you like," Isaac responded, hauling himself out of the sofa. "I'm going to bed. You can sleep here or wherever. We can talk more later if you want. But know this: Phoebe is my lawyer."

Chapter 24

The next morning, a faint scratching at the front door startled me as I readied myself to go to the office. Isaac was still holed up in our bedroom, probably waiting for me to clear out before emerging, and hadn't heard it. The first thing that came to my mind was that Silva had returned. Bracing myself, I yanked open the door and found Nilo curled up and purring on our welcome mat. He slithered past me into the apartment, padded to our bedroom, and yowled at the door. An instant later, the door flew open, and Isaac cried out with joy, gathering Nilo into his arms and kissing him again and again.

"Oh, my precious little Nilo," Isaac said, his eyes bright with tears. "Where did you find him?"

I pointed at the open doorway. "He was there on the doormat. He must have snuck out when Phoebe was distracted like the detective said."

Isaac held Nilo up and gazed at him, his tears giving way to an emotion-filled smile, hardly believing his eyes. An instant later, his smile evaporated. "His collar is missing."

"What?" I came over to him and confirmed what he was saying.

He put Nilo in our bedroom and shut the door, then turned to me. "First your pendant; now Nilo's collar. That means the bastard was here again."

"I'll call the detective when I get to the office."

"I should go stay at a friend's place." Anxiety was etched onto Isaac's forehead. "I don't feel safe here anymore."

"Let me talk to the detective first, then we'll decide what to do. If we can prove Silva violated his parole, he'll be arrested and put away for a while. In the meantime, you should go to work as usual, and I'll report the trespass to management so they can keep a closer eye on the building." I started for the door.

"Wait! What about rehab?"

"I'll look for a program once I clear it with Ed."

I sped up the stairs to my office, closed the door, and punched in Detective Bey's number. The call went straight to voicemail, and I left her an urgent message asking for a call back. Moving on, I called Vlad into the room to get a rundown on the progress of my cases while I was away, noting he seemed more fidgety than usual. Saint-Cloud had settled at an amount much less than our four clients expected. They'd threatened to sue us for malpractice while at the same time accepting their settlement checks and cashing them. Ed was out all week on a series of depositions in Bakersfield, and the rest of the staff had been holding down the fort as best they could, waiting for my return. Much as I regretted it, I decided rehab would have to wait until after Ed got back.

Once we finished our status meeting, I asked Vlad to close the door, and I cut direct to the chase.

"By any chance, did Mr. Silva happen to come by here while I was gone?"

Vlad blinked and glanced to one side, then shook his head. "He called here a couple of times when you first went away."

"What did he say?"

Vlad shrugged. "He wanted to talk to you. He was surprised

you weren't here. Stuff like that. Ed finally told him to stop calling."

"Is that it?" I asked.

"Well, yeah. After that, he stopped."

"And he never came by?"

Vlad pursed his lips and shook his head.

"The guy's got my new cell phone number, Vlad. He tracked me down, to my parents' home in Los Angeles, and he goddamn knows where I live. Where do you suppose he got all that information?"

"How should I know?" Vlad stammered. He was pumping his legs and gripping the armrest of his chair.

"If you had anything to do with it, I'll find out. You know that, don't you?"

"I mean, I *might* have let something slip, but I didn't purposely give him any of your private information or anything like that."

Just as I was about to respond, my telephone rang, and I snatched up the receiver. It was Detective Bey, calling me with an update. I asked Vlad to step outside my office and wait while I finished.

"We spoke with the charming Mr. Silva earlier this morning at his hotel," Bey said, edging in the descriptive barb.

"And?"

"He has an alibi, which we were able to verify."

"What alibi?"

"He was out of town all weekend, staying with a cousin of his in San Diego. We spoke with the cousin. We also spoke with the desk clerk at the Headlands Hotel. It all checks out."

I took in the information, feeling a surge of emotions ranging from anger to confusion. "I forgot to tell you he's on parole," I said.

"We know; he told us. I didn't think it was necessary to speak with his PO, as he didn't leave the state. Did you have a chance to inspect your apartment?"

"There's no question someone rifled through our drawers," I said. "But nothing's missing. The main development is that our cat showed up this morning, right outside our apartment door."

"Ah! Well, then, he must have slipped out when your attorney visited the night before."

"I don't think so. His collar is missing. Plus, that doesn't explain the drawers."

"To be honest, Mr. Mendes, we don't have much to go on here. I'm inclined to finalize my report and close things out on our end. If you notice anything else unusual, you can let us know, and I'll reconsider. Otherwise, let's hope this is a case of all's well that ends well. Are you okay with that?"

I swung my chair around in frustration. "Yes, fine, I'll telephone you if anything else comes up."

"There was one more thing, Mr. Mendes."

"What?"

"According to Mr. Silva, you and he are in a relationship."

I should have expected it. Why wouldn't Silva mention that? But somehow it caught me off guard.

"If I read him right," she continued, "there's even something of a rivalry between him and Mr. Perez. Is that correct?"

"No, that's not correct. *He* may see it that way," I said haltingly, "but it's all in his head really."

"Is it?"

"I told you he was a disgruntled client. He became obsessed with me, and when I rebuffed him, he continued to pursue me."

"So you're not in a relationship with him?" Bey persisted.

"You know, detective, I'm not comfortable with where this conversation is going. So let's call it a day for now. I'll call you if we have anything else for you."

I ended the call and waited a few minutes to regain my composure. The situation had the potential to spiral out of control, and I didn't know what to do, given the emotional volatility of everyone involved. I needed someone to confide in, someone who could give me some solid advice, and it couldn't wait until the next week. So I ran through my options, picked up the phone, hesitated, then called my father, who was wrapping up an early morning meeting at the synagogue.

"Abba, I've got a problem," I started, then froze.

"It must be some problem for you to be calling me at ten in the morning on a Monday."

"I'm really stuck, Abba. I feel like my life is falling apart." I broke down as the words spilled out.

"Have you had another relapse, *hijo*?"

"No, Abba, not that. It's *everything*. I'm sorry, I should be able to handle it. I should be stronger. But for some reason, I can't get things right. I need your help."

There was a moment of silence when I thought the call had dropped.

"Abba?"

"I'll fly up this afternoon," he said.

"No, Abba! I didn't mean you had to come here. I'm fine with us speaking over the telephone."

"If things are that bad, son, it's best we discuss them face to face. Do you think you can hang on until then?"

"Yes, Abba, thank you; I can hang on. Just get me your flight details once you're booked, and I'll pick you up at the airport."

As I hung up, I felt a mix of relief and trepidation at the prospect of baring my soul to my father in person. But it had to be done if I was to avoid a complete meltdown. Still, I needed some solid legal advice as well. So I called Phoebe, who was between hearings at Immigration Court. Sensing my distress, she agreed to meet me in one of the attorney breakout rooms during the lunch recess. Having worked out a plan of action, I called Vlad back into my office.

"Okay, I confess," he blurted out, holding up his hands as he walked in. "I *did* give Silva your new cell number. The guy cornered me outside after work, looking like he was about to off himself, and I felt sorry for him. So I did it. I'm sorry. I also told him you'd gone out of town for a while, probably to Los Angeles where you're from. But that's it; I swear it. He must have figured out the rest on his own."

I was furious; what he was telling me constituted a total breach of trust. I could hardly bring myself to look at him.

"Gather up your things," I said coldly. "Take the rest of the week off while I discuss your future at this firm with Ed."

A moment later, the door clicked shut behind me.

Silva was waiting for me across from Bix. I'd intended to cut through Gold Alley to Sansome where the Immigration Court building was located, but abruptly changed course when I spotted him reclining against a brick wall in a white linen *guayabera*, fresh-pressed tan trousers, and white *huaraches*. His hair had grown out since I'd last seen him, and he was sporting a day or two of stubble, all of which lent him a rakish look. He caught up with me at the corner of Montgomery and Jackson, came around in front of me, and put out his hand.

"I was worried, Marc," he said, inches from my face. "You disappeared without a word. I was afraid something bad had happened to you."

"Nothing happened. I just needed to get away, like I told you. I wasn't aware I had to clear it with you in advance." I pushed past him and powered down the sidewalk.

"Why did you tell the police I broke into your apartment?" he called out.

I spun around. "Did you?"

"No, of course not! I don't even know where you live. Are you trying to get me arrested, or what?"

"I don't have time for this, Alejandro. I'm late for a meeting."

"Come over to my place after work. I want us to talk about the other night. Plus, I need to give you back your necklace. You left it behind."

"No, Alejandro." I interrupted. "We're not going to talk about the other night. And stop coming around, please. We're done."

"But your necklace—"

"Keep the damned necklace! Consider it a parting gift."

"I'm not going to just go away, Marc. Not after what's happened between us. Not after everything I confided in you."

"Get out of my way."

"You're going to Immigration Court, aren't you?" he asked, his voice turning hard. "For your boyfriend's thing."

All the control I'd been mustering crumbled at those words.

"How do you know about that?" I snapped.

"It's public information, isn't it?"

"Who told you?"

Silva shrugged. "Doesn't matter. Anyway, I guess you'll be more available once he's gone. Because there's no way he's going to win his case."

I'd never felt like killing anyone before, not in my entire life. But at that moment, the thought entered my mind. It took all I had to master my emotions and wrest control of myself. Once I was steady, I looked him straight in the eye and, as calmly as I could, said, "Stay the fuck away from Isaac and me. I won't tell you again."

Then I sped away from him, zigzagging through a couple of side alleys to throw him off my trail, and emerged catty-corner to the Immigration Court building. Looking in all directions to make sure he hadn't followed me, I ran across the street and ducked inside. A few minutes later, I was locked in a room with Phoebe. Isaac had already informed her about Nilo's reappearance, and she was aware Bey had closed the investigation.

"I know it was Silva, Phoebe," I said.

"That's as may be. But without evidence directly implicating him, the police can't do anything more about it."

"Silva interrogated my paralegal while I was away. That's how he found out I'd gone to Los Angeles."

"Your paralegal told him where you were?"

"Yes, he did; he confessed as much. He may also have told him about Isaac's immigration case. His girlfriend works in the clerk's office here. I'm just speculating about that, though. I did have some papers about the case in my drawers at home that Silva might have seen. Either way, he knows."

Phoebe shook her head. "None of that's a crime, unfortunately."

"I know that. The problem is he keeps coming around, interfering in my life. Anywhere I go, there he is. I just ran into him on the sidewalk on my way here to see you. He won't leave us alone, and I'm worried about how that might affect Isaac and his case."

"I told you before you should run as fast and as far from Mr. Silva as you can, didn't I? That was my advice then, and it's still my advice today. Don't meet him and don't take his calls, and let's hope he gets the message and goes away."

"You also said we could file a restraining order against him," I prompted.

"That was before I learned more about the situation from Isaac." She paused and arched an eyebrow at me. "Mr. Silva could contest the restraining order. Are you prepared to have all the sordid details of your association with him aired in open court? Or to have the matter referred to the Ethics Committee of the state bar because he was a client?"

"Not particularly."

"I thought not." Phoebe nodded curtly. "Again, I repeat, my advice is that you completely shut him out. The man is on parole. If he does anything other than to follow you around, then he'll end up back in prison, and you'll be free of him. Hopefully, things will not come to that, and he'll simply go away."

Isaac and I picked up my father at Oakland International Airport and drove straight home. After an emotional arrival, our drive back was, for the most part, silent, with my father exchanging a few pleasantries with Isaac while I plotted out my conversation with him. Isaac had been surprised I'd called on my father and was even, for some reason, a bit angry. But when I filled him in on the latest developments with Bey and Vlad, and their effects on my emotional stability, he understood and supported the visit.

Isaac prepared a quick dinner over which my father updated us on family matters. When we finished, my father withdrew to the living room with a cup of coffee, and I helped Isaac clear the table, stalling a bit.

"Leave this to me," Isaac said, lifting a dinner plate at the living room. "Go on. I'll be in the bedroom."

I found my father standing at the picture window, watching the sun starting its dip into the ocean behind the bridge. I came up next to him and placed my hand on his back.

"This really is a lovely view." He turned to me. There was a smile on his face, but his eyes looked sad.

"Thank you for coming, Abba," I said.

He nodded at the bridge. "Shall we take a walk?"

"Where? You mean there?"

"It's not far, is it?"

"It looks closer than it is. About an hour's walk, give or take."

He shrugged. "That's perfect."

We strolled along the water's edge, through the industrial buildings of Fort Mason; along Marina Boulevard, where green lawns meet the waters of the bay; past the monumental Palace of Fine Arts; and across Crissy Field, the former airfield turned waterfront park. The breeze was bracing, and the advancing darkness helped loosen my tongue. In the hour it took for us to walk from my apartment to the Golden Gate Bridge, I poured my guts out to my father for the first time in my thirty-six years. I spoke about my adolescent struggles with my sexuality, the depths of guilt I'd experienced, and the dark secrets I'd guarded. My knees nearly buckled from nerves as I divulged the truth to him about what had *really* happened in Israel to Simon, the searing anguish I'd suffered from keeping it all bottled inside for decades, and my retreat into substance abuse and debauchery to camouflage the pain. I didn't hold anything back; I spoke, and he listened.

After securing my solemn pledge to come clean with Simon's parents about what happened to their son, he asked me to elaborate about the protective shell I'd crawled into after my first stint in rehab, how Isaac had helped draw me out and had been there every step of the way, loving me and supporting my recovery.

When I finally got to the topic of Silva, I broke into tears as I confessed everything that had happened with him and how I felt my life had gone into an irreversible nosedive.

We paused at the entry to the bridge, which rose like a giant orange arthropod above us. I was talked out by then, and my father had yet to offer a single word of advice. He gazed at me, his dark, piercing eyes filled with a mix of emotions, working out what to say. Then, glancing over his shoulder at the distant skyline, he took me by the hand and led me onto the bridge.

We carried on along the pedestrian walkway and stopped in the middle. My father looked out once again at the skyline and held out his hand.

"It's beautiful, isn't it? This view of San Francisco at night."

I followed his line of sight, looking through tears at the

distorted city lights, the rotating beacon of Alcatraz, the Oakland Bay Bridge beyond. It had been so long since I'd seen it all from this vantage. He was right. It *was* beautiful.

"It's beautiful because of the darkness," he said, pausing a moment to let his words sink in. "If it were not for the darkness, we would not perceive the shining lights."

"It's beautiful in the daytime, too, Abba," I said.

"Yes, it is. But that's a different view." He pointed at the lights. "*This*, my son, is the night view." He turned to me. "But it would *not* be beautiful without the lights. It would just be dark."

I nodded and wiped my face with the back of my sleeve, trying to work out the syllogism.

"My point is one needs *both* the darkness and the light—in perfect balance—to appreciate the beauty of this view. Do you understand me?"

"I think so, Abba."

"The daytime view is something else entirely. It's much less nuanced."

"Yes, I suppose."

"It's the same with us," he continued. "We are all made up of both darkness and light. You know this from *cheder* as the *yetzer hara* and the *yetzer hatov*: the dark inclination and the good inclination; the ego and the spirit. Our *hahamim* tell us that we are *all* born with the dark inclination and that Hashem instills the good inclination in us when we come of age. After that, it is a lifelong battle between these two forces. Spiritual and emotional maturity result when one effectively turns down the volume on the darkness, one's ego, and turns up the volume on the light, one's spirit, to get them into proper balance. Do you follow me?"

"Yes, Abba, I'm with you."

"In some, the darkness is much stronger than in others. For those unfortunate souls, even after Hashem gifts them with the good inclination, they are never able to fully conquer their egos. They exist in a state of perpetual adolescence, driven by their appetites, their animal instincts, always fearing, always protecting, always subjective, never objective, until they are finally able to, God willing, master themselves."

"You're talking about me."

He placed his hand on my shoulder. "The ego has always been strong in you, my son, more so than in Jacob. I've sensed this from the beginning. I've prayed that you would find the strength to control it, to find your balance. I knew you were struggling, but I never knew how much until now. I'm just sorry you never came to me before. I could have helped you."

"You could have offered," I said, gazing across the bay.

"That was a boundary I wasn't going to cross without an invitation from you. It's that way with Hashem. He's always there for us, but *we* must first approach him and ask for his help. As you've done now."

Tears stung my eyes. "Abba, I was doing better. A *lot* better, thanks to Isaac. Everything in my life seemed sorted."

My father nodded. "I appreciate that young man much more now," he said. "But the battle is yours, not Isaac's. Instead of winning the war yourself, you've been sheltering in the safety of your relationship. If you wish to truly take control, you must face your demons head-on and, as the psalmist says, lift up your eyes to the hills for your strength."

He raised his head and gazed over my shoulder in the direction we'd come from. "It seems we're being followed."

I turned and saw Silva standing a couple of yards away, dressed in ankle-length jeans and a blue-and-white striped T-shirt. He was reclining against the rail, staring at us.

"Would that happen to be the other young man we've been discussing?" my father asked.

"Yes, that's him."

"Speak with him," he said.

"My lawyer said I should ignore him."

"Know who you are, my son. Establish your boundaries and communicate them to him, human to human."

I felt his hand at my back.

Silva stood away from the rail as I approached him. His eyes were shining in the reflected light of the bridge. It was the most vulnerable I'd ever seen him.

"Why are you still following me, Alejandro?" I asked in as gentle a voice as I could muster.

"Who's that man?" he asked, looking past me down the bridge.

"That's my father. He came up from Los Angeles to see me."

Silva nodded, then met my gaze again.

"I'm sorry I allowed things to get out of control between us, Alejandro," I said, maintaining my even tone. "It's my fault, mainly."

"Nothing's out of control, Marc. Not all relationships start out smoothly. Ours had a rocky start, that's all. But we can get past that and have something beautiful."

"But that's the thing, Alejandro. There is no *we*."

"Of course, there is," he insisted, returning his hands to the bridge's railings.

"No, Alejandro, there's only a *you* and a *me*. Something happened between us that shouldn't have. It's something I regret, and it can never happen again."

"But why do you regret it? You liked it."

"I can't go into all of that now. I just need you to respect my decision. Isaac is my partner. He and I are the only *we*. We've built a life together—a good life. We've had a difficult patch, but we're getting through it. You can understand that, can't you?"

"But I'm better for you than he is," Silva insisted. "When's the last time someone pleased you the way I did? Never!"

"Sex isn't everything, Alejandro."

"No, but it's important. And if I read you right, you and I are more compatible in that way than you and he are."

"Maybe if you and I had met before under different circumstances, things might have worked out differently. But you came too late. I'm sorry. This really has to be good-bye."

"What if he gets deported? Can we get together then?"

"Isaac is *not* going to get deported, Alejandro." I paused for a moment in thought. "How do you know about that anyway?"

"Your secretary guy told me. Cost me a couple of fifties. And then I went and read through the file at Immigration Court. The hearing's coming up pretty fast."

I looked back at my father. He was watching us from a distance with a serene expression.

"With respect, Alejandro," I said, turning back to Silva, "I'm not going to ask again. If you really care for me, if you're anything better than a homewrecker, you'll let me get on with my life, and you'll get on with yours. This is the end of the story."

Silva lowered his gaze to the glistening pavement. After a beat, he nodded and turned around. I rejoined my father, who drew me close, and we watched as Silva receded into the distance.

Chapter 25

Between the fourteen days I spent in rehab followed by several weeks of therapy, NA meetings, and regular exercise, the day of Isaac's hearing crept up on us. I awoke to a kiss on the cheek and found him peering down at me with a nervous smile, dressed in his best suit, dark gray with light gray pinstripes.

"I woke up at five this morning and couldn't go back to sleep," he said, stepping into the sunlight streaming through the bedroom window. "How do I look?"

"You look great." I rubbed the sleep out of my eyes. "How much time have we got?"

"About half an hour. Phoebe's coming over. She said we could ride with her." He fidgeted with one of his sleeves.

I sat up in bed. "How are you feeling?"

"Anxious as hell, but I'll be all right. How about you? Are you okay?"

"I'm all right," I said.

He sat on the bed, and I pulled him toward me and held him. Things had gotten much better between us in the days after my showdown with Silva, which seemed to have done the trick—we hadn't heard from him since. Best of all, Isaac had received me warmly after my stint in rehab and had been as supportive as ever, which meant the world to me. We still had a long way to go to get back to normal, but I was determined to do whatever was necessary to make things work, come what may.

When I finally let go, Isaac made a show of smoothing his hair, trying his best to look as nonchalant as possible. "You'd better get up," he said, "unless you're planning on going to court in your skivvies."

I quickly showered, dressed, and emerged into the living room. Isaac was standing at the picture window, looking out at the bay. He was cradling Nilo in the crook of his arm and stroking him behind one ear.

"I'll never get over that view," I said, coming up behind him, "the way the light plays off the headlands in the morning."

"Yeah . . ." he said without turning around. He let Nilo slide out of his arms and plop to the carpet. Nilo cast a puzzled glance at us, then crept away, leaving the two of us alone. "You don't suppose we'll find a view like this in Canada, do you?"

We were interrupted by the three-toned chime of the intercom.

"That must be Phoebe," Isaac said with a sigh of resignation.

I stepped to the intercom and looked over my shoulder at him. "I understand Vancouver has a lovely bay. And there's always Lake Ontario, I guess." I flipped on the intercom. "Come on up, Phoebe," I said, buzzing her into the lobby.

I walked back over to Isaac and put my arms around him. We stood like that for a couple of minutes, both of us lost in our thoughts, when we were interrupted again by the chime.

I strode back to the intercom. "You didn't get lost, did you?" I said into the speaker.

"I beg your pardon?" came Phoebe's perturbed voice.

Just then, a pounding on our front door reverberated throughout the apartment. Nilo shot out from underneath the sofa and took refuge in the kitchen, and Isaac turned around and crinkled his brow at the door.

"Um, sorry, Phoebe. I thought you were someone else." I buzzed her in and headed for the foyer. "You're not expecting anyone else, are you?" I asked Isaac.

He shook his head and shrugged.

The apartment was shaken by a thunderous knock. Flinging open the door, I revealed my father, his arm raised in mid-knock, and my mother standing by his side wearing dark glasses.

"We aren't late, are we?" my mother asked, adjusting her floral wrap dress and black cardigan.

"Ima, Abba, what are you . . .?"

Isaac joined me at the door. "Mrs. Mendes, Rabbi, come in!"

My mother slipped past my father and put her arms around me, locking me in a maternal embrace. My father walked into the apartment, shook hands with Isaac, and waited his turn to hug me. When my mother finally moved on to Isaac, my father stepped forward. He regarded me with an expression that was full of love and curiosity.

"Hello, Abba." I pulled him into an embrace and kissed his woolly cheek.

"How are you feeling, son?" He drew back his head and searched my face.

"I'm much better now, Abba, thank you. Things have stabilized. Thank God."

He cocked his head a bit and nodded. His staring made me uncomfortable.

"Today's Isaac's hearing," I explained to them, changing the subject.

"Of course it is," my mother said. "That's why we're here."

"We debated whether this should be a surprise visit," my father added, addressing Isaac.

Isaac's eyes misted over with emotion. "Thank you. You didn't have to come, but thank you. Both of you."

"Your timing couldn't have been better," I said. "Isaac's lawyer is on her way up right now."

"Isaac's lawyer is here now," came Phoebe's voice from the doorway.

We quickly exchanged introductions. Then the driving arrangements were made—Isaac would ride with Phoebe, and my parents would ride with me—and we were out the door on our way to Immigration Court.

"She's an interesting woman," my mother said of Phoebe as we drove to the courthouse. "Don't you think so, Gabriel?"

"I don't know," my father said. "We've only just met her."

"I meant the way she dresses, the way she carries herself. Is she a good lawyer, Marc?"

"She's excellent," I answered. "Plus, she and Isaac click."

"That's important," said my father, "that a client and his lawyer should get on well. How she's dressed doesn't matter, Hannah."

"Are we nearly there, Marc? I'm feeling a little carsick," my mother said, signaling the close of the matter.

"We're here," I said as I swung the car into the parking garage adjacent to the courthouse.

We joined Phoebe and Isaac, who were waiting in front of the building. Isaac looked calm enough, but I could see he was furtively wringing his hands behind his back. I sprinted over to him and threw my arm around his shoulder.

The five of us rode up in the elevator. My father struck up a conversation with Phoebe about retirement investment strategies, or some such nonlegal matter, while my mother looked on behind her dark glasses. When the elevator reached the eighth floor, the doors opened onto a crowded hallway. We moved into the throng and instantly became the center of attention as different people exchanged greetings with Isaac and shook hands with him. I recognized some of them from the firm where he worked; others I knew from his astronomy group.

Phoebe worked her way to one of the benches against the wall, shooed a few people away, and climbed onto it, her head poking up above the crowd.

"May I have your attention, please," she called out. "Those

of you who are here for the Isaac Perez hearing, kindly move down to the other end of the hall and gather in front of the courtroom with the number eight-dash-fifteen posted on the door. The hearing will be starting shortly."

One of the security guards helped her off the bench, and she beckoned Isaac over and whispered in his ear. He nodded, and the two of them walked arm in arm to the courtroom door. As the group followed them *en masse*, I directed my parents to wait on a bench until things were under control. Then I pushed past Isaac's supporters and stood next to him and Phoebe.

"Everybody, please lower your voices," Phoebe said. A hush fell over the crowd. "Thank you very much. Now then, my name is Phoebe Thistlewig; I'm Isaac's attorney. We'd like to thank you for your presence here this morning. We realize that for some of you, coming here today represented quite a sacrifice. Please believe me when I tell you your attendance here is not only greatly appreciated, but it's important for Isaac's case as well."

At that moment, Mindy Blair, the attorney for the immigration service, stepped into the hall from a side door. She halted as she was confronted by the mob in front of the courtroom. Her usually bland expression contorted into one of dismay. She pushed her way through the crowd and approached Phoebe, her eyes ablaze. "May I ask what you're doing?"

"Certainly you may," Phoebe responded and turned back to the crowd. "As I was saying, I will shortly enter the courtroom with Isaac. All of you should follow quietly and take your seats in as orderly a fashion as possible. Once all seats have been taken, please begin lining up against the walls, and when the walls have all been lined, those of you who remain will have to wait out here in the hallway."

"Are all these people witnesses?" Mindy Blair asked.

"There are only two witnesses on my list, Ms. Blair," Phoebe said.

"That's my point."

"Since we're agreed on that, might I suggest we cease wasting valuable time?" Phoebe opened the door and extended her hand.

Blair shook her head and moved into the courtroom. Phoebe held the door open for Isaac and me, and we moved to the front of the room, holding hands. I gave Isaac a good luck kiss on the cheek, placed my coat across three seats in the front row, and went outside to find my parents. When we returned, the clerk was at his desk, wagging his head at the crowd. Phoebe and Isaac were seated at the defense table, and Mindy Blair was furiously pacing in front of hers. Phoebe and Isaac had indeed accomplished what they'd set out to do: the courtroom was packed, standing room only, and several of Isaac's supporters were left milling about in the hallway.

A few minutes later, the courtroom buzzer sounded, and Judge Tanaka entered the room. He stood by the back door for a moment, slipping on his robe and staring at the crowd. Then he slowly approached the bench.

"Poor man," my father whispered. "This is going to be interesting."

"Good morning, counselors," Tanaka said.

"Good morning, Your Honor," Phoebe and Ms. Blair responded in unison.

"May I ask who all of these people are?"

"These people are supporters of the respondent, Mr. Perez," Phoebe explained.

Tanaka looked around the room. "Why are there so many of them, Ms. Thistlewig?"

"Your Honor, I'm going to request that all these people leave the courtroom immediately," Ms. Blair said.

"On what grounds, Ms. Blair?" Tanaka asked.

"Well, just look at them, Your Honor," she answered. "There isn't any place for them to sit."

"I see. Your request is denied, Ms. Blair. Ms. Thistlewig, I'm awaiting your response."

"Your Honor, given that Mr. Perez worked for several years in a community legal clinic in Los Angeles and more recently at a law firm here in San Francisco with a robust pro bono practice, he has amassed many friends and supporters. They have come here in appreciation of the work he has done and in a show of support for his cause."

"Thank you, Ms. Thistlewig. Mr. Zane, please take a head count of these people and pass a sheet of paper around the room on which they can record their names and addresses. I will then enter the information on the record. Once that has been done, they must all leave the courtroom, all except those who will be testifying as witnesses in this matter and the members of Mr. Perez's family. Agreed?"

Phoebe and Ms. Blair agreed, and we spent the next quarter of an hour gathering the names and addresses of everyone who had shown up. Only when the courtroom was evacuated of everyone except Isaac, the lawyers, my parents and me, did Tanaka come back out and switch on his tape recorder.

"We're back on the record in the Matter of Respondent Isaac Edgar Perez, case number A98-589-437. This is Judge James Tanaka of the United States Immigration Court. It is the 31st of August, 1997. The respondent is present, as are his counsel and counsel for the Service. Please state your appearances for the record."

"Phoebe Thistlewig for the respondent."

"Mindy Blair for the Service."

"Ms. Thistlewig, how will you be proceeding today?" Tanaka asked.

"Your Honor, the respondent has filed an amended Application for Asylum and for Withholding of Removal, as well as a binder of documents that shall serve as evidence at our hearing. We have also served trial counsel with a copy of the same. Has the court had an opportunity to review the Application and Evidence?"

"Yes, Counsel." Tanaka hefted a fat binder above his head. "I've gone through all of it. What's your pleasure at this time?"

"Respondent is ready to proceed in the matter."

"Does the Service have any objections, Ms. Blair?" Tanaka asked.

"Not at all, Your Honor. Let's get this show on the superhighway." Ms. Blair glanced at Isaac before returning to her notes.

"All right, then, if you're ready, Ms. Thistlewig," Tanaka said, "you may begin your direct."

Chapter 26

"Thank you, Your Honor." Phoebe turned to Isaac. "Please state your complete name for the record, spelling your first, middle, and last names."

"Isaac, I-S-A-A-C; Edgar, E-D-G-A-R; Perez, P-E-R-E-Z."

"Mr. Perez, how did you arrive in the United States?"

"How do you mean?" Isaac asked.

"Was it by air, by water, by land?"

"By land."

"Which route did you take?"

"I made my way from San Salvador, through Guatemala and Mexico, and then crossed the border into California."

"By what means of transportation did you arrive? Car, bus, train?"

"We took a car to the Guatemalan border, a bus to the Mexican border, then a train from the Mexican border to Mexico City. We waited in Mexico City for a few days and then rode in the back of a big truck until we reached Tijuana. A couple weeks later, at night, we crossed into the United States on foot, near San Ysidro."

"When you say *we*, to whom are you referring?"

"There was a group of us traveling together."

"You all knew each other?"

"No. I didn't know any of the others. But the same person was escorting all of us. Each of us had made our own separate arrangement with him."

"You're referring now to the *coyote*, the person who made the travel arrangements?"

Isaac nodded.

"Please answer yes or no for the record, Mr. Perez," Tanaka said. "The tape machine can't record nonverbal responses such as nodding or shaking of the head."

"My answer is yes. I was referring to the coyote."

"Thank you, Mr. Perez," Phoebe said. "Now then, were you inspected by the United States Immigration Service at the time of your entry?"

"Was I inspected?"

"Yes, in other words, were you given permission to enter the United States by a US Immigration Officer at the US–Mexico border, or did you present any kind of a visa to a US Immigration Officer at the border prior to entering the United States?"

"No, we just jumped a fence and ran to meet someone waiting for us on the other side."

"And did you, in fact, meet someone on the other side of the fence?"

"No. I was caught by the border police."

"Do you remember the date you were apprehended?"

"Objection," Ms. Blair said. "The witness said caught, not apprehended."

Phoebe turned a full ninety degrees in her chair toward Ms. Blair. "You're not serious, are you?"

"Counsel, please," Tanaka said. "Direct your comments to the bench."

"Yes, Your Honor. But really—"

"That objection is overruled. Ms. Blair, I don't want to hear any more of that type of objection. You may answer the question, Mr. Perez."

"I've forgotten it already," Isaac said, visibly flustered by the proceedings.

"The question," Tanaka said, "was whether or not you remembered the date you were apprehended."

"Right. Yes, clearly: February 14, 1986. St. Valentine's Day."

"Not a very happy Valentine's Day, was it?" Phoebe asked, casting a sidelong glance at Ms. Blair.

"Objection," Ms. Blair said.

Phoebe threw up her hands. "I withdraw the question."

"It wasn't exactly a question, was it, Ms. Thistlewig?" Tanaka said.

"In any event, Your Honor, I've withdrawn whatever it was. May I proceed with my direct?"

"Please."

"Thank you. Mr. Perez, what happened after you were apprehended?"

"I was released on bond."

"Who posted the bond?"

"The coyote, I guess. I don't remember his name. It's probably in the file."

"And why did you come to the United States?"

"To escape the political persecution in my country."

"Objection," Ms. Blair interjected. "The witness is stating a legal conclusion."

"Sustained. The answer is stricken. Ask another question, Ms. Thistlewig."

"What happened to you in El Salvador that made you come to the United States?" Phoebe asked.

"My brothers and father were killed, and my mother was afraid I would be next. So she sent me away."

"Objection. Nonresponsive. The question was what happened to him, not what happened to his father and brothers."

"Your Honor," Phoebe said, waving a sheaf of legal authority, "the law is clear that fear of persecution based on membership in a persecuted family class is a legitimate basis for an asylum claim."

"Nevertheless, Ms. Thistlewig," Tanaka answered, "the question, *your* question actually, was what happened to him, was it not?"

"His brothers and father being killed isn't something that happened to him? Mr. Perez was a member of a family targeted for persecution."

"That remains to be proven, counsel. That's your burden at this hearing. Objection sustained. Ask your next question, please."

"I have another objection, Your Honor," Ms. Blair said.

"Enough, Ms. Blair," Tanaka said. "The court sustained your last objection. The witness's answer is stricken."

"Your Honor, with respect, I would like to make my second objection for the record."

"Request denied, Ms. Blair. Your office can take it up on appeal. Continue, Ms. Thistlewig."

"Thank you, Your Honor. Mr. Perez, did anything happen to you personally while you were in El Salvador, anything that frightened you and made you want to leave the country?"

Isaac looked down at the table for a moment. His lower lip disappeared into his mouth and then puckered out.

"Mr. Perez, are you with us?" Tanaka said.

Isaac nodded. "Yes . . . something happened."

"Please tell the court what happened to you personally," Phoebe said.

"One afternoon, it was just after New Year's in 1986, me and my older brother Arturo—he taught at the university I attended—we were coming home from school one afternoon when the bus we were on was stopped by some soldiers who had set up a roadblock."

"Objection, Your Honor," Ms. Blair said. "This is obviously going to be a narrative."

"The court will be going off the record," said Tanaka into the microphone. He switched off the tape recorder, removed his glasses, and glared at Ms. Blair. "Ms. Blair, are you going to be the cause of a two-day hearing?"

"Not me, Your Honor." She stood up. "I've made a legitimate objection. According to the Federal Rules of Evidence—"

"Don't lecture this court, Ms. Blair. I know the law. But this information will come out one way or the other, either by way of a narrative or by way of a blow-by-blow question and response format. You do understand that, I hope."

"Well, yes—"

"And you don't see a jury here that might be confused by a narrative answer, do you?"

"No, Your Honor, you're the finder of fact here, but—"

"That's correct. I'm glad you understand that. Now then, please allow Counsel to complete her direct and reserve your objections only for the most egregious violations of the Federal Rules of Evidence. Do we understand each other?"

"Yes, Judge." Ms. Blair sat down, took up her pen, and poised it over her notepad.

"Thank you." Tanaka switched the tape machine back on and continued: "We're back on the record. The Service's last objection is overruled. Go on, Ms. Thistlewig."

Phoebe cleared her throat. "Mr. Perez, you've stated the bus on which you and your brother Arturo were riding was stopped by some soldiers, is that correct?"

"Yes, that's right."

"What happened next?"

"The bus driver got off to see what the problem was and was shot dead on the spot by someone wearing a uniform."

"Did you actually see this?"

"Yes, through the window of the bus."

"Do you know the identity of the person in the uniform who shot the bus driver?"

"No," Isaac answered, his eyes fixed on the wood-paneled wall of the courtroom. "It was a young guy, a teenager. He was part of a group of a half-dozen uniformed young men. I heard the others refer to him as *Mi General*, or My General."

"You could hear that from inside the bus?"

"No, later, after they took us off the bus."

"What happened next?"

"Some of the passengers panicked and tried to jump out the windows of the bus. Arturo and I did our best to keep calm. But when the soldiers noticed the other passengers were escaping, they stormed the bus and herded us off at gunpoint."

"And then what happened?"

"They ordered us to stand against a nearby shack."

"What were you feeling at this point?"

"I was terrified. I tried my best to keep calm, but I'd never been so afraid in my life. We weren't sure what they wanted, whether they were going to forcibly recruit us into the army, whether they wanted to interrogate us, or whether they were going to kill us like they had the bus driver."

"Do you have any idea why these people targeted the bus you were in?"

"Most likely because my brother and some of the others on the bus belonged to a university teachers' union with political ties to a left-leaning party called *Andes 21 de Julio*. The government considered the universities to be incubators for leftist revolutionary groups, and it blamed the teachers and professors for allowing it."

Judge Tanaka cleared his throat and leaned forward. "Mr. Perez, are you suggesting these men were acting at the behest of the Salvadoran government?"

"Well, they were wearing government-issued army uniforms. I didn't know them personally, but I think it's fair to conclude that people wearing army uniforms are in the army; that is, unless someone can prove otherwise."

"Bravo, Mr. Perez," said Phoebe, gifting him an approving smile, "we'll make a lawyer of you yet."

Tanaka shook a finger at her. "Decorum, Ms. Thistlewig, remember your decorum."

Ms. Blair rolled her eyes and buried her head in her notes.

"These soldiers, Mr. Perez," Tanaka said, "and, please forgive me, counsel, for taking over your direct examination for a moment."

Phoebe placed her hand on her heart and bowed deferentially.

"These soldiers, did they mistreat you physically, or did they just detain you?"

Isaac frowned and whispered something to Phoebe. After a moment of thought, she placed her hand on his shoulder and spoke into his ear. Isaac's face clouded over and, from where I was seated, I could tell he was close to tears.

"Do you need a moment, Mr. Perez?" Tanaka asked.

"This next part's difficult for me to talk about, sir."

"All right, then take your time."

"Thank you, Your Honor." Isaac drew in a long breath and let it out slowly. He looked over his shoulder at me and snuck in a half wave before turning back to finish his story. "My brother Arturo, Your Honor, may he rest in peace, was always the diplomat of the family, the peacemaker. Everyone liked him because he knew how to—well, he just had this way of making things better, that's all." Isaac rubbed at his face with the back of his sleeve. "Anyway, he tried to reason with the soldier nearest him. I can still hear his last words: *Hermanos, por favor, no hagan esto.* Brothers, please don't do this."

Isaac fell silent a moment. I could see his jaw clenching and unclenching. Then he looked up at Tanaka and spoke through gritted teeth. "The soldier smashed Arturo's head with the back of his rifle . . . hard . . . I was close enough to hear the crack . . . then he fell face down in the dirt. The soldier kept hitting him again and again . . . it was awful. I wanted to do something . . .

anything . . . to scream at the soldier to stop. But I just stood there frozen . . . like a complete dummy." He looked down at the table. "Then two others . . . two other soldiers . . . they. . . they . . ." his voice trailed off. Phoebe touched his hand, urging him to continue.

"They what, Mr. Perez?" Tanaka said.

Isaac looked up and stared into the middle distance, conjuring up the memory. "They took turns kicking . . . really kicking . . . my brother's head. Like it was a football. Until . . ." He looked down at the table again. "Until it didn't . . . until it didn't look like a head anymore."

The courtroom fell quiet, and everyone edged forward on their seats, Mindy Blair included.

"A gunshot went off," Isaac continued after a long pause, cocking his head to one side as if hearing it in the distance. "It startled everyone, even the soldiers. The one they called 'Mi General' had fired his pistol in the air. He shouted at the soldiers . . . told them to stop playing. To get to work . . . But Arturo . . . my brother . . . he was dead. Murdered."

Isaac lifted tear-filled eyes to Tanaka. "Your Honor asked me if the soldiers physically mistreated me personally. Well, the answer is no. The only reason I can think of for that is that some miracle happened that saved me."

"What miracle was that, Mr. Perez?" Tanaka said.

"The soldiers started arguing with each other about something. A few minutes later, it turned into a big fistfight. Then they started shooting at each other, and I, along with the rest of the passengers, scattered in every direction. I ran and ran, through neighborhoods, through fields, and up into the hills, and I hid there until it got dark. I was shaking . . . hungry . . . exhausted. I ended up passing out under a tree. When it got light, I found my way back home, keeping away from the main roads. The next day, my mother hired a coyote to take me out of the country. She'd lost one son; she didn't want to lose me, too . . .

her baby. Five weeks later, I crossed the border into the States."

I glanced over at my parents. Tears were streaming down my mother's cheeks, and she dabbed at them with a handkerchief, gazing at Isaac with one of the most pained expressions I'd ever seen on her face. My father was sitting forward on the bench, tugging at his beard, following the proceeding like someone watching a tennis match—as if he were presiding over the hearing himself.

"What happened to the rest of your family?" Phoebe asked.

"A few months later, my father and my second brother were killed in a bomb blast in San Salvador's city center. My mother died a couple of months ago, here in San Francisco."

"Do you have any other close family relatives anywhere in the world?"

"No."

"I'm sorry to hear that." Phoebe touched Isaac's arm, looking close to tears herself, then glanced down at her papers and sifted through them, collecting her thoughts. "Your Honor?"

"Yes, counsel?" Tanaka said, his voice barely audible.

"If I may, I'd like to turn now to respondent's second ground for his asylum claim."

"Your Honor," Ms. Blair said, tossing a glance over her shoulder at the back of the courtroom, "the Service is willing to stipulate that the respondent is a homosexual; that since coming to the United States, he has been living an openly homosexual lifestyle; that he's in a long-term relationship, etcetera, etcetera. We don't believe there is any need to go into all of the minutiae."

Phoebe rose to her feet. "Your Honor, I really must object to Ms. Blair's callous and condescending characterization of Mr. Perez's life as mere minutiae."

"Fine," Tanaka said, "Ms. Blair, please avoid using condescending language. Now please sit, Ms. Thistlewig. Does the respondent accept the Service's stipulation?"

At that moment, the door to the courtroom creaked open,

and I nearly blacked out from rage as I took in the sight of Silva creeping inside, sporting a pair of Wayfarers. Everyone in the courtroom turned to look at him as he sat at the back, looking for all the world like a Hollywood star—perfect hair, dark gray wool trousers, suspenders, and a nicely fitted navy blue shirt open at the collar. My eye was immediately drawn to the Star of David pendant displayed around his neck. I looked back at Isaac. He'd seen it, too. His face turned crimson, and I saw knives in his eyes. Phoebe also looked fit to blow a gasket, having been thrown off her stride by the unwelcome interruption. She tossed an irritated glance at me, and my father grasped my arm.

"Does the respondent accept the Service's stipulation?" repeated Tanaka.

"The Service withdraws the stipulation for the moment, if we may, Your Honor," Ms. Blair blurted out. "And we'd like to request a brief recess."

All of us turned back to the proceedings, surprised by the government's sudden change of tack and still thrown by Silva's appearance on the scene.

"On what grounds, Ms. Blair?" Tanaka asked.

"Our rebuttal witness has only just arrived," Blair said, gesturing toward Silva, who removed his sunglasses and stood up. "I'd like a few minutes to confer with him."

"Your Honor," Phoebe said. "I must strenuously object. The Service did not advise us of any such witness." She held up her witness list.

"That's true, Ms. Blair." Tanaka skimmed his copy. "I don't see a rebuttal witness on your list."

"It was all very last minute, Your Honor, and we weren't even sure he was going to be able to make it to the hearing."

Tanaka looked up at Silva, still standing with his hands in his pockets, his face devoid of any expression.

"Sir, please state your name for the record," Tanaka said.

"Your Honor!" Phoebe said.

"It's my turn now, Ms. Thistlewig, if you don't mind," Tanaka responded.

"But this is most irregular, Your Honor, to be surprised in this manner by a witness of whom we had no advance notice."

"I am aware of that, Ms. Thistlewig," Tanaka said. "May I continue?"

Phoebe sat down and lowered her head to say something to Isaac, who looked close to tears.

"Noting no further response from respondent's attorney," Tanaka said, "I repeat my question to the gentleman who appeared in the courtroom following the Service's proposed stipulation, whom Ms. Blair has identified as her rebuttal witness: Sir, please state your full name for the record."

"Alejandro Jesus Silva, Your Honor," Silva said in a resonant voice that carried throughout the courtroom.

"Thank you, Mr. Silva," Tanaka responded. "Please sit while I confer with the lawyers off the record in my chambers."

He switched off his tape machine and signaled for Phoebe and Blair to follow him. Phoebe whispered something to Isaac and squeezed his arm as she rose from the table, and he nodded his agreement.

Isaac rested his head on crossed arms. I looked back at Silva, who pulled a smug smile and lifted his eyebrows at me. I swung back around and mastered the urge to confront him, especially as he'd been identified as a witness. The last thing I needed was a tampering allegation leveled against me.

"What's happening?" my mother whispered to my father.

He took her hand and patted it. "The judge called a recess to discuss a surprise witness with the lawyers."

"May I?" I asked the clerk, pointing at Isaac.

"Be my guest," he answered.

I crossed the bar and placed my hand on Isaac's back.

"Are you all right?" I asked in a low voice.

"What's he doing here?" Isaac asked through clenched teeth.

"I have no idea. But I don't imagine Tanaka will let him testify without any advance notice."

"But he can if he wants to, can't he? He's the judge."

"Well, yes, but—"

At that moment, Phoebe came out of chambers, followed by Ms. Blair, who exited the courtroom through a side door. I could tell by her stony expression and controlled movements that Phoebe was worried.

"Gentlemen, follow me," she said.

I took Isaac's hand, and we walked behind her past my parents, past Silva, and out the door to the breakout room across the hall.

"As you know, gentlemen, we had planned to offer evidence about Isaac's openly gay lifestyle, as this was relevant to our asylum claim, given El Salvador's appalling human rights record and the country's social hostility to homosexual men. That evidence was meant to include testimony from yourself, Mr. Mendes, regarding your shared life with Isaac."

"But the government's lawyer said she was willing to stipulate to all that," Isaac said.

"The operative word here is *was*," Phoebe said. "Now that Mr. Silva has put in an appearance, the lovely Ms. Blair is daring us to present that evidence so that she can machine-gun it down with whatever he, Mr. Silva, has to say."

"But she can't just put on a surprise witness," I said.

Phoebe looked first at Isaac, then at me. "We'd have grounds for an appeal if the judge were to allow it over my objection. And he very well may do so. Alternatively, Ms. Blair has offered to dispense with the witness if we withdraw that particular ground for our claim. It's up to us."

"Screw that!" I said. "I say we put on our evidence. Even if Silva were to testify, you could easily impeach him. The guy's a convicted felon."

Phoebe shrugged. "Ms. Blair consented to our having a

word with Mr. Silva before we decide how to play this. It's most irregular. But it *would* be helpful to know what's coming."

Isaac nodded at this.

"No," I warned.

"I want to talk to him," Isaac said.

"I don't think we should," I countered. "We already know what he's going to say. Plus, he has this way of getting into a person's head—"

"Bring him in here, please, Phoebe," Isaac said.

Phoebe disappeared from the room, and Isaac turned away from me, shutting out any further conversation between us. A moment later, Phoebe reappeared with Silva. She directed him to sit at one end of the table.

"I want to speak with him in private," Isaac said as Phoebe reached for her chair, "with Marc."

Phoebe cocked her head at him; Silva nodded his agreement, and I felt my blood pressure spike.

"It won't take long," Isaac said.

"I don't recommend this," Phoebe warned.

"It's okay, Phoebe." Isaac offered her a weary smile. "I'll call you back inside in a moment."

She regarded him for a beat, then nodded in resignation and slipped out the door.

"Alone at last," Silva said, crossing his arms. "Just the three of us."

"Cut the comedy," Isaac said.

"It wasn't a joke," Silva responded.

"What do you think you're doing?" I asked him.

Isaac held up his palm at me and shook his head, then looked back at Silva.

"Give Marc his pendant, please," he said, pointing at Silva's open collar.

Silva's hand shot up to the six-pointed star, and he caressed it between his fingertips. "He gave it to me."

Isaac turned to me, incredulous. "You gave it to him?"

"He was trying to lure me back to his hotel to retrieve it," I explained. "So I told him he could keep it to have done with him."

Isaac looked back at Silva. "That star was a gift from me to Marc. It was never meant for you. Give it back." He held out his hand.

One side of Silva's mouth pulled up into a smile. He buttoned the top button of his shirt and hid the pendant from view. "You gave it to him; he gave it to me; now it's mine. That's how it works. Right, Marc?"

"You're a real son of a bitch, you know that?" I said, with as much venom as I could muster.

Silva smiled and addressed Isaac: "It's like the situation with Marc. He was yours; now he's mine. Or he soon will be, once you've lost this case and they've deported you."

"When are you going to get it through your thick head that I'm not interested in you?" I shouted. "Just give it up and go away. Let us live our lives."

"Has he *really* told you everything that happened between us?" Silva asked Isaac.

"That's none of your business," Isaac said. "What matters is what he just told you: Leave us alone."

"He's only saying that because you're still here. Between the two of us, he prefers me, and he knows it. Sexually, psychologically, I'm more of a match for him than you ever were. And once you're gone, it's *my* show."

"Just leave, Alejandro," I growled, having lost any vestige of restraint.

"Leave, stay, it really doesn't matter, does it? If I get to tell the judge my story, I win, even if his lawyer impeaches my testimony. And if his lawyer accepts Ms. Blair's condition to leave out all the gay stuff to shut me up, I still win. Either way, he's bound to lose and be deported. Then you and I, Marc, can press the restart button." He turned to Isaac. "This is game over, amigo."

Isaac stared at Silva in the silence that followed until Silva started to squirm. I opened my mouth to say something but thought the better of it and kept quiet. After a charged moment, Isaac pointed to the door.

"Go," he said to Silva.

I expected Silva to protest or at least to hit back with a clever retort. Instead, he rose from the table and glanced briefly at me before swaggering victoriously out the door. An instant later, Phoebe was in the room.

"Accept the lawyer's condition," Isaac instructed her. "The sooner that guy is out of here, the better."

"We're back on the record," Tanaka said. "Following a conference in chambers, counsel for the petitioner has agreed with the Service to withdraw petitioner's claim for asylum on the grounds of his homosexuality. Is that correct, Ms. Thistlewig?"

"Yes, it is, Your Honor," Phoebe said, holding up her head, trying her best to maintain the appearance of control.

"Is that correct, Ms. Blair?"

"Yes, Your Honor."

"In that case, the Service's rebuttal witness, Mr. Silva, is dismissed."

"Thank you, Your Honor," Silva said, executing a curt bow and slipping out the door.

An audible sigh of relief arose from the front row, and my father reached down and squeezed my hand.

"Ms. Thistlewig, the floor is yours," Tanaka said.

"Thank you, Your Honor." Phoebe shuffled through her papers. "We'd now like to direct the court's attention to respondent's exhibits A through H. These documents include reports from such watchdog groups as Amnesty International;

they detail the discrimination and personal danger daily encountered in El Salvador by members of various persecuted social groups because of their political opinions, whether actual or perceived. Included among these persecuted social groups are politically active families, such as respondent's."

"The court notes the documents and has previously reviewed them," Tanaka said.

"Thank you, Your Honor. Respondent requests these exhibits be moved into evidence as respondent's A through H."

"Any objection from the Service?"

"None, Your Honor."

"Very well, then. The exhibits are hereby accepted and marked respondent's A through H." Tanaka handed a binder to his clerk and lifted his eyebrows at Phoebe. "Does the Respondent rest?"

"For the time being, Your Honor." Phoebe reordered her materials in preparation for the cross-examination. "Of course, we reserve the right to redirect."

"Of course," Tanaka echoed. "Ms. Blair, does the Service wish to cross-examine the witness?"

"Thank you, Your Honor, yes." Ms. Blair grabbed her notepad and stood up. "Mr. Perez, what is your understanding of the geopolitical conditions of your native region of Central America during the early 1980s?"

"I don't understand your question," Isaac said. "What is my understanding of what?"

"The geopolitical conditions of Central America in the early 1980s."

"I still don't know what you're asking. Each country in Central America has a different political situation. Nicaragua was controlled by leftist revolutionaries; El Salvador by a right-wing government and was fighting a civil war; Costa Rica has had a stable democracy for a long time; Guatemala's civil war was just getting underway; Belize and Panama . . . What do you mean by geopolitical?"

"Never mind," Blair said. "Let's stick with El Salvador. What was the political situation there?"

"Objection," Phoebe said. "Asked and answered. He already said that El Salvador was in the midst of a civil war."

"Overruled," Tanaka said. "Now, please, Ms. Thistlewig, don't you start."

"Forgive me, Your Honor."

"Done. Mr. Perez, you may answer the question."

Isaac nodded and drew a breath. "At the start of the civil war," he started, "the country was in the hands of a right-wing military junta that enforced harsh strictures on dissent. The junta was eventually replaced by a provisional civilian government that continued many of the policies of the junta and was supported by the United States. The FMLN was the major opposition party. It was a leftist party with a guerrilla wing that received backing from the Soviet Union, Cuba, and Nicaragua. These two groups were the main players in the civil war, and the people were pretty much evenly split in their support for either of the two groups. This led to a civil war that lasted ten or twelve years. What else would you like to know?"

"What was the political platform of the ruling government?"

"I beg your pardon?"

"Objection," Phoebe said. "Irrelevant."

"It's very relevant, Your Honor," Blair countered. "The respondent claims fear of persecution in part because he was a member of a family that held political views in opposition to those held by the government. Therefore, the respondent's understanding of those political views is relevant to his credibility."

"I'll allow it," Tanaka said. "Answer the question, Mr. Perez."

"I'm not sure they even had a platform," he said.

"Okay . . ." Blair said, "then can you tell me what the major aims of the FMLN were?"

"Land redistribution, social justice."

"What do you mean by social justice?"

"The adoption of laws to protect workers from exploitation by their employers, the implementation of a system to provide adequate food and shelter for the poor and unemployed, those sorts of things."

"How do you know about these aims?"

"These things were everyday topics of conversation at that time. It was all that was ever discussed on television and in the newspapers and in people's homes."

"But you yourself were never a member of the FMLN, were you?"

"No, I wasn't."

"In fact, you were not a member of, or affiliated with, *any* political party or action group of any kind, were you?"

"No."

"And nobody in your family was in, or affiliated with, the FMLN or any other political party or action group, were they?"

"As I testified earlier, my brother was a member of a university teachers' union with political ties to *Andes 21 de Julio*."

"Yes, you said that," Blair said in a voice as arid as the Kalahari. She flipped through the pages of a binder. "Did you happen to submit any evidence of this alleged membership?"

"I don't think we did." Isaac looked at Phoebe, who shook her head.

"Well then," Blair said, "why don't you enlighten us about this party *Andes 21 de Julio*. What were their major aims? What were they fighting for?"

"I'm not sure. I think the same things as the FMLN."

"In fact, you have no idea what *Andes 21 de Julio* is, do you, Mr. Perez?"

"I'm not sure. But—"

"Aren't you, maybe, just making all of this up to shore up your case?"

"I'm not making anything up," Isaac stammered.

"Objection, argumentative." Phoebe's face flushed.

"Sustained," Tanaka said. "Next question, Ms. Blair."

Blair flashed her teeth and moved closer to the defense table. "Isn't it possible, Mr. Perez, that your family was not targeted at all? That you and your family just happened to be in the wrong place at the wrong time? After all, your country was in the middle of a civil war. There were bound to be casualties. Isn't that possible?"

"Objection!" Phoebe said. "Counsel just threw no less than three separate questions at my client. It's clear she's trying to harry and confuse him."

"I'll allow it this time," Tanaka said. "Ms. Blair, please ask your questions one at a time. Mr. Perez, please answer the question."

Isaac sat quietly. Unblinking.

"Mr. Perez, the question," Tanaka repeated. "Please answer."

Isaac closed his eyes and lowered his chin to his chest.

Judge Tanaka peered over his glasses at him. "Ms. Thistlewig, is there something wrong with your client?"

Phoebe leaned in Isaac's direction and said something to him. He slowly shook his head. She waved me over. "Your Honor," she said, "May we take a short break?"

"Five minutes, Ms. Thistlewig. We're going off the record." Tanaka switched off the tape recorder, flung off his robe, and disappeared from the courtroom.

"What's wrong?" I asked, putting my hand on Isaac's shoulder.

"Outside, both of you," Phoebe said. She stalked out of the room. I pulled Isaac up by the arm, and we followed in her wake.

In the empty hallway, Isaac and I waited silently for Phoebe to speak. She paced up and down, her heels going *click-click* on the Formica tile, pausing only occasionally to glance at us before resuming her pacing. I took Isaac by the hand and led him to one of the benches lining the hallway. Suddenly, Phoebe snapped her fingers and approached us.

"I don't mean to be defeatist, young man," she said, shoving me aside with her rump and sitting down next to Isaac, "but we're going to lose this one. I can sense it. First, the Silva debacle, and now this."

"I'm sorry, Phoebe," Isaac murmured, "but I couldn't stand the way that woman was calling me a liar."

"Now, now," she said, "there's no need for apologies. Anyone would have reacted the same way. Only the worst of us are hard as leather. That said, I don't see any point in continuing with this farce. You're not going to be able to satisfy them with what they want because you're no expert in Salvadoran politics. And, really, there's no requirement that you should be."

"So what's he supposed to do?" I asked.

"I was getting to that, Mr. Mendes." Phoebe continued without looking at me. "Fortunately, we have plenty of material to work with on appeal. So, if you're in agreement, I suggest we aim toward concluding this hearing as quickly as possible. Are you with me?"

Isaac nodded, his eyes focused intensely and exclusively on her eyes.

A loud squeak echoed through the hall as the clerk opened the courtroom door and stepped into the hall. "Excuse me, folks, but the judge is ready."

"Thank you, Mr. Zane, we're coming now," Phoebe said.

The clerk withdrew, closing the door behind him.

"Listen to me clearly, Isaac," Phoebe said, rising from the bench, "from now on, I want your responses to consist entirely of the following words: *yes*, *no*, and *I don't know*. I'll take care of the rest. Yes?"

"Okay," Isaac answered and followed Phoebe into the courtroom.

"Back on the record." Tanaka switched on the tape machine before everyone had finished taking their places. "Ms. Blair, repeat your last question, please."

Blair strode over to the defense table and stared down at Isaac. "Isn't it possible, Mr. Perez, that your family was not targeted at all?"

Isaac slowly pushed his chair away from the counsel table and stood up. Phoebe and I flashed a questioning look at each other. Only a few inches of airspace now separated Blair's face from his. Phoebe made an abortive hand movement, suppressing the instinct to yank Isaac into his chair by his shirtsleeve. Blair inched forward toward him, and Judge Tanaka looked over the top of his glasses at them.

"Mr. Perez," Tanaka said, "may I ask what you are doing?"

"I'm standing to answer the question."

"May I ask why?"

Isaac frowned at Tanaka. "This lawyer got up and moved to my side of the room," he said. "I can't exactly see her very well to answer her question when she's towering over me."

Tanaka tossed his pencil into the air. It clattered as it landed next to the microphone on the bench. "Ms. Blair, move back to your side of the room. Mr. Perez answer the question, if you will."

"May I remain standing, Your Honor?"

"If you wish to stand, you may stand."

"Thank you very much. So my answer is *no*."

"Your answer to what is *no*?" Tanaka asked, raising an eyebrow.

"That's my answer to her last question."

Blair's cross-examination of Isaac continued in this halting manner for another quarter of an hour. Once she was finished, Phoebe declined to redirect. Instead, she spent the next half hour arguing the equities of Isaac's asylum case from her exhibits. Once she had finished, she announced that she was resting.

"Very well, Ms. Thistlewig," Tanaka said, eyeing the clock. "Will you be delivering a closing argument? Or are you happy for me to render my verdict based on your presentation? We're nearing the two hours you promised."

"I most certainly intend to deliver a closing, Your Honor, if it pleases the court," Phoebe said.

"Ms. Blair, does the Service have something prepared?"

Mindy Blair waved a piece of paper. "It's right here, Your Honor."

Tanaka crossed his arms and leaned back in his chair and nodded at Phoebe. "All right, then. Proceed with your closing, counsel."

"Thank you, Your Honor."

Phoebe rose from her chair and scanned the courtroom, making eye contact with everyone there. Then she looked at the judge.

"Your Honor, you have before you today an exemplary young man. As you know, I have been practicing before you for the past ten years. Never in those ten years have I ever seen a respondent who has filled a courtroom to the breaking point with friends, supporters, and admirers. And, dare I say it, I doubt that Your Honor has seen such an impressive show of support either. Only an exemplary person could attract that level of admiration. And the reason for that? In the twelve years since he arrived on our fair shores, Isaac—for Isaac is what I call the respondent, Your Honor—has dedicated his life to serving others. The very week after he arrived, before he could even utter a complete sentence in the English language, Isaac offered himself as a volunteer at a legal clinic, where he worked five hours a day, six days a week, helping to process the asylum applications of others in the Los Angeles Central American community. And not only their asylum applications, but their applications for employment authorization, medical screening, and housing benefits as well. In his work, he has helped victims of domestic violence, torture survivors, individuals with physical and mental disabilities, elders, displaced juveniles, and lesbian, gay, bisexual, and transgender workers who have suffered discrimination on the job. I repeat, Your Honor, the young man before you did all of this as a volunteer—that's *unpaid*. Whereas others may have sought paid employment straightaway, Isaac chose first to help others. Only an exemplary person would have done such a thing. What is most remarkable here is that whilst working at that legal clinic, this young man *simultaneously* studied English as a second language, which he has mastered; earned himself a paralegal certificate by attending evening classes; and, in due course, sought part-time paid employment at a law office. Again, most exemplary."

She continued, "Following the completion of his studies and his relocation to San Francisco with his long-term partner, Mr. Mendes, Isaac found employment, not at a high-powered litigation firm, but at this city's premier public interest firm, continuing his *oeuvre*, if you will, of service to his fellow man. In short, Your Honor, you have before you today a hard-working, selfless young man who has tirelessly served others, has never received or requested a single penny of government assistance, and has never been in trouble with the law. Whilst you may or may not agree that he is entitled to the benefits he seeks before you today, Your Honor, you cannot deny that Isaac Perez—whom I am so proud to count as a dear friend—is a most exemplary young man and that this country would be all the poorer if it were to send him away."

Phoebe placed her hand on Isaac's shoulder and looked down at him with a tender expression, then slowly sat down. Isaac smiled at her and nodded.

"Thank you, Ms. Thistlewig," Tanaka said. "Ms. Blair, over to you."

Not bothering to stand, Ms. Blair delivered a halfhearted and truncated closing argument. I felt as if she was merely repeating the same canned argument she made, day in, day out, hearing after hearing, ad infinitum. Judging from Tanaka's seeming lack of interest in her words as he scribbled notes and paged through benchbook after benchbook, never bothering to look up, I believe I wasn't far off the mark.

After talking for around five minutes, Ms. Blair fell silent. All of us waited for Tanaka's decision while he continued attending to his notes and benchbooks. He finally raised his head and removed his half-glasses. He studied the large wall clock and then addressed his clerk.

"Mr. Zane, has counsel for the next case signed in yet?"

"Not yet, Your Honor."

"All right, then I believe I'll have time to issue my ruling now. Are all parties ready?"

Both Phoebe and Blair indicated their readiness, and Tanaka switched on his tape machine again.

"Back on the record," he said, putting on his glasses. "The court has heard from both the respondent and the Service. First of all, I would like to congratulate Mr. Perez on his accomplishments. It's not often I have before me individuals who have dedicated their lives to serving others in as selfless a manner as you have. I am also impressed by the fact that in the eleven years since you arrived, you've managed to master the English language and earn a college-level certificate in legal studies. I say without reservation that this country would be lucky to have you.

"However, what counts here is not my personal opinion, or the personal opinions of your many character witnesses and admirers, or the personal opinion of your able lawyer and advocate, Ms. Thistlewig. What counts here is the law. The Act states that for me to grant you asylum in the United States, you must prove to me that you have a credible fear of persecution were you to be returned to your home country because of your membership in a particular class. You have presented evidence here that demonstrates that you were present during the murder of some individuals, including your brother, by uniformed men you believe were in the Salvadoran military. You also presented evidence that your father and other brother were killed in a bomb blast. And you presented evidence that your mother sent you away from El Salvador because she was afraid you also would be killed. What you have failed to present to me is: (a) that you are a member of any persecuted class of persons and (b) that you have a reasonable fear of being persecuted in any way were you to be returned to El Salvador. Furthermore, even if you had been considered a target by the Salvadoran government during your country's civil war, that war is now over. The government has changed. And many of the former enemies in your country now sit side by side in the legislature. I am sure you and your lawyer are aware of this. I certainly am."

"Your Honor," Phoebe ventured, raising her hand, "I respectfully object."

Tanaka's mouth dropped a bit. Judges were not typically interrupted when ruling from the bench, and I could see Tanaka was no exception. "What is it, counsel?"

"No evidence was introduced by either party regarding the present composition of the government of El Salvador. With respect, the law does not permit you to consider evidence not presented at the hearing, and you certainly are not allowed to introduce it yourself at this time. So I move for a mistrial."

"Your motion is denied, counsel," Tanaka said. "I am going to allow myself to consider what is common knowledge and will take judicial notice of it for the purpose of these proceedings. Respectfully or not, counsel, please don't interrupt me again. As I was saying, I don't find that you, Mr. Perez, have a reasonable and credible fear of persecution were you to be returned to your native El Salvador.

"Furthermore, notwithstanding the fact your attorney has withdrawn the sexual orientation basis of your claim, I *would* like to say a few words about this for the record. I find no evidence of systematic persecution of homosexuals by the present government of El Salvador. There are no laws on the books there that make homosexual acts illegal or punishable by law. In fact, I understand that gay bars have begun to thrive in the capital city of San Salvador, which is where you are from. The acts of violence against homosexuals in El Salvador cited in the materials put out by Amnesty International and the other watchdog groups, which your lawyer cleverly snuck into evidence, appear to me to be random acts committed by bigoted and intolerant citizens against their homosexual countrymen. There is nothing exceptional about acts such as these. They happen in this country all the time, even in this fair city, and I am not aware of any of *our* citizens seeking asylum in other countries because of the random acts of violence committed against homosexuals in the United States.

"So then, while it pains me to do so, I am going to deny your Application for Asylum and for Withholding of Removal for the reasons I have cited in the record. Perhaps, Mr. Perez, you and your partner Mr. Mendes will be able to make a satisfactory life for yourselves in El Salvador.

"Ms. Thistlewig, I assume you are reserving your right to file a Notice of Intent to Appeal for your client?"

"I most certainly am," Phoebe said, gathering her binders and notes and stuffing them into her satchel. "We are also requesting that the court grant voluntary departure in this matter, in the event the appeal is either not filed or fails."

"That request is granted based on the evidence in the record," Tanaka said. "A copy of my ruling will be available Monday afternoon. Good luck, Mr. Perez."

And with that, Tanaka flew out of the courtroom, leaving his clerk to deal with the formalities.

Chapter 27

Phoebe moved to the clerk's desk, making a visible effort to avoid physical contact with Ms. Blair, who was trying to scurry out of the courtroom by the side door. There was an odd moment when they faced off over a narrow strip of carpet separating the two of them. Ms. Blair capitulated with a sarcastic flourish, and Phoebe squeezed past her.

Isaac swung around in his chair and surprised me with a broad smile. He melodramatically passed his hand over his forehead in the age-old sign of relief and waved me forward.

"Wow!" he said when I reached him, "I've never felt so damned good about losing in my entire life." He hugged me tight, and we swayed a bit before he finally released me; I'd never seen him so giddy before. "What a relief," he said.

Phoebe joined us, putting down her bag and placing her hands on our shoulders. "You two seem awfully happy," she said. "I expected the opposite."

"He's relieved," I explained with a smile. "Can you believe it?"

"It's like a weight's been lifted from my shoulders," Isaac said. "I don't know what I'm going to feel like tomorrow morning, but right now I'm happy. Thanks, Phoebe." He kissed me on the cheek. "I'm hungry," he said with a grin.

"Lunch is on me," Phoebe announced. "For both of you."

"All right, then," Isaac said, rubbing his hands together.

"Let's go."

"Sounds great, thank you," I said. "Is it all right if I bring my parents along? I'll cover them, of course."

"Certainly, you may," Phoebe said. "I know just the place."

She sidled over to my father, who was standing to one side with my mother, waiting for us. "Rabbi, I know a fabulous kosher Israeli restaurant off Union Square. The atmosphere is quite nice, and the food is lovely. I'd be honored to have you and your wife join us."

My father smiled at Phoebe. "That's very thoughtful of you, Ms. Thistlewig."

"Oh, please, Rabbi, there's no need to stand on ceremony with me." Her hand danced on his arm. "Call me Phoebe, please. You as well, Mrs. Mendes."

"Well, then, yes," my father said, "I believe we *will* join you."

My mother was pursing her lips in the background. I moved next to her and put my arm around her shoulder. "Doing all right, Ima?"

"I don't know what everyone's so happy about," she whispered. "Isaac lost, didn't he? And then there was that incident with that awful man."

"He's glad it's over, Ima. The pressure of it all was killing him. Me, too."

Isaac joined us and gave my mother a hug, and the three of us, Isaac and me on either side of my mother with our arms linked, followed Phoebe and my father out of the courtroom.

The courthouse was only five blocks from my office. With Ed's support, I'd been working on a substantially reduced schedule in the lead-up to Isaac's hearing, and it had been a couple of days since I'd last checked in. So as we exited the courthouse, I felt a sudden urge to go see him.

"Do you all mind if I catch up with you at the restaurant?" I said. "I'm really sorry, but I've got to go to my office for a few minutes."

Isaac cut his eyes at me. "Do you have to do that now?"

"It'll only take a couple of minutes, I promise."

Phoebe put her arm around Isaac and pulled him close. They looked like an old mismatched couple. "The restaurant's called Balagan," she announced.

"Yes," I said, "I know the place."

The sidewalks were jammed with the lunchtime crowd, and it took me double the usual time to maneuver my way to the office. When I arrived, I found Ed signing for a courier delivery at reception. He looked up at me as I walked into the building and beckoned me into the boardroom.

"I'm just back from Isaac's hearing," I said as he closed the door behind us. "My folks flew up from Los Angeles, and now they're all waiting for me to join them for lunch."

"How did it go?"

"Fine," I said. "We lost."

"I'm sorry to hear that, Marc." He patted my arm.

"Silva showed up."

Ed raised his eyebrows.

"The guy just won't go away. He wanted to testify against us."

"Jesus Christ!"

"We sent him packing," I explained. "But he may have influenced the outcome."

"Maybe he's after money. Have you thought about that?"

I gazed across the room and considered that for a moment. "No, it hadn't crossed my mind."

"It's what we do, Marc, day in, day out. Make the guy an offer—through a third party if you need to."

I nodded.

"He might go for it," Ed said.

"I'll think about it. In any case, Ed, I just wanted to swing by and thank you for allowing me the space to deal with everything I've had on my plate lately. I'm hoping things will start to improve."

"Let's hope so," he said absently, casting a glance around the boardroom. After a moment, he looked back at me. "What are you and Isaac going to do now? And where do things stand between us?"

"I don't know yet."

"I assume if he has to leave, you'll go with him."

"That's always been the plan. But as things stand, I have no idea what we're going to do. A lot is up in the air."

"I see," Ed said.

"Outside of my family, you'll be the first to know when things become clearer. Meanwhile, now that the hearing is out of the way, and I'm in a better headspace, I'll return to my normal schedule and responsibilities."

"That's good to know," he said. He put out his hand, and I grasped it. But instead of shaking my hand, he clasped it with his other hand and held it tight. "Welcome back, Marc, for as long as it lasts."

Ed's kindness moved me, and in that moment I felt genuine affection toward him. I pulled him close and hugged him. When I released him a few seconds later, he stepped back, a flabbergasted smile teetering awkwardly on his face.

"What did I do to deserve that?" he asked.

"Everything, Ed. Everything."

Feeling buoyant, I bounded up the stairs to my office, noting Vlad's empty desk with mixed feelings. I shuffled through a stack of mail on my desk and came across an envelope from the Canadian Embassy. I sliced it open with a flick of my wrist and skimmed the letter inside. It was an invitation to an interview for me at the Canadian consulate in Los Angeles at the end of January. A panicky feeling crept over me at the absence of Isaac's name. I quickly went through the remaining envelopes and found an identical letter addressed to Isaac. Just then, my cell phone fired off. It was Isaac.

"Nobody wants to start eating until you get here," he said. "And I'm starving. What are you doing?"

"Sorry! I'm on my way now," I said, trying my best to sound upbeat.

I stuffed the letters into my coat and ran out the door.

Fifteen minutes later, I arrived at the restaurant. My father and Phoebe were seated at one end of the table, engaged in an animated conversation. My mother and Isaac were at the other end glumly picking at a plate of baba ganoush, Isaac with an olive, my mother with a piece of stale pita bread. I plopped into an empty chair.

"I'm *so* sorry," I said sheepishly. "You should have started without me."

"I told you!" Isaac said to the rest of them. "He wasn't going to mind." He got up and walked over to one of the waitresses who had sped past our table, balancing a couple of steaming plates of chicken soup.

"What happened to you?" my mother asked. "You forgot about us, or what?"

"I got hung up at the office. I'm sorry, Ima." I kissed her and snatched up a piece of pita bread, smearing it with baba ganoush.

Isaac returned to his seat. "The food's coming now," he declared. He looked in the direction of Phoebe and my father and leaned across the table to me. "They seem to have hit it off."

"Marc," Phoebe said, "your father and I have been comparing the procedures between rabbinical court and immigration court. It's really quite fascinating."

"You should invite her to observe one of your proceedings, Gabriel," my mother remarked dryly. "I'm sure she'd enjoy that."

My father regarded my mother over the top of his glasses. Phoebe blinked at her for a moment, then looked at Isaac and at me with a befuddled smile. "Oh, dear," she said, "I do hope our hunger isn't going to lead to fisticuffs."

Before my mother could shoot off a retort, the food arrived, and her desire to eat overrode her instinct to fight. Taking her cue, we each turned to our meals.

Once we'd finished our main courses, I pulled out the letters from the embassy and waved them in the air.

"Oh, my Lord," Phoebe exclaimed. "Already?"

"What are those?" my mother asked. She removed her dark glasses and squinted at the envelopes.

Isaac snatched one of them out of my hand and ripped it open. He scanned it, mouthing the words to himself, an incredulous smile spreading across his face.

"What is it, Marc?" my father said.

Isaac held up the letter for everyone to see. "It's the interview," he said, "at the Canadian consulate. It's less than five months away."

"Why, that's wonderful," my mother said.

"Congratulations," my father added. "Good news at last."

"It's scheduled at the Canadian consulate in Los Angeles," I said. "So we'll probably be dropping in for another visit."

Phoebe squinted at the letter Isaac was holding up and looked at the one in my hand. "May I please see those?"

We handed her the letters, and she read through them, her jaw tensing as she compared the two. When she finished, she folded them neatly, slid them back into their envelopes, and looked up at us with a polite smile. "Yes," she said, "I do believe congratulations are in order—for both of you."

"What's the matter?" I asked.

"It may be nothing. We can discuss the details later."

"Is there a problem, Ms. Thistlewig?" my mother asked.

"Hannah," my father said, "she said they'd discuss it later."

"Hannah, Hannah," my mother repeated irritably. "If there's a problem, they might as well know now."

"Phoebe, do you see something wrong?" Isaac asked.

Poor Phoebe glanced around the table, then snatched up the letters. "There are two letters here."

"That's right," I said, "one for Isaac and one for me."

"It strikes me as odd. You filed one application, yet you receive two letters."

"Actually, I posted two applications together with one cover letter."

"But I prepared the applications," she explained. "Yours was meant to be filed as the principal application, as head of the household, and Isaac's as your dependent."

"Yes, and I prepared a second set modeled on yours, but presented the other way around. That way, if my application failed, Isaac could be considered the principal applicant with me as his dependent spouse. We talked about that."

"Oh, my," my mother said. "This sounds complicated."

"But you didn't tell me you were going to submit *both* sets," Phoebe said, looking flustered. "It wasn't supposed to be like that."

"I explained it all in my cover letter—that we were filing as one family unit."

Phoebe handed me the letters. "Well, evidently, they didn't see it that way."

"The appointments are on the same date and at the same time," Isaac said. "That must mean something."

Phoebe nodded. "I may be reading too much into it. But I think it's worth sending a follow-up letter to the consulate to clarify the issue."

Once we were back home and alone, Isaac migrated to the living room sofa and collapsed into it. He stared out the window at the bay, pale and unblinking, his dress shirt rumpled and his hair sticking up here and there. I brought him a glass of water and sat next to him.

"Are you all right?" I asked, smoothing his hair.

"I don't know." He took a sip of water and set aside the glass. "I feel all mixed up inside. So many different feelings: happy, sad, mad, frustrated, hopeful. It's like . . . as if my life were collapsing and blossoming at the same time. I don't know how to work it all out in my head."

"I know how that feels." I reached for the water glass and drained it. "But at least we have a plan."

Isaac sat up and unbuttoned his shirt. "Not really. What we have are contingencies."

"Canada's not a plan?"

"Canada's a contingency. We don't know that we're going to be approved. And even if we are, we don't know what we're going to do if and when we ever get there."

"We have time to figure it all out. Right now, we should just be thankful the hard part is over."

"I don't think it is." Isaac drew up his legs on the sofa and sat cross-legged.

"What do you mean?"

"Your admirer is still out there." Isaac gestured toward the door. "That's a disaster waiting to happen. It makes me nervous, not to mention how angry I am at the thought of him interfering."

"Ed thinks we should offer him money to make him go away."

"No way! We're not going to reward that bastard for trying

to ruin our lives. That fuckhead probably cost me my hearing."

"Maybe. Although it seems the judge would have ruled against us either way."

Isaac waved off my comment. "In any case, Phoebe thinks it's best if we ignore him, and I agree."

"If we don't do something, he's liable to follow us to Canada."

"Don't do anything, Marc! I say we leave it to the universe to take care of him. And let's do our best to carry on as normal, okay?"

"Yes, okay."

"Do you promise?"

"I swear it."

Chapter 28

Isaac and I showed up for our appointment at the Canadian consulate and were interviewed separately over our protests. Isaac walked out with an approval. I didn't.

"I'm not certain you're entirely suitable for Canada," my interviewing officer had explained. "That's a judgment call the immigration rules empower me to make."

"Why wouldn't I be?"

Her eye had flickered at an envelope sitting to one side of my application materials. "Some new evidence has come to light."

"What new evidence?"

"I'm not at liberty to say just yet," she said, sliding the envelope out of view. "What I *can* say, Mr. Mendes, is it's obvious to me you're not interested in the least in emigrating to Canada. Isn't that right? Canada isn't there to solve your relationship problems. Our doors are wide open to people who are keen to come to Canada because they want to become part of our society, because they like our country."

The interviewer had averted her eyes and pretended to pick a piece of lint off her blazer; then she looked back at me. "We'll let you know," she'd said, switching off her computer.

I met Isaac in the waiting room and explained what had happened. His elation quickly turned to anger, and I worried he would endanger his approval by saying or doing something he was going to regret later.

"Come on, let's go." I pulled him by the arm. "Let's talk outside."

As we rode down in the elevator, he continued to rant.

"Isaac," I said once we were outside the building, "did you by any chance mention to anyone that we were applying to Canada?"

"No! Why?"

"Not to anyone? Not at work, not to any of your friends?"

Isaac shook his head, carefully scouring his memory. After a beat, he looked up at me, his eyes opening wide. "Actually, I did mention it to Ingrid and Christianne, the Canadian women."

"When?" I asked.

"When we first received the interview notices."

"Why would you do that? We weren't supposed to tell anyone."

"I know; I'm sorry. I was so excited I was bursting to share the news with someone. But I didn't tell anyone else, I promise."

"How did they sound when you told them?"

"Ingrid sounded pretty happy. Christianne, not that much. Do you think the new evidence could have come from them?"

"I don't know. But they gave Silva their number at the restaurant, remember? And I'm pretty sure he was in contact with them because he mentioned something to me about the baby. They may have told him about the interview."

"Silva again! That motherfucker!" Isaac kicked a concrete planter in frustration. "Who knows what he might have said to these people about you—about us."

"It's best if we avoid jumping to conclusions," I said, pulling out my cell phone. "Why don't we call Phoebe and tell her what happened? She may be able to investigate."

Isaac grabbed the phone out of my hand and punched in her number.

"Hello, Phoebe, it's Isaac. If you're there, please pick up.

It's—Oh hi, Phoebe. Thank God you're there. Yes, we just finished, but we have a situation. Marc will explain everything to you."

He shoved the telephone at me, and I explained everything to Phoebe.

"I see," Phoebe said after a pause. "What was the officer's name?"

"Navarro, I think. She said they'd let me know at some point—by mail, I guess. She wasn't too clear."

"That doesn't sound right," she said. "I'll send a letter to the Consul General straightaway."

"Do you think that's a good idea?"

"Of course, it's a good idea. That's why I'm suggesting it."

"What's she saying?" Isaac pressed his head against the cell phone.

"But won't that just aggravate the situation?" I asked, moving away from Isaac. "What if they decide to withdraw Isaac's approval?"

"If they were to take back Isaac's approval after we filed a letter of complaint, we'd have good cause to challenge the reversal as retaliatory. So, no, that's not going to happen. As for your case, I think the sooner we fire off a letter to the consul, the better. But it's up to you, of course."

"I don't know . . ."

"Let me talk to her." Isaac grabbed the phone out of my hand. "Phoebe, do whatever you think is best, okay? We won't get back to the city until late tonight, so we'll call you in the morning if that's all right. Yes, thank you. Bye."

I stared at him as he powered down the phone, bewildered by his attitude.

"Why are you bothered?" he asked. "Someone had to make the decision."

"We could have at least discussed the pros and cons, the possible risks—"

"Let Phoebe handle it, okay? She's the one with experience in these things, not you and certainly not me."

"Fine, Phoebe can handle it." I sighed. "In the meantime, what do we do?"

Isaac took me by the arm and dragged me toward the parking garage. "In the meantime, we go home."

"This is the letter I faxed to the consulate. I've made a copy for each of you."

Phoebe placed the duplicate letters on her desk, one in front of each of us. Isaac looked down at the one in front of him. I picked up my copy and scanned it.

"You'll notice I've addressed it directly to the Consul General," Phoebe said.

"Do you think it will do any good?" Isaac asked.

"It might," Phoebe said. "At any rate, it could come in handy in the event of an appeal."

I fell back in my chair and groaned. "Just what we need: more uncertainty, more delays."

Phoebe lowered her eyes at me. "It's not as bleak as all that."

"Looks that way to me," I said. "Letters of complaint, possible appeals—it seems pretty bleak."

Phoebe removed her glasses and peered down her nose at me. "Really, Marc, you never fail to surprise me. Have you forgotten the success of Isaac's interview? Your primary problem is solved; Isaac will soon have legal status in Canada. That's what this was all about, wasn't it? Your case was always secondary."

"I wouldn't call it secondary," I grumbled.

"Yes, that's right," Phoebe said, "play the semanticist. I am sure that will help matters."

"Phoebe, please, he didn't mean anything by that," Isaac said. "He's just frustrated, that's all. We both are."

"I realize that, of course," Phoebe said. "But my point here is he's an American citizen. He can enter Canada for months at a time, as a visitor, or for an indefinite number of years as a professional under the NAFTA treaty. Besides that, once you've entered the country, you will be entitled to file a petition on his behalf, and with more right to do so than now, since you will be doing so as a full-fledged permanent resident of Canada."

"I imagine that would take quite a while," I noted.

Phoebe cast a sidelong glance at me and continued. "Of course, the most convenient scenario would have been for the two of you to obtain status at the same time. But if you cannot, it's not the end-all, and it certainly isn't bleak." She pried her eyes away from Isaac and focused her gaze on me, somewhere in the region of my forehead. "At this point, Isaac's future is more certain; thus, I would think yours is as well."

"I'm happy about that," I said. "I just want to avoid a scenario where Isaac and I are forced to separate while I find a way to regularize my stay in Canada."

"That's right, Phoebe," Isaac agreed. "We don't want to be separated."

"And as I said, you needn't be. Marc has plenty of options. And now that *your* issue is settled for all intents, you can begin making your plans. I expect you'll receive your landing papers soon."

A couple of days later, Phoebe called us during dinner and broke the news that she'd spoken to a supervisor at the consulate. He'd confirmed the additional evidence they'd received was, as she put it, a "poison pen" letter from one Alejandro Silva. Isaac's hands trembled when he heard this, and he gripped the sides of the dinner table to control them. I had no words. Silva was destined to be a plague on our relationship, regardless of what happened.

I lowered my head to the table, on the verge of tears.

"Fortunately," Phoebe said, "I had an opportunity to explain the situation. I was even able to fax across information I extracted from Mr. Silva's criminal case file, confirming he's a convicted felon."

Isaac looked up at that.

"How did that go over?" I asked.

"Very well, in fact," Phoebe answered. "The officer told me they'd probably disregard the letter and base their decision on the evidence we submitted. The good thing is I was able to press home that they should consider your case in light of your common-law relationship with a, now, soon-to-be resident of Canada, and he was receptive to that. Overall, it was a positive call. I think we can be cautiously optimistic."

After the call ended, Isaac sat staring at the top of the table. I wrapped my arms around him and held him, both for him and for myself. After a moment, he stood up, and my arms dropped away. He collected our half-empty dishes and withdrew into the kitchen. I didn't hear the sounds that usually followed—clinking cutlery, running water, cabinets opening and closing. The apartment was silent as death. Resisting the urge to see if he was all right, I decided to give Isaac the space he needed to process his emotions.

I drifted to the living room to watch the sunset and, for the first time in ten years, I breathed a prayer.

Two weeks after our interview, on a crisp February afternoon, a courier arrived at my office with two packages from the Canadian consulate. I contemplated them for a few seconds before picking up the telephone and calling Isaac at work. When I told him what had arrived, the line went silent.

"Are you still there?" I asked.

"You did say two packages, right?"

"Yeah, one addressed to each of us. Do you think we should call Phoebe?"

"Is there any difference between the packages? Anything obvious?"

I cradled the receiver against my shoulder and compared the two packages, using my two hands as balances.

"They seem identical from the outside."

"Then open them."

I ripped open the one addressed to Isaac and extracted a cover letter and a certificate bearing the title: *Record of Landing*. I quickly read through the cover letter.

"It's a certificate and a letter that says you can enter Canada as a new immigrant anytime within the next 365 days."

"What about yours? What does it say?"

"I haven't opened it yet."

"What are you waiting for? Open it already!"

I picked up the package and fingered the cardboard tab. I drew a deep breath and yanked hard, causing the contents to eject from the package and fly halfway across the room. "Oh, shit!"

"What happened?" Isaac yelled through the phone. "Marc, what is it? What does it say?"

I cocked my head at the documents scattered across the parquet floor, afraid to touch them. "Hold on a second," I said and set the squawking receiver on the desk.

I picked up the strewn papers and examined the cover letter. It was identical to Isaac's. I flipped the page and found my *Record of Landing*. Suppressing the urge to scream, I snatched up the receiver.

"I got it!"

"Are you serious?" he said. "What's it say?"

"I'm fucking approved!" I jumped up from my chair. "We're going to Canada."

We agreed to meet at the SF MOMA, which was halfway between my office and Isaac's. Trying my best to retain my composure for a few minutes more, I informed Ed I'd be out the rest of the afternoon and headed for the stairs. I had to grasp the railing as I descended to avoid passing out from the excitement. Susan pulled off her headset and watched me as I staggered past her desk and moved to the door on wobbly legs. Once outside, I waited until I'd turned the corner before letting out a loud and long whoop. A group of university students seated in the window of Kells, downing pints of Guinness, stared in amazement as I ran screaming past their window, tears coursing down my cheeks.

Chapter 29

Isaac and I spent the next few weeks researching our move and nervously plotting and replotting our exit date. At the behest of my parents—more or less—we settled on Montreal, although I had to make it clear to them I wouldn't be joining a religious community. Still, they were happy we would be local to people they were friends with, as one never knew when that might come in handy.

Everything was proceeding smoothly. Then one afternoon in mid-May, I received a message on my office voicemail from Detective Bey, asking me to call her regarding Alejandro Silva. I was taken aback at the sound of his name, as it had been some time since we'd seen or heard from him. I'd started to believe he had finally taken the hint and fucked off.

I snatched up the telephone and called Isaac at work. I told him about Bey's call, and he fell silent for a few moments. Neither of us could imagine why she would be calling me about Silva but agreed it was best to call her back. I did so and waited with my heart in my throat as another detective tracked her down. When she finally came to the telephone, I was totally unprepared for what she told me.

"Mr. Mendes, we're trying to ID the body of a homicide victim we discovered last night, and we believe you might be able to help us."

"A body?" I asked, puzzled. "You said something about Alejandro Silva in your message."

"That's correct."

"You don't think Silva had something to do with it, do you?"

There was a long silence on the line, then: "We believe it's Alejandro Silva's body we found. At least that's what our initial fingerprint check tells us. But he's still just a John Doe until we get a personal ID. We thought you might be able to help us out."

"Why me?"

Detective Bey let out a sigh. "We found one of your business cards in the victim's back pocket. That's the only thing we found on him."

Bey was waiting for me in front of the criminal courts building when Isaac and I arrived. He'd insisted on coming along, and I was grateful for the support. The detective looked askance at my extended hand when I offered it to her and told us to follow her around to the back of the building where the coroner's office was located.

"One of our officers found the body stuffed into an abandoned dumpster behind the Headlands Hotel. He'd been dead for quite some time," she explained. "Someone called in an anonymous tip."

"How did he die?" Isaac asked.

"From trauma to the head," she said, holding open the door to the coroner's office for me. "He was battered to death with a heavy object. Wait here."

Isaac and I waited in the lobby for a few minutes before Bey returned and called us inside. We followed her down a long, narrow stainless steel-paneled corridor. We turned left into a cold lime green room where a coroner's clerk was waiting for us next to a sheet-draped body.

Bey stepped around to the other side of the corpse and signaled to the clerk. He pulled back the sheet and exposed the body to the sternum. I caught my breath. It was Silva. The upper right side of his head was partially caved in, his once-handsome face now grotesquely contorted in death. But the birthmark on his left cheek was unmistakable. Isaac stepped forward and peered down at him.

"Well?" Bey said, watching my every expression.

I nodded. "It's Silva," I confirmed, feeling my knees buckling.

She signaled the clerk to cover up the body. Isaac moved to my side and grabbed my arm to keep me from keeling over.

"Are there any suspects?" I asked once I'd recovered from the initial shock.

Bey eyed me with a cynical smile. "What do you think?"

"I'd like to see the coroner's report, if I may," I said, determined not to be intimidated by Bey's attempt at passive interrogation.

"Sure, why not?" she said. "Let's go back out to the front. I'll bring it to you."

Isaac and I waited a few more minutes in the lobby, neither of us saying a word until Bey returned with the report. I paged through it and handed it back to her.

"Have you reviewed the victim's criminal record, Detective?"

"Of course. He was arrested a few years back for a homicide, as you know, and he's been picked up a couple of times in the last few months for hustling in the Tenderloin."

"He was hustling?" Isaac asked.

"Yep."

"Great." Isaac sat down and shook his head.

"The guy he was convicted of killing *also* died from a blow to his head," I noted.

Bey crossed her arms. "Is that so?"

"Look it up in the homicide report," I said. "Maybe someone's trying to send a message."

Bey considered this for a moment.

"I suggest," I said pointedly, "that you add to your suspect list anyone who might have had a motive to take revenge against Mr. Silva for the killing. You might actually find the right person."

"Maybe it was those drug dealers," Isaac said, turning to me.

"What drug dealers?" Bey shot back.

I looked at Isaac, then back at Bey. "Silva once told me in confidence that a couple of drug dealers from Oakland had killed his roommate and then framed him for the crime—something about a drug deal gone wrong. They threatened to kill him if he ever told anyone."

"And you're only mentioning this now?" Bey asked, her voice dripping sarcasm.

"I mentioned it months ago to our lawyer, Ms. Thistlewig. You can check it out with her."

I glanced at Isaac. He was gazing at the floor, listening.

"I never believed the story myself," I said. "Neither did Ms. Thistlewig. We considered it another one of Silva's tricks to gain my sympathy. So we didn't give it much thought. Besides that, he'd asked me not to tell anyone."

Bey blinked at me, trying to get her head around what she was hearing, now that I'd shaken her neat assumption that I had anything to do with Silva's murder. She produced a steno pad and spent another quarter of an hour taking down the additional information for her investigation.

"We'll have a few more questions, of course, Mr. Mendes," she said, putting away her notes. "Can you swing by the station tomorrow afternoon? You too, Mr. Perez."

"Why me?" Isaac asked. "I'm not a suspect, am I?"

"Not at all. We're just interested in getting your perspective."

"I'll pass on that, thanks," Isaac said.

"Likewise," I said. "I've answered enough questions already."

I pulled an extra business card from my inside pocket and dropped it on the counter in front of her. "Call me when you're done with the body. If you have any trouble locating a next of kin who gives a shit, I'd like to make arrangements to have him buried properly." I walked out of the office without waiting for a response and ran to my car with Isaac trailing behind.

My eyes filled with tears as we drove home, and I was having trouble making out the road in front of me. I kept seeing Silva's corpse on the gurney, feeling against reason that I was somehow to blame for his ignoble end. I tried to suppress the sobs that threatened to unsteady me. After a few minutes, I gave up the struggle, pulled to the side of the road, and broke down. Isaac stared at me with an embarrassed expression as I wept bitter tears for Alejandro Silva.

Chapter 30

Three months after discovering Silva's body, the police suspended any further investigation, closed his file, and it became a cold case. Nothing had come of any of their leads, and all potential suspects had unshakable alibis. So that was that.

It took Isaac much longer to forgive me for my emotional outburst. He couldn't understand why I would feel any pity for a person he saw as the monster who'd upended our lives for nearly two years. I didn't understand it myself. But I preferred not to delve too deeply, especially as we were in the middle of planning our new lives in Canada. We couldn't afford any more emotional upset. So I put it down to a human reaction and left it at that. Surprisingly, the one thing Isaac didn't hold against me was my offer to pay for Silva's burial. *That* he was on board with.

The nearer the day of our departure came, the more furious the pace of our planning became. And as we dismantled our lives in the United States—resigning jobs, selling cars, packing our personal effects, giving up our beautiful apartment, entrusting Nilo to my mother, saying good-bye to family and friends, and, most difficult of all, meeting with Simon's parents to tell them the truth about their son's death—Isaac and I gradually grew close to each other again. We resumed sleeping in the same bed, talking long into the night, and making love with a renewed passion. Things had returned to the way they'd been before, except I couldn't help noticing that the light had gone out of Isaac's smile. He'd been profoundly wounded, and I feared the damage was permanent. My father urged me to be patient. So much had happened to Isaac and me in such a short space of time, it was only natural that we'd been affected—both of us. But time was a great physician, my father assured me, and we would eventually heal.

Ten months to the day after Isaac's hearing, on a frosty December morning, he and I were seated in SFO's international departures lounge, waiting to board our flight to Montreal. Phoebe had accompanied us and was conversing with Isaac in hushed tones while I sat on the other side of him, holding his hand. With fifteen minutes to go before they opened the gate, Phoebe came around to my side and patted my arm.

"You seem lost in thought," she observed. "This is supposed to be a happy day."

I offered her a warm smile. I was genuinely happy she was there and grateful that she'd been with us every step of the way. "I *am* happy, Phoebe."

"Then why so glum?"

"I'm not glum, just a bit apprehensive. About the future, I guess."

"The future is bright! For both of you," she said.

"I'm sure it is. But it's completely uncertain what course it's going to take once we get there." I shrugged. "I don't do uncertain very well."

"Consider it a fresh start," she said. "Not many of us get to have one of those. You have your education and your experience, which nobody can take away. You have more than sufficient financial resources, and you're both sharp as tacks. I'm confident you'll be on your feet and thriving in no time at all." She smiled at Isaac, and he nodded in response.

I looked around the terminal and let out a sigh.

"You don't seem convinced," Phoebe said.

"No, you're right, Phoebe. I'm sure we'll be fine. I was just reflecting on this whole leaving thing: It's like my father and my grandfather before him, and the unknown ancestors that preceded even them, emigrating, expatriating. It's a lifestyle that's been forced on us. For them, it was because they were Jewish; for me, it's because I'm gay. It's like a curse."

"Now, now," Phoebe said. "It won't do to feel sorry for yourself. The law will evolve in due course, and cases like yours and Isaac's will be a thing of the past. I'm sure of it."

"Maybe."

"In any case," Phoebe pulled three plastic cups out of her bag and distributed them to us, "today is a day of celebration!" She then produced a bottle of sparkling apple juice and popped the cork, drawing the attention of a gate agent who moved in our direction as Phoebe poured a cup for each of us and raised her own.

"A toast to new beginnings!" she called out, her voice ringing off the walls.

The moment we'd both wished for and dreaded was finally upon us; both of us were strapped into our seats, about to take off on a nonstop flight of no return. Once the plane was in the air, there would be no turning back for Isaac. He would be unable to return to the United States until he became a Canadian citizen, which would be no earlier than four years after our arrival in Montreal. Acutely aware of the finality of the whole thing, neither of us spoke a word as we sped down the runway, each of us keeping our thoughts to ourselves.

The plane took off over the Pacific, making a long, drawn-out turn and doubling back over the peninsula. Isaac, who was seated next to the window, peered out at the city as it passed beneath the ascending plane. I could see his reflection in the acrylic, his eyes darting over the landscape, and I sensed him picking out the familiar landmarks: Twin Peaks, Market Street, the Transamerica Tower, Telegraph Hill, Alcatraz Island, which by then was just a tiny spot of land in the middle of the diminishing bay. As we ascended over the Marin Headlands, Isaac turned to me.

"Here," he said, pressing into my hands a little gift-wrapped box that he produced out of his jacket. "To our new life."

Surprised by the gesture, I held the box up to the light streaming in from the window and smiled at the glitter-speckled paper and the tiny rainbows printed on the ribbon.

"What is it?" I asked, putting it to my ear and shaking it.

"Open it and see."

Excited, I gave him a quick peck on the cheek and turned to untie the ribbon, trying my best not to tear it. Then, carefully pulling back the paper, my breath caught at the sight of a familiar-looking blue velvet jewelry box. A flash of prickly heat shot up my spine as I stared at the little blue box in my trembling hand. I slowly raised my eyes to Isaac, who was watching me with a blank expression.

"Consider it a gift from the universe," he said, nudging my hand.

I glanced at the box again and, after a moment's hesitation, unlatched and pried it open. Reaching inside, I extracted a delicate platinum chain upon which dangled a Star of David pendant. *My* Star of David pendant. I immediately returned it to the box and shoved it into my rucksack, then turned to Isaac. His face had hardened into an inscrutable mask.

"But how?" I whispered, terrified of the answer.

He held my gaze for a beat, then turned away and peered out the window. "Don't ask."

A few moments later, the light in the cabin dimmed as the plane entered a large bank of clouds, and the city, the bay, and the hills disappeared. Even after the clouds obscured the view, Isaac continued to stare out the window. I reached over and touched his hand. It was cold and limp. Still, Isaac continued to look out the window as the plane leveled off at its cruising altitude and carried us away into the darkening eastern sky.

Acknowledgements

The Fitful Sleep of Immigrants began life twenty years ago as an intended memoir penned in exile. As I drafted the source material over the course of a long, dark Toronto winter, deeply bitter at having been ejected from my country of birth due to marriage inequality, it became clear to me that a memoir forged in anger made for an unpleasant read. I was simply too close to the material and lacked sufficient objectivity to produce anything better than 200,000 words worth of sour grapes. And so, reluctantly, I shoved the manuscript into a drawer and forgot about it.

Two decades later, I came across the material, dusted it off, and began the painful process of reimagining *Immigrants* as a novel, albeit inspired by the events that led my life partner and me to leave our lives in San Francisco and emigrate to Canada. And so began the novel's long journey from initial draft to innumerable rewrites and on to publication which I could not have possibly accomplished alone.

I would therefore like to humbly thank the following people for supporting and collaborating in the development of this latest incarnation of *Immigrants*:

Wanda Whitely for tearing into an early draft (in the nicest way) and leaving me to reassemble the pieces and plug up the holes;

Gabriel Burrow, editor extraordinaire, for his skill in buffing out the rougher edges without sacrificing the grit;

Michael Nava for acquiring the novel on behalf of Amble Press and providing invaluable feedback that vastly improved the narrative;

Ann McMan for her brilliantly arresting book cover;

Salem West, Publisher for Bywater Books and Amble Press, who brought it all together;

And, most especially, my (now) husband William Campos-Ortega for his unflagging love, support, and grammatical skills.

About the Author

Orlando Ortega-Medina was born in Los Angeles to immigrants from Cuba. He studied English Literature at UCLA and earned a Juris Doctor law degree from Southwestern University School of Law. At university, he won the National Society of Arts and Letters Award for Short Stories.

Following his admission to the bar, Ortega-Medina practiced criminal defense in Los Angeles under the tutelage of Attorney Kenneth Kahn, of *The Falcon and the Snowman* fame. After four years, Ortega-Medina moved his practice to San Francisco, where he transitioned to representing clients in appeals, post-conviction relief, and deportation defense.

In 1999, Ortega-Medina and his life partner expatriated to Canada. And in 2005, taking advantage of Canada's recognition of same-sex marriage, they were among the first same-sex couples to marry at Montreal's Hotel de Ville.

Ortega-Medina's short story collection *Jerusalem Ablaze* was shortlisted for The Polari First Book Prize (2017). In 2018, he was named the Marilyn Hassid Emerging Author for the Houston Jewish Book & Arts Festival. He is the author of prior novels, *The Death of Baseball* (2019) and *The Savior of 6th Street* (2020). Ortega-Medina lives in London.

Amble Press, an imprint of Bywater Books, publishes fiction and narrative nonfiction by LGBTQ writers, with a primary, though not exclusive, focus on LGBTQ writers of color. For more information on our titles, authors, and mission, please visit our website.

www.amblepressbooks.com